W9-BWX-965

LEGENDS OF THE HORSECLANS . . .

Robert Adams' "Battle at Kahlkopolis"—In the war-torn Southern Kingdom of the Ehleenoee, can the allies of the Confederation defeat the bandit hordes . . . even with the aid of a strategy never before seen in those lands?

Andre Norton's "Rider on a Mountain"—Alone and pursued, she would find unexpected allies who were far from human. . . .

Joel Rosenberg's "The Last Time"—He was the last lawman, and with Milo Morai's aid, he would face his enemy in the last shootout a Horseclansman would ever face.

John Steakley's "The Swordsman Smada"—Twentieth-century Americans, they woke in a world not their own—the world of the Horseclans, where only a quick blade would keep them from sudden death!

Join Robert Adams and his fellow writers in these sword-swinging new adventures of Horseclans derring-do!

☉ SIGNET SCIENCE FICTION

The Bestselling HORSECLANS Series by Robert Adams

(0451)

☐ **THE COMING OF THE HORSECLANS (Horseclans #1).** After two hundred years of searching for other immortals, the Undying High Lord Milo Morai has returned to the Horseclans to fulfill an ancient prophecy and lead them to their destined homeland by the sea. (137485—$2.95)

☐ **SWORDS OF THE HORSECLANS (Horseclans #2).** Led by an ancient and evil intelligence, the wave of destruction is thundering down upon the Confederation forces. Milo must call upon his allies in a desperate attempt to save his people from seemingly certain doom . . . (140257—$2.95)

☐ **REVENGE OF THE HORSECLANS (Horseclans #3).** Bili, the eldest son of the Thoheeks of Morguhn, has been summoned to claim his inheritance after years of soldiering in the Middle Kingdoms. Yet his reign could end before it begins, for the old Ehleen nobility and the priests of the ancient region are planting the seeds of rebellion . . . (133064—$2.95)

☐ **A CAT OF SILVERY HUE (Horseclans #4).** Lord Milo must call upon his very best; for only with the aid of men like Bili Morguhn, whose skill with axe, sword, and mind control makes him a natural clan leader, can Milo hope to contain the menace of the Ehleenee rebels and save civilization from destruction . . . (133056—$2.95)

☐ **THE SAVAGE MOUNTAINS (Horseclans #5).** Milo Morai is ready to take the next step in his master plan to reunite all the tribes which centuries ago formed a single, powerful nation known as the United States of America. (129342—$2.95)

☐ **THE PATRIMONY: (Horseclans #6).** Although young Horseclansman Tim Sanderz has returned to claim his rightful inheritance as leader of Sanderz-Vawn, his stepmother wants to see her own Ehleen son as ruler in Vawn. But there is far more at stake than the leadership of Sanderz-Vawn, for the Confederation's deadliest enemy is again at work . . . (133005—$2.95)*

Prices slightly higher in Canada

Buy them at your local bookstore or use this convenient coupon for ordering.

NEW AMERICAN LIBRARY,
P.O. Box 999, Bergenfield, New Jersey 07621

Please send me the books I have checked above. I am enclosing $_____ (please add $1.00 to this order to cover postage and handling). Send check or money order—no cash or C.O.D.'s. Prices and numbers subject to change without notice.

Name_____

Address_____

City_____ Zip Code_____

Allow 4-6 weeks for delivery.
This offer is subject to withdrawal without notice.

ROBERT ADAMS
FRIENDS OF THE HORSECLANS

EDITED BY ROBERT ADAMS
AND PAMELA CRIPPEN ADAMS

A SIGNET BOOK

NEW AMERICAN LIBRARY

PUBLISHED BY
THE NEW AMERICAN LIBRARY
OF CANADA LIMITED

NAL PENGUIN BOOKS ARE AVAILABLE AT QUANTITY DISCOUNTS WHEN
USED TO PROMOTE PRODUCTS OR SERVICES. FOR INFORMATION
PLEASE WRITE TO PREMIUM MARKETING DIVISION, NAL PENGUIN
INC., 1633 BROADWAY, NEW YORK, NEW YORK 10019.

Copyright © 1987 by Robert Adams and Pamela Adams

All rights reserved

First Printing, April, 1987

2 3   4   5   6   7   8   9

SIGNET TRADEMARK REG U S PAT OFF AND FOREIGN COUNTRIES
REGISTERED TRADEMARK — MARCA REGISTRADA
HECHO EN WINNIPEG, CANADA

SIGNET, SIGNET CLASSIC, MENTOR, ONYX, PLUME, MERIDIAN
AND NAL BOOKS are published in Canada by The New American
Library of Canada, Limited, 81 Mack Avenue, Scarborough,
Ontario, Canada M1L 1M8
PRINTED IN CANADA
COVER PRINTED IN U.S.A.

To the contributors, without whom none of this would have been possible

Contents

Introduction

"Mr. Adams, sir, where do you get your ideas?"

I often am sorely tempted to answer, "Why, from the Heroic Adventures Division of the Ideas for Writers Company up in West Putrid, Massachusetts, of course." But I don't, no, I go through the old process of trying to explain mental creativity to folks whose minds are not bent that way and so cannot understand me. Actually, to those of you readers who can understand it, it's simple and miraculous: the germ of HORSECLANS came from a dream; after that, I have just written the kind of thing that I would like to read, and, apparently, my reading tastes match those of a fairish number of other readers.

Naturally, my own experiences of life, nearly fifty years of reading both fiction and nonfiction, observation and a soaring imagination are also necessities in producing books of the sorts I write. A good memory is a distinct asset, too. The larger and the more diverse the personally owned reference library, the better, I feel, and this is why I have to keep moving into larger houses every few years.

I wrote the first HORSECLANS book in late 1973 and sold it in 1974. It was published by Pinnacle Books, Inc., and released in June 1975. The second book in the series was released in 1976 and the third in 1977. I parted company with Pinnacle in 1978, and the fourth book in the series (as well as all succeeding ones, plus new editions of the first three) was published by Signet Books. Book fifteen was published by Signet in July 1986. I have recently completed the sixteenth and am at work on the seventeenth. Something over three million HORSECLANS books are now in print from Signet alone, and so I thought that the time had come to let other writers into my world, other professionals who also happened to be admirers of HORSECLANS. This was the genesis of *Friends of the Horseclans*.

I just might have been able to carry off this project alone, but it would have gone much more slowly and been much more difficult without the enthusiastic assistance of my coeditor and, incidentally, wife, Pamela Crippen Adams.

To date, HORSECLANS covers some thousand years and so is rife with loose, dangling story ends and gaping, blank spaces; I am slowly tagging onto a few of the former and filling a few of the latter, but I would have to live and write for another fifty-odd years in order to do it all. Therefore, I am getting help from my friends, the twelve friends whose splendid work you will read in these following pages.

Battle at Kahlkopolis

by Robert Adams

With the retreat of the late, unlamented King Zastros' huge army from Karaleenos back into what once had been the Southern Kingdom of the Ehleenoee, the surviving *thoheeksee* of the kingdom set about putting their hereditary lands to order and productivity, filling titles vacated by war, civil war, assassinations, suicides and disease, and in general preparing the southerly territories for the merger with the victorious Confederation of the High Lord, Milos of Morai.

Chief mover and the closest thing to a king that the Southern Ehleenoee now owned was *Thoheeks* Grahvos *tohee* Mehseepolis *keh* Eepseelospolis. After taking into consideration all of the varied infamy that had taken place in the former capital, Thrahkohnpolis, Grahvos had declared the new center of the soon-to-be Southern Confederated *Thoheekseeahnee* to be situated at his own principal city of Mehseepolis.

Now that city was become a seething boil of activity—sections of old walls being demolished, the city environs being expanded and new walls going up to enclose them, troops camped far and wide around the city, existing public (and not a few private) buildings become beehives with the comings and the goings of Ehleenoee nobility, their retainers and their staffs, as well as the host of attendant functionaries necessary to the operation of this new capital city.

One day, some years after the announcement of the new capital city, two noblemen sought audience with *Thoheeks* Grahvos and his advisers. The one of these two was a greybeard, the other a far younger man, but the shapes and angles of the faces—eyes, noses, chins, cheekbones—clearly denoted kinship between the two, close kinship. The old man was tall—almost six feet—his physique big-boned and no

11

doubt once very powerful, with the scars of a proven warrior, at least a couple of which looked to be fairly new.

The harried assistant chamberlain knew that he had seen this man or someone much like him before, but could not just then place who or where or when, and the petitioner refused to state his name or rank, only saying that he was a man who had been unjustly treated and was seeking redress of the new government. The only other word he deigned to send in to the *thoheeksee* was cryptic.

"Ask the present lord of Hwailehpolis if he recalls aught of a stallion, a dead man's sword and a bag of gold."

When, on his second or third trip into the meeting room, the assistant remembered to ask this odd question, *Thoheeks* Vikos of Hwailehpolis leaped to his feet and grabbed both the man's shoulders, hard, demanding, "Where is this man? What would you estimate his age? Is he come alone or did others bring him?"

When the now-trembling functionary had scuttled off to fetch back the oldster, Vikos explained his actions to his curious peers.

"It was after that debacle at Ahrbahkootchee, in the early days of the civil war. I had fought through that black day as an ensign in my late brother's troop of horse, and in the wake of our rout by King Rahndos' war-elephants, I like full many another found myself unhorsed and hunted like a wild beast through the swamps of the bottom lands. It was nearing dusk and I was half-wading, half-swimming yet another pool when I heard horsemen crashing through the brush close by to me. Breaking off a long, hollow reed, I went underwater, as I had done right often that terrifying day, but I knew that if they came at all close, I was done this time, for the water of the pool was clear almost to the bottom, not murky as had been so many others, nor was the spot I had to go down very deep—perhaps three feet, perhaps less.

"Suddenly, I became aware that the legs of a big horse were directly beside my body, and, not liking the thought of a probing spear pinning me to the bottom, to gasp out my life under the water, I resignedly surfaced, that I might at least die with air in my lungs.

"I looked up into the eyes of none other than *Komees* Pahvlos Feelohpóhlehmos, himself!

"In a voice that only I could hear, he growled, 'Stay

down, damn fool boy!' Then he shouted to the nearing troopers, 'You fools, search that thick brush, up there where the stream debouches. This pool is clear as crystal, nothing in it save fish and crayfish, so I'm giving my stallion a drink of it.'

"Then the *komees* deliberately set his horse to roiling the sediments of the bottom, clouding the water, while he did the same with the butt of his lance. He dropped a sheathed, jeweled sword upon me, and when I brought my face up to where I could see him, he tossed me a small, heavy bag and said, 'You may well be the last of your House, after this day, young Vikos. There is a bit of gold and a good sword. Wait until full dark and then head northwest; what's left of the rebel army is withdrawing south and southeast. If you can make it up to Iron Mountain, you'll be safe. And the next time you choose a warleader, try to choose one with at least a fighting chance to win. God keep you now.' "

Thoheeks Grahvos nodded. "Yes, it sounds of a piece with all else I know of the man. For all his ferocity and expertise in the waging of war for the three kings he served in his long career, still was he ever noted to be just and, when possible, merciful. Strange, I'd assumed him dead, legally murdered by Zastros as were the most of his peers. It's good to know that at least this one of the better sort survived the long bloodletting. Who was his overlord, anyway? If he'll take the proper oaths, *Komees* Pahvlos the Warlike would make us a good *thoheeks*, say I."

"And so," concluded old *Komees* Pahvlos, "when it was become obvious that these usurping scum were determined to not only deny young Ahramos here his lawful patrimonies, but to take his very life as well, had they the chance, I knew that stronger measures were required, my lords.

"Could but a single warrior do it alone, it were done already. Old, I assuredly am—close to seventy years old— but I still am tough and the hilt of my good sword has not become a stranger to my hand. But a disciplined, well-armed and -led force will be necessary to dislodge this foul kakistocracy that presently squat in Ahramos' principal city and control his rightful lands. And due to reverses, I no longer own the wherewithal to hire on fighting men, equip and mount and supply them with the necessities of warfare."

"But I will wager, *Strahteegos Komees* Pahvlos," said *Thoheeks* Grahvos, "that nothing has robbed you of your old abilities to lead armies, plan winning battles and improvise stunning tactics on the spur of the moment. I had meant to ask you to take oaths to this council and the Confederation, then assume one of the still-vacant *thoheekseeahnee*, but if you'll indeed take those oaths, I have a better, far more useful task in mind for you, now."

Chief Pawl Vawn of Vawn sat at a table in a tent in the camp of *Seentahgmahrtees* Tomos Gonsalos, senior officer of those Confederation forces sent south to aid the *thoheeksee* in securing and maintaining peace. With them at table sat *Ahnteeseentahgmahrtees* of Infantry Guhsz Hehluh, and *Thoheeks* Portos, figurehead commander of these alien troops deep in the heart of the former Southern Kingdom.

A meal had been eaten while the men talked, and now, while a bottle of sweet wine circulated, the Horseclansman asked, "If this Pahvlos is such a slambang *strahteegos* and all, how come he didn't tromp you all proper for his king and end it all before it got started?"

"Oh, he did, he did, my good Pawl," said Portos, "in the beginning, years ago. I was a part of that rebel army, then, I know. It required years and the—then unknown—help of the Witchmen to put Zastros' army back together in a shape fit to once more face *Komees* Pahvlos; and that, finally, we did not have to face him was a great relief to full many a one of us, believe me. By that time, all of the ancient royal line was extinct and *Thoheeks* Fahrkos, who had seized the crown and the capital, had dismissed the royal *strahteegoee*. Most of the remaining royal troops—the only regular forces the kingdom had had—deserted, then marched away with their officers, so all Fahrkos had when we brought him to bay was his personal warband, such as it was."

"Even so," put in the greying Freefighter officer, Guhsz Hehluh, "before I put me and my Keebai boys under the orders of some whitebeard doddard, I'll know a bit more about him. You Kindred and Ehleenee can do what you wants, but if I mislike the sound or the smell of this Count Pahvlos, why me and mine we'll just hike back up to Kehnooryos Ahteenahs and tell High Lord Milo to find us other fights or sell us back our contract."

But within bare days, Guhsz Hehluh was trumpeting the
praises of the new Grand *Strahteegos* who, with his small
entourage, had ridden out and found the Freefighters at drill.
After sitting his horse by Hehluh's in the hot sun, swatting at
flies and knowledgeably discussing the strengths and weaknesses
of pike formations and the proper marshaling of infantry,
Pahvlos had actually dismounted and hunkered in the dust of
the drill field to sketch with a horny forefinger positions and
movements of an intricate maneuver.

To Tomos Gonsalos, Pahvlos remarked, "It's basically a
good unit you command, here, Colonel. I'd take you and
them just as they are now, were you not a mite shy of
infantry and a mite over supplied with cavalry. To rectify that
situation, I'll be brigading your regiment with two more, all
infantry, all veterans, too, no grassgreen plowboys.

"I think that both you and your other officers will get
along well with Colonel Bizahros, who commands the Eighth
Foot, from the outset; but Colonel Ahzprinos, commander of
the reorganized Fifth Foot, is another matter entirely.

"Understand me, Lord Tomos, Ahzprinos is a good warrior, a fine commander in all ways, else I'd not choose him to
serve under me. But he also is loud, brash and sometimes
overbearing to the point of arrogance. Nonetheless, I can get
along with him and I'll be expecting my subordinates to do so
too."

And so, in the weeks that followed, the Confederation
troops and the two regiments of former Southern Kingdom
foot drilled and marched and drilled some more under the
critical eye of *Komees* Pahvlos, while all awaited the arrival
of the war-elephants from the far-western *thoheekseeahnee*
where they had been bred and trained for centuries, making do
in the meantime with the three beasts that had survived King
Zastros' disastrous march north.

These three survivors were not the huge, fully war-trained
bull elephants now on the march from the west, but rather the
smaller, more docile cow elephants, mostly utilized for draught
purposes. That they were used by *Komees* Pahvlos at all was
a testament to the extraordinary control of them exercised by
the Horseclansman Gil Djohnz, who could get out of the
three cows performances of an order that the old *strahteegos*
had never before seen in all his long years of service with
elephant-equipped armies. Watching Djohnz and his two

Horseclansmen assistants put the trio of elephants through their paces had reduced native Ehleenoee *feelahksee* to a state of despair and set them to mumbling darkly of sorcery and witchcraft.

The old commander was greatly impressed with Horseclansmen, in general, for never before had it been his pleasure to own such a splendid and versatile mounted force as the squadron of medium-heavy horse under Chief Pawl of Vawn. Southern Kingdom horse traditionally came in three varieties— light horse or lancers, heavy horse, most of whom were noblemen, and irregulars, who frequently were archers and usually recruited from the barbarian mountain tribes and were often undependable, to say the least.

But these nothern horsemen were very dependable; moreover, they could fulfill the functions of at least two of the three—they could lay down a heavy and accurate arrow storm, then case their bows and deliver a hard, effective charge against the unit their arrows had weakened and disorganized. Serving in conjunction with such troops, Pahvlos could easily ken just how they and their forefathers had so readily rolled over the armies of Kehnooryos Ehlahs, Karaleenos and assorted far-northern barbarian principalities.

Nor was the reinforced squadron that *Thoheeks* Portos had brought down from the north your normal unit of lancers, either. To Pahvlos' way of thinking, they were become true heavy horse, and he used them as such, obtaining from *Thoheeks* Grahvos a half-squadron of old-fashioned light-horse lancers to take over the scouting, flank-guarding and messenger functions of traditional light-horse usage.

To *Thoheeks* Portos' questions regarding the reassignment of function of his squadron, the old *strahteegos* answered, "My lord *Thoheeks*, to my way of thinking, if you put a man up on a sixteen-hand courser all armored with steel and boiled leather, the man himself protected by a thigh-length hauberk and steel helm and armed with lance and saber and light axe and long shield, then that man is no longer a mere lancer, but a medium-heavy horseman at the very least. Your so-called lancers differ from Lord Pawl's force only in that his are equipped with bows rather than lances, carry targes instead of shields."

Although inordinately pleased with all of his cavalry, both native and alien, *Komees* Pahvlos was not quite certain what to make of or do with the most singular pikemen of Lord Guhsz Hehluh. Unless they chanced to be the foot-guards of a king or some other high, powerful, wealthy nobleman or of a walled city, Southern Kingdom pikemen simply were not armored—save for a light helmet of stiffened leather with strips of steel and a thick jack of leather, plus a pair of leather gauntlets which were occasionally reinforced with metal—and only the steadier, more dependable front ranks were provided with a body shield to be erected before them where they knelt or crouched to angle their pikes. Traditionally, of course, they had died in droves whenever push came to shove; such was and had always been expected.

But not so in the case of the big, mostly fair-skinned, thick-thewed barbarians commanded by Lord Guhsz. Only the cheek-guards and chin-slings of their helmets were of leather, the rest—crown-bowls, segmented nape-guards and bar-nasals—being of good-quality steel. Their burly bodies were guarded to the waists and their bulging arms to the elbow by steel scales sewn and riveted to padded canvas jacks; both their high-cuffed gauntlets and their leathern kilts were thickly sewn with steel mail, and, below a steel-plate knee-cop, their shins and calves were protected with sets of splint-armor riveted inside their boot linings.

Moreover, each and every one of these pikemen carried a slightly outbowed, rectangular shield a good two feet wide and near twice that in length, and on the command, each man of a formation could raise that shield a bit above his head in such a manner as to over- and underlap those of his fellows and provide a roof that could turn an arrow storm as adroitly as a roof of clay tiles turned a rainstorm.

Nor were these the only differences in the equipage of the alien foot and those of the Southern Kingdom. Aside from his fifteen-foot pike, your average pikeman bore no weapons other than a utility and eating knife, while not a one of Lord Guhsz's men but did not also bear a heavy, double-edged sword about a foot and a half in its sharp-pointed blade, one or more shorter dirks or daggers, sometimes even a short-hafted belt-axe, one of the sort that could be either tool or missile or weapon.

Burdened as they were, the old *strahteegos* had doubted that these overprotected, overarmed, overequipped pikemen could maintain the needful pace on the march or in a broad-front charge. But that had been before he put them to it; after he had, he knew the—to him, near incredible—facts of the matter. It was at that point that his formerly rock-firm opinions began to undergo a change and he began to wonder just why so many generations of his forebears had callously, needlessly sacrificed so many pikemen with the excuse, now proven false, that proper armor and secondary weapons would decrease mobility. Colonel Bizahros agreed with him, but Colonel Ahzprinos did not, flatly, unequivocally and at very great length.

So, the *eeahtrohsee*, with their bandages and ointments, their saws and other surgical devices, arrived. The artificiers were assigned, the quartermasters and the cooks, the smiths, the farriers, the wagoners and the muleskinners. Finally, *Strahteegos Komees* Pahvlos, tired of waiting and drilling, announced to the Council that he intended to start on his campaign with only the three cow elephants he already had, wanting to get the business over and done before the autumn rains arrived to complicate things for a field army.

Mainahkos Klehpteekos and Ahreekos Krehohpoleeos had risen fast and high from their origins as common troopers in the first, almost-extirpated army of *Thoheeks* Zastros. That both men were savage and completely unprincipled had helped, that they were good warleaders and inordinately lucky had helped even more. During the years of howling chaos in the Southern Kingdom, they and the heterogeneous packs of deserters, banditti, escaped criminals, shanghaied peasants and stray psychopaths they had led had sometimes signed on as a mercenary force to first one then another army of the battling lords.

Sometimes they had given the service for which they had been paid. But more often they had either deserted in mass or turned their coats at a crucial point, especially if the ongoing battle showed signs of being a close one. At length, so odious had their reputation become that no lord or city—no matter how desperate—would even consider hiring them on; at that point, they followed their basic inclinations, becoming out-and-out warlords, they and their lawless band of ruffians at open war against the world.

When at long last Zastros had made himself High King and, after scouring the length and breadth of the land of soldiers and men of military age, had marched his half-million and more north, out of the kingdom, on the road to his death in Karaleenos, the two warlords had found themselves in pigs' paradise, able now to prey not only on villages and travelers and isolated estates, but on walled towns and cities, as well.

They had behaved in their usual, bestial fashion at the intakings of the first few of these urban sites—by then, all but defenseless, despite their walls, what with their once-garrisons now marching north behind the Green Dragon banner of High King Zastros—first raping, plundering, torturing, then killing whole populations until the streets ran with gore, and finally burning everything combustible in the stinking charnel house they had made of the towns.

Then, of a day, a broken nobleman who had joined the bandit-army to avoid starving had had words with the two warlords and slowly convinced them of the sagacity of those words. For all that they and their followers were become wealthy beyond their wildest dreams of avarice, each succeeding victory had cost them men—and men of fighting age and strength were become almost as precious as rubies in this land stripped of warrior stock by Zastros' strenuous recruitments. Moreover, scattered and fast-moving survivors of those intakings had spread the word of the atrocities far and wide, so that all walled enclosures within weeks of marching time were doing everything possible to strengthen their existing defenses and had put aside any previous thoughts of trying to deal with the marauders on a near-peaceful basis.

So, although it went hard against the grain, the warlords had begun to rein in their savages, dealing gently—by their personal lights—with the inhabitants of those places that opened the gates without a fight and showed a willingness to treat. Mainahkhos and Ahreekos even took it upon themselves to move against, either recruiting or wiping out, numerous smaller bands of their own ilk then lurking about the countryside. Then they began to recruit from the remaining garrisons of the smaller towns and cities, and slowly their howling pack of human predators metamorphosed into a real, more or less organized army.

By the day, three years ago, that they had appeared under the walls of the city of Kahlkopolis, onetime seat of the *Thoheeksee* of Kahlkhos, the few straggling hundreds of ill-

or sketchily armed bandits were become an impressive, very threatening sight, indeed.

All classes of infantry marched in their ranks, fully armed and equipped, heavy cavalry rode in that column, with light cavalry on the wings and riding guard on the awesome siege train. Only elephants were lacking, and this deficiency was partly alleviated through use of old-fashioned mule-drawn warcarts as archery platforms—the stout, armored cart bodies, with scytheblades set in the wheel hubs and the big mules all hung with mail having proven almost as effective as elephants at the task of smashing in infantry formations for years before the pachyderms had been adapted to warfare.

The last *thoheeks*, Klawdos, was by then five years dead, a casualty of the civil war, along with all his male kin. His wife and infant son had disappeared shortly after his death, and the city was then being held by a distant cousin of the ancient line, a bastard with little claim to noble blood, even less to military experience. So, when he ordered the gates to be closed and the walls to be manned by the pitifully few men he owned to defend them, what was left of the city council did the only reasonable thing: they murdered him.

Since then, Mainahkos had been *thoheeks* in all save only name, having seen to it that the city councilmen quickly followed their victim into death, by one means or another. He had been upon the teetering verge of declaring himself *Thoheeks* Mainahkos Klehftis of Klehftispolis (as he and his men had become "respectable," he had adopted the new surname, and now no man who was undesirous of a messy, agonizing and brutally protracted demise ever called the warlord Klehpteekos—"the thief") when he had learned that the son of his legal predecessor still lived.

He and his fellow warlord had both chanced to be out of the city when the boy had come nosing about in company with some arrogant dotard, but they had been gone beyond recall when the would-be *thoheeks* had returned, and he had had the fools who had allowed their escape flayed alive and rolled in salt for their stupidity. Those cured skins still hung in a prominent place in his hall of audience, a silent, savage warning to his surviving followers.

As the would-be *thoheeks* sat at meat with his principal officer-advisers and his longtime partner, Ahreekos (who had never bothered to change his surname, still reveling in the

cognomen of "Butcher," although he was grown now far too
fat to do much real fighting of any nature), the topic of the
discussion was that army which they had had word was even
now advancing against them from the southeast.

In answer to a query from Mainahkhos, the heavy cavalry
commander, one Stehrghiahnos—who had been born and
reared the heir to a *vahrohneeskos*, though he had forfeited
title and lands and very nearly life itself through too early a
support of the then-rebel *Thoheeks* Zastros—said cautiously,
"My lord, it might be as well to essay a meeting with these
commanders. After all, my lord's claim to this *thoheekseeahn*
is as good as any; he has been a good lord and owns the
support of the people of the city, at least."

Ahreekhos nodded agreement. "He's right, you know,
Mainahkhos. From whatall my scouts have told me, that
army a-coming ain't one I'd of cared to face three years
agone, even, when we were at full strength, much less now.
And they got them elephants, too, at least three of the crit-
ters, prob'ly more.

"Why not send out Stehrghiahnos, there, and a couple
more fellers and let them palaver with this *strahteegos*, huh?
Ain't nuthin to be lost by that, is it? Old *Thoheeks* Grahvos
and them is making new *thoheeksee* and *komeesee* and such
all over the place, and, like's just been said, you got you as
good a claim to this here city and all as anybody has. Could
be, you say you'll stand a-hint *Thoheeks* Grahvos and them,
won't be no battle a-tall."

Mainahkhos shrugged. "Hell, that's right, ain't a damn
thing lost by talking with them bastids . . . but I want the
levy and all raised at the same time, too. And send word to
old Ratface Billisos to brang up every swingin' dick he can
lay claws to from the western *komeeseeahnee*, too, and all the
mounts what he can beg, borror or steel, too."

Strateegos *Thoheeks* Pahvlos received Stehrghiahnos, of
course, but treated him with the contempt that he felt a renegade
nobleman deserved. When he had heard him out, he shrugged
and spoke.

"Were the house indeed extinct, there might possibly be a
bare modicum of sense in what you have said, but it is not
extinct. Here, at this very table, sits the rightful *Thoheeks* of
Kahlkos." He nodded his white head in the direction of young

Ahramos, who sat stiffly and blankfaced in his dusty, fieldbrowned armor, his plain helm and sheathed sword on the tabletop before him.

From where he stood (Pahvlos had deliberately proffered no chair or stool), Stehrghiahnos eyed the husky boy critically, then said, "We might avoid a general, assuredly-costly battle, you know, my lord *Thoheeks*, by the simple, old-fashioned expedient of arranging a session-in-arms between the present *Thoheeks* of Kahlkos and this pretender your present here . . . ?"

"Cow-flop!" the old man snorted in scorn, adding, "In addition to being an arrant traitor to your class and your breeding, you seem to possess all the native intelligence of a braying ass . . . And I warn you, sirrah, if you make the mistake of drawing that blade, I'll see you lose that hand a joint an hour before you leave this camp!

"To begin, *Thoheeks* Ahramos here, far from being some pretender, is the rightful overlord of Kahlkos, *Thoheeks* by birth; as such, he deserves and is being afforded the firm support of every loyal, right-thinking nobleman of this new Confederated *Thoheekseeahnee* . . . which is precisely why I and my army are here.

"The sort of resolution you've suggested does not apply to this situation. It was considered legal only for cases wherein both contenders owned equal birthright claim or no claim at all. Besides, no gentleman—no *true* gentleman—of my army is going to go forth to meet a common bandit chief on terms of equality . . . and I find it significant of just how far down the ladder you have descended that you would even suggest so dishonorable a course to me and *Thoheeks* Ahramos."

Strahteegos Thoheeks Pahvlos' original order of battle had been to place the armored pikemen of Hehluh and Bizahros at the center of his line, retaining the unarmored pikemen of Ahzprinos as a reserve and placing half of the Horseclan medium-heavy cavalry on each wing to provide enfilading archery against any aggressive movements on the part of the enemy. He did not intend to advance until the opposing force had been bled a bit at trying to break his line.

Report of probing cavalry patrols and information gleaned from captives as well as a few loyalists who had managed to flee the city had assured the old soldier that, although outnumbered, his was much the better, more reliable army.

The broad, verdant plain surrounding the city was the logical place for any battle. True, it was not all open ground, there were a few copses here and there, a few folds of the landscape, but none large enough or deep enough to allow for ambushes or unpleasant surprises for any save the smallest of units.

A week after the visit of Stehrghiahnos to his camp, the elderly *strahteegos* was apprised by a sweating, bleeding galloper that a detachment of his far-ranging lancers had made contact—violent contact—with an estimated two thousand men, mixed horse and foot, who were apparently guarding a long wagon train, a large herd of cattle and a smaller herd of horses and mules. The newcomers were marching west to east in the direction of Kahlkopolis.

Grinning like a winter wolf, *Thoheeks* Pahvlos dispatched *Thoheeks* Portos and a mounted force consisting of both the heavy and the medium-heavy cavalry. As an afterthought, he reinforced the units of lancers which were ambling about just beyond bowshot of the city walls, lest someone in there get the idea of riding forth to succor the obvious supply train.

A bit after nightfall, *Thoheeks* Portos rode into camp to report few casualties to his own force, most of the foemen dead and the few survivors scattered and running hard. His troopers were bringing in the wagons and the horse herd, but had left the scrawny cattle to wander at will.

At dawn, a herald was sent to the main gate of the city to summon Stehrghiahnos. When that renegade dismounted before Pahvlos' pavilion, ranged beyond the hitching rail were a number of wooden stakes, each crowned with a livid, blood-streaked head—the sharp features and prominent, outthrust incisors which had given Ratface Billisos his name were on one of those ghastly heads, and that fact gave Stehrgiahnos the clear, indisputable message that there would be no reinforcements or resupply no matter how long his overlord waited.

Pahvlos' words were short and brusque. "Yesterday, Master Stehrghiahnos, my cavalry intercepted and extirpated the western contingent of your chief's bandit band. We captured some two hundred head of horses and mules, considerable amounts of arms and armor and horse gear, and above fifty wagon- and wainloads of supplies, as well as so many cattle that we had to leave the most of them running loose around the site of the battle.

"You had best advise your chief that he will not now be reinforced or supplied, so he had best come to battle with me as soon as possible, before his force within the city begins to suffer and be weakened by starvation and disease. Not that *Thoheeks* Ahramos and I give a damn how many bandits and renegades starve or suffer or waste away of the pox or the bloody flux, but we want no undue suffering to befall the innocent, the noncombatants within the city."

Screened by a long file of mounted lancers who, under orders, were raising as much dust as possible in their slow progress, Gil Djohnz and the elephant Sunshine led the way toward the assigned position. Sunshine, Tulip and Newgrass were all armored for the coming battle, but their huge, distinctively shaped bodies had for the nonce been covered with sheets of a dull-colored cloth, while the heavy, cumbersome wood-and-leather archer boxes had been dismounted and now were being borne in their wake by the teams of archers who would occupy them.

After the third or fourth time he slipped and stumbled on the broken, uneven footing, Gil found himself steadied and lifted easily back onto his feet by the gentle but powerful trunk of Sunshine. "You are silly to try to walk, Man-Gil," the pachyderm mindspoke him. "Your poor little feet will be sore beyond bearing tonight. Those men yonder are astride their horses, so why do you not ride Sunshine?"

Gil sighed. Sunshine was as stubborn as any mule when she chose to be. "It is still as I have said ere this, sister-mine: High as you are, if I mount you, anyone watching from the other army will know that at least one elephant is in this area, and it is our plan that they not know such until we are ready to attack them."

"Silly!" Sunshine mindspoke. "Two-legs are surely the very silliest of creatures. Fighting is the silliest of two-leg pastimes, and Sunshine is herself silly for taking part in such silliness; she only does so because she loves you, Gil."

At that same moment, seven huge, tawny felines were but just arrived in position to the rear of the cavalry reserve of the bandit army. They crouched within a tiny copse, their sleek bodies unmoving, their colors blending well with the dead leaves that covered the ground.

One of the prairiecats—for such they were, come south as part of the Horseclans force—meshed his mind with those of two others to gain sufficient strength for farspeak and beamed out, "We are where you said we should be. The horses cannot smell us . . . yet. But I fear the wind soon may shift . . . ?"

Strahteegos Thoheeks Pahvlos' well-concocted plan of battle had to be severely altered. With the bandit army formed up in position, it became clear that in order to avoid having his center outflanked by the center of the enemy, he must either stretch his lines of armored pikemen to suicidal thinness or commit the unarmored pikemen of Ahzprinos—for the umpteenth time he cursed the old-fashioned, obstinate, obtuse officer and his failure to emulate the other two pike regiments.

At length, the *strahteegos* made what he felt to be the best of a bad situation. He extended the regiments of Hehluh and Bizahros to a depth of only six men, but then he ordered the first and second battalions of Ahzprinos' regiment to form up two men deep immediately behind the armored regiments.

Of course, this left him damn-all reserve—one battalion of old-style pikemen, the headquarters guard of heavy horse and a scattering of lancers—but it would have to do.

Nor was he formed up any too soon. Out from both wings of the bandit army came clattering the warcarts—barded to the fetlocks as they were, there was no way to determine just how heavily or fully the pairs of big mules were armored, only safe to assume that they were; three men stood in each jouncing, springless cart, two archers and a spearman; the man responsible for guiding the pair was mounted on the near-side mule, fully armored and bearing shield and sword or axe. The carts kept a good distance from each other lest the steel blades projecting from each wheelhub become entangled with another set or, worse, cripple a mule.

Pahvlos saw immediately that there were not enough of the armored warcarts to tempt even such an amateur as the bandit chief to send them head-on against the massed pikes and hope to get any of them back. Anyone knew that the cavalry on the wings could easily ride deadly rings around such slow, cumbersome conveyances, and that left only a couple of alternative uses for the archaic weapons: an attempt to drive between wing and center and take the pikemen on the flank or a series of passes back and forth across the front while raining the pikemen they assumed to be unarmored and shieldless with darts and arrows.

It was the latter. In staggered lines, the warcarts were drawn, clattering and bouncing, the length of the formations of pikemen, expending quantities of arrows for precious few casualties. As the first line of warcarts reached the end of that first pass and began to wheel about, however, they got an unexpected and very sharp taste of similar medicine to that they had been so lavishly dispensing. Chief Pawl Vawn of Vawn, commanding the left wing, treated the carts and mules to such an arrow storm that some quarter of the carts were unable to return to the raking of the pikelines. Nor did the carts receive any less from the Horseclansmen under Tomos Gonsalos on the right wing.

With it patently clear that the warcarts were doing no significant damage to his front, *Strahteegos* Pahvlos sent *Thoheeks* Portos' heavy lancers out from the rear area and in a wide swing around his own right to deliver a crushing, crashing charge against the units of heavy horse and irregulars making up the left wing of the bandit army. That charge thudded home with a racket that could be heard even within the old warrior's pavilion. The heavy lancers fought bravely for a few minutes after the initial assault, but then a banner went down and, with loud lamentations, they began to disengage piecemeal and withdraw. Sensing victory within grasping distance, the bandits' entire left wing quitted their positions to stream out in pursuit.

And no sooner had the cavalry left their assigned flank areas than up out of a brushy gully filed Sunshine, Tulip and Newgrass. Speedily, the cloth shroudings were stripped away, the heavy, unwieldy, metal-shod boxes lifted up onto the broad backs and strapped in place. Then the boxes were manned by the archers, Gil Djohnz and the other two were lifted by the elephants to the saddles just behind the domes of the huge heads, and those still gathered about on the ground affixed the last pieces of the pachyderms' armor and uncased the broad- and heavy-bladed swords—six feet and more in length—each elephant would swing in the initial attack.

All of these preparations were well rehearsed and so took less than five minutes in the accomplishment, then the three huge beasts set out in line abreast at a walk which the trailing and flanking horsemen had some difficulty in matching for speed over the broken ground.

Much of Mainahkos' "infantry" was no such thing, rather were the most of them a broad cross-section of civilian men impressed off streets at sword's point and handed a pike or a spear before being hustled willy-nilly into an aggregation of similar unfortunates, then marched out to add depth to the pikeline. To these, the mere sight of the three behemoths fast bearing down upon them, swinging two-*meetrah* blades and supported by a horde of horsemen, was all that was needful to evoke instant panic.

Pawl, Chief of Clan Vawn, farspoke but a single thought, "Now, cat-brother!"

With bloodcurdling squalls, the seven mighty cats burst out of the tiny copse and sped toward the ranks of the now-mounting cavalry reserve. Broadbeaming hideous mind-pictures of blood and equine death, never ceasing their cacophonies of snarls, growls, squalls and howls, the felines rapidly bore down upon the horses and men.

The harried, wounded commander of the warcarts had never before heard of such a thing! Leaving their secure position, the entire four-hundred-yard length of the enemy pikeline was advancing, moving at a brisk walk, their pikes still presented—an array of winking steel points that projected well ahead of the marching lines. The miserable infantry simply did not advance against armored warcarts! Basically a less than imaginative man, the commander did the only thing he could just then think to do—he headed back to whence he and his force had come.

But before the carts could reach their objective, their own infantry had boiled forward, out of formation, to block the way. Deeply contemptuous of footmen at even the best of times, the commander led his survivors in carving a gory path through these up unto the moment that a terrified man smote him such a blow with a poleaxe as to hurl him to the ground just at the proper time and place to be decapitated by the sharp, blood-streaked, whirling blades projecting from the hub of his own warcart.

*   *   *

Portos and his squadron abruptly turned, raised the ''fallen'' banner and hacked a good half of their pursuers out of the saddle before said pursuers broke and fled. At that juncture, Portos halted his force, formed them up and directed them at the nearest protrusion of the roiling, confused mass of men that had formerly been the enemy's center.

But the projection had recoalesced with the main mass by the time the heavy horse reached it, so quick-thinking Portos rode on into the chaos that had lately been the rear areas of the bandit army. After leaving half the squadron to interdict the road leading to the city, the grim officer used the other half to strike the rear and flank of those units still guarding the right wing of the bandit army only bare moments before those units were assaulted all along the front by Chief Pawl Vawn's Horseclansmen.

With the precipitate retreat of the warcarts, *Strahteegos Thoheeks* Pahvlos ordered the drums to roll the signal, whereupon the pikemen dropped their shields, lowered their long, heavy pikes to lowguard-present—waist-level—and increased their pace to a trot, though maintaining proper interval and formation up to the very moment that their steel points sank into soft flesh or grated upon armor and bone.

Although the slaughter continued on for some hours more on that bloody field, the charge of the pikemen had ended the Battle of Kahlkopolis.

A Vision of Honor

by Sharon Green

Sharon Green writes: "I've been reading science fiction since the age of twelve, began writing it even before then, but never got serious about my writing until five years ago. I read a speech of Robert Heinlein's that said, 'Don't talk about it, do it!' So I did. Once turned on, it hasn't stopped yet." Sharon is the author of three series and two singleton books, and this is her second short story to appear in an anthology edited by Robert Adams.

Late-afternoon sunlight spread thickly through the wide windows of the large stone room, creating pools on the flags through which the five laughing young people strode. Four men and a girl they were, all clearly kin, all nearly of a size save for the girl, who was half a head shorter than the smallest. The clothing they wore was richly stitched and patterned, well cut from costly bolts of brightly colored cloth, dress-up for those of noble blood and just short of brand-new. Not many came to their father's house who merited such a peacock parade, and their laughter stemmed from looking at each other in linen and silk and velvet rather than in leather and scale or plate. They hadn't been told who the visitors were, and their laughter was half eager curiosity.

"It may well be some other count of Father's acquaintance who comes seeking a strong husband for his eldest daughter," one of the four young men offered, his handsome face creased into a grin. "His sons will have gone off to war and not survived, and now he must have a son-in-law to rule after him. The girl will be stunningly lovely, and the count will have heard of my exploits in the Middle Kingdoms, and will therefore ask me to accept her."

"She will more likely be fat and ugly, and her father will ask *me*, little brother," said a second, his own laughter joining that of the others. "Surviving the wars in the Middle Kingdoms is scarcely a guarantee that the following peace at home will also be survived—or filled with pleasure."

"I feel a great deal of relief that my company has already been recalled from the taverns where they spend their leave," said a third, eldest of the four and fully as amused. "As we depart in two days to seek our next commission, there will be no need for me to give fanciful excuses to our father's guests as to why it would be impossible for me to wed his skinny, homely daughter. Should you wish to join me, brothers, my company will welcome your swords."

"And what of *my* sword, Dharrehn?" the girl asked with an impish grin, fully sharing the mood of the men. "Although there are no sons with which *I* might be threatened, it would please me to ride with your company. I have no exploits in the wars to boast of as do you and our brothers, and for that reason feel deprived."

Captain Dharrehn Cambehl paused to look at his sister, considering the girl he had discovered when he had returned with his company to his father's city to allow them a time of well-earned leave. Although she wore an ankle-length brown woolen shift with yellow silk tunic beneath out of deference to their father's wishes, she could most often be found in leather and chain mail, armed and armored nearly as well as her brothers, the skill she had somehow acquired clearly in evidence while she trained. Had his shaven head been allowed to sprout, the hair would have been a light brown similar to her now neatly combed tresses, the eyes he inspected her with a pale blue just like her own. Saucy and harmless-looking and nicely well-rounded, he thought, and how few of his men would find fault with *that*.

"In *no* manner have you been deprived, Lisah," he replied after a moment, allowing his approval to be clearly seen by her. "Considering that in conjunction with your weapons skill, my company would soon be decimated were I to allow you to join us, and that before any commission was accepted. The number of high noblemen hereabout continue to be as few as they were?"

"They do indeed," the girl agreed happily, a brief look of annoyance flashing when her left hand failed to find a hilt to

rest on. "For that reason alone have I not been pestered while
training at war skills, with our arms masters and also with our
brothers when they briefly returned home from the wars.
Father will not even consider those who *are* about; therefore
has there been no need of my personally refusing them. And I
do no more than rag you, brother, for I have no true wish to
join your company. If you would have the truth, I have
already begun to form a company of my own."

Her brothers were so quick to exclaim in shock that the girl
laughed in delight, pleased that the surprise she had planned
to give them had not been discovered before she might spring
it. Brothers were, at times, worse than fathers, and yet their
approval remained important to her.

"Few capable men would be attracted to the banner of an
inexperienced girl, Lisah," her brother Dharrehn protested,
overriding the comments of the others. "A company must be
led by a man whose leadership qualities and tactical skills
have been well proven, not by one who has seen no more
than practice battle."

"My company will be led by exactly such a man," the girl
agreed, folding her hands before her in pleased comfort that
caused even greater agitation in her brothers. "Some three
months agone, I made the acquaintance of one Hwarruhn
Fredrix, former captain of the Red Horse Company, those
who were sent to death for so little reason. You may perhaps
have heard of how badly they were done."

Nods came from all four of her brothers, their upset quiet-
ing in the face of unpalatable memories. A year earlier the
Red Horse Company had taken hire with Duke Steev of
Vincetburk, a man who had had ambitions for expansion
unmentioned to the company he had hired. They had been
told that they were to guard his borders against rumored
attack by the duke's neighbor, Baron Rhich Djones, an upstart newcomer with few swords and less gold, but great
intentions. The baron was to have been unlikely to appear
with too great a force, therefore was the single company to
have been sufficient to halt him; were their numbers to prove
insufficient, however, a rider was to be sent back and the
balance of the duke's forces would quickly ride to their
assistance.

The Red Horse Company had established their camp headquarters in the pretty little vale they had been ordered to by

the duke, disliking the open position but saying little as they had been told that the duke's border lay just beyond the gentle swell of land not far ahead of them. It had been deemed best that they not show themselves too ostentatiously, merely patrol the border as a silent, forceful warning against foolishness, and their commission had included a comfortable extra to replace the loot they were unlikely to have the opportunity of securing. All in all the commission had seemed much like a leave with wages, and consideration of the brevity of the hire had kept most of the experienced campaigners of the company from fretting over the possible loss of the company's fighting edge.

Captain Fredrix had been too old a hand at surviving, however, to allow his men to grow even the least bit sloppy—which surely saved what small number of lives were not lost with the rest. When one of the mounted patrols came haring back with word of the force which marched against them, a force a good deal larger than any they had been told to expect, a rider was sent back for reinforcements and the company was quickly formed up, for all the good it did. The advancing host came on slowly until they had nearly reached the vale, and then they put heel to horseflesh and streamed over the rise and down upon the mere hundreds of the company, cavalry alone far outnumbering the defenders.

Captain Fredrix cursed the obscenely low and open position he was required to defend even as his men spurred forward in answering attack, hoping to down enough of the invaders close enough to the rise to entangle any following gallopers incautious enough to follow at full speed—and to render near useless the enemy's archers. The two forces came together with the clash of plate and the ring of swords, the fury of shouted curses and the finality of dying screams, and all the while they fought, the Red Horse Company awaited the arrival of the reinforcements they knew would soon be there. The duke's forces had their field camp no more than a few miles away while they played at maneuvers, and the rider sent would surely bring them as quickly as humanly possible.

Or so most of them died expecting. When relief finally did come and the attacking forces withdrew to regroup against the new threat, Hwarruhn Fredrix let his sword fall to the end of its knot and slumped in his kak a very long while, too exhausted even to fall to the ground. When the ringing in his ears eased and he was able to force his deadened arms to raise his visor, the sight which greeted him took the life from his spirit as well. Dead and dying lay all about, messily hacked corpses and writhing wounded alike, his once proud company mown like summer wheat. Even his banner was down and lost, the flag and the man holding it trampled to mud, and it came at last to the captain to wonder on the length of time it had taken assistance to reach them. He continued to think upon the matter even as he resheathed his sword and forced his achingly stiff body to dismount so that he might see to those of his men who still lived, but it needed the arrival at the duke's field camp before the truth of the thing was discovered.

The captain and three of his survivors, having at last brought their wounded to the camp doctors, came upon another wounded they had not expected to encounter. It was the boy they had sent to bring the duke's host to their aid, and they were told by a doctor that his bleeding body had been the first to be brought in, right after the host had marched. He was not expected to live, and most were surprised that he had survived even that long.

It quickly turned out that the boy lived only so that he might speak to his captain a final time, his indominable will refusing to allow his murdered body the surcease it yearned for. Captain Fredrix leaned low with his ear to the boy's lips for quite some time, and when he straightened, the boy's spirit at last gone to Wind, his face was a mask of fury. The duke had laughingly told the boy all, for the boy was not to have survived to repeat the tale; at the end of it he had been sworded beneath his armor, in the lower back, by one of those who stood with him in the duke's presence.

The Red Horse Company had been given hire with the expectation that none of them would survive, and it had not been the duke's lands they had been ordered to camp on.

Duke Steev, hungry for the lands held by Baron Rhich but unwilling to give warning to their other neighbors who would be victimized after the baron, had hatched a scheme which would make it appear that it was the baron attacking and the duke merely defending. The Red Horse Company had been placed not on the duke's land but on the baron's, and word of it had been sent to the baron in a roundabout manner, luring him forth in great anger with his host. The vale had been close enough to the duke's lands so that afterward he might claim that it *was* on his lands that the attack had taken place, and the scheme called for the slaughtered bodies of the Red Horse Company for the duke to grow enraged over. Enraged enough to lead his own host against the murderers of a new, peaceful company that had just taken hire with him.

And, of course, for that reason could not ride out too soon to give support to those who were meant to be slaughtered. When the boy had made to return to his company and reveal the truth to them, he had been sworded and thrown to the side, where he might die and take the truth with him.

"I have heard it said that Captain Fredrix attempted to reach the duke to give proper thanks for such a hire," Dharrehn mused, his fingers pulling at his lower lip the while his eyes glittered. "It seems unfortunate that Baron Rhich, well aware of the duke's intentions, had already done for him and his with companies taken on for another purpose, not to speak of his own levy and those of a number of neighbors. Hacking a corpse is not nearly so satisfying as causing one. For what reason has he not raised another company of his own?"

"At first he lacked the heart, and then he lacked the gold," the girl replied, nodding agreement with the sentiments her brother had voiced. "Mother's jewels have long been mine to do with as I saw fit, and what might be more fitting than to raise a company with them? I will merely be a member of that company, and not the only female among them. There will be three of us to begin with, and later there will certainly be more."

"I believe she means to corrupt and recruit every female she comes across," one of the four said with a sigh, sending the others a covert wink. "What, then, will we do for wives when we return at last to take up land and raise heirs?"

"Clearly, Fhill, we will each need to personally engage a company and carry one off," Dharrehn responded with a matching sigh, the twinkle in his eyes belying his mock sadness. "Our own sister will have made such effort necessary, and she with none who burns to do the same with her."

"Ah, but there *is* such a one," the youngest of the five interrupted, a wicked grin helping him to break the silence he had held till then. "Due to this cursed thigh wound I have been home longer than you others, and recently the hidden truth has been revealed to me by one who shall remain nameless."

"There *is* no hidden truth, Jahk, and that you should know even though fighters gossip like the eldest of retired ladies," the girl snapped, more annoyed than embarrassed that her other brothers immediately pricked up their ears like alerted herd stallions. "I would wed a savage before I would so much as smile at the dandified oaf!"

"Baron Kalvehn Theros' eldest son Lhestuh haunts our halls in preference to visiting what battles are about in leather and plate," Jahk confided to his brothers, paying no mind to the wrath of a sister who would not, after all, raise weapon to a brother who continued to limp and therefore lacked his natural balance. "He yearns to take our sister to wife, and although our father has refused to allow it and his intended has sworn to alter him in such a way as to make the doing futile should he ever approach her again, he continues to sulk about glaring at all who are thoroughly male, hoping the presence of his hired bullies will frighten them away. He wishes them gone before they clap eyes to his beloved, you see, for he fears they will carry her off as he lacks the courage to do. Many wagers have been made as to whether his sword has ever so much as scented blood."

"I have come to the belief that he wishes me to tread on him in full armor and spurred boots," the girl said sourly, now unmindful of the chuckling her brothers indulged in. "When he dies he is most unlikely to be sent to Wind, for that would spread the inner stench of him too far. Thank Sun our father had long since given me leave to do as I would with my life, else would I surely have found it necessary to spill the blood of a guest—after Father had been petitioned to death by him."

"Speaking of guests, by now the reception lacks only the presence of us five," remarked Fhill, nodding toward the closed double doors across the wide hall. "All niceties aside, I find myself curious as to who our visitors are. They must have crept within the house like thieves for none to know who they might be."

"It seems that Father alone knows them," Dharrehn said with his own share of curiosity, also looking toward the doors. "As we all know full well that hanging back in the face of the unknown merely allows one's enemies to creep up behind one, I believe we should now continue as we earlier began. Even proposed marriages should be faced with bravery rather than cowardice."

The others laughed their agreement even as they again began their advance, and soon they reached the doors to the reception room. No house guards or servants stood before these doors, as they were used only by members of the family, therefore did Dharrehn and his next younger brother Bhen open them as they reached them, then allowed the servants within to see to them from there. In two lines did the five move forward into the surprisingly large gathering, making their way through the greetings of men and women who should surely have had other things than wine-swilling to occupy them at so early an hour of the day. So thought Lisah from her place between Fhill and Jahk, behind Dharrehn and Bhen, pleased to be in the company of her beloved brothers, yet not so pleased to have been called away from axe lessons. The pesky weapon had till then gotten much the better of her, and the summons had come just when she had begun to see a glimmer of hope of reversing that. In battle one occasionally needed to use what weapon came to hand rather than what weapon one preferred, and to fail to learn the use of them all was surely an excellent way to ask to go prematurely to Wind.

"Ah, there they are at last," came their father's deep, calm voice from a point beyond Dharrehn and Bhen, a place not easily seen by Lisah from where she walked. "Four of nine sons, my lords, and hidden in their midst my only daughter."

At which words the two who walked before moved each to one side, and the girl was able to see her father and the three men who stood with him. The one nearest her sire and to his right was not quite of an age with him, the one to the stranger's right seemed a bit older, and the third was a good deal younger than the others, perhaps Dharrehn's age. Beside the third and youngest sat the reason the clustering guests failed to cluster too closely about the four, an extremely lovely reason that brought a smile of delight to Lisah. The prairie cat was full-grown although young, and her long-fanged, sharp-toothed grin of amusement was being misinterpreted by those who looked at her. Seated, her brownish-gray head rose easily above elbow level of the man despite his

size, and Lisah thought again how good it would be once the
new company was formed. *Her* company would have cat-
brothers and -sisters as well as horse-brothers and -sisters,
just as the wandering Clans had had all those years ago,
unlike most Kindred of the present day.

". . . and last but certainly not least is my youngest son,
Jahk, home recovering from wounds I'm told were gotten
under rather admirable circumstances," her father was saying
as her thoughts left the company-to-be and returned to where
her body stood. "The circumstances were not described to
me by *this* rapscallion, who has so far avoided discussing the
matter, but by other sources a father of sons learns to cultivate. It seems a truism that those who do best are least
willing to speak of it."

"Which is as it should be," the man beside her father
chuckled, accepting Jahk's bow with a nod of his head. "If
fighting men were to spend their time regaling audiences with
details of their exploits, they would find precious little time to
add to those exploits. Is that not so, Captain Cambehl?"

"As my lord *Ahrkeethoheeks* undoubtedly knows from
personal experience," Dharrehn replied with a bow of his
own, surprising Lisah. More often were Middle Kingdoms
titles used by her brothers, and the use of a Karaleenos title
could mean no other thing than that this was *their* archduke,
the renowned Bili of Morguhn, Bili the Axe! Lisah looked at
the big, light-haired, light-eyed man with something close
to awe, wondering if she might somewhere find the courage
to question him concerning her difficulties with the weapon
that was considered more a weapon-brother to him than mere
inanimate metal. In Bili of Morguhn's hands the axe lived,
and Lisah had long believed that this was due to more than
his magnificent size and strength.

"As all of us here are likely to know," the Archduke Bili
said with the faintest of smiles, looking about him. "Your
father *Komees* Sahm was a source of delight to storytellers
before his return here to claim his patrimony, as was *Thoheeks*
Hwill of Dunkahn before his own return. As the names of
you and your brothers are scarcely unknown in this, your own
day, Captain, neither is the name of *Thoheeks* Hwill's heir,
Bryahn, who now stands beside him. His cat-sister, Wind
Whisper, is too young to have joined him in battle, yet not so

her sire, Iron Claws. Had we days and weeks, the exploits of
those two would make excellent telling.''

"Certainly those of Iron Claws," their youngest guest put
in with a laugh, paying no mind to the very evident awe of
Bhen and Jahk. "My own exploits, such as they were, simply
accompanied his, at times with a great deal of reluctance.
One sword and four sets of claws, even accompanied by
teeth, should not have accomplished half of what they did.''

"Iron Claws offers the tale with a considerable difference
of opinion, most especially concerning the value of that
sword," remarked *Thoheeks* Hwill with bland amusement,
sending no more than a glance to his heir. "As a father of
sons I, too, found it necessary to cultivate other sources, and
the best of them is the prairiecat. No cat of my acquaintance
suffers from reticence where battles are concerned.''

"Which is also as it should be," said the *Ahrkeethoheeks*
Bili into the gentle, agreeing laughter. "Members of the Cat
Clan are justifiably proud of their battle prowess, and had we
claws and fangs of our own, perhaps our reticence, too,
would be overcome. But we've scarcely come here to speak
of battles and cat-brothers. Is there not one last introduction
to be made, *Komees* Sahm?''

"Indeed there is, my lord," said his host, turning with a
smile of pride to the girl, who had, till then, done no more
than join in the general laughter. "It pleases me to present
my daughter Lisah, youngest of all my get save Jahk, who
has grown to more than adequate womanhood despite having
been surrounded by naught save brothers and a father all of
her life. Her mother was carried off by fever not long after
bearing my last son; therefore has there been a dearth of
womanly guidance for her.''

"Surely there were female servants who assisted in raising
so delightful-looking a girl," protested *Thoheeks* Hwill as
Lisah bowed to the Archduke Bili, the duke's steel-gray eyes
seeming well pleased. "She appears quite mannerly and properly modest, a far cry from the outspokenness of too many
other girls about these days, who consider their opinion the
equal of a man's.''

"My daughter is well able to appreciate the company in
which she finds herself, *Thoheeks* Hwill," *Komees* Sahm said
hurriedly, seeing the raising of his daughter's brows and
knowing well what the gesture meant. "She, like her broth-

ers, has participated in war training, a thing which became necessary when the female servants in charge of her as a child declared themselves incapable of coping with her . . . manner. Arms masters tend to view such a manner with different sight.''

"And most often produce a far less fascinating product,'' put in Bryahn of Dunkahn, his lighter gray eyes showing a matching interest to his father's. "I must be sure to send my thanks to the High Lord Milo for his suggestion.''

"You find her acceptable, then,'' the Archduke Bili said with approval, nodding his agreement. "The High Lord will be very pleased, and I, myself, am able to recommend a woman with war skills without reservation. Should your own skills exceed hers, that is, which be more of a caution than a reservation. Some men, I hear, prefer it t'other way about.''

Again there was general laughter, but this time the girl Lisah failed to share in it. There was an oddness floating about which seemed just beyond the bounds of comprehension, and Lisah had never been one to allow the incomprehensible to pass without questioning it.

"There was a suggestion made by the High Lord Milo which concerns me?'' she asked as the laughter wound down, looking at her father's guests and then directly at her father. "And for what have I been found acceptable?''

"For a truly great honor, daughter,'' replied the *komees* with a wide smile, stepping forward to put an embracing arm about the girl. "The High Lord has had his attention brought to the fact that an inordinate number of nobly born girls in our district are husbandless, and that despite the two and three wives taken by the surviving noble sons and fathers. For that reason has he asked his nobles in more densely male-populated districts, such as *Thoheeks* Hwill's demesne, that they seek for wives a time in ours, to even the numbers which have fallen so far out of balance. The *thoheeks'* heir Bryahn now searches for a wife, and his presence greatly honors us, most especially as it comes at the express request of the High Lord.''

"The High Lord Milo asked that they come *here*?'' Dharrehn inquired with a good deal of surprise, in the process misinterpreting his sister's suddden silence. "Father, is there a reason for that you have never spoken to us of?''

"The *ahrkeethoheeks* tells me there appears to be a reason

I, myself, never before considered," the *komees* responded, his great pleasure evident in his voice. "We all of us know how strongly mindspeak talent runs in our family, but what we failed to know was that the High Lord was aware of it as well. For many years he had hoped to see a merging between our family and that of *Thoheeks* Hwill, the Dunkahn line being fully as strong in mindspeak as we, and now such a merging has become possible. The first issue of the union will be more eagerly awaited by the High Lord, I am told by Archduke Bili, than by the sire and dam."

This time nothing of the laughter touched Lisah, who was scarcely even aware of it. She was, instead, wrestling with a problem there could be but one solution to, considering her nature and the manner in which she had been raised. Her brothers had been correct about the awkwardness of the thing and her father was certain to be disappointed, but happily not forever. When the laughter was done, she smiled all about her.

"Should that be so, I find it a great relief that the High Lord is Undying," she announced to those who listened politely to her words. "He will then find little difficulty in awaiting issue which will not appear till my return. I regret the necessity, my lords, yet must I plead previous commitments."

Little of a visual nature could at first be seen on the faces about her, a phenomenon certainly caused, unbeknownst to the girl, by stunned shock. All eight were men of the world, and as such knew the way of the wagging of that world; to have been attacked with weapons there at the reception would not have caused a fraction of similar agitation. Lisah, who had known no more than her father's court all her life, smiled even more broadly with relief at how well they accepted the disappointment, understanding nothing of the sudden, extremely amused look Sir Bryahn attempted to swallow. The prairiecat Wind Whisper also chuckled inside her mind, as though she and the man had exchanged certain thoughts, and then Count Sahm's arm tightened about his daughter.

"Lisah, child, clearly you have somehow misunderstood the situation," he began, searching, in accordance with his kindly nature and the love he felt for his only daughter, for a manner in which to explain the truth without giving hurt. "Sir Bryahn seeks a wife *now*, not some time in the future, and as I have already given my permission for the union, there can be no previous commitments. The matter has already been settled.''

"But, Father, I have given my word based on your word," the girl protested, feeling the deepening upset in all four of her brothers, who yet stood silent rather than support her when she was so clearly in the right. "Was I not told that my life was mine to do with as I pleased, and have not all of my brothers been permitted to ride forth to sharpen their battle skills in actual combat? Just recently I have arranged to do the same, and will ride with the Crimson Cat Company now being formed. Was there not a proposed marriage for Dharrehn when his company was first formed, and did he not decline due to previous commitments? I do no more than the same.''

A great many looks were then exchanged between the eight men, some clearly wishing that the High Lord Milo had *not* expressed such keen interest in the matter. Although unused to protests of that sort from women raised to the knowledge that they would one day wed at their fathers' direction, they remained men of honor who could well appreciate the girl's arguments. Duke Hwill of Dunkahn, most often short-tempered with "flighty, mouth-flapping females," knew at once that this girl was not the same, that the giving of her word was looked upon as a Sword Oath, and became even more determined that such a prize would not be lost to his son.

"You misunderstand, girl, in believing your brothers were 'permitted' to ride forth to sharpen their battle skills," he said with less gruffness than his usual manner, drawing Lisah's light blue gaze. "Male children are *required* to do so among the Dunkahns, and I doubt not that the same holds true for Cambehl sons. Daughters, however, are another matter entirely, for one man may get many heirs on two or three wives, but one woman may have no more than one birth at a time, no matter the number of husbands. Battle was made for men, girl, and we would none of us wish to see you lost to it.''

"Your outlook is more than understandable, child," Count Sahm added at once, grateful to Duke Hwill for the assistance of his words. "With the blood of Clan Maiden warriors so thick in your veins, scarcely could you see the matter elsewise. You must, however, make the effort to recall that my word to

you was not as you stated it. You were told that *in the
absence of acceptable suitors* your life was yours to direct, a
qualification which no longer obtains. Do you contend that
the thing was not put to you in such a way?''

Lisah stared silently up at her father, helpless to deny the
statement, for it was certainly true. That she had failed to
place significance on the qualification was certainly not the
fault of her sire, yet was it inarguably his fault that such a
qualification had been added to begin with. In a few brief
moments she had grown to feel that all those about her
attacked at once with weapons she was totally unfamiliar
with, but her training and basic nature disallowed surrender,
or falling without a final effort.

"And the fact that I have already committed myself, just as
Dharrehn had?'' she said, unaware of the sadness in her
father at the stiffness of her tone and bearing. "There was
another qualification, perhaps, allowing his word to be honored the while mine need not be?''

Again there was an exchange of glances, nearly to the
point of embarrassment, yet her father refused to allow himself to avoid her gaze.

"Lisah, child, the qualification had no need to be spoken
of aloud," he said, this time sparing her no more than he
would have one of his sons. "Dharrehn is a man, the while
you are not.''

The words struck her more harshly than a bucket of ice
water for predawn wakening, a clear-cut statement of preju-
dice she had never before encountered. The arms masters
who had trained her had never demanded less from her
because of her sex, and she had never understood that this
had been done because her life was precious to them. To
demand less would have been to give less, and to their
minds her due was all they were capable of giving. Lisah, the
girl trained up with men and by men and now a woman,
found comprehension completely beyond her.

"I see," she said, even more stiffly than before, meeting
the eyes of none about her, the lie spoken automatically and
without conscious thought. "I regret that I must now ask to
be excused, my lords. An—illness has settled upon me of a
sudden, and I fear I would be no fit company for guests who
do my father honor with their presence.''

None attempted to halt the girl as she turned and made her

unheeding way through the balance of the guests, some of whom had been near enough to hear what had transpired, but most sighed for her distress. *Komees* Sahm of the Cambehl line, a man who had inspired songs with the ferocity of his battle skills while still a very young man, sighed more deeply than the others, causing Duke Hwill to step to his side and clap him gently on the shoulder in commiseration.

"She will not long be so filled with upset, my friend," he assured the man, who surely felt that he had somehow betrayed one of his own blood. "I now see the wisdom in the manner in which my own girls were raised, and you must recall that your duty lies in seeing her well wed, not well battle-companioned. She is more than bright, and will soon come to understand that you wish only the best for her."

"And I will see that she receives not one whit less," said Bryahn of Dunkahn, stepping forward to stand beside his sire. "I had not hoped to find a wife I both desired and respected, and now that I have I will certainly see that she has no regrets over our union. Wind Whisper has assured me that I am unlikely to find better to bear my kittens, and I would be a fool to disregard such sound advice."

"You are all surely correct," the count allowed with a final sigh, unable to keep from chuckling at having his future grandsons termed "kittens." "The girl will retire early, perhaps with tears, and in the morning will be capable again of smiles. The hour of the day remains early, yet is the feast I promised now ready for consumption. Shall we drink a bit more, or retire to the tables?"

"Drink, I trust, is also available at your board, and we have traveled far in the days just past," said *Thoheeks* Hwill with a second, stronger shoulder clap, grinning in anticipation. "I have heard many things said of the table you set, and the least of them brings instant watering to my mouth."

"Not to speak of the fact that we must, this night, return Archduke Bili to the camp where most of our escort waits," said Bryahn, also agrin at his father's well-known penchant for fine food. "He accompanied us at the High Lord's request merely to perform introductions, and now must return home with all possible speed."

"But not without first fortifying myself for the journey," the *ahrkeethoheeks* put in, a faint smile on him for the fact known only to himself that his presence had not been merely for introductions. The High Lord Milo's keen interest would need to be satisfied, and this he was now able to do.

"There was little need to camp your escort a full mile from my city, my lords." Count Sahm repeated what he had much earlier said, only this time with unarguable firmness as he began to lead the way to his dining hall. "You will, of course, fetch the balance of them back with you after the *ahrkeethoheeks* is on his way, for there will then no longer be a need for speedy departure. My city may be small, yet is it certainly capable of . . ."

His words trailed off as he and his guests and his sons quitted the room, followed at a discreet distance by those other guests who were the city's notables. Not all, however, followed with eager anticipation, for there are all sorts of things which might be anticipated. One guest, a man with weak chin and burning eyes, a man who delighted in always being well dressed and never leaving in doubt his excellent upbringing, held his ground in thought while the others followed, then turned and left the reception room by another door. What he anticipated might not be eaten, but after its successful completion it would certainly need to be swallowed.

Full dark had long since descended when Lisah slipped into the deserted stables, laboring to keep herself from rattling. Her mare, White Feet, already expected her, and was not far from stamping in eagerness.

"Why must we be silent, sister?" the mare asked with mindspeak as the girl slipped into the stall, turning her head to watch the arrival. "And why is your chain wrapped rather than upon you?"

"We must be silent for the reason that some men seem capable only of speaking of honor, not of practicing it," the girl replied in the same way, setting her burden down before reaching for her saddle. "Also, my chain must be wrapped rather than worn, for I have never before worn it on our nightly excursions just without the city's walls. A last, brisk gallop before retiring is something to be expected of us; an armored gallop is not."

Which was why she wore no more than boiled leather beneath her swordbelt, her chain mail and bow and shafts and darts carefully wrapped for dropping over the wall. Once she had passed through the gate she would reclaim the bundles, and gave thanks to Sacred Sun that it was chain rather than plate she needed to drop. Chain would cause enough of a racket, but plate would be heard all the way to her destination.

When Lisah had left the reception room to return to her apartment, it was not to shed the tears her father had made mention of. Warriors are more often trained to think and react than to weep, and Lisah had been trained as a warrior. Her floors endured much striding back and forth as she strove to understand what had been done to her, and at long, long last she had reached a conclusion she had not sooner been able to bring herself to.

Her father's sense of honor had been overcome by flattering attention, the sort he had never before been exposed to. His sense of the right had been warped in the light of the expressed wishes of the High Lord Milo, wishes no man would be expected to ignore.

Lisah had shaken her head at that conclusion, her smoldering anger aimed at the Undying Lord rather than at her beloved father. Never would her father have broken his word if he had not had his head turned so completely, the proof of which was clearly to be seen in his last remarks. She was to believe it mattered that she was female while Dharrehn was not? When had such a difference mattered before, most especially to their father? And why had her brothers not supported her, as they none of them had ever failed to do in the past? Two had fallen in battle and three were away as the four now home would soon be again, but never had any of them refused to aid in her training, all standing firmly behind her right when some wide-bottomed city matron attempted to take it from her with catty criticism.

No, her brothers had been intimidated at mention of the High Lord, and her father had been flattered blind, and now they thought she would add to the dishonor by breaking a word which had been accepted as given. Were she to do such a thing her father would never forgive himself nor her, for he was certain to return to his senses as soon as his high-noble guests were gone. It was *her* duty to see that they were not dishonored, a duty she was most pleased to accept, and should the High Lord be displeased enough to wish vengeance, his wrath would fall only on her. She knew very little about the Undying High Lord, having never before considered him at any great length, yet knew well enough that she had no fear of him. The years she had lived had not been many, yet had there been sufficient of them to show her there was *no* man she feared.

Lisah had then begun to gather her things, having spent enough hours bringing herself to the realization that she must give her father a small bit of embarrassment to save him from more and worse. She would simply join the Crimson Cat Company sooner than expected, and that would be that. Her father's "guests" would depart quickly enough when they found her gone, and when she returned home with true battle experience, all would be even better than it had been. She should really have been gone on her way years earlier, at the age her brothers had first left, but she had let her father's oft-mentioned loneliness keep her home at his side. Now it would fall to Jahk to ease that loneliness, for he was the youngest and she had already had her turn.

She encountered no difficulty with the gate guards, who merely bid her a pleasant ride as always, and also had no difficulty in locating what had previously been dropped over the wall a good distance from the gate. She quickly dismounted, tied her awkward gear to White Feet equally as quickly, then set off obliquely for the road, wasting none of the precious little time she would have. She knew well enough it would have been wiser donning her armor before seeking the road, but without a dresser she would be some time adjusting it all, and when her usual ride-length elapsed without her return, the city guard would be quickly mounted and sent after her. She would need to be well away before that happened, and well concealed before she stopped. The full moon was nearly bright enough to read by, which would make remaining undetected that much more difficult.

Lisah and White Feet both had sufficient time to wish they had been able to bring a pack mule, when the road curved enough to present them with an unexpected sight. Through the darkness and her mare's insistences that she was a war-trained destrier and *not* a great, sexless Northorse, Lisah caught sight of what seemed to be a battle, between perhaps fifteen defenders and nearly twice that number of attackers. As she rode nearer, wondering which side was in the right and therefore the side she should join, the clang of weapons grew clearer and also the curses and screams of the wounded. It was an insane melee, swirling like a dance of death 'neath the moon, and then the madness music turned them so that she had not the least of doubts who was there.

A great axe swung, seemingly without effort, taking both head and shoulder from a man, and a great, silent cat leaped upon another, removing face and life together. Her father's guests were under attack, and still outnumbered despite their efforts.

Without further pause Lisah turned in her saddle, yanked on the slipknots securing the bundles to her kak, turned back to unsheathe her sword, and was encouraging White Feet in her forward leap almost before her gear had hit ground. Who the attackers might be was still unclear, outlaws having been discouraged from the area years agone, but it mattered no more than that scale remained bundled rather than worn.

The approach of horse and girl was as silent as possible, fully as silent as her arrival behind the attackers was noisy. White Feet then screamed challenge as she voiced the Cambehl cry, leading the attackers to believe that they, in turn, were being attacked, and so they were, but not by the large force they at first imagined. Their attention, however, was diverted long enough for half a dozen of their number to be accounted for by their erstwhile victims, and another two downed by the unexpected new arrivals. Lisah's blade took the arm from one cleanly before the backswing opened his throat, and White Feet's teeth sank into a roan neck much like her own but scarcely as well trained. The frightened, wounded horse screamed and reared, unseating its rider into the midst of the still-raging destriers of the intended victims, and steel-shod hooves quickly stamped the life from him.

From that point on the battle was turned about, as Lisah quickly saw would have been the case even had she not arrived. The attackers were, for the most part, riffraff from the city, none fully armored and few even in boiled leather, the sort who counted a battle won merely because they possessed superior numbers. Those they had hoped to overwhelm were fully armored, well-mounted, experienced warriors, unimpressed by mere numbers and coolly pleased by the unexpected diversion. Duke Hwill, especially, chortled with pleasure as he lay about him with a well-crimsoned blade, then laughed aloud when Lisah's swing took the guts from one who had chosen to face her rather than him. The craven screamed with pain and disbelief as he tumbled from the saddle, leaving the battle in a way he had not expected. He had thought to save his life by running, but had chosen the wrong route.

Others also attempted to flee once the tide had clearly turned, but their efforts proved no more successful. A small number of the nobles' escort, led by Sir Bryahn, pursued them back up the trail, and a few moments later a shrill, high scream rent the darkness. With none left to face their weapons, Lisah and the balance of the party trotted after pursuers and pursued to see what had occurred, and found that the fleeing few had led their would-be victims to the one who had set the attack. The dog had sat his horse well away from the battle rather than join it or lead it, and had attempted Sir Bryahn's back while the Dunkahn heir was engaged with the last of the cur's followers. Sir Bryahn's plate had turned the weak, craven blow, and then Sir Bryahn had turned, to smash the skull of the thinly armored fool with the edge of his blade, bringing forth a scream shrill as a woman's even before the blow landed. Afterward the man was no longer able to scream, his unmoving body and wide-staring eyes making that clear.

Lisah looked down at the body of Lhestuh Theros where it lay sprawled on the ground, moonlight washing it to a purity it had never had in life, and felt somewhat shaken. She and her brothers had laughed at Lhestuh's attempted pursuit of her, never dreaming that the fool would go to such lengths to remove other suitors from his path. She truly should have departed the city a good deal sooner, to avoid a happening such as that if for no other reason. Had any of her father's guests been harmed because of the attack, the fault would have been hers.

The girl silently bespoke White Feet, and the mare backed from the press of men and horses, then the two quietly paced back to the place Lisah's gear had been left. White Feet's thoughts were a satisfied swirl of battle pleasure and high interest in the war stallions she had fought beside, but Lisah was more concerned with wiping her blade on her leather-covered thigh as best she could before sheathing it. As she halted before her bundles and dismounted her thoughts were already taking her up the road to her earlier-chosen destination, the place where her company was gathering, a destination suddenly centered about with worry. She had been considering it a haven and an opportunity not to be equaled, but would it instead become a nightmare?

White Feet's soft nose nuzzled her hands as she stood in the moonlit dark, staring down at gear her eyes failed to see. She knew it was more than time she left her father's city, Lhestuh's nauseating attempt enough to convince her of that had she needed convincing, but the attack had brought her another, brand-new thought to consider. Captain Fredrix had been so achingly heart-sick to be leader of and a part of another company that he hadn't balked long over allowing her to join the one she had proposed to fund, but her brother Dharrehn's words now rose up in her mind to cloud her joyful confidence.

My company would soon be decimated, were I to allow you to join us, he had said, and that before any commission was accepted. And in no manner have you been deprived, Lisah.

Would such a thing occur in *her* company, the one she had so long dreamed about? Would there be those like Lhestuh, willing to go to any lengths to possess her? Returning to the city was out of the question, but if she could not join the Crimson Cat Company, where, then, would she go? Was there no place in all that world she might call home?

"You should not have ridden off so quickly, Lisah," a voice came from behind her, calm and even. "We have not yet had opportunity to thank you for your assistance."

The girl turned to see Sir Bryahn Dunkahn astride his war stallion, both pairs of eyes resting on her with interest. A third, yellow pair regarded her from beside the stallion, a long red tongue leaving off its paw-cleaning for the purpose. Lisah felt the chuckling in the mind of Wind Whisper, but as the prairiecat made no attempt to bespeak her, she also remained silent. Her eyes returned, instead, to the Dunkahn heir, but found that the man now looked on the bundles behind her, the odd smile on his face saying that he knew what lay wrapped in them. With helm already doffed he had no more to do than dismount, and then he stood facing her.

"The reason for your being abroad at this hour of the night is no longer a mystery," he said, removing his gauntlets as he looked down at her. "As you so clearly prefer riding off to wedding me, I wonder that you took the time and trouble to aid us."

"You happen to be my father's guests," the girl returned stiffly, finding herself growing annoyed at the easiness of the man's manner. Would that all men responded to her as this one; she would then find it possible to ride with her company till she was gray and bent. "No matter my own feelings and opinions, assisting the guests of my father is a duty. To behave differently would be dishonorable."

"Ah, I see," he said, nodding with the same odd lightness behind his sobriety. "To have failed to assist us would have been dishonorable, but disobeying your father's wishes is not. The matter is now clear to me."

"I scarcely disobey my father's true wishes," Lisah replied as haughtily as she might, praying to Sun and Wind that the blush hot on her cheeks might not be visible to the awful man who continued to regard her. "When he returns to his senses he will find it again possible to admit that one may not withdraw one's word with honor, and that duty must be attended to even if unpalatable. I now do no more than honor my word and attend to duty."

The girl began to turn from him then, intending to retrieve her gear and replace it on her mare, but a big hand came to her arm, halting her.

"You speak of honor and duty as though well familiar with them, girl, yet does your understanding of the two seem rather flimsy to me," Sir Bryahn said, the lightness gone from him, his voice filled more with steel. "Should it be your wish to run petulantly from your true duty like some spoiled, pouting child, you may do so, but you may not tarnish the word 'honor' by linking it to such an act. There is no slightest trace of honor or duty in what you do."

"How dare you!" Lisah hissed, her right palm aching to be clapped to her hilt. Had the swine been other than her father's guest she would surely have drawn on him, and that despite the plate he wore. His helm had been left behind on his kak, the doing of a fool if ever there was one. One of her arms masters had taught her a ploy . . .

"I dare quite easily," the beast returned, folding metaled arms across metaled chest. "Have you never been taught that a child's first duty is to its sire and family, not to its own desires? From what I have already learned of your father, I would strongly doubt that the omission was his. Think you are alone in wishing to do one thing, while needing to do another? We all of us do as we must, and therein lies true honor.''

"Your words make as much sense as the cawing of a crow," the girl pronounced, hoping to push the man into drawing on her instead. "I most certainly am aware of my duty to my family and my father, which is one reason why I ride from here as I do. Had my father been in his right senses, never would he have spoken to me as he did, insisting that I withdraw an already-given word. It was he I learned the meaning of honor from, and none of this 'he is male, you are female' foolishness. Honor is the same for all.''

"Indeed it is," Sir Bryahn allowed, nodding carefully. "It is, however, not *seen* the same by all, most especially not by one who lacks full knowledge. All Kindred family members know that a daughter must wed at her father's direction, the while a son need not do the same. Our combined escort numbers a full two hundred men, girl, a large number of them Kindred. Should you doubt my word, you may put the question to each and every one of them."

Lisah stood wordless at this revelation, having no need to do as Bryahn had suggested. The man's mind was just then fully open to her as it had not previously been, and the truth in his words shone forth from his thoughts as the moon shone forth from the sky. In no manner was it a lie he spoke, and she abruptly felt that to have been chopped with his sword would have been far kinder.

"But—then—my having left would be no other thing than dishonorable," she whispered, raising one hand to her whirling head. "And yet, what else is one to do when faced with such—*injustice*? How does one find an honorable course in such a morass, even should there be one? And how very unlikely it is that there is one; honor, in all probability, will prove to be no more than illusion.''

The tormented girl turned to bury her fists and face in the mane of her mare, bitter disappointment and the pain of incomprehension slicing her from within. All things she had ever been taught were now suspect, for how many other hidden snares might there be among them? Freedom was not freedom and words might be broken at will, and each time her father had told her that she was the most precious of all his get, he had surely lied. She was the least precious of all,

for she was female, unfit, even, to have the full truth spoken
to her.

"Honor is no illusion, Lisah, nor are you faced with the
sort of injustice you currently picture," Sir Bryahn's voice
came, now gentle and filled with compassion. "As I said
earlier, one without full knowledge merely sees it differently."

"In what other manner is one to see it?" the girl demanded, disillusionment making the words harsh, her fists
still tight in the mane. "To disobey my father would be
dishonorable, but to obey him would be to dishonor my
word, and dishonor as well my sense of pride. Am I a mule,
to be given to the first man my current owner approves of, to
be bred for the pleasure of a distant herdmaster? Perhaps you
picture yourself a mule, my lord. I most emphatically do
not."

"Hardly a mule, Lisah, for mules cannot be bred," was
the reply, spoken in a voice which strove not to be amused.
"And also do I believe that the High Lord would be ag-
grieved to hear himself referred to as a herdmaster. He, like
us, does as he must, for the entire Confederation is his
concern. Our concerns are more modest, however, and what
you have said is entirely wrong. Have you the courage to give
heed to a truth which disagrees with your sense of the proper?"

"I no longer have a sense of the proper," the girl returned,
freeing one hand to stroke her mare. "You may speak whatever words you will, for I care not."

"Moping suits you not at all, girl," the man retorted, firmly
taking Lisah by the arms and turning her to face him. "Much
do I prefer your smile, and perhaps we may return it to you.
Let us speak first of what you see as injustice. You believe
your father should not have the right to marry his daughter to
the man of his choice?"

"When that daughter's brothers may do as they please?"
Lisah replied with a sound of disdain. "Certainly not."

"Ah, but that daughter's brothers may *not* do as they
please," Bryahn pounced, a faint gleam in his moon-silvered
gray eyes. "They do indeed have the right to choose their
own wives, but there are other things they have no choice
whatsoever in. Should your brothers all have chosen to remain at home, sniffing the flowers in the fields and forests
rather than riding off to hone their battle skills, would they
have been permitted to do so?"

"After the disinheritance, certainly," Lisah grudged, attempting to picture a wandering flower-sniffer as Clan Chief rather than an acclaimed warrior. She recalled having said that her brothers had been *permitted* to ride off to battle; "required" might indeed be a more accurate word.

"And yet, I doubt that needing to ride off to battle strikes you as too terrible a fate," Bryahn said, grinning at the answer Lisah had given. "Perhaps we would do better discussing another aspect of a man's duty to sire and Clan. Is your brother Captain Dharrehn your father's heir?"

"My brother Tohm is heir, with Djorj after him," Lisah replied, curious as to the reason for the question. "Dharrehn is third-eldest now, with Arthuh gone to Wind."

"As I was third-eldest of five," Bryahn said with a nod. "Your brother captains a company he has great pride in, but I would have you tell me what would be required of him were he suddenly to become eldest, named heir, and summoned home."

The girl stared in considerable dismay, never before having considered the point, and the man who watched her nodded again.

"I believe you understand," he said, faint satisfaction evident. "Should he be named heir and summoned home he would need to go, likely without his beloved company, possibly with them in escort, but he no longer their captain. Duty to sire and Clan would require him to reclaim his word concerning all other commitments, and none would think any the less of him for it. I, too, was faced with such a thing when my eldest brother fell, leaving me the last of the five. My father had begun to feel the weight of his years, and had no wish to cause discord among my sisters' husbands. You may see now that you were not singled out as one whose given word had no meaning. One who is duty-bound has no choice in the matter."

Lisah digested the words spoken to her as she stared at a plate-covered chest, some measure of composure returned but by no means all. Matters seemed less black than they had; however, less black was more often gray than white.

"I still see no hint of the smile I seek," Bryahn said, and then his hand came to her chin to raise her face. "I would have preferred not mentioning this, but there is one additional thing a man has no choice in. Should he find the woman who would make him the best of wives, he must be sure not to release his already-acknowledged claim on her. Should he do so, his father might well claim her in his stead, and then rather than wife, she would be mother to him. My father was delighted with the skill you showed during the attack, and told me that sight of you has made him feel young again. Surely you can see now that I have no choice save to press my claim for you, Lisah. I could not bear having you become my mother.''

Despite her previous upset, Lisah could not help but smile at that, so foolishly outrageous was the picture evoked. That the situation described was more than possible seemed to add to the humor of it, and the two smiled widely at each other. It came to Lisah then that perhaps her lot was not quite as bad as she had thought it to be; as she could not join her company and had no wish to remain longer in her father's city, she needed to find *some* destination that would suit her. This Bryahn of Dunkahn was still unknown to her, but his words had brought a clearer sight of her proper path, the one to take her through the morass with honor intact. There *was* one other point, however. . . .

''I seem to hear the echo of 'herdmaster' in your thoughts,'' Bryahn observed, deliberately putting his arms about her and drawing her close. ''The position of herd stallion has always been considered more noble than brood mare; however, no herd stallion worth his salt would allow a passel of yapping, panting observers to bring distress to his favorite mare. What say we have five or six before we let on that we've done more than nod to each other?''

This time Lisah laughed full out, wishing that the chest she was being held against was not encased in blasted metal. On second thought, Sacred Sun had done right well by her, and perhaps her father had done the same. This man not only saw through to problems clearly, he made the effort to show *her* the solutions.

''Would you truly keep the Undying High Lord at arm's length merely to please a brood mare?'' she asked, oddly eager to hear what his reply would be. ''I feel it only fair to warn you that should he appear at the wrong moment, demanding to see our issue, I am quite likely to take a sword or dirk and determine for myself just how undying he truly is.''

''I somehow have no doubt that you would, my girl,''

Bryahn laughed even as he winced at the thought, his arms tightening carefully about that leather-clad bundle that was now undeniably his. "But no, I would not keep the High Lord at arm's length for a brood mare. For my beloved wife who is a vision of loveliness, however, I would do that and a thousand times more."

He lowered his face to take the first taste of her lips then, his mind now showing the pulsing heat he felt for her which he had earlier covered, and Lisah was more than willing to join in the effort. To him she was a vision of loveliness, but to her he was far more than that. To her he was clearly a vision of honor—and even more, one who rode with prairiecats. Surely, before the first of his issue was required of her, there would be opportunity to ride with a cat into one or two *small* battles. . . .

Wind Whisper laughed with a great deal of amusement, but Bryahn was far too distracted with other doings to hear.

Rider on a Mountain

by Andre Norton

Precisely how do you go about introducing one of the top seven living science fiction and fantasy writers in the world, an extant legend, who has produced over two hundred works, a fabulous lady whose literary art introduced so many current readers to the field back in the early fifties, has continued to entrance them as they matured and now is introducing their children to the same Norton magic? The following, "Rider on a Mountain," is an original, never-before-published Andre Norton story, written in my HORSECLANS world for this anthology. I feel deeply honored and blessed to be able to offer it for your pleasure.

Nancee pushed back under a screen of drooping willow branches. The wad of wet clothing she had snatched from the stream launched a runnel of water between her small breasts. Her skin was roughened by more than just gully breeze as she quivered and shook from raw bursts of fear and pain in her head. This was not hearing—though she was also dimly aware of shouts and cries from the camp over the hill behind—this was rather a feeling which racked her slim, near-childish frame.

There was pain and death, and also a wild excitement and need to cause both pain and death—running with it a cold calculation which was like a stab between her narrow shoulders, a greed which fed upon attack, the lust for death. She crouched, as frozen as a rabbit cornered by a tree cat, the sandy gravel of the river's edge grating against her legs and buttocks.

That mind thread of pain arose to torment—then snapped as might a cord pulled too tightly. She smothered an answering cry with her hand, her teeth scraping her knuckles. Someone had died—someone close to her. Now the triumphant greed wreathed about like the smoke of a wild fire. If she stayed here—

She had learned well wariness and resolution during the past half year. Now she burrowed yet farther into the thickness of the willows until she had her back to the trunk of the largest, the rough bark grinding into her shoulders.

Would the raiders come questing along the stream? Did they realize that one of their prey was missing? She began to pull on the limp dampness of her clothing. How soon?

Would they come pounding over the hill where the river made a turn, or would they ride upstream in the stream bed itself?—the water ran shallow enough. She chewed on her lower lip.

Loincloth, then divided shirt weighted with water, but still smelling of horse and her own sweat, the shirt which her fingers fumbled so that she could hardly fit lashing cords to hole.

She squeezed the water out of her hair and knotted back the lank strands with a greasy thong, trying the while to stifle her hard breathing as she forced herself to accept the worst which must have happened—inwardly marveling that she had this small fragment of time still unhunted. She must prepare—

For Dik Romlee. Her lips stretched in a mirthless line.

Nancee studied the ground around her. Weapons? She remembered the Horseclans woman with whom she had shared a fresh roasted rabbit only two days ago. Then she and her uncle had still been part of the caravan, before Dik showed his hand. That prairie rover had had weapons in plenty, a knife hilt showing an inch or two above boottop, another at her belt, a sword of deadly promise, a bow—

The girl wiped her sweating hands on the skirt. She had nothing but those hands and her teeth. And she might well consider herself already captive. Except she was a Lowree of the House of Bradd.

Her head jerked as she raised her pointed chin. A Lowree was not truly mastered except by death. If she could not defend herself she could use those same teeth to open her own veins. Did not the Song of the House of Bradd tell of just such a deed when Mairee of the Sun Hair was taken by the Lord of Kain? Little good *he* got from that!

Firmly she closed her mind to that other's cold triumph, which beat at her as if a fist thudded into her face. She tried to pick up any call, the slightest hint of message from Uncle Roth, from Hari or Mik. There was only blankness to answer. So she was truly alone—

But she was startled out of that grim thought for a moment by a high squealing sound, a battle cry of another kind. Boldhoof—they had the greatest treasure left to Bradd's line, the giant Northhorse. She could use—

Only she could not. The Horseclan guards could bespeak their mounts at will. With the Northhorse Nancee had no such a bond. Her mindspeak was limited more to a sensing of emotion—the identification of those who had been long known to her. She could not now stir Boldhoof into any rebellion which would count. Rather did she already feel the reassurance which was flooding the camp. That mind which had betrayed itself with greed and cruelty was now striving to bring the huge horse into obedience. And Dik would certainly win. She had seen him with animals before. It was the one part of his character she could not understand, for it was not part of the evil which walked two-legged under his name.

He would not be satisfied with the loot he had taken, the deaths which already answered the steel of his followers. Her body would not lie there and he would come seeking—

Nancee dropped to her belly, her head raised only inches from the gravelly soil, as she began to wriggle from the temporary shelter she had found farther along under the screen of the willows. This was another hunt in which she was the quarry, only this time there were none of those who had been with her before.

Back in the east where Bradd's Hold had once stood tall and defiant against the sky there had been swords in a plenty. Until that black-mouthed traitor Dik Romlee had caught them from their blind side—where they had had no watchful eyes, since no man expected treason from an oathed kinsman.

Uncle Roth, his right arm useless from the witch curse Dik must have laid upon him, had gotten the two of them out and away. She might not be as dear to him as a daughter in truth, but it was from her body—Nancee levered herself up a fraction on one elbow and listened with ear and mind. Yes, only she could birth an heir the kin would accept. And Dik was sure to lay within her his treacherous seed should he take her. Her outstretched fingers dug painfully into the gravel and she pulled determinedly ahead.

Still there gnawed upon her that belief that they would come a-hunting. What chance had she against the foul pack of them? Already they had accomplished half their plan. Dik had maneuvered the Traders' trail chief into leaving them behind, spreading his tale of their being outlawed in the west on Uncle Roth's first trip hither—that the Horseclans would not treat with any from a train giving them shelter. It was Dik's word against her uncle's. And Dik's hand deep in a money purse as he said it all. Gold pieces were few on the frontier—those looted from Roth's own strongbox had sentenced him to death in the end.

She turned her head to the river, of which she sighted only a little between the well-leaved branches. There was an inner core there with a current, but she could not swim. With a piece of the dried storm wrack which was between the rocks farther on could she hold herself afloat? Yet she would be in the open, easy for them to take.

Tentatively she tried a mindsend toward the hidden camp. And snapped it free and away as she breathed fast and shallowly. No one there except those who followed Dik. But not even Dik now—which meant—

She could look ahead to that pile of drift which had drawn her this far. No spear, no bow, no keen-bladed knife. What she might have—

Her hand loosed its tight grip upon the gravel and she made a quick grab with hooked fingers which closed iron-tight on a length of sun-and-wind-dried sapling.

What Nancee jerked into her willow screen was bone-yellowed wood ending in a mass of snapped and broken roots. She broke off several of those and hefted her find. A club of sorts—at least the best weapon she was to find except for some water-smooth stone. But a sorry and useless thing with which to meet a well-armed raider.

Yet they were not going to take her until—

She started, one hand dropping back to the ground to steady herself, her eyes wide in her sun-browned face. What—

"Where are the wagons, two-legs? This one is sore-pawed—also hungry—"

No foggy beam of hate or fear or calculating menace—this

was as clear in her head as if she heard it by ear instead of by
mind!

"Two-legs—"

Again that imperative and irritated call. She hunched over
the crude club, her hands rubbing along its length. Then there
came a quiver of leaves ahead, a swinging of branches, and a
fur-covered head arose into her line of astounded sight.

She had seen tree cats in plenty, and Uncle Roth had had in
the presence chamber of the hold two rugs made from great
cat beasts with spotted hides for which he had traded some
years back. But this was—

Nancee drew a deep breath, and a little of her hold on the
club loosened. Here was one of those great cat people with
whom the Horseclans had a treaty-of-assistance. Of that she
had heard even before she had come to envy the caravan
guards and talked as much as she could with Oonaa, the
archer.

"Cat lord—" She spoke in a hoarse whisper. She was no
woman of the Clans; this furred death before her had no
kincall for her. But what had Dik done which had given him
the power to call such into his service? The Horseclans alone
shared shelter with the cats.

"Where is the wagon?" Once again the clear words in her
head.

"No wagon." She spoke aloud, but perhaps the cat could
understand speech too, for it stared with great green eyes at
her, the grayish brindle of its fur seeming to fade into the
maze of branches wherein it crouched.

"This one is sore-pawed—this one is hungry—" There
was a low throaty growl to underline that. "This one wishes
to ride—"

"There is nothing to ride," she returned bitterly, and then,
wondering if she could indeed communicate without words
which it might not understand, she tried to form the message
in her mind, haltingly, as one would speak a language of
which one knew but a phrase or two. She pictured the camp
as she had seen it last before she had sought the stream. Then
deliberately she beamed what she had not seen but what was
clear to her mind had happened—the complete killing raid led
by Dik.

Again the cat growled, and it pulled back under the willow
boughs until she feared it was going. Why she should cling to

this one animal which might mean her no good, she could not have said. But she felt that she could not bear to let it go.

"Those will be coming—" She mind-pictured Dik striding confidently toward the willows, satisfied that the easiest part of his massacre and pillage waited before him.

"This one will kill if any two-legs tries to—" The words in her mind faded out, but she was aware of movement against the gravel, of seeing a paw—outsize for even the large animal before her—rise claws curved as if already dug into flesh to tear.

"These hunt cats—" She pictured the hide Dik had had made into a cloak and wore proudly.

The young prairiecat spat and whipped out with that uplifted paw to scrape a fall of leaves from a willow branch.

"This one is of the blood of Dark Slayer. No two-legs can—"

"They can stand at a distance," she interrupted that boastful claim, "and fill you full of arrows. Dik is a master archer." Deliberately, as she had tried earlier to project what she had deemed had happened to their camp, so did she now mind-picture a gray-brown body well covered with quills which snapped wildly from side to side as a wounded animal expired under feathered death.

"So." There was an odd note in that. The cat mask again came farther into view—the yellow eyes only slits, the mouth open enough to show the whole armanent of fangs. Though Nancee knew that the cat was hardly yet out of cubhood, still there was something about it which held her in a kind of awe.

"Would you wait here for this two-legged killer of his kind?" came the quick demand then. "He will fill *you* with his arrows or take a blade to cut you down."

"The cat warrior knows of a better place?" Out of her resigned belief that she faced an already lost battle a small hope arose.

"This way." The swaying of the branches was all which remained to mark the cat's retreat. Because she could think of nothing better she followed, trying as well as she might to go without disturbing the branches and so betray her path to any who might watch from the hilltop.

However, the screen lasted until she was faced by a stand of grass where a number of bruised stems showed her a new trail. Keeping to her hands and knees, Nancee followed.

In the wall of the hill here there was a break—perhaps some spring storm long ago had eaten away the bank. A tree of greater girth than the willows among which she had taken refuge lay crown downward, its withered and broken tangle of roots uphill. To one side of the trunk there was a scatter of earth and a large hole from which came a musky stench that nearly made her gag.

"The black killer thing is gone," sharp into her mind came the "voice" of the cat. "That one has left a hidden way of its own. Crawl, two-legs, and you will see. I do not think that those you fear can look into the earth itself. Crawl!"

Obediently she crawled forward into the evil-smelling pit in the soil. She found it large enough that she could still keep to hand and knees, but it was dark and she had only a very faint scrape of claw now and then to let her know she still followed the cat.

There came an abrupt change as ahead she saw daylight, which was dimmed nearly at once by the cat shouldering its way through. So she came, head foremost, into another stand of grass and brush, warned in time to slither belly down under this other natural cover.

Nancee found herself looking down into the small hollow where they had pitched camp. The first hues of sunset were at her back as she skulked behind a bush to peer through.

Three bundles of red-splashed clothing had been rolled aside. Mik, Hari, and Uncle Roth, she was sure, and had no desire to see them closer and prove her identification right. Three men hunkered on their heels after the way of prairie barbarians. They had ripped open the supply bags and were wolfing down the nearly stone-hard rolls of travel meat, chewing with determined force.

Dik was not there. A ripple of foreboding ran up her spine. Only too well she could guess what occupied the man she had come to loathe. Snooping into the willows—hunting—*her*!

There was the pound of a huge hoof on the ground. Even where she lay in hiding she could feel the force of that through the earth. Boldhoof, the one treasure Uncle Roth had held fast to, was impatient. Large and armed as she was with hoof and teeth, the mare was generally even of temperament. Nancee had had those soft lips pluck a round marble of maple sugar from her palm and knew she had nothing to fear from the tall mountain of a horse.

The Northhorses were not unknown here in the southern lands, but those who had them gave them great care. None were bred here, being sold only by tribes who were so jealous of their monopoly that they would not ever offer a stallion to be bought by an outsider.

They would not have gained Boldhoof even, had it not been that her former owner had died of the coughing sickness two months back and Uncle Roth had claimed the animal as burial price. The secret he discovered within a day thereafter he had shared only with Nancee. Though Dik might have discovered it by some spying. Boldhoof was in foal! And should she throw a colt, why then their family fortune could be established as soon as the foal appeared.

Hate was bitter water in Nancee's mouth as she watched the outlaws below. Though they seemed at such ease she was certain that they must have sentries out and perhaps even men on the search with Dik. She counted seven horses—most of them the smaller mounts known to the prairie men. If those were of the Horseclans breed—

She could no longer see anything of the cat, who had gone to earth making itself invisible, its brindled fur one with the earth and the sun-browned grass. Again the girl heard and felt the impatient stamp of Boldhoof. Never had she longed so much for anything before as she wished she could communicate with the huge mare. These rogues had picketed her, but they could not guess the strength beneath that well-groomed hide. Perhaps a single sharp pull would free—

"The evil two-legs!" A flash of warning cut through her own thoughts sharply enough to immoblize her for a moment.

"Sooooo—" That word was drawn out to become the hiss of a serpent.

She turned her head unwillingly, still hoping against hope. Looked up. Dik had fulfilled his claim as an expert hunter. He stood there, his unsheathed sword gripped in his hand. Nancee knew the meaning of that threat. Dik could use his sword like a throwing knife. She had seen him win a handful of good silver bits doing just that. One swing and she would be pinned to the ground—and he could place that unwieldy spear exactly where he chose.

"Lady of the House of Bradd!" He made the greeting a jeer, and in his eyes she could read exactly what she knew would be there. "You have been overshy. But all is well now. Come to me!'' His soft slur of speech ended with a snap like that of a whip.

She could be a fool and defy that order—and lose everything by being mishandled and perhaps even thrown down to those stinking men huddled around the fire. Or one could rise as Nancee did now, her attention on Dik, wary and waiting for his next move.

''Lady of Bradd''—again his leer and the tone of the words was like a blow—''it would seem that you come late to our meeting. But that you do come is as it should be.'' He spoke without the slur of the frontiersman, the garbling of an underling; he might be some man of name in exile.

''There is no Bradd,'' she found her voice to say flatly. ''As you well know. Roth had no kin land anymore.''

''Which is the same as saying that you are also landless—but that you are lordless is a different matter, my lady. The man who takes you will have his rights, as you are heiress now and there is more fighting in the east. Even as we stay here there could be a reversal of all which has happened and you could call yourself duchess and first lady in Bradd.''

Her lips twisted in a grimace. ''That will never be.''

''Ah.'' He was smiling, a smile which carried with it the chill of deepest winter. '' 'Never' is a word no true man takes for surety. Come!'' Again that snap of order, this time fortified with jerk of the swordblade, beckoning her to him.

She rubbed one wrist against the other, remembering her plan born out of the wildest fear at the riverbank. In that camp there would be other weapons than her own teeth. Again that death lay beyond was nothing to fear—life, on the other hand, was promised enduring horror.

Nancee took two steps farther and then was rocked by the message which flashed into her head:

''Two-legs, why do you what this piece of stinking guts and evil thought orders you?''

The cat! ''Go,'' she found wit enough to return, watching Dik. If the renegade had any mindspeak the creature from the prairies might already have brought a sad fate upon itself. ''Go—this one is a killer-of-all, men and animals both. He would wear your hide with pride. Go before he comes to hunt you!''

''There will be a hunting, yes, a good hunting!'' The answer seemed as loud to her as if the prairiecat had shouted it aloud in human-formed words. "Be you ready for that hunting."

She took another short step. There had been no change in that twisted leer with which Dik was regarding her. She was almost sure that he had no mindtouch ability. "Go before he discovers—"

There was no answer—nothing she could touch which suggested that the cat was still within range. So, for all its confidence in battle, it had indeed followed the prudent way she had suggested. But deep in her there was another small taste of death—she was wholly alone.

"Lookit, Ed. Th' boss has him th' ladybird, all nice and easy!" One of the men by the fire had arisen and was staring upslope at them.

"What yuh do now, boss? Bed her and make yurself High Lord—"

"What I do is my concern." Again the arrogance of a high-kin man, and something in the note of that wiped all the gap-toothed smiles from the faces of his followers.

Nancee's chin went up a fraction. She might be wearing clothes stinking from months of travel, her hair hanging in wet tails about her head and shoulders, but the manners of the great hall were hers, and now they provided her with a kind of armor, keeping away the horrors which might still face her here.

She had only one thing to depend upon—Dik would seem to have some ambitions laid back in the war-torn country from which she and Uncle Roth had been fleeing. It was true that if Bradd still held any power the man who wed her could sit in the high seat there. But that anyone would now fasten on such a thought made her weigh Dik's plans the lighter. There was nothing left in the once-rich land which would be worth even a clipped silver piece now. Yet it was still this belief she sensed in the renegade which gave her any kind of a chance.

Without looking back over her shoulder she spoke again:

"Kehlee of the Peaks squats in the ruins of Bradd—unless he has swept the land of everything, even sold our people to slavers. Do you go up against Kehlee's squadron with this army of yours?" From some inner strength she produced that same flat tone which denied him any thought of having imprisoned more than just her body.

"We shall see." He did not sound as if he had any fears of her dismal suggestion being truth. "Harz, over with you and let the lady sit there."

The man directly before her did move and with a will, which suggested that Dik ruled his own following if he did not play overlord in the east. Nancee seated herself with the same sweep of skirts she would have used back in the House of Bradd. Dik had returned his sword to its sheath; now he made a gesture, and the others of his noisome force shuffled away, allowing him good room to seat himself not too far from his captive.

He now held to her part of a dry and crumbling journey cake, one end of which was covered with thick grease. "Eat!"

She longed to lean forward and throw it into his face, but she ate, the rancid taste giving her queasiness.

"You are wiser than that meat over there." He spoke clearly, as if determined to make her see the very depths into which she had fallen, perhaps thinking so to cow her further as he gestured to the tangled bodies at the other side of the hollow. "I think we shall deal well with one another." Now he reached into a saddlebag and brought out a length of dark dried meat, from which he cut a mouth-shaped piece, flipping it into his open jaws with a turn of the knife.

The knife had been riding in his boottop. Nancee made note of that. Then she heard the heavy stamp of Boldhoof's foot. The Northhorse—if they were lean of loot this outlaw force had at least that bit of luck—there was also what rode in the two panniers. Those had not been loosened from their pack across the mare's broad back before the raiders had struck.

Metal, always good for sale to the skillful smiths of the Horseclans—some of it dug with her own hands when their small party had chanced upon one of the old ruins before they had joined the wagon train, that train where Dik had enough interest with the wagon boss to get them cut off and left behind, ripe for his taking.

"Two-legs—"

That voice which she imagined was gone with its owner when she had been taken captive again sounded in her head. There was no change in Dik's expression as he watched her.

Dared she believe that she was the only one here that the prairiecat could reach?

She took the chance. "Cat-one, this is death for you. Get away while you can."

Nancee chewed and swallowed. Again she heard a heavy stamp from the picket line. The other mounts were moving uneasily. Then one gave a shrill whinny which brought Dik's head around.

"What's to do with those horses, Mish?"

One of the men who had slouched away from the fire spat over his shoulder.

"Jus' spooked—they's bin doin' that for a while. Tree cat hanging around maybe. Tha's like 'em."

"See to it." Dik did not raise his voice, but there was a bite in it.

He turned back to Nancee. "Tree cat," he repeated slowly as if trying to impress on her the dangers which might be piled mountain-high against anyone in this wild country. "Get one of them on your trail, lady, and you'll know what ill luck really means."

Defiance was on the tip of Nancee's tongue, but she swallowed hasty words. She must let him believe that he had won—at least for now. Perhaps he had, unless she had such courage as that of Mairee.

One of the horses flung up its head and uttered a startling loud neigh. Boldhoof stamped as if in some answer known only to the equine kind.

"Cat-one—" Nancee's thought was sharp. "If this is your doing—"

All the men in the bowl had turned to look at the picket line now. Two had swords out, and a third was fitting an arrow to the string of his bow. Even Dik had half turned his back on her, though she did not believe that she dared move without his seeing.

"Cat-one—these are ready for the kill!" She could not be sure what game the half-grown cub was playing nor why, but she was sure that the prairiecat was behind it all.

"Get it!" Dik's order grated and sent the men into action, though she noted that they moved slowly, watching the brush and the two trees between which the picket line had been anchored.

Nancee measured the distance between her and Dik. His

attention was now all for the horse line, and he had drawn his own sword. That knife in his boottop—dared she try for it?

As if the hidden clan cat read her purpose, only half-formed as it was, mind to mind, there came a squall as nerve-racking as any sound she had ever heard, and the horses, including Boldhoof, went into wild lunging at the ropes. That of the Northhorse parted as if it were made of tapestry thread and the huge mare swung around, shouldering its smaller neighbors apart, leading to the break-free of one of those. At the same time Nancee flung her own light body forward. Her shoulder struck behind Dik's knees, sending the man staggering for a step or two, but not before she had jerked that boot knife free, its hilt fitting into her hand as if it had been made for her alone.

The men pulled back as Boldhoof reared and dropped both hoofs together with a ground-shaking force. While two of the other horses, now free, ran up and away over the edge of the hollow, their fellows flailed out with hooves and jerked their heads against the confinement of the ropes which held them.

"Whar's tha' double-be-damned cat?" shouted the archer, his bow swinging from side to side as he tried to find some target.

They were all looking upward into the trees, endeavoring to sight the menace. Yet, save for the threshing of lower limbs caused by the jerking of the picket line below, there was nothing to be sighted.

Dik had regained his balance and swung around, his eyes narrowed, the intent look of the hunter on his bristle-cheeked face. He took a single stride to where Nancee was regaining her feet, the knife in her hands.

"What kind of damned witchery—" he began, and then his hand flashed out. Before she could dodge or try to defend herself his fist struck her chin, not full on as he had intended, for some providence allowed her to jerk her head back in time, but with force enough to send her spinning backward, the world a whirl of pain and light around her.

She fell right enough, and part of her waited for the second blow she was sure would come. Instead there was a hoarse shout and her dazed head and misty sight could not warn her. There was the heavy smell of horse scent, and with it the odor of raw fear.

Over her loomed a trampling monster. A great head bowed,

and jaws opened and closed again on her hunched shoulder. She was dragged upward, though her feet did not quite leave the ground, and so she passed into a darkness through which came only faintly for the second time the yowl of a cat.

Pain in her back and her feet reached into the dark and brought her out again. She was near stifled by the heavy smell of horse sweat, but she forced her eyes open. Yet, she was being drawn along the ground, backward, unable to see where she might be taken. And it was Boldhoof's mouth which had closed upon her, the mare's giant strength seemingly little disturbed by the burden of the slight body she had gathered from the ground.

There was a whistling flight of an arrow, the kind used to frighten game into a stampede during which the stragglers could be picked off. Yet Boldhoof paid no attention to the shaft, which must have passed near by the sound of it.

Nancee was half-conscious—the pain in her shoulder where the great teeth gripped her and the bruising of her body dragged along the ground made her sick—but she held on to the small portion of awareness she had. Surely one of the men back there would use an arrow to better purpose soon—

For the third time the battle cry of a cat rang out, and this time from close to her, from the air, as if some furred warrior had grown wings.

"Two-legs, let the good horse free you and then join me here!"

Somehow that reached her in spite of the pain of her body and the near blankness of her mind brought about by Dik's blow. She was freed suddenly from that crushing of her shoulder, and she slumped, unable to move. Then she could have screamed, perhaps she did, as something tangled fiercely in her hair and pulled up her head. There was a furred body behind her; she caught only a glimpse or two of it as it endeavored to keep its hold in her hair.

Somehow she got to her knees, and that torturing grasp on her hair loosened. She flailed out with one arm, and her hand struck against a stone-firm pillar seemingly covered with damp hide. Grasping at that, she strove to come erect, though she had to lean against the foreleg of the Northhorse to do that.

"Two-legs, there is no time for resting. Get you up!"

Nancee wavered along Boldhoof's side, and her hand hit

against one of the panniers which had still beladen the horse. Apparently the raiders had not stripped their prize. That voice in her head provided the energy she must have. As it impressed "Climb" on her, Nancee strove to fight her way up over the pannier onto the broad back. There was a flash of gray-brown and the young prairiecat was there also, crowding against her.

Boldhoof went into a rocking trot and then such a gallop as Nancee would never have expected the heavy animal could produce. She lay on that back, her fingers laced in the belts which held the panniers, while the cat flattened itself beside her.

"The voiceless horses of those have run," it cast into her mind. "This good mountain stepped on two of the bad two-legs—perhaps neither will rise again. This is better than the wagon—but we shall find that, two-legs, and Frog Hunter shall be among the bold ones—with another name—you shall see. I am Rider of the Mountain that runs—"

She managed to raise her head a fraction. There was the flow of air about them; truly Boldhoof was running now. Nancee listened for a sound of pursuit; she was not able as yet to look back. Surely Dik would not let them go so easily!

"Dik—" she said aloud, forgetting the difference now between mindspeech and that from the lips. "He will follow."

There was an odd feeling in her mind. If perhaps the cub laughed so among his peers, that was what she sensed now.

"The loud two-legs was stepped upon by this great mountain."

To be stepped upon by Boldhoof—could she wish a more successful fate for Dik Romlee? Her mind still seemed hazy, but she held on to the fact that they did seem to be free and moving at a wind-raising rate of speed. But how had Boldhoof had the luck to break loose just at that right moment?

"This one called upon the Mountain." There was a burst of pride and satisfaction in the mindtouch from the cat. "The lesser horses were told to run and shown this one's claws. Run they did. But the Mountain came with Rider!"

She shook her head a little and winched at the resulting flash of pain. That the cats of the clans talked with both man and mount was well known. However, those furred and hoofed ones were familiar from birth with each other and with the humans of the tribes. Boldhoof came from a country where horses were truly dumb beasts.

"Only because two-legs have no speech either," returned the cat crisply. "Ask now what this one thinks."

Tentatively Nancee denied her headache and her uneasiness at being a part of this flight. She tried to reach out to contact Boldhoof.

There was a sensation of pleasure and freedom, of being a mistress of herself—and with it a small, almost humble touch for Nancee. The girl pulled herself up higher and could not help but stare at the large maned head before her, twining her fingers harder into the straps of the panniers. The ears on the head twitched, then slanted directly back as if pointing to her.

She filled her own mind, that part of it she hoped would be a passage to Boldhoof, with thanks and return pleasure.

"Now"—that was the cat cutting in impatiently—"we go to the clan. This Mountain will carry us safely and we can find the trail where there is no reason to hide. Let all see Rider and no more will he be a kitten-cubbling to wagon-ride!"

Nancee laughed shakily. They had forded a river where the water had risen high enough to wet the pannier and Boldhoof's barrel, and the whole of the wide-open country lay before them. To go to the clan—why not? She had no kin—

"Save Rider," the cat cut in sharply.

"And Boldhoof," she agreed. "Two who fight very well and are valiant company. Agreed—let us now seek this clan of yours, Rider of a Moving Mountain!"

Maureen Birnbaum on the Art of War (as told to Bitsy Spiegelman Fein)

by George Alec Effinger

George Alec Effinger, widely known as one of today's finest science fiction writers, lives in New Orleans, Louisiana. Among his many fine works are *What Entropy Means to Me*, *Heroics*, *Felicia*, *The Bird of Time*, and more short stories than there is room to mention, including his Muffy Birnbaum stories, one of which is printed here. Enjoy!

I had never been so deliriously, deliciously giddy in my life. I had only been married for three hours, and already everything was like happening exactly as I had hoped and dreamed since childhood. My whole family and all my friends agreed that Josh was a real catch. He was an M.D., a newly graduated family practitioner. As a wedding present, his Uncle Mort Fein announced that he was retiring and like turning his long-established Queens practice over to my new husband. My legs turned weak for yet another time; Uncle Mort's patients were all well-to-do and terribly loyal, and the gift also saved Josh and me a considerable amount of money that we assumed we'd have to borrow to get Josh's office set up, not to mention the long years it would otherwise have taken to develop a good practice from scratch. It was as if Uncle Mort had, with one stroke, like fully insured our futures. On top of that, Mums shook loose a considerable sum from her "holdings," as she called them. All the rest of

*my family and Josh's family followed suit. I felt a little guilty
about being exhilarated by all those dollar signs, but Josh
said it was perfectly normal to be dazzled by such a windfall.
He said that he was, too.*

*Right after the reception we caught a plane to our honey-
moon vacation in Bermuda. Josh's younger sister is like a
travel agent; she made all the arrangements and used her
pull to get us a terrific discount, even though it was the height
of the season. I don't have a single memory of the flight
itself. We flew first-class, of course; and as soon as the flight
attendants learned we were newlyweds, they started hitting us
with champagne, even before the plane pulled away from the
terminal building. The bubbly wine and the pressure in the
cabin combined to relax me so much that my next conscious
memory is of Josh holding me in his arms and trying to
unlock the door to our honeymoon suite. Like I don't even
recall checking in, you know? "Josh, honey," I go, showing
my down-to-earth level-headed side right at the beginning of
our new partnership, "put me down, unlock the door, open
it, and then, like, pick me up again."*

*"You're brilliant and beautiful, Betsy." Josh can never
bring himself to use my old high school and college nickname.*

*I kissed him. Then, after he'd opened the door and carried
me across the threshold, he put me gently down on the
gigantic bed. He gave me a comic leer, and I giggled. Then
we looked at each other. Neither of us could think of anything
to say or do. Like, what came next?*

*"Well," goes my darling, "how does it feel to be Mrs. Dr.
Josh Fein, King of Queens with eyes cast rapaciously toward
Manhattan?"*

*"Cast your eyes rapaciously toward me and nobody or
nothing else," I go. I took a few deep breaths and let myself
calm down. That's when I noticed how absolutely beautiful
our suite was, and the view through the picture windows of
the gardens and the sea beyond. "Josh," I go, "let me go
into the bathroom and put on something more romantic. I
packed some special things and I've like planned this moment
ever since eighth grade."*

*He smiled at me. "All right," he goes. "I'll open the
champagne and turn down the bed." He wiggled his eye-
brows at me suggestively. I giggled again. Josh just cracks
me up.*

I grabbed one of my suitcases and went into the bathroom. I had a little trouble with my dress, and I struggled with it for a moment. Then I heard a voice go, "You need some like help with that?" It hadn't been Josh's voice. I whirled around.

Damn it to hell if it wasn't Muffy—I mean, Maureen—Birnbaum. I could see by her outfit that she'd just come back from one of her nauseating exploits. I remembered the promise I'd made myself when she'd left a huge emerald to reimburse me for an old debt. She thought she was playing a joke on me with that gem, but it got me into no end of trouble. I declared that the next time I saw the girl, I was like going to break her face for her.

Well, I didn't. Instead, I went straight for her pure-and-innocent eyes.

Maureen reacted more quickly than you'd think such a like full-figured girl could. Her fist came up in this long, clean arc and detonated on the point of my chin. I thought I heard a little grinding of bone. The world went black and I was falling over backward, watching bright red points of light glimmering like fireflies in the gloom. I heard Maureen from a long distance away. "Bitsy, hell, Bitsy! Oh, wow, I didn't mean to hit you. Not so hard, I mean. I got you, you'll be all right. You'll have maybe just a bad bruise, that's all. Come on. Like, shake it off!" She threw cold water on me, for which I could have killed her. In a couple of minutes I was a little better. I found that I was sitting on the edge of the bathtub. Maureen was regarding me anxiously from her perch on the beige chenille-covered toilet lid.

"God damn, Muffy," I go, gingerly feeling my jaw, "I'm on my honeymoon, and now I'll probably have to like take all my meals through a straw." I couldn't imagine how we ever could have been friends.

"It'll be worth it, to hear the story I've got this time," she goes. I really wanted to hand her head to her, but I was still stunned.

"You die, bitch," was all I could hoarsely murmur.

"Calm down, Bitsy," she goes. "You want to like change outfits? Get out of that geeky schmatte and I'll find your little bit of nothing in here."

I did as she said, wobbling my jaw every now and then, feeling my head pound and throb as I wriggled out of my $380 Neiman-Marcus "schmatte."

"This like what you wanted?" goes Maureen, extending the drop-dead lavender gauzy chemise-and-panty set. *" 'Victoria's Secret'? I don't know them, but I do know their secret: they know you don't have any like boobs."*

My right hand clenched slowly into a hard fist.

Maureen just laughed. *"Hey, ease up, Bitsy. You always zinged me about my fat ass, I always zinged you about being titless."*

"Yeah," I muttered. That's when I first really noticed what she *was* wearing: leather pants tucked into high boots, very butch; a sleeveless quilted cotton shirt covered with chain mail, I mean, for God's sake; and some kind of crested helmet pushed back on her head. She wore her old sword— the one she'd picked up on Mars—on one hip. On the other hip she had a new sword, bigger, and like a dagger. She had a spear and a large sack made of some rough, filthy material. She looked like a combination of Santa Claus and Joan of Arc. Can you believe it? Sometimes I doubt she really has these adventures. I think like she goes away for a year or more and makes up some ridiculous Mardi Gras outfit and comes back just to see how much she can annoy me. She's either a for-sure scientific enigma or she's really like psycho, you know? *"For Christ's sake, Muffy, where have you been!"*

She grinned at me. She never grinned before; she'd smile or she'd laugh, but she never grinned. She was losing that fine edge the Greenberg School had labored so long and so futilely to apply to her. *"Run the shower so Mr. Honeybunch doesn't wonder what's going on in here."*

I reached behind myself and turned on the taps full blast.

"Good," she goes. *"Now, wait until you hear this story. And if you call me Muffy again, I'll brain you."*

I was ready, *believe* me, I was *more* than ready to hang up my sword; but, like, two things occurred to me. The first was that there wouldn't be anybody to look out for the wretched and downtrodden on all these planets without me, and the second was that every time I have an adventure I meet a real cute boy. That was better odds than I used to get at the Greenberg School. So I didn't retire Ol' Betsy after all. I decided to go for one last shot at finding Mars and Prince Van. I mean, like, it wasn't *his* fault that I got lost, was it? Let's be fair about this, now.

I put together another full-on collection of wearables, crammed into two Oh-They're-Just-Something-I-Stumbled-Over bags that leaped at my throat from a page in the Bean catalog. I decided on the college-sophomore look. You know: too old to be a *total* squid, but still young enough so that the Mandatory Party Rule is still in effect. I had on a beige shirtdress with blue pins, a 'schmere sweater tied around my neck, and a pair of raggedy old Pumas on my feet. Come nightfall, I looked into the sky and felt a tug toward the God of War. I barely had to whoosh myself; like it was almost whooshed for me. The going was getting easier every time I tried it.

But, goddammit, the steering was as slippery as it ever was. Right from the second when I blammed into a big old tree, I knew I'd missed Mars again. And Mars is like a *big place*, right? You'd think it'd be easy enough to hit. Well, let's see *you* try it. Get back to me on that.

Anyway, where I did end up, I was smushed against this tree. I couldn't tell you what *kind* of tree, except it had bark—it had bark in my mouth, jammed into my nose, cutting up my knees. I was thinking, "Maureen Birnbaum killed by tree. Details on the hour." The tree was like making no move to back off, so *I* did. I looked around and there were no witnesses, so I didn't feel like such a total wheeze.

There was a dusty dirt road behind me, winding through the trees. I didn't know which way I ought to go, so I thought I'd just kind of sit down with my Bean bags and wait for someone to come along. So it figures, as soon as I sit down, my *imagination* starts to work—maybe I'm all alone on this planet with like a road.

Chill out, *Maureen*. In a few minutes I hear a lot of clanking and bumping and rattling. Traffic sounds. No I-95 traffic sounds, you know, but at least *some* creatures were hustling their buns toward me. I asked myself, I go, "Maureen, is that necessarily like a good thing?" So I take my bags and my sword and hide out behind this clump of underbrush. A few minutes later I see this little parade. There's a bunch of Schwarzenegger types wearing hacked-up outfits, riding these big old horses that looked like a cross between a Clydesdale and a Peterbilt tractor. The men were all carrying swords and battleaxes and stuff.

They are fighting men. I have no problem with that. I got out from under the underbrush. "Hey," I go.

Three of these totally bluff guys leap on me—from their *horses*—and bring me up in front of their leader. They yammer at me in some language, it could have been Greek for all I knew.

Finally the leader, who's still up on his horse so I have to lean way back just to see his face—which was a *cute* face, in a sort of fierce and determined way, mature and all—this man leans down and gives me one of those amused little smiles. He goes, "May I ask your name, miss?"

I go, "You can call me Maureen, but I've bailed out of all those sexist mister-and-miss things."

He nodded pleasantly, but one of his young friends mutters something that sounded like "brahbehrnuh." Now, my *God*, Bitsy, you know I'm the last person in the *world* that would burn a bra. Without good underwired support, a fighting woman is just plain asking for trouble. Halfway through the action she'd be nearly *helpless*, what with the harmonic motion of her boobs interfering with her swordplay. I spun around real fast to see who'd made that little remark, but they looked at me all wide-eyed and innocent. Their leader goes, "Forgive them, they haven't met many twentieth-century women, and those they *have* met were without exception hostile."

"A typical generalization," I go. This is where I got all haughty. In the back of my mind, though, certain questions are just like *crying out* to be asked. "Where the hell *am* I?" seemed like a good start.

This man with the dark skin and the bright eyes goes, "You're a trifle north of the Kingdom of New Kuhmbuhluhn, east on the road from the ducal seat of Tchaimbuhsburk."

"I meant what *planet* is this?" I go.

He shrugged. "Earth," he goes. "What did you expect?"

"Earth? Then something's wrong."

"What year do you think it is?"

I'm like easy to get along with, so I told him. He says it was now more than eight hundred years since civilization had been destroyed in a nuclear holocaust. I looked at his weapons and his men's armor and the whole knobby barbarian influence on this band of merry men. I didn't have any trouble believing him. I mean, it couldn't be that they were only making, you know, a daring fashion statement or something. Instead of traveling through *space*, I'd traveled through *time*. Prince Van and you, Bitsy, and my allowance were many hundreds of years in the past, dead and buried. I paused a moment for emotion.

"My name is Milo," goes the leader. He saw that I was sort of like all *aufgeshaken*, you know? He looked down from his horse and shook his head, evidently deciding what he was going to do with me.

"You don't have to do *anything* with me," I go. "I can take care of myself."

Milo nodded. "I was just curious about how you got here."

"I don't know."

"Well, you've walked into the middle of a war. We have to keep moving; I plan to catch up with my army in the next few days. Maybe I'd better detail one of my men to take you to a safe—"

"Hold on, Milo, old buddy," I go. I've never met anyone else named Milo. The only Milo I'd ever even heard of was the Venus de. "I don't need you to look out for me. You don't have to send one of your men—if that's, you know, the right word for them—to escort me anywhere."

"You appear to be very independent, Miss Birnbaum." He gave me another smile.

I went immediately from merely haughty to fully stoked. "Get off that goddam *elephant!*" I yelled at him. I was stalking back to the bush to get Ol' Betsy. We were going to see about this right now. I was so mad I didn't even like ask myself how he knew my last name.

I'm waving my trusty blade in his face and the three soldiers are just laughing their filthy, scungy heads off. Milo raised a hand and they stopped. He held a locked case in his other hand. "I haven't used one of these in centuries," he goes, taking a beautiful, gleaming saber from the case. Its basket hilt's not jewel-encrusted like mine, but I can see it's a nifty piece of work. "Toledo," he goes. "That wouldn't mean anything to the troopers of my Confederation, but perhaps you'll appreciate it."

"Appreciate *this*," I go. I salute him, spend a twelfth of a second *en garde*, and then lunge, apparently for his chest. I really meant to cut his wrist on the inside, but he saw that coming. He parried Quarte, with his blade nearly vertical, and merely tilted his forearm from the elbow, knocking my blade aside. His riposte came so damn fast that he almost got me. Milo shot his fist straight toward my chest, making a quick, short slash. I was forced to parry Quinte, which God only knows I'm not *good* at. My sword hand was high, near eye level. I caught his attack okay, turned my wrist over, and lunged at him. The two of us went back and forth like that for a few minutes. I knew right off that like maybe I'd made a mistake. This guy Milo was no Martian monster, for sure, and I didn't have low gravity on my side. Milo could have diced me up any time he wanted. I'm just real, real glad he didn't *want* to. Really.

Still, I was holding my own, you know, if only just barely. I could pick up on a murmured conversation behind me, the three hairball soldiers making comments. I like to think they were sort of astonished by how well I was handling their commanding officer. I hoped they couldn't see that Milo was carrying me.

That is, like he carried me for a while until I made a dumb goof. He feinted at my wrist, then bent his elbow and brought his point up and cut at my left shoulder. I wasn't sure what to do, and I parried wrong. Before I could attack, he scored with a remise, putting his saber completely through my shoulder just above the armpit.

"*Goddammit!*" I yelled. "*Goddam son of a bitch!*" I was hopping around in pain and swearing like a, well, trooper. I dropped Ol' Betsy and clutched my shoulder. A little blood spurted out and stained my brand-new shirtdress. I hadn't worn it more than a couple of hours. Milo was really sorry. He put his sword down and hurried to me.

"Are you all right?" he goes.

I just glared at him. "It hurts like homemade *hell*," I go.

"Let me see," he goes.

"Are you *kidding* me? Here, just take all my clothes off and examine my booboo. Fat chance, buster."

"I'm just—"

"I know, I know. It's all my fault, I'm just being unreasonable, I asked for it. That's what Daddy tells me all the time. *Ouch.*"

His eyes narrowed a bit. "Take your hand away, at least."

I did. The wound had stopped bleeding already.

Milo gave me a long, thoughtful look. "Lift up the material and tell me what you see."

I did. "It's *healed!*" I go. I was amazed, if you want to know the truth.

Milo rubbed his jaw with one hand. "I'd be grateful if you'd travel with me for a few days," he goes. "I'd like to talk with you about a few matters that are important to this world."

That was better. It showed he was a gentleman and not just some kind of gross, chauvinist Captain Future. "Will I get to see some of your war?" I go.

"You won't be able to avoid it."

"Neat. Let me get my things." One of the soldiers helped stow my two bags on his huge horse. Milo lifted me up to his saddle, and I clung to him as we rode. His beautiful chestnut stallion was so big I couldn't get my legs around it. I felt like I was doing splits on a gym floor, for Christ's sake.

Milo talked as we traveled. Apparently, some upstart had formed a pocket kingdom he called Kehnooryees Ahkeeyuh, or New Achaea. This bozo, who crowned himself King Pahleebohaitees I, worked for a while making allies and raising an army. He merged the city of Ritchmuhnd and several nearby villages, and called the result his capital, Kehnooryees Spahrtuh. His Union of Pure-Blooded Ehleenee let the Undying High Lord Milo know that it was dropping out of his Confederation. Not only that, but like it was making a beasty *pain* of itself by raiding the prosperous lands to the north and west. It was all the combined forces of the Confederation, the Kindred dragoons of the Middle Kingdoms, the Ahrmehnee troops, and the Moon Maiden archers could do to contain the rebellion. It still wasn't clear if they could defeat it. Milo expected me to know what the hell he was talking about, but like I was lost from Word One, I'm sure.

A few hours later we whammed into the tail end of his army. The soldiers all cheered for Milo like he was Napoleon or What's-His-Name MacArthur or something. I could definitely handle inspiring that kind of reaction, but all my adventures have been one-on-one, you know, and like this was my first for-real war. Milo wanted to know which side I was going to be on, his or this bogue King Pahleebohaitees' Union. I go, "I know who *you* are, what's this Union?"

"Just renegade Ehleenee," he goes.

That like decided it for me. "Illini?" I go, with a suitable *avant*-barf expression. "Oh my *God*, that's like the Big Ten! Pammy, my stepmother, you know, she gave me three harsh rules about finding a husband: One, marry Yale first; if you can't get Yale, marry Princeton; if you can't get Yale or Princeton, devote yourself to a life of public service, like Mother Teresa. I'll never have a house in Newport if I hang around with Illini ag-school jocks. *Urrr*."

Milo just shook his head again. He said something in that other language to one of the soldiers, then he turned back to me. "Just go with Duhlainee; he'll take you to the armorer. You're very good with that saber, but it won't help you very much against the weapons you'll be seeing soon."

The armorer fixed me up with just what I wanted. I got a *crushin'* longsword, lighter than what Milo carried. I could barely lift one of those big suckers off the ground, but I could swing the smaller sword with both hands. I figured like I'd be a hell of a lot quicker on the draw than those big zods. One of those guys takes a hack with his sword, he needs five minutes to recover for another swipe. Meanwhile, I could shred him with a combo of point and edge work. I also took this tasty dirk and a spear. I wanted a helmet, too—an open-faced helmet with the nosepiece like the ancient Greeks wore, okay? With the spear and the helmet I'd look just so *kill*, like Athena, who was fully ruff and a legend in her own time.

"Nosepiece," the armorer goes, in this fractured language they called Mehrikan. I could barely make out what he was like saying. "You got a big nose on you to protect."

I just gave him my Number Eight Smile—icy, totally aggro, *Warning to Others: This Is Dangerous Territory*. "You want to like do your job? I don't *need* your constructive criticism."

He shrugged. "What about your shield?"

I hadn't planned to carry one; I was going to use both hands on the sword, right? I told him, and his eyes got wider. He muttered something under his breath: "Ahnaiyeestah." I found out it meant "without a shield," and that's what that bunch called me from then on: Mahreenah Ahnaiyeestah. My *nom de guerre*, can you believe it?

I also got this way rad draped white gown that I could wear with my crested helmet and spear and like *really* do the Athena number; and I was fitted with *this* outfit, the leathers and the chain mail, for battle. I was all set. Now we were like waiting for Milo's scouts, who were hauling ass all over the countryside looking for the Union army.

So a couple of days later, still moving east, we got a frantic report: like the advance guards of *Thoheeks* Djaik Morguhn's Red Eagle warriors made contact with these hungry Pure-Blood Union foragers. "I didn't want to fight a battle here," goes Milo. "And, I'll wager, neither did Senior *Strahteegos* Lahmbrohs, our shrewd enemy. But look at the map; it is a coincidence, nothing more, forced on us by geography. This town is the junction of all the main roads for many miles around. I hoped that we would pass through it well ahead of the Union troops. I wanted to put my army between Lahmbrohs and his source of supply, far away in Karaleenos. There's nothing to be gained by wishing it was otherwise. I'll reinforce Djaik Morguhn and hope that Lahmbrohs chooses to disengage. There are more favorable places to come to grips." Milo looks at Prince Bili, Djaik's older brother, and Bili nods. I didn't like offer any advice, 'cause like I didn't have any. In Milo's tent, it all looked like toy soldiers on a gameboard, but it was really weird on account of I knew men had already started to die for real.

Milo sent out his orders. *Thoheeks* Djaik was to hurry to bail out his advance unit and do what he could to slow down the withdrawal of Lahmbrohs and his Union rebels. Meanwhile, the Confederate units, scattered all across the damn countryside, would zoom up as fast as their mammoth horses could carry them.

I was like just hot to get into my first battle, you know, but everybody I talked to kept saying, "Just wait, you'll see." Nobody would tell me *what* I'd see, and I thought maybe they didn't want to fight. That was dumb. I should have known better. They were all brave dudes—*stark* was their word—and they'd tussle every time they had to. It was only like they could think of other things they'd rather be doing. I know about that: I was very popular on Saturday nights. I mean, it was that Athena look that did it. And it was the Athena look plus the spear and the longsword that kept them from bipping my boobs, too. See, you don't feel up a warrior woman. Not if you don't want people calling you Lefty for the rest of your life, I'm sure.

In the middle of the next morning, Milo got another report from Djaik Morguhn—he had sent a third of his infantry and cavalry to the town, under Strahteegos Kehrtuhs Hwiltuhn. Hwiltuhn was ordered to see what the Union *strahteegos* planned to do, and to like head back toward our main body when he got that news. Things sort of didn't work out the way Milo and Djaik planned. Hwiltuhn did as he was told, but like when he got to the town, the battle was already boiling and he couldn't fall back. A whole horde of Ehleenee hodads were riding into town from the other direction, but most of the Union troops were like still quite a ways away. Old Hwiltuhn was famous for staying in fights when other leaders might decide to retreat. His men loved him for his guts and his totally hot-blooded but battle-wise experience. Hwiltuhn sent word that whether Milo wanted it or not, the fighting *was* going to happen around this sleepy town. He said he'd like try to slow the enemy up as much as possible while Milo got the rest of the Confederation army to the front lines. He was busily sheltering his men in a thin forest across a bare field from the Ehleenee when a few arrows from the Union *kahtahfrahktoee* fell around them. One skanky arrow caught old Hwiltuhn in the throat, and he fell right to the ground, like totally dead. No others of his men were wounded. The battle was like begun, okay?

Milo let out this long, deep breath when he heard the news. "Kehrt was a good man," he goes, "one of the best." He shook his head a couple of times, and like that was *it*. He couldn't spare more time grieving for his old friend, there was warlording to do.

I had my own horse now, a small mare I called Mr. Ed. You're totally not going to believe *why* I called her Mr. Ed. Because I could *talk* to her. No, Bitsy, she wasn't a talking horse; she was like a *telepathic* horse. I heard her voice in my head, and she heard me. It like freaked me out at first; but we made friends fast, and she told me she'd been in battle before and I wouldn't have to like worry about leading her around, she'd know what I wanted and the best way to get there. We still had to catch up with the forward troops in the town, so Mr. Ed and I had a while to just kind of gossip, you know? Like you and I used to do. Turns out Milo with his tubular silver-streaked black hair was already married. I would have bet a million dollars that he was, but I had these *hopes*, okay?

Later that afternoon we came up to the town. Kehrtuhs Hwiltuhn's men had tried to hold their positions, but like there were just too many Ehleenee slimeballs pouring down on them. The bad guys seemed to have an ocean of reinforcements. Sooner or later the Confederation had to like back off, and they retreated at last right through the town.

Now like you remember my daddy, don't you, sweetie? The original Great Social Undertaking, dressed up like a WASP to get insight into the Goyische Experience. When he was told to put down his pencil and turn in his answer booklet, though, he figures out he's really hep to this way rad life. He has become an honest-and-true Them, I'm sure, okay? Like he traded his Abraham & Straus credit card for one that says *Penney's*, you should forgive the language. He got rid of the sexy Giorgio Armani after-shave I gave him for his birthday and started using Old Spice, like a *grandfather*, for God's sake. And he joined *clubs*, said it was good for business. He turned into—and I totally lost my lunches for two weeks when I heard this—one of those freaky guys who run around in toy uniforms carrying toy weapons and recreating historically heavyweight battles nobody hardly remembers anymore. Little puffs of white smoke and like dudes valiantly clutching their chests and going "Oooh, I'm dead," then they got to lie around on the wet grass till everybody else is either dead, too, or historically captured or accepting someone else's sword or something. Daddy clutched his chest a lot, 'cause dudes with more seniority got to be the hotshot conquerors. That didn't bother him any. A few more years he'd be General Sherman or George Washington, but he'd have to *die* his way into the good roles.

I got to watch these crispo mishmoshes, over and over. I learned some history and got like sunburnt and rained on. That's how when Milo and me and his army rode up to reinforce Kehrtuhs Hwiltuhn's panicky men, I made an observation that saved the Confederacy a bunch of time. I sat on a hilltop with Old Man Morai and it hit me like a kablooie from Athena or even Zeus himself: I pointed to another hilltop. I go, "That's *Little Round Top!*"

Milo goes, "Excuse me?"

"Little Round Top. I used to trudge all over this land with my daddy. I know this place. I've studied every square inch a million times. That's Little Round Top, this is Cemetery Ridge we're stuck on, that's—"

"That must be Seminary Ridge," Milo goes in a quiet voice that for him was wild and crazy excitement.

"And the town is—"

"Getzburk."

"Gettysburg."

"That's right," Milo goes.

"Nothing new under the sun," I go.

"The geography makes the armies come together in the same place, for the same reasons. It really isn't such a huge coincidence."

"We'll like ponder it all later," I go. "Right now we've got a battle to fight. We'll see how close to real life it plays out."

"Sister Mahreenah, this *is* real life," he goes.

"Depends," I go. He was going to have to prove it to me, step by step. Then I started having like doubts, you know? "Oh my *God*! And you're the Confederacy, and the Confederacy *lost* the Battle of Gettysburg." I was scared, because I'll be the first one to admit that I don't always win. In fact, I was so insecure in those days, I thought of myself as the Black Hole of Victory, where winning was sucked down and lost forever, and defeat got bigger and blacker all around me.

"I assure you," Milo goes with a gentle smile, "the fact that *we're* the Confederation fighting a *Union* army at Gettysburg *is* mere coincidence. If I recall my ancient history correctly, it was Meade's Army of the Potomac that occupied this part of the battlefield, and Lee's Army of Northern Virginia that attacked from *Strahteegos* Lahmbrohs' position. The words Confederacy and Union have been switched around, that's all."

"I'll like believe all that when I see them try Pickett's Charge, I'm sure, you know?"

"I doubt that they will," Milo goes. "It was an act of desperation back then. The chances of it happening again are very slight."

Yeah, right. Gag me with a supernova, okay? I mean, that was one *hell* of a bloody fight, thousands and thousands of dudes shot to like *bits*. And for what I'd seen—okay?—our "futuristic" medical team was just as primitive and clumsy as during the Civil War. You know, like no Demerol and no anesthetic and amputations done in the *dirt* with a *hacksaw*. If Milo hadn't told me that I was immortal, right, and all my

wounds would heal *immediately*, I would have been nervous.
Being immortal kind of lets you relax. I just felt sad for like
all the troops who *weren't* undying, you know? All I could do
that night was go up and down the Confederate line going,
"Where are you from, soldier?" and "There, there, everything will work out *just* fine." I felt like a crud.

One of these broad-shouldered madmen comes up to El
Supremo and goes, "God-Milo, will we be attacking on the
morrow?"

Old God-Milo gives his handsome head a little shake and
goes, "No, Sekstuhn, we have almost an impregnable defensive formation here. We'll make the Union *kath-ahrohee*
come to us, if they want to."

Another thing, sweetie: It sure does make a warrior woman's mind rest totally easy to hear she's like *impregnable*.

Anyway, when Sekstuhn took the news back to his buddies, I go, "*God*-Milo?"

Milo just shrugged with an embarrassed smile on his face.
"What can I say?" he goes. "Being immortal impresses my
men as godlike."

"There is no god but Milo, and Prince Bili is his prophet,"
I go. "Let's see you make a *tree*, I'm *so sure*."

"Get some rest, Mahreenah."

So I go, "*Bag it*, Milo." But I did catch some Z's.

The next morning, before first light, the whole Confederate
line was buzzing with activity. We all ate a light breakfast
and drank plenty of water; there probably wouldn't be any
time to like stop and *refresh* ourselves during the battle. We
checked over our weapons and horses and waited. After a
while, right, we checked them again. We were all restless,
you know, waiting for the Ehleenee to like get their act
together.

If I'd known what I was going to witness—and be a part
of—I might *totally* have bailed out of there before dawn. I
still have nightmares, you know? There was only one word to
describe the fighting: totally *B-L-O-O-D-B-A-T-H*. I mean, it
was one thing to lop the heads off green Martians and great
apes, 'cause they were just *storybook* things to me. I didn't
even *believe* in them while I was like cutting them to shreds.
But maiming and killing *people*, that was completely Mondo
Bummer.

The Union army had this idea, see, that they could bust

through our lines. They were overconfident and they were like such total *jels* that they kept bonking themselves on our strong points. They'd make a charge at the left end of the line, squirm their way almost to the top of Cemetery Ridge, and then realize too late that they were *no way* going to cut through King Gilbuht's Harzburkers. The Blue Bear guys would work the Union butts until the Ehleenee would all go screaming *EEK!* back down the ridge. Then they'd try the Zunburk boys in the middle of the line. Same thing, like *tell* me about it. All morning that went on, back and forth. I held back at the beginning, trying to get the rhythm of it. Then I saw that the spazzy Greeks were working up to another run at the left. I kicked up Mr. Ed and went charging down on them. I don't know what got into me. I just got carried away, so *beat* me. I was lucky that the folks from the Duchy of Vawn got all revved, too, and came hollering and thundering behind me. In a minute I could hear them chanting: "Mahreenah Ahnaiyeestah! Mahreenah Ahnaiyeestah!" Like I was totally Sergeant York or somebody, I'm sure.

We slammed into the Ehleenee in a peach orchard. I didn't have *time* to be nervous, it was all I could do to stay *alive*. The first Union geek who took a run at me, I caught his sword on mine and turned it to the inside. While he was struggling to wind it back up, I just jabbed the point of my longsword through his throat. It was so easy I laughed. Felt like spearing a *marshmallow* on the end of a *stick* or something.

A big cheer went up. I was a *hero!* I thought, "Maureen honey, you've *done* your part. Why don't you just trot yourself back up the hill and take ten?" But Mr. Ed was sending me these *awful* bloodlusty images. She was just itching to tromple somebody, I'm totally sure. It was like if *I* wanted to go back, I'd have to do it on *foot*, because Mr. Ed was not about to leave the battle. So I stayed, too. Horse and rider are one, I'm telling you, and you can't just *leave* your four-legged friend in the middle of a battlefield—Bad Show, Just Not Done.

I stood in the stirrups and nearly decapitated another Ehleenee slimeball before he could even unlimber his swordarm. Another cheer went up. I turned to flash the boys a courageous smile. While my head was turned, *jeez*, two of the bad guys came at me and like I never even *saw* them. One huge brawny Vawn person behind me spurred up and took out the nearer of the Ehleenee. He had time to deflect the second Ehleenee's swordthurst, but he deflected it right *at* me. I felt this way gross pain, like I'd been slashed right where my neck meets my shoulder. Didn't break any bones, but it *hurt* like holy hell. I went through my screaming and swearing number again, and I got a worried message from Mr. Ed. The Vawn cutie who came to my rescue turned around and supported me in the saddle while I gnashed my teeth and acted like *wholly* unladylike.

But then the bleeding stopped, and even *wickeder*: the wound closed and the pain went away. I thought I heard shouting from the axe-and-blade boys *before*; you should have like heard them when I showed I was, you know, halfway immortal myself. "Mahreenah! Mahreenah!" I could have totally sold them *anything* from then on. But business called.

I led the *Thoheeks* of Vawn's brigade into the midst of the Ehleenee; and finally, after I'd sort of accounted for a dozen or so of the mega-nerds, they decided to book it out of there. We let them go and turned to reform on the ridge. No time to rest, though, 'cause like *another* batch of Union zods were trying us to the north. I let Mr. Ed take me to the action. It seemed to me that this battle was like shaping up just the same as the Civil War battle. No biggie, the defensive lines were in the same places, for the same reasons, you know? Cemetery Hill and Cemetery Ridge were the logical places to make a stand. Well, I knew that sooner or later, the Union was going to try the right again, making a bid for Cemetery Hill and Culp's Hill. I just didn't know *when*. All this time the fighting must have been *Heat City* down at Devil's Den, and I warned Milo to send some boys down to fully case it around.

About now I see this old, old dude walking up the back of the ridge. I go, "Just what we need, I'm sure, a *spy*." So I bounce over to him and I go, "My good man."

"This's the battle, ain't it?" he goes.

Total Dudley. "Yup," I go.

"I come here to help out."

Now, it is *slightly* obvious to me that Nathan Hale here is like *completely* ancient, seventy years old and gray and grizzled, with this dinged-up old sword over his shoulder. I thought it was sweet of him to offer, but a warrior woman and leader like myself can't take the time to watch after these like *sightseers*. I start to open my mouth to tell him, you know, that we all appreciated his *guts* and all, *but* . . .

He rushes past me, whips his sword in a circle over his dumb-bunny bald head, and hacks down an Ehleenee son of a bitch who had almost snuck up on me. I blinked at the geezer, you know, totally freaked, but I didn't know what to say. He looked up at me. Finally I go, "Very good. Carry on," like I was this rockin' steady Milo Morai type, which I'm not when I've almost been killed.

I didn't see much of Grandpa until after the battle. He went on to collect three totally hairy wounds for himself and whole slews of new notches on his sword. Whoa *Nelly*, life in the old fox yet, I'm sure.

So it was like that all morning and all afternoon: one surge after another, dinking one part of our lines and then another. We met each charge, though, and the shouting and clanging of swords and the death-cries of Union and Confederate dudes were fully ready to drive me dizzy. There was nothing to do but hang in there and put up a good fight, especially when your *horse* wants to gallop into the heaviest part of the action, right, and doesn't know the meaning of the word "retreat." *I* knew the meaning, but Mr. Ed must have been absent the day they were teaching *that* one.

The Moon Maidens were our artillery all this time, but Milo couldn't spare any infantry to like support them. They softened up the Ehleenee with their arrow showers well before the enemy got into sword range, so every rush up the side of the hills cost the Union plenty even *before* they touched steel with us. As the sun set, *Strahteegos* Lahmbrohs, the Dim Bulb, had a big part of his army like totally lying on their bellies all along the ridge, really just yards from the Confederate positions. The Ehleenee had gotten within feet— okay, within inches sometimes—of overrunning our brave dudes, but every time, just at the maximum moment, the Union rebels lost their drive, or the Confederate regulars and their Freefighter pals found like a new hardness of will. At last, that part of Lahmbrohs' strength was totally used up, and the men hung on to the side of the ridge, waiting for dawn and another order to like attack.

But Lahmbrohs was not ready to call it quits just on account of *night* was coming on, okay? He made one last push against the far right of the line, like on Cemetery and Culp's hills. That attack was more successful, like they actually broke through the defense and charged into the unprotected Moon Maidens. I was still mounted and ready, although I was about to like *rolf*, for sure, I was so totally wasted. I didn't know if I could handle another fight, but I go, "Maureen, honey, *go* for it, party hearty." Mr. Ed, bless her little heart, was right with me, so off we went to save Moon Maidens. I mean, they never so much as laid a "*hi*" on me before the battle, but I'm not one to like be all stuck-up about something like that, you know? Right.

Well, there was one furious fight in the twilight. The Moon Maidens stood their ground like good little girls, and pelted the Greeks with like a nonstop *hailstorm* of deadly arrows. A Pitzburker veteran told me like he'd never seen *anything* so terrible and bloody. I never even had a chance to use my sword—the Moon Maidens were skewering their attackers faster than reinforcements could get close. After a while there were no more Ehleenee willing to like stand up against these like *totally* excellent archers.

Night fell, but wouldn't you like know it, I wasn't done yet. I was leading Mr. Ed down to a stream to water her, right, with four or five other tired Confederate buddies, and like we look up and on the other side of the water there's this lame bunch of Union men. So we went at it right there, hand-to-hand, and it didn't take long to totally *burn* those dudes. We didn't get one scratch between us. It was just like this pointless hassle that kept me from supper and had me fully edged, I'm sure.

There was a strategy meeting in Milo's tent, set up all secure behind our lines. Milo talked, we listened. He goes, "Tell your soldiers that they all did a fine job today, but the battle isn't over yet."

Prince Byruhn of New Kuhmbuhluhn goes, "Where do you think Lahmbrohs will hit us tomorrow?"

"He failed today on both flanks, again and again," Milo goes. "I am almost certain that he will concentrate on our center, at dawn."

"He still has a couple of thousand men spread out on the face of Cemetery Hill," said *Strahteegos* Klaytuhn of Pitzburk.

"I haven't forgotten them. They won't get any sleep tonight, and they're exhausted. When the sun comes up, the fighting between your Freefighters and those weary Union boys will start up by itself. I don't expect they will stay in the battle very long. They are almost spent as it is."

So I go, "Then it's like the center I have to worry about, right?"

Milo gave me a warm smile. He goes, "Our center is where our best men are, covered by squadrons of Moon Maidens, in a solidly dug-in position, high uphill from the attacking Ehleenee."

"Pickett's Charge," I go, fully freaked but like *knowing* that it was coming all the time.

"Pickett's Charge," goes Milo.

I kind of like remembered something I learned from Daddy. General Longstreet had told Robert E. Lee that no fifteen thousand men ever put on any battlefield in history could take our position. I was like really hoping he was right, you know?

The meeting ended a little after that, and then it was nighty-night, y'all.

Come the morning, Milo was like totally right about his first prediction: The Ehleenee on the hillside made these *completely* wimpy swipes at the Pitzburkers, then gave up and bailed, happy trails. They probably had the best chance of getting out of Gettysburg—I mean, Getzburk—alive or something, I don't know.

All that's left is the charge itself. I sat Mr. Ed in the center of our line. I could like hear the wailing voice of the bloody God of War in my head, but the God of War sounded just like, you know, that Freddy Mercury, the lead singer of Queen. First I could hear him doing "We will, we will *rock* you!" But it totally wasn't like any fun to watch what was going on. That's all we did, was *watch*. Like the Moon Maidens picked off every one of the poor bastards while they were crossing the low ground. Freddy Mercury shifted right into "Another one bites the dust." Suddenly like everything went *quiet*. None of our boys were shouting or anything, and you know none of the Ehleenee were in a mood to whoop it up, for sure. It was weird, the silence I mean, and I felt this creepy tingly feeling. I go, "Maureen, like this is *so* ill." But there was nothing to do but watch. They kept coming on like lemmings, hustling their buns to suicide. "Gross, gross, *gross*," I go. They kept coming.

Then the Moon Maidens let fly, and the air was like totally filled with the zeeping of their bowstrings and the whooshing of the arrows. The Ehleenee hodads were coming through it in nice, straight lines, like they wanted to impress us with their *neatness*, I'm *so sure*. But the arrows punched gaps in their lines, more gaps every second as the Union lines marched nearer. As more of them went down, the Greeks who were like still alive like, you know, started to amble back to safety. They got punctured while they were retreating, too.

Then it was all over. Little Freddy was singing "We are the champions!" in my pea brain. Maybe half of the Ehleenee were still alive, running for their lives. The Battle of Getzburk was like *history*, in more ways than one, like for sure. We watched them as they fled. Our boys were celebrating, and the commanders looked on, you know, *proudly* and all.

At supper, Milo came by to talk to me a little bit. He goes, "You were an inspiration to our men, Mahreenah."

I go, "It was like nothing, God-Milo."

"Will you go on with us? This battle is done, but there will be many more before the war is won."

I like chewed my lip, pretending to think about it. "Milo," I go at last, "there are many worlds and many oppressed peoples, and it is my sacred duty like to *stand up* for the little clods wherever they're being, you know, like forced to eat *dirt*."

"I understand. I wish you well in your crusade."

"Thanks. And good luck to you." I didn't know what else to say, but I thought of a question. "Am I like, you know, *really* immortal?"

"You are in *this* universe. I can't say if you are anywhere else. Perhaps you're not truly traveling from world to world, but from parallel reality to parallel reality."

That made me think. I figured I better not try any crankin' heroics until I checked things out. I like didn't want to find out the *hard* way, right, that whoa, I'm *not* immortal on Venus of Ganymede or ancient Babylon if I turned up there. I ought to like test every place by socking myself in the nose and watching how long it takes to stop bleeding, I'm sure. I didn't know what to do, but Milo had planted a grody seed of doubt, you know?

I gave him this zingy salute, I go, "Seeyabye," and then I whooshed on out of there.

*   *   *

*And like right into my honeymoon suite. This is where you
and I came in. Maureen came to the end of her story and she
was totally right: I was amazed. I was also like still stunned
from the sock on the jaw she gave me, which I am never, ever
going to forget. I just put that on the bill with the heartache
and suffering she'd caused me in the past. I'd collect on it all
someday, for sure.*

*She was going to climb out the bathroom window, but I
stopped her. She goes, "What* now?" *like I've been making
demands on her.*

*I go, "Maureen, you're still cruising the Solar System like
some kind of kid on summer vacation. I mean, look at
it—Maureen Birnbaum, Tacky Girl Beast. You're getting muscles, honey. If you start growing a mustache, you should
seriously think about passing the heavy responsibility to
someone else. A guy, maybe." She glowered at me like
really threatening, but I held up a hand. "Look at* me.
*Happily married Bitsy Spiegelman Fein, settled wife and
planning maybe to be a mother, if you ever let me spend some
time alone with Josh. Real adult stuff, real adult hopes and
dreams. Who are* you? *Still Muffy Birnbaum, the One-Woman
Mercenary Army. It's* not *chic, sweetie. It doesn't fit you at
all. And you know what else doesn't fit? Look at us in the
mirror. What do you see?"*

She goes, "I see you, *you zod, and me."*

*I go, "I see me, twenty-two years old. I see you, and you
look the same as you did when you were a junior at the
Greenberg School."*

She goes, "I do?"

I go, "Uh huh."

She goes, "Whoa, get back! Maybe I really am *immortal."*

*I go, "Maybe you really are a case of arrested develop-
ment." I had to duck fast after that one. She grabbed her
spear and her bag and everything and like thundered out of
the bathroom. Too late I tried to stop her. "Muffy! No!" I
yelled.*

*She was already crossing the suite to the front door. My
darling Josh was standing there in his boxer shorts, socks,
and garters, holding two glasses of champagne. He had a
peculiar look on his face. The front door slammed shut after
Maureen. I looked back at Josh. He turned to me, trying to*

like make sense out of the apparition that escaped his bath-room. I go, "That was Muffy Birnbaum, sweetheart. You've heard me speak of her."

He goes, "Right."

I took one of the glasses from him and drained the cham-pagne in one long gulp. I didn't mention Maureen again. What Josh didn't know wouldn't barf him out. Loose Lips Sink Ships, like I'm totally sure.

The Last Time

by Joel Rosenberg

Joel Rosenberg has established himself not only as a science fiction writer but as a fantasy writer as well, thereby driving librarians and book cataloguers to distraction. He lives in Connecticut with his wife, Felicia Herman, and the traditional writer's cats, two at last count. His first novel, *The Sleeping Dragon*, the first in his Guardian of the Flame fantasy series, is in its sixth printing; the two following volumes are doing equally well. His most recent novel, *Emile and the Dutchman*, is part of his long-term plan to reinvent space opera.

There was a last time for everything, the last gunfighter thought, sitting astride his horse.

Not that he meant this time, of course, but someday the last Clan Lehvee sheriff would ride out and perhaps never return, leaving the world to the goddam swordsmen.

"Keep a weather eye on the horizon, Dunkahn," the big man said, dismounting from his horse and kneeling next to the ashes of the fleeing dirtmen's fire.

"Yes," Dunkahn Lehvee said sullenly. Then, at the other's arched eyebrow, he tried again, this time forcing the resentment from his voice: "I will."

Of course he would keep an eye open, even if that meant squinting painfully in the direction of the setting sun. He didn't want to be here, but hardly meant that he wanted to leave himself open to ambush by the dirtmen they were chasing.

This wasn't the sort of thing he had wanted. Not ever. But it was a matter of tradition, perhaps of necessity. His many-times-great-grandfather, before the Blast, had been what the ancients called a ''sheriff''; while the original functions of the office had long been lost in travels of the Kindred, the office, the blackened badge, and the pistol had been handed on; it was a family tradition.

It weighed heavily—literally.

The crude leather pistol belt wasn't a bad example as it hung on his hip, its weight threatening to cut him in two. It wasn't supposed to have been his yet, but his father, Micah, had died last year in an idiotic accident, his chest crushed when his horse had fallen and rolled over him.

It wasn't right. The responsibility shouldn't be his.

Not with only fifteen summers behind him.

His hand fell to the strap holding down the butt of the ancient weapon, his blunt fingers feeling at the runes that Kindred had long lost the ability to decipher.

It felt strange under his hand. And that was more than passing strange in itself. Under Micah's instruction, he had dry-fired it perhaps ten thousand times, practiced with it for hours and hours, ritualistically cleaning and oiling it after each such use.

Never, of course, had he placed it loaded in its holster. The pistol and seven cartridges had been handed down to him by his father, Mikah, as he lay dying; Dunkahn had intended to hand all down to his son. Never, that is, until this morning, when Chief Milo of Morai had wakened him, saying formally: ''Sheriff Lehvee, there has been a shooting.''

There has been a shooting. The words felt strange on his tongue as he tried them out silently. The last time that had been said it had been to his grandfather, when the Kindred's travel had brought them up against a band of roving raiders with rifles. Simon, who had inherited twenty-three bullets from his father, had tracked them down; when he returned to the Lehvee encampment, there were only seven.

Someday, perhaps, a Lehvee sheriff would fire the last round. There was, after all, a last time for everything.

Dunkahn Lehvee, of course, had never fired a shot in anger. Not even with a hornbow; he was renowned among Clan Lehvee as perhaps the worst bowman that the Kindred had ever produced. His skills with a sword were similar; with a lance, he was only passable, and that was only because of the almost instinctive way that his dappled mare responded instantly to almost microscopic nudgings of his knees and twitching of the reins. If he didn't know better, he would have thought that Sunflower could read his mind.

How was he with a pistol? He didn't know, despite all the hours of practice. The pistol was supposed to be a symbol, not a weapon. To actually have to *use* the pistol was something he had considered only idly.

And for what? To avenge a God-forsaken Braizhoor horsethief, his woman, and their cubs? Ridiculous. Granted, dirtmen had to be persuaded that attacking Kindred was a fatal mistake, but the point could have been made another way. Still, he didn't like the memory of the large hole in what had been little Ahrthuh Braizhoor's chest. Braizhoor cubs were cute, just like all little children. Why had the dirtmen shot the little one?

That wasn't right. Nothing wrong with killing a full-grown Braizhoor, but a baby? That wasn't right.

"Chief Milo?" he asked from the back of his horse, while the big, black-haired man knelt next to the ashes of the campfire. "How long?"

Milo Morai eyed him levelly. "More than a moment, less than a year." With a grace that belied his size, the big man swung to the back of his brown gelding and kicked it into a slow walk, leading the two packhorses while Dunkahn led their two spare mounts.

Riding toward a setting sun felt strange. The long travels of the Kindred were always to the east, occasionally veering north or south, but never west. The *morning* sun had been created to beat into one's eyes; the afternoon sun was supposed to warm one's back.

Milo Morai's eyes didn't meet Dunkahn's as they rode. Not that there was anything shy about the big man, but eyes fixed on the next stand of trees or rocky outcropping had no time for the courtesy of looking at the one he was addressing.

They rode in silence as the darkness slowly fell; before the light totally faded, Milo called a halt and they made a rude camp in a stand of trees at the edge of the forest, although he relaxed visibly only after Dunkahn had climbed the tallest of the leafy giants in an attempt to spot their quarry.

There was sign of them—they had clearly entered the forest and were likely camped somewhere along the trail—but they were clearly not near. Yet.

Supper was a swig of water and a few mouthfuls of pemmican for the humans and water for the horses, who were hobbled to graze nearby. Good Horseclans ponies, they wouldn't wander far, and would sound an alarm if anything approached. Except for Sunflower; Dunkahn patted her solid neck and let her roam free, knowing that she would return at his whistle.

The two men took to their furs. Dunkahn eyed the sky; it was a clear night, stars burning overhead like distant campfires.

"Are you sure that you won't lend me the pistol?" Chief Milo asked from the dark.

It had been a shock to Dunkahn when Morai had made that suggestion two days before, before they had set out on the trail of the fleeing murderers. After several gentle repetitions, it wasn't shocking anymore. He wasn't certain why Morai kept it up; didn't repeating the same silly question bore the older man?

"No," Dunkahn responded gently. "Only the Sheriff of Clan Lehvee or his heir may touch the badge of office," he said, reflexively bringing his thumb up to touch the blackened shield pinned to his rough leather vest, "or the pistol that backs up his au-thor-ity," he finished, stumbling over the old English word that wasn't Merikan.

"Understood." Morai nodded. "I'd really like to take a look at the rounds, though. Probably most don't fire, after all this time. Although your ancestor did choose well; Remington Archivals were designed and packed to have an indefinite shelf life."

Dunkahn wondered, again, where such knowledge came from. If knowledge it was, and not mere braggadocio; Chief Milo often let go pieces of information that it would seem he couldn't possibly have come by. But Milo Morai didn't impress Dunkahn as a braggart.

And while it simply had never been done for another to touch the sheriff's tools of office, looking was something else, Dunkahn decided.

Dunkahn burrowed into his furs and took the spare round from his belt pouch, holding it in the palm of his hand as he walked over to Morai. Sealed in something like intestine, only thinner, brass shone brightly in the moonlight.

Dunkahn had never seen prettier metalworking; the smiths that had built the pistol and rounds must have been true wizards, indeed.

But they and their magics were long since gone. The world was left to the damn bowmen and swordsmen.

"Looks good." Morai shrugged as Dunkahn returned to his furs. "Can't tell by looking, but some have clearly survived the centuries." He patted at the hornbow strapped to his saddle and hitched across his belt at his sword. "But maybe we'll have to rely on this."

"*I* will not," Dunkahn said. "Without offense intended."

"Nor taken, boy. Nor taken."

Technically, Milo Morai had no obligation to take to the trail with Dunkahn, but the boy had been loath to spurn the big man's offer of help. Really, it should have been a whole raiding party sent after the dirtmen—three of them now pulling a string of Braizhoor ponies, to judge by trail signs—but there had been the bulletholes, recognized by Bard Sami; tradition required that the Sheriff of Clan Lehvee go after gunmen.

Gunmen. The word felt strange in his mind. "How do you know?"

"About what, Dunkahn?"

"That the bullets that the dirtmen used were ancient? Isn't it possible that some of the old wizards are still around?" Even in his sixteen years, Dunkahn Lehvee had seen things he wouldn't have credited as possible.

Although he didn't really believe in the magic of gunpowder.

Morai shook his head. "Not likely, boy. Besides," he went on as though to himself, "if it was of recent manufacture, they'd be back to ball and powder, not Geco-BATs, of all things. But the plastic caps left behind nailed it down: the rounds are old Geco-BATs."

Again, something that sounded strange. A gecko was a lizard; a bat, a flying creature. That one would name a bullet after a bat was reasonable; but why would anyone name it after a lizard?

"How do you know about all this? And why did you insist on accompanying me?"

Milo Morai was silent for a moment. "I won't answer the first; it's private clan business. As to the second, boy, if there are more bullets and gunpowder around than your ancient handgun, Clan Morai is definitely interested." Dunkahn could almost hear him smile. "When you get older, Dunkahn, you'll learn that there are such things that man was not meant to know. Now, sleep.''

Dunkahn slept.

Morning came in with the threat of a storm. Which wasn't good; a plains storm would wipe away any trace of a trail and assure that their meandering quarry would escape.

They rode quickly, thoughts of "gecko-bats" and "ball and powder" running through Dunkahn's head as they rode single-file down the narrow trail through the forest. Ball and powder . . . was it possible . . .

"Are you a wizard, Chief Milo?" he finally asked. "Could you make more of my bullets?"

"Me?" Milo Morai chuckled. "No. Hardly." He shrugged. "I talked too much last night, eh? It matters little. Just leave it there's . . . a road down which humanity has traveled before, and one of the important way stations leads to things like that piece of iron on your hip—and to things far worse, as much more dangerous that that as that is more dangerous than a bee sting.''

Morai spoke as though he'd given the speech several thousands of times before, but hardly expected to be believed. "You're the last of your ilk, Sheriff—whoa, there.''

The big man suddenly reined in his horse and vaulted lightly to the trail, retrieving the core of an apple, which he held in the palm of his hand. It was dirty and browned, and the flies swarming over it had yet to carry off much. "What do you make of this, Sheriff Lehvee?"

Dunkahn shrugged. "There's someone on this trail not far ahead of us, and that's for certain," he said. "And they don't know that we're following them, or—''

"*Not necesssarily*," a harsh voice snarled from the woods. "If ye don't move, we might let ye live—for a while." From behind the bulk of an old oak a short, grimy man in a dirtman's ragged tunic stepped, followed by two others, who were even filthier, if such a thing were possible. "Although we'll pro'ly havta kill the big 'un quickly," he added in a clear afterthought. "Ye both know what these are, eh?"

Each of the three held a pistol clutched awkwardly in his hand. "Tol' ya, I did," the second dirtman said, "that if'n we killed a couple of 'em and lef' a trail they'd havta send the sheriff after us.''

"And here 'e is, eh?"

"Be still, Dunkahn. They're not going to shoot." Milo Morai stood easily, the weight on the balls of his feet.

"Oh?" The third dirtman gestured threateningly with his pistol. "And what makes ye say that?"

"You're after the magic of gunpowder, aren't you? And you think that the sheriff here has that."

The man gave a gap-toothed smile. "And aren't ye the clever one? He'll tell us, after he sees ye roasting over a slow fire. If not, we'll start on his own toes."

Finally, it had started to make sense.

They had heard about the one Horseclansman who had an ancient magic weapon, and assumed that he had the ability to make more. Actually, that made sense; a man knew how to make a bow or lance, and most knew something of smithing, although only few were expert enough to be swordmakers. Somehow or other, they must have stumbled across an ancient cache of the weapons; they wanted more ammunition and thought that the sheriff was the way to it.

"Be still, Dunkahn," the big man repeated. "They're not going to shoot you because they think that you know how to make more bullets. And they're not going to shoot me, either."

The taller of the three men nudged his neighbor again. "A bright one, he is. And why should we let you live?"

The big man smiled. "Because you just think that the boy knows the secret. I do know it."

One snickered, while another gestured Morai to silence. "Shaddap. I think he be serious, even if ye don't. And what does it hurt to wait awhile?"

Morai nodded. "And I'll be happy to tell you—*now, Dunkahn.*"

The big man drew his sword and lunged for the nearest of the three.

Time seemed to slow.

There is a last time for everything, he thought, as he clawed at the strap holding his pistol in its holster.

His vision narrowed, until the whole universe was the smallest of the three dirtmen, the one swinging his gun to bear on Dunkahn.

As he had done ten thousand times in practice, Dunkahn gripped the handle of the pistol smoothly, drawing it from his holster, his thumb pulling the hammer back as he brought it into line.

Trained reflexes took over; left hand clamped around and steadying his right, he brought the pistol up and centered the smaller man's chests in his sights as he jerked on the trigger, twice.

The sound of the pistol firing was a thunderclap that echoed through his body, but the only effect was twin explosions of bark and splinters from the tree next to the small man, which jerked his arm up and sent his own shot wild.

Out of the corner of his eye, Dunkahn could see Morai, moving with a grace that belied his bulk, his sword drawn and held out in front of him, ducking under the shot of the second man; Milo Morai speared him through the chest and kicked the man from his wet blade as the third dirtman brought his gun in line.

Squeeze, don't pull, he could hear his father say as he brought the gun up and pulled hard on the trigger, just as the other fired, dumping Morai to the ground with wounded arm and a muffled moan, just as a red flower appeared in the dirtman's chest, instantly turning into a gout of blood, and Dunkahn followed up with another shot that knocked the dirtman off his feet.

A gun-wielding hand peeked out from behind the tree; Dunkahn took aim and fired at it, once, twice, three times, until the gun clicked empty.

The familiar *snick* of the hammer on an empty chamber sent his left hand clawing for his belt pouch while his right thumbed the cylinder open and sent the empty brass tumbling.

There is a last time for everything, the last gunfighter thought as his trembling fingers fitted the last round into the chamber. The dirtman walked around from behind the tree, his gun held lightly, smiling.

"No more bullets, eh?" he said, smiling happily as he brought his own gun up. "Well, I've only got one more me'self," he said, bringing up his own weapon and aiming it at the boy's face.

There is a last time for everything, Dunkahn Lehvee thought, as he brought up his own pistol, took careful aim, and fired, just as thunder tore his own chest apart.

His second-to-last thought was that Milo Morai had not been lying—that for whatever reason, the big man *could* have brought guns and powder back into the world, but had decided not to; Morai really meant that he didn't want the world traveling down the same route as it had last time, that guns, powder, and the skills to make them led to far worse than this.

His last tortured thought was to wonder how Milo Morai could possibly be right.

High Road of the Lost Men

by Brad Linaweaver

Brad Linaweaver began his career as a professional writer in the areas of journalism and political opinion, but soon found that he preferred more honest forms of fantasy. In 1983, he was a Nebula finalist for his first work of fiction, "Moon of Ice," that ran in *Amazing Magazine*. He is currently expanding the tale into his first novel for Arbor House. He has also appeared in *Magic in Ithkar*. While awaiting several other anthology appearances, he lives in Georgia with his wife, Cari; stepdaughter, Morgan; and a miniature prairiecat named Puff.

During the time of the cracking of the plateau, there were many who were cast down, and others crushed by a rain of boulders. The fortunate ones escaped the Night of Fire. Among these were Kindred, Confederation nobles, Ehleenee, Freefighters, prairiecats, Moon Maidens, Soormehlyuhn, and Ahrmehnee, as well as sundry wild animals, birds, and even Ganiks, who lived to see a red sun hanging, as a distant torch, above the dust-shrouded crags of what remained. One survivor was the traveling bard Noplis, who sang of the Day of Doom thereafter.

He had not been the most popular of raconteurs before this time. The night before the disaster, he had been in the camp of Von, a chieftain in the mighty army that was Sir Geros' to command, where the storyteller was recounting deeds of the High Lord Milo. The largest prairiecat in camp, Flatear—so called because his left ear had been broken since birth—had little patience with the artificial means by which humans entertain themselves. Unable to restrain himself, he mindspoke thus:

"Here is a two-leg who speaks at length regarding matters of which he knows less than a cub. Were it not that our Chief Graypaw and Chief Von saw some use in these word mists, I'd be for sending all tellers of tales to finish their days in the yurt of the old and sick."

"Hold there, cat-brother," said Von, quick to mediate, for his reputation as a diplomat was as widely appreciated as his record of fighting prowess. "This bard is welcome with any Kindred clan, and we should show proper manners. Though I'll admit"— here Von winked at Noplis—"'tis unlikely he's had firsthand experience with the matters of which he sings."

The poor man could do naught but agree. "Such is my admiration for the High Lord," said he, "that I sought to give an impression, or overview, of his campaigns, without bogging down in details."

"True words from the two-leg at last!" was Flatear's opinion. Noplis knew that cats do not smile, but he could not shake the feeling that this feline's permanent grin was at his expense.

"Relax, friend bard," said Von, slapping the slight man on the back with a force that almost sent him reeling into the camp's fire. "Would seem you've made a conquest of your furry critic, all in all." At this, the company burst into raucous laughter. Noplis was at least a professional. He had the sense to join in.

Von's concubine scratched behind Flatear's good ear, and Noplis wondered if he saw jealousy in the face of the large cat's female lying at the opposite end of the camp, carefully watching all that happened. Perhaps he'd been singing for his supper one night too many, he considered, if such odd fantasies could cross his mind unbidden. Human faces were a better source for potential drama, and he could not help but notice that a dark Moon Maiden watched the fair concubine with undisguised lust. But young Ethera's loyalty was to Von, and even were this not so, she seemed disinclined to frolic with her own.

"My lords," announced Noplis, his voice cracking a bit, eyes searching out Flatear, "I'd be happy to tell another tale, or cease withal, if such be the camp's pleasure."

"Fair is fair," shouted Terrell, one of Von's most trusted lieutenants. "If Flatear be unsatisfied with two-legged amusement, mayhap he'd regale us with a story of his own?"

Halfway through the night, and surfeited on heavy wine, these clansmen were eager to laugh at anything that was at someone else's expense; the basis of high humor, after all. But Flatear was a wily beast, well versed in the affairs of men, and able to protect his own sensibilities.

The great cat played along: "I've seen horses overcome dangers to test the mettle of anything living, and my cat-brothers and I have not spent all our time purring at a warm fire. Any story of the Kindred should be of interest to you, but it's been my experience that two-legs are only interested in other two-legs." This inspired a chuckle or two, but the more thoughtful took a moment to reflect on whether or not they had been insulted. Paying no heed to the response, Flatear continued: "I'll tell of a two-leg deserving a respect from all clan brothers, if Chief Von does not object to being singled out by one who witnessed his bravery."

"Pay close attention, Noplis," said Berti, the cook, "and you'll have something to sing about."

A flicker of resentment crossed the bard's face, but then he realized that one of the convenient things about prairiecats—even a mean old sourpuss such as Flatear—was that they do not fret over ownership of an idea or the telling of an event.

Observing that Von had settled down beside Ethera, a flagon of wine in his large-knuckled hand, Flatear went on: "Von and I were hunting meat where pickings were scarce. Winter was prowling near, our breath was on the air, and frost was on the ground. Most game had gone farther south. There was in the region an old grizzly bear who was faring no better in his search for sustenance. Besides coming across the spoor of the grizzly, I'd also found a pile of dried wolf shit. 'Tis not mutton or pork,' said Von, 'but a sweet find nonetheless, with a welcome odor indeed,' and I was certain that a fine two-leg had taken leave of his senses. He proceeded to make a fire—where would a two-leg be without the flame?—and mixing the old dung with herbs he carried in a pouch, he made a stinking mixture which he smeared over his body."

"Ha, he must have stunk like a Ganik!" said good old Noplis, instantly regretting his ill-chosen words as the deafening silence assailed him. Even Flatear was stunned into speechlessness, a rare occurrence indeed.

But once more was Chief Von's reputation for diplomacy

proven merited. "A fine jest," said he, "and one you will no doubt add when you make this tale your own. For the nonce, I think we'd appreciate the uninterrupted flow of Flatear's narrative, eh?"

With long, pink tongue licking his chops, Flatear turned his baleful gaze from his least favorite bard in all the world and resumed mindspeaking: "When his body was covered in the putrid solution, he spread what was left across the frost-covered ground in the direction of the bear's cave; then we gathered all the leaves that we could find—I still can taste the dry flavor—and Von lay upon the ground. We covered him with the leaves! Then we waited to greet the wind—and it obliged us by blowing in the direction of the cave. I held back, out of sight and scent, ready to help when need be.

"That old bear was as hungry for Von's appetizer as were we for him. With a carelessness borne of hope that he was creeping up on a lone wolf, the bear walked straight toward the hiding place."

There was a low, appreciative murmuring from those assembled. Most knew that Flatear and Von had had adventures together before they came to prominence with the forces of Sir Geros. Some had heard this story before, but all were entranced at the description of their chief's daring.

"One wrong step from that big four-paws and this clan would never have known the guidance of a sensible leader, brothers. Von had spread his wolf scent with care, so as to guide the bear's movements. When the bulk of his adversary was directly over the trap, he struck with that very knife you see at his side now. I hurried to join the kill." As Flatear was the swiftest prairiecat of Von's clan, none doubted the speed with which this was accomplished. "I needn't have bothered. With one straight thrust of that long knife, he pierced the grizzly's heart, and his one danger remaining was to roll clear before two tons of bear flesh fell into a pool of its own hot blood! That's an act of bravery you don't see every day, wandering bard. If you sing of that, see that you tell it truly."

Noplis had nothing else to say that night but for repeated thanks at the generous offerings of food he received despite his less than successful showing. At first, he felt some degree of resentment at the brusque prairiecat, but as he thought upon it he came to agree that his critic had a point. There was no substitute for the proximity of a subject. It wasn't that the

bard had not faced danger before—almost impossible not to
do in these perilous times—but that when danger loomed
near, it was his habit to find matters demanding his immediate attention at a further remove. So accomplished was he at
running that it had once been suggested that he might be of
immeasurable value as a messenger, but when considering the
brief life span offered by that profession, he concluded that
he should apply his abilities to the more demanding rigors of
the storyteller's art.

The one trouble with excessive caution, of course, is that
the world pays no heed to the plan. How could Noplis have
foreseen that the very next day he would be caught in the
cataclysm of an earthquake because of insane machinations
by a few Witchmen? Afterward, Noplis would have to agree
that firsthand experience adds a dimension of verisimilitude
to one's poetry, but at the time itself, the only thought in his
head would be a raw animal urge to survive at any cost.

It began when the earth shook. That part was bad enough,
but what bothered Noplis the most was that the horizon he
was observing to his left suddenly wasn't there any longer.
The ground was shaking badly by then. Unable to flee,
stomach turning over, Noplis prayed that the world return to
normal. Instead of tranquillity, he was rewarded by fireballs
that tore through the sky in his direction. His instinct to throw
himself to the ground was thwarted by the ground moving
away—or at least so it seemed, as the earth crumpled beneath
his feet. One white-hot rock, the size of four horses, came
close enough that he felt the heat on the back of his neck
before the stone plunged into a nearby stream. The steam
resulting from that immersion drifted in Noplis' direction,
reducing his visibility. This was just as well, as he had no
desire to see more—but the hot mist made it difficult to
breathe.

By now, the shaking of the ground was at its peak. Somehow Noplis avoided broken bones, although he almost fell
into a crevice that yawned open a few feet from where he was
trying to maintain his balance. In the midst of chaos, soaring
above the cacophony of roars and rumbles below, and the
whooshing of rocks above, was a veritable symphony of
mindspeak. The bard was one who had the gift developed to
the point where he could farspeak. The telepathic cries for
help added an unusual counterpoint to the earthquake: Real

voices could not be heard for more than a few seconds, constantly drowned out by the grating of stone on stone.

After several attempts to stand, Noplis finally gave up, electing to remain flat upon the ground. He was too tired to get up again. Idly he wondered if the earthquake was a punishment for the previous night's artistic inadequacy. If so, it didn't have a very good aim.

The ordeal finally ended. Opening his eyes, Noplis discovered that he was alone. Not a tree was standing as far as he could see. Near at hand was a huge slab of basalt and granite, with streaks of red and brown slashing across it—mineral deposits that made him think that the earth was bleeding. The air was full of dust, enough to make him cough as he rose woozily to his feet.

And there was something else amiss. He didn't even notice it at first, but when he did, it sent shivers down his back. The symphony of mindspeak was over. He heard not a note, not a word, not a yell. There were no voices.

His head felt as though it had been split in twain. Even so, he called out . . . and the sound of his own voice hurt his temples. For many lonely minutes he cried out, alone. Then came a welcome, mindspoken greeting: "Stay where you are. I can reach you."

Right away, he knew who it was. His fellow survivor was Flatear.

Whenever he was bored, the Judge would look at himself in a mirror. In fact, he kept mirrors expressly for that purpose. Today he used a round one, with a yellow stain across the top, and one crack running diagonally across the pitted surface. It was one of his best mirrors.

The wrinkled face returned his gaze with large, watery eyes, the color of an eel—his healthiest feature. The protuberance extending from his right cheekbone was still growing, almost imperceptibly lengthening since last he'd taken inventory. It curved over the pulpy indentation where once his nose had been, almost seeming to be a replacement for that organ. He referred to the growth as a beak when he was around the Ganiks, pleased that his head had a birdlike appearance. That, combined with the feathers growing from his thin neck to his twisted shoulder blades, completed the image by which he convinced them that he was an emissary of their god, Ndaindjerd. The absence of a nose had proven a positive boon where that stinking rabble of ghouls was concerned. How convenient for him that they would not eat bird or beast.

As for the rest of the Judge's visage, it was a catalogue of the putrescent, scars of old diseases making a cobweb pattern across his forehead as if they were strings to a mask. Blue-gray flesh hung upon the skull without softening the contours beneath. He had no chin to speak of, the ears were barely noticeable lumps, and his mouth was the worst part: a few lonesome teeth, sharp as fangs, at odd angles to the ugly purple color of the gums. *Yes,* thought the Judge, *you're looking good.*

He thought of himself as Lucifer, fallen from the Center, the ultimate renegade of the Witchmen. He liked that label for his old associates precisely because they hated it. Witches. Across the sad and empty centuries, he had come to loathe his colleagues far more than he did their various enemies. The world the Center would recreate was not for him, any more than was the world that did exist. So he had aspired to something else that would be entirely his. Experimenting in secret with a genetic project of his own, he had secured the services of an assistant named Davidson, a biochemistry man.

Weary of transferring from one body to another, jealous of the High Lord, Milo Morai, and all others blessed with natural longevity, hating everything built by Dr. Sternheimer, the Judge had projected his mind into an artificially developed body. The good news was that the experiment worked, in that the transfer was complete, and that the body did not age . . . exactly. The bad news was that he couldn't get out of the horribly changing, ever more freakish shell. He'd bought himself a ticket to hell.

When Davidson saw the results of the experiment, he made the mistake of saying: "You are a great man, Doctor. Unwilling to settle for the status quo, you took a self-critical approach, the glory of our scientific method! Despite a few unexpected side effects, with this experiment you open the door to a renaissance. Surely the time has come to share this good news with everyone!" Davidson might have said more had he not been strangled on the spot. The new body was strong, at least. It was the death of the Doctor and the birth of the Judge.

Under the circumstances, he decided to make the best of his lot. One thing he had learned was that the general population agreed on very little, but an opinion that bound men together, however different their creeds, was: Ganiks are the scum of the earth. Brutish, superstitious, unintelligent, disorganized, disloyal, slavering cannibals . . . what possible use could they be to anyone, themselves included? He decided then and there that they were the folk he needed. His knowledge of their customs made it child's play to convince them of his divinity. They learned to call him by the name he had given himself: the Judge. He didn't need many of them at first—just a few bullies and their herds.

On the last mission he had carried out when he still inhabited a human body, he'd stumbled upon an underground base in almost perfect condition. He surmised that the original occupants had suffocated perhaps as far back as the Great Change. It was like finding an Egyptian pyramid with all its relics intact. Naturally he kept the find to himself, never knowing when it might come in handy. Today it was *his* base. So far as the Center was concerned, he had died in a failed experiment, and taken Davidson with him.

It took months to put his new home in order. If the equipment had not been protected in a virtual vacuum, he wasn't sure what he would have done. As it was, he restarted the generators, turned the lights on, found some functional weapons in the armory, and even discovered Muzak tapes kept in their own airtight container. He reasoned that men of a thousand years ago must have prized this music very highly; because although the Judge remembered a good bit about the twentieth century, he had forgotten other things.

He had the most fun finding his "children," scaring them first, recruiting afterward. It was Home Sweet Home.

As he preened in front of the little round mirror, there was no way for the Judge to know that, elsewhere, Dr. Braun and Major Corbett had set off explosive charges at the entrance to caves above a volcano, for motives entirely irrelevant to the actual consequences. So far as the Judge could tell, the earthquake that began to knock down the plateau beneath which resided his base was from natural causes. Then again, on several occasions, he had joked to the witless Ganiks around him (he enjoyed talking to himself) that were the earth to split wide open, he would suspect that the Center was behind it, because "they have the qualifications once required by the Army Corps of Engineers." At the moment, however, the Judge was shaken as thoroughly as if he were in a Mixmaster, and he watched his precious mirror fall to the floor and shatter.

The Judge's Hold withstood the tremors. It had been built to survive nuclear war . . . and had. Within minutes, a bruised Ganik crawled into his presence, fell at his feet, and using one of the forms of address that his teacher insisted upon, said: "Oh, mighty one who looks down from on high, a dozen men were killed in a cave-in in Sector 8."

"Is there other damage?"

The Ganik shrugged. Well, that would do for a no.

"How long will it take to clear the exit?"

"Only a few hours, as you have taught us the engineering ways."

"You're a smart one, all right. Give the order to collect the bodies if they can be located. Waste not, want not. And most important of all, report to me on how many mirrors I have left."

"By Sun, Wind and Steel," said Von, wiping grit from his eyes. "How many can hear me? Call out, or mindspeak!"

"Danger increases," interrupted the prairiecat Swifteye, mate to Flatear. "We must flee the fires."

"I can see that, cat-sister," said Von, "but survivors there may be whom we can save."

White-hot rocks were still falling, albeit smaller ones than before. The fires ignited by these were rushing together, forming one large curtain of red-and-yellow death. The only direction left was off the plateau, but that way was little better than the fire. The terrain was slowly collapsing about them, and no sure footing was possible.

"Follow me, all who can hear my voice or beaming!" called out the chief. Swifteye sent out farspeak, and everyone else converging on the spot added his or her beacon to the call: "LET ALL WHO SURVIVED COME WITH US." Every rolling pebble or far-off thunder added to their terror.

Berti the cook had a broken leg and arm and was bleeding from his chest. Terrell's boot splints had protected his ankles from being cracked; he was now withdrawing these bands of metal and using them as splints for his friend's bones, while the cook retained his good humor, between racking coughs, by insisting that he was better off than the Moon Maiden beside him, whose wound had been terminal: a broken neck.

When the ragtag group was ready to travel, Von went in the lead, checking out the treacherous incline that dared his every footstep. Swifteye was at his side, sending out messages to Flatear—messages that were not answered. Von was the first to see Blackhoof, a noble warhorse, trapped beneath a mound of earth. Only the head and one hoof protruded, and it was evident from the angle of the hoof that the leg was broken. The horse mindspoke a simple message, all the more eloquent for its simple plea.

As Von started toward the horse, Ethera's arm reached out for him. He had not known until that moment that she lived. "My chief," she said, as he touched her lovely face, so wonderfully whole and unmarked, "no one loved Blackhoof more than I, but you risk your life to climb down there. Would it not be best to end his suffering with an arrow?" She gestured at one good bow and several steel-tipped arrows that had survived.

"My soul flies now that I see you live, dear one. But I will not dispatch yonder steed without a proper farewell. He bore me in battle, and that's an end to it."

Blackhoof's eyes were huge in pain, his nostrils flaring; but he beamed an emotion of such pure joy at the coming of a kinsman, and this man in particular, that the danger seemed to recede before such camaraderie. An aftershock surprised everyone, and Von fell, sliding the last ten feet of rock-strewn slope to come up hard against the sweating flank of the horse. Putting out a big hand, he patted the wet, dark neck of his steed. They looked into each other's eyes, and exchanged something beyond words or mindspeak, before Von cut his friend's artery.

The chief of the clan didn't have to make the climb back up alone. Ethera had come to join him, and helped support his large frame, bruised from the sliding.

By some miracle, the survivors made it the rest of the way without further mishap, although Terrell needed extra help with Berti, who was fading in and out of consciousness. Periodically a wild animal would scamper or gallop by them, so close that some of the Kindred could almost touch it. The greater fear drowned all smaller instincts.

Only when they'd reached the base of the plateau, and dusk was closing in, did they finally take a count of their numbers. The horses and ponies were presumed dead or run off. From a party of twenty warriors, thirty-five clanswomen, six prairiecats, and five Moon Maidens, their numbers were reduced to eight men, ten women, two cats . . . and none of the Moon Maidens. Von kept up their spirits with: "We don't know that any be dead we didn't see with our own eyes. Others may be lost from us, as we are lost from other clans."

"Wouldn't we have received mindspeak?" asked a young girl."

"Nothing is certain," Von insisted.

Further discussion would most certainly have involved plans to reconnoiter and set up camp. Foraging would be no problem with all the fresh food so newly descended from the plateau. Their deliberations never got anywhere, because they were ambushed!

Exhausted as they were from the arduous journey, they still had the strength to put up resistance. The nature of the enemy was so completely unexpected, however, that it delayed their response. The enemy was a short, hairy Ganik, but what was worse, he carried a weapon the likes of which none of the Horseclansmen had ever seen.

The noise from the strange weapon was frightening; in fact, they feared that the earthshaking had started again. Even more frightening were the smoke and sparks thrown by the strange weapon. None of the clansmen were harmed, however; and the idea of a Ganik deliberately shooting to miss was almost as inconceivable as his using an incomprehensible weapon in the first place. Before Von could give orders to rush the enemy, a giant of a man, almost nine feet in height, appeared from around a boulder to their right, blocking their only avenue of escape, since none wished to challenge the unknown weapon to their left.

"Don't give hard time," shouted the giant. "Bigboy hurt when ground shook. Back hurts. Ribs hurt. Don't fight or Bigboy hurt you bad." The Horseclansmen stood still, several thanking Wind that they could understand the strange language of the Ganiks. Somehow it made the bad situation a little better.

"Hey, shaggy man," taunted Terrell. "Aren't you afraid

that your demon, Plooshun, will feed your guts to your children for sinning against him? He will strike you down for using that strange weapon!''

Von was surprised. He knew that Terrell spoke many languages, but he hadn't realized that his young lieutenant knew so much about the Ganiks and their strange beliefs. Terrell's words were having good effect on their first captor— the little man was sweating heavily, and cursing in his coarse dialect. However, before they could take advantage of the Ganik's fear, the giant shouted again.

''Leave him be! Bigboy talk now,'' he cried. ''Come. The Judge decide what happens to you now.'' The Horseclansmen still might have succeeded in rushing the enemy, despite their weakened state. Swifteye mindspoke to Von, assuring him that nothing could prevent her from tearing out the throat of whichever Ganik he assigned. Then suddenly a small army of Ganiks appeared, creeping forth from among the shadows.

Von broadbeamed a silent warning to his people: ''Had they meant but to kill us, they'd have done so ere now. Wait for a better chance. We'll bathe the ground in blood before we enter their stewpots, I promise it.'' His people, more angry and frustrated than exhausted, eager to meet a tangible enemy after enduring natural disaster, agreed with their chief. They would bide their time.

So it was that Horseclansmen were introduced to the peculiar legal practices of a renegade Witchman.

The earthquake had played a game upon Noplis. Miserable over his latest performance, even obsessed with it, all the forces of nature had risen up to remove the would-be entertainer from his no doubt grateful audience. At least, it felt that way to him. If the earthquake were a bard itself, it could have done no better than to leave the singer of woeful tales with but one companion: his most severe critic, Flatear. Surely the earthquake had too blatant a sense of irony to be a first-rate artist.

''Sacred Sun is barely visible,'' observed the prairiecat. A feline's excellent night vision was of no use in a sky befouled with debris. On top of that, the big cat was continually sneezing in Noplis' direction.

If the Witchmen were driven to learn the secrets of how mutant telepathy worked, it was something taken for granted by the Kindred, as natural a part of their daily lives as breathing or eating. Something about the earthquake was interfering with both the cat's and the bard's farspeak, although they could still communicate one-to-one. Was it magnetic disturbance released from the earth? Was it smoke and dust in the air? Whatever the reason, long-range telepathy was impeded in this locality.

"Last mindcall was over there," observed the prairiecat, his good ear twitching in the direction of the wall of rock that had been vomited from the bowels of the plateau only a short distance from Noplis.

"Then we can't follow," moaned the bard, "and the other way lies certain death." The wall of fire was a safe distance from them, but how much longer that would last neither dared venture a guess.

"We must find another route or perish," said Flatear, already moving with grace and precision along the side of the new barrier. "There needs be an opening somewhere," insisted the cat. "Help me look, two-legs."

Well into the afternoon they searched, the inferno blazing nearer, a reminder of the urgency of their plight. There was little opportunity for the exchange of bantering words, and no breath was wasted. Search, hope, move swiftly . . . or die.

It wasn't exactly friendship that was formed by the ordeal, but there was a lessening of enmity. Treating a companion as an enemy is a luxury that danger does not allow.

The fire crept nearer, hot and hungry for them; the wall of rock remained impervious; the great eye of the sun was ever more occluded by the shroud of dust. Over and over, Noplis said a silent prayer: *Let me not lose courage before this brave prairiecat.* He had not even noticed that his prayer had changed from a screaming, hysterical plea of: *Get me out of here!*

They found a dead mountain pony. All they could salvage of his gear was a coil of rope. As Noplis worked at this task, he received a surprise. "Two-legs," beamed Flatear, his tongue hanging from his mouth, perspiring, "if I don't have another chance to tell you truly, I like one thing about your songs."

"You do?" asked Noplis, a sudden weight removed from his heart.

"You pronounce names correctly."

* * *

The Judge had been in a bad humor. Earthquakes tended to do that to him. The last occasion he had felt this way had been four hundred years earlier, during the submergence of Florida. Between his phenomenal memory and love of history, it was natural that he had made the joke: "Well, this will put a real dent in the tourist industry." Alas, the technicians at the Center were no more likely to laugh at his humor than were the vaguely human forms that made up his new community, but at least he didn't expect anything from the latter.

His mood was instantly lightened by glad tidings. "We've found Milo-men," said a Ganik, using a term that his master had taught him.

"Splendid! At times like this, nothing is so welcome as a trial."

The closet in which he kept his handmade vestments and favorite mirror (a floor-length one) had survived the tremors. Hurrying there, he eagerly reached out clawlike hands to fondle a moldy black robe—yet another reason to be grateful that his olfactory senses didn't work—and draped the garment around his bony frame. Even more absurd was the makeshift wig, once the working end of an old mop. One had to make do. Outfitted in the splendor of his office, he proceeded to court.

Bigboy always had trouble entering what had been the operations room a millennium ago but now served as the courtroom. Once inside, there was ample room for him; but despite a sloppy job of enlargement, the doorway still represented a tight squeeze. When there was to be a trial, the giant knew that the Judge would insist on his playing the role of something called "Abailiff." Bigboy stood close to the olive-green wall, and waited.

Von was standing in the center of the room. When he closed his eyes, little sparkles of light danced behind the lids, and his balance was uncertain. How delightful it would be to simply lie down upon the hard floor . . . and sleep forever. With a start, he opened his eyes. No, he would not succumb; through force of will he would be as formidable as ever. The enemy would not claim his people or himself while life beat within the veins of any member of the Horseclans.

Yet no amount of bravado could completely remove the

sour memories of being brought into this Hold. Down a flight of metal stairs, assailed by the stench of shaggy men's unwashed bodies—so concentrated that it was indescribably revolting—they had been forced to march. Their weapons and supplies were dumped in a pile at the foot of the stairs. The scene was bathed in merciless white light from the ceiling. This made it more of a torment, because it was all too easy to see the shaggies clearly; and some of the Ganik females, with an even more noxious odor than their mates, poked and prodded them. Disarmed and surrounded by such as these, Von had to wonder if he had made the right decision. The machine gun remained a persuasive argument.

The sound of a dull thud attracted his attention. Berti had collapsed at Terrell's feet. "Let me help," said Ethera, but before she could take a step, a swarm of Ganiks surrounded the fallen man and made off with him. There was nothing Terrell could do, but he tried nonetheless. His attempt to hold on to his friend was met by one hamhock of a hand lifting him by the shoulders. Bigboy was the most alert giant Von had ever seen.

"Bigboy!" shouted Von. "Tell your chief Judge that should butchery befall our kinsman, he will answer to me, anon."

The laughter of these part-men is said to be able to curdle milk. Von had to agree with that assessment as he listened to them snort and snuffle in a parody of mirth.

When the Judge entered the room, there was an end to levity. Von could see why. On first sight, there was little that could be more startling than the human monster that addressed the assembly: "In honor of our guests, I will speak in their language. Translations are available upon request. Now, which one of you is the theologian?" Nothing amused the Judge more than bafflement on the part of others. "Come, come, I mean the one of your group who knew about the Ganik demon, Plooshuhn, that forbids these, my children, to smelt ore or work bronze."

Bigboy pointed to Terrell, who maintained a stony silence. "That's all right," said the Judge. "I don't expect cooperation. Are you impressed that my giant remembers you? Of all the monsters I've collected in Muhkohee lands, he's my favorite. He's smarter than my children, if truth be told." Here the Judge pointed first to a small band of large, hairless

Ganiks, then to the far larger number of small, hair-covered ones.

"*What* are you?" asked Von, his voice a threat.

"You are the leader of your side; I the leader of mine."

"Ganiks don't have leaders, just bullies, until they fall and are eaten," said Terrell.

"Bravo, the scholar breaks his silence. I am flattered that you contribute to the discussion. I am their leader. Perhaps it is due to my being a special envoy from one of their gods. Why, I even chat with Kahlohdjee, chief of their deities, now and again. The future belongs to the Ohrgahnikahnsehrva-shuhnee. As for this theological question, you don't appreciate the subtle nuances of High Church Ganik worship. They are not allowed to make anything interesting; but they are allowed to steal and use interesting things made by other people. In the long-ago days, they would have found many professions suited to these nice distinctions."

Swifteye mindspoke to Von: "A Witchman."

Von replied: "He could be naught else."

The Judge grimaced, his version of a smile. "By your face, Chief Von, I sense that I'm failing to convince you. Very well, I'll admit the truth: I am their leader because I am inedible. You asked what I was. I am no man, so behave."

"What would you have of us?" demanded Ethera.

The Judge hopped over to one of the Ganiks, reached out his long fingers, and triumphantly held up a squirming white louse. "See this? Their bodies are crawling with fleas and lice. They like it because it's what they know. I want to broaden their outlook, bring out their potential."

"If you choose to live with Ganiks, you're lower than they," said Ethera.

"A woman who thinks that she thinks! Very good. I am an expert on parasites, my lady, and eminently qualified to lead. A thousand years ago, they had their own city—Paris I believe it was called. But enough history."

A fat Ganik entered the chamber—Von wondered how long the man could avoid being on the menu of his leaner brothers—carrying something wrapped in a brown cloth, a red stain on the bottom. The Judge was given the now dripping parcel, which he opened to reveal a gelatinous object that he held with some difficulty between two fingers and thumb, as it was very slippery, and took a bite out of the end, pulling and chewing before he could separate a piece of the rubberlike material. There was a splatter of blood.

"I won't watch," screamed Ethera, covering her eyes.

"May I have a knife for this?" asked the Judge of the room at large. "A Horseclansman's liver is tasty, but tough." He looked straight at Von and said: "I've picked up a few bad habits, but when in Rome, do as the Romans. Of course, you don't know anything more about Rome than Paris, but—"

Von's discipline was forgotten as one of the prairiecats, Firepaw, leapt toward the Judge and bit into his arm with three-inch-long fangs. Once again, it was Bigboy who was first to react, throwing the cat with such force that its back was broken, legs quivering in death agony.

Several things happened at once: Swifteye pleaded for a command from her chief, flashing the thought that she had seen Chief Graypaw crushed beneath a rockslide, and was sure that Flatear was dead, as well. With no reason left for living, the cat wished to join the fray, but with the sanction of an order. Von was busy commanding that everyone resist temptation, Swifteye included. Until that machine gun was neutralized, he couldn't take the risk. The Judge was as concerned over the gun as anyone. "Stop!" he shouted, as the nervous Ganik debated whether or not he should open fire. "Look!" cried the Judge, holding out his mangled arm to reveal that not one single drop of blood had been spilled. Several Ganiks fell on their faces in reverential swoons. "This always impresses them," said the Judge, winking at Von.

"It's fascinating to watch your expressions as you play with telepathy," said the Judge, his mouth full. He had retrieved his meal from the floor. Swallowing by turning his head at an inhuman angle, and jerking his head in the process, he continued with better enunciation: "No need to be upset. You'll end up as your friend did. They won't eat your dead cat, of course. They really aren't the best material with which to bring back civilization, but they are all I have . . . and they do obey."

A chair was brought for the Judge. When he was sitting, the folds of his robe draped about him, it appeared that his vulture's head and emaciated arms grew out of a black obelisk. "Please note, if you will, the oversized head of the Ganik. You'd almost think that he had some intelligence. The overbite of his teeth help to correct that impression, as it makes him appear a caricature of the stupid. Here, then, is the creature I would bring into civilization. To accomplish this unlikely task will require repeated demonstrations of the court's justice.''

Pointing at Terrell, he accused: ''You, theologian, have Ahrmehnee blood. I can spot it a mile away. Have not the Ahrmehnee collected heads from these poor brutes? You, Chief Von, chieftain of this sorry little band, have you not put Ganiks to the sword more times than you can count?''

Von would rise to a mental challenge as readily as a physical one. ''Aye, I've slain shaggies, and proud of it remain. Any who eat their own kind are less than men.'' Von pointedly looked at the soggy mess in the Judge's hand.

''Thank you for your candor,'' replied the Judge. ''One of the first things you must learn about Law, however, is that only the accused is on trial. The moral stature of the authorities should not be brought into question, as the inspiring edifice of our justice is based on the rule of Law and not of men.'' Munching heartily upon Berti's liver, the Judge persisted in the high purpose he had set himself.

''My dear barbarians,'' said the Judge, ''it's not your fault that you're uncouth mutants. You can't help misunderstanding that you have wronged the Shaggy Men, as you call them. The reason that my children are better able to appreciate a proper ethical code is that they have a custom neither practiced by you nor by the fools at the Center. They are cannibals. Since justice is a social concept, and rests on the welfare of the group, the highest form of justice places the group first. Cannibalism is not the death of the group; it is merely rough on individual members.

''You may wonder what role the court has to play. When individuals in one group suffer at the hands of individuals from another, the barbaric response is to bring in the notion of honor, and reduce the grievances to an individual level. True justice requires a disinterested third party to find one group entirely guilty, exonerate the other group entirely, and make certain that individuals suffer the penalty. It may be pointed out that I am not an entirely disinterested party, but to this I can only respond that nothing is perfect. We have a system that works.''

''You speak wickedness and call it justice,'' said Von.

"From your point of view, that is a reasonable conclusion. Mine is a loftier perspective. All of you must die for your crimes against the Ganiks. True, the Ganiks have committed crimes as well, but they are not on trial; and no social purpose would be served if we viewed the case in individual terms. Coming at it from the other direction, it would surely be utopian to put everyone on trial at the same time. No one would be left to discharge the office of executioner.'' The Judge swallowed the last of his macabre meal.

There are silences so complete that they defy the idea of sound. The courtroom was like that for at least a minute, until the low growling of Swifteye begin to fill the spaces.

"You mutants cannot learn the error of your ways, but you can serve as an object lesson to my children. The superstition of an earlier age's inquisition was to save the individual's soul. A later age was enlightened enough to admit the real objective of torture: welfare of the greater number. Your deaths will be of benefit to these poor shaggies on two levels: spiritual and physical.''

"'Tis justice when two-legs eats two-legs,'' Swifteye beamed to Von, who could only nod in grim agreement.

"Civilization was never an easy proposition. It prided itself on having left the primitive rites of sacrifice behind, and clucked its collective tongue over the simplistic codes of savages. Lord Milo believes in personal responsibility. How terribly unsophisticated of him! Justice teaches that the more people alive, the greater the number to be sacrificed! One virgin girl sliced open to irrigate the crops won't do for a civilized man. Such a paltry sacrifice is an insult to his morality. For him, whole cities must be reduced to fertilizer; and not to grow food, but to feed his guilty conscience. The best enemy is one in which you see a reflection of yourself. We are all killers in here. That is a fact. Another is that there is no higher morality than joyous self-sacrifice. Despite my lofty ideals, I fall short of this noble ideal. For me, the best I can accomplish this evening is to sacrifice the selves of others.''

"Do we eat now?'' asked the ugliest Ganik present.

"Trial first, eat afterward,'' answered the Judge, annoyed.

"You eat now,'' said the Ganik, pointing to the sticky remains of the poor cook smeared on his master's hands. The Judge believed in spare the rod and spoil the Ganik. Producing a standard military-issue revolver from within the folds of his cloak, he blew the sucker away.

This was not a smart move. It wasn't that other impatient ones were sidling over to the fresh meat; the problem was a crack that appeared in the ceiling. Some plaster fell in the center of the room.

"It appears that I've been overzealous in disciplining my children," muttered the Judge, appraising the damage above. During the course of his heated monologue, he had completely forgotten about the earthquake. Now he remembered why he had been leery of the machine gun being used earlier. He'd thought the threat of the weapon, and the greater numbers of his gang, would be sufficient to stave off trouble. He was wrong.

Von realized the same danger from the machine gun at that instant. He needed no further impetus. Nerves on edge, black rage surging up in every breast, the Kindred attacked. As the Judge hesitated between a response to the assault and giving an order to the gunner *not* to fire, the panicky Ganik with the machine gun went berserk and started firing with wild abandon.

Given the respective positions of everyone there, and the full clip of ammo in the machine gun, the one crazy Ganik could have wiped out the entire population within the courtroom. For one mad moment, the Judge tried to shoot his own man with the handgun, but Swifteye was already all over him by then, and his gun went sliding across the smooth floor. The barrage of lead was terminated from an unexpected quarter.

"Flatear!" shouted Terrell, first to see the welcome sight, as the great prairiecat sprang from the corridor into the chamber of death, ripping the gunner to shreds. Close behind came Noplis, arms full of weapons taken from the pile near the stairs.

The fat Ganik who had brought the Judge the liver slipped on blood, the leavings of that unwholesome supper. With an animal cry to match a prairiecat's yowl, Von went for the man, and was busy snapping the fellow's neck before Bigboy could come to the rescue. The befuddled giant was not acting swiftly now; he could not figure out which way to turn. Finally deciding that the Judge was important, the giant pulled Swifteye away from her prey, and was about to throw her, as he had done with the other cat, when Noplis shot an arrow into the huge man's unprotected thigh. The giant never finished his maneuver, and it was Swifteye's turn to attack.

Elbowing the frenzied animal away, and finally backhanding her so that she was temporarily stunned, the giant began loping toward one of his human opponents. But it was not the archer he sought. The leader, Von, was his target. Bigboy roared a death curse.

As the towering shadow fell across the Horseclans chief, it was joined by another shadow: Flatear, finished with the Ganik, enraged over Swifteye, sank his claws into the giant's hide. Von turned to help his feline ally, but already the giant had fallen, and Flatear was keeping him prone as sharp fangs worried at the gore-bespattered flesh of the big neck. Another shadow fell across the duo, and Swifteye joined her mate in the kill. As Von saw the blood drain from Bigboy's face, he returned to his primary objective: passing judgment on the Judge.

The Judge was not thinking about Von. He was staring with mounting horror at the ceiling. More cracks were appearing. Bullet holes in the walls were also producing a spreading network of cracks. It just wasn't fair. The base had survived up until now. He hadn't even picked his jury yet.

With any degree of military discipline worth the name, the Ganiks would have prevailed. But the Judge had only been able to give them the appearance of soldiers. The reality was somewhat different. The shaggy men and women were fighting each other in a frenzied scramble to flee the base.

Von's flesh crawled as he wrapped his hand around the Judge's scrawny neck, lifted him from where he'd lain, and forced him back into his chair. There were puddles on the floor, but the liquid wasn't blood—rather something like stagnant water.

With his other hand, Von lifted a sword, grateful to Noplis for the delivery, and drove it straight through the Judge's midsection, until the blade imbedded itself in the floor. Amazingly, this did not kill; but it pinned him to the spot. Picking the wig up from where it had fallen, Von replaced the smelly thing on the Judge's head, then stood back, admiring his handiwork. The human monster struggled, as would a bug, in a vain attempt to free himself.

" 'Tis no easy task returning your 'justice' in full measure, but methinks your throne will do as a place to receive it," said Von—and then he laughed the loud, clean laugh of certainty.

The Judge screamed. It was part cackling, part retching. Slowly the room was emptied of Ganiks, and Von's warriors gathered around their foe. "Ere now, words came from you like maggots from a carcass," said Von. "What have you to say before we quit this stinking hole?"

"If you kill me, you'll remove the moral conscience of the future. I was only practicing the politics of reality, but it appears that I should have made a better choice than Ganiks. We might work together! What do you say we build a new society together?"

Noplis, suddenly more useful than he'd ever dreamed possible, figured out how to turn off the lights, and they left the Judge babbling in the dark about how he could have been a contender.

They tasted good fresh air when they stepped outside, and even the leaden sky of the first night after the earthquake appeared to them as the open vaults of paradise in comparison to where they had been. Von insisted on waiting until the final cave-in, rumblings of which increased as a promise that the Judge would retire soon.

Noplis finally had an appreciative audience for his every word—and the story was all the better told without his usual singsong delivery. He described how Flatear and he had found themselves caught between the flame and the rock, when they reached the edge of a cliff. With rope they had taken from a dead mountain pony, the bard was able to swing down a dizzying ten feet to a ledge below; then the rope was tied to Flatear, and the prairiecat was able to jump within a margin of safety. As night set in, they used some of the rope to make torches, but this light soon proved unnecessary as they detected an illumination showing through a small hole in the rubble.

Clearing this away, they found a tunnel that led directly to the base. They took the short cut. "The spoor of so many unbathed two-legs was a better guide than the underground sun," mindspoke Flatear.

Like corpuscles in a vein, they were drawn to the source of continued life within the ruined plateau, and came out in a place with a sign that read "Sector 8." Dead Ganiks were in there, but living ones were clearing an entrance to get at them, no doubt with feeding in mind.

"We heard your mindspeak," said Noplis, "a relief after the long silence. We followed that, and in so doing, learned of your peril."

"Could not you have let us know that you lived?" asked Ethera.

"Originally, communication was impossible. The earthquake cut us off in ways we do not understand. When we found you, anon, and you were in the clutches of these vermin, we trusted in stealth."

"Guards there were in the man-tunnel," said Von.

"Flatear killed the Ganiks in the corridor," said Noplis, respect for the feline infusing his voice. With the discovery that his telepathy was working again, the prairiecat had delighted in clouding the minds of the guards, one at a time, before dispatching them.

Suddenly there was a loud crash from within the mountain. Dust puffed out the entrance to below. Several men cheered.

"The Judge is dead," said Ethera.

Then Noplis said what Flatear would later agree were the wisest words the bard had ever spoken: "Thanks be to all the gods."

Yelloweye

by Steven Barnes

Steven Barnes is one of those rare writers equally at home in both books and television. He has written two novels, *Streetlethal* and *The Kundalini Equation*; collaborated on two others with Larry Niven, *Dream Park* and *The Descent of Anansi*, and has yet another collaboration coming out this fall, cowritten with both Niven and Jerry Pournelle, called *The Legacy of Heorot*. He has also written several television screenplays, mostly for *Twilight Zone*. In his copious spare time, he both instructs and studies various forms of the martial arts, among them Tae Kwon Do, Kempo Karate, Kali Stickfighting, and Aikido.

He currently lives in Los Angeles with his wife, Toni, and their daughter, Lauren, two dogs, a cat, and a houseful of tame, invisible Tyrannousaurs (*Caveat* Burglar).

Winter was dying softly in the 'Ginni mountains. Under the soft, insistent touch of sunlight, the milky ice crystals melted into water. It trickled down, formed shallow, rapid streams that cut through the banks of snow, whispered promises of spring.

Hoofprints dappled the snow. Here goats and sheep foraged for winter grass under the watchful eyes of their herdmaster. In places the hoofprints were scattered, barely impressions in the sparkling white carpet. Where the herd had been guided back and forth regularly the trail cut deep, exposing rock and dark earth below.

A rabbit lay burrowed into the snow, nose pressed against a skewed fence of barren twigs. Its coloration made it nearly invisible, but its pink eyes were nervous, frightened. The smell of Man was strong here. Man, and . . . something else. Something terrifying. An unfamiliar sound wound its way through the trees. The rabbit paused, ears perked.

Paused for a moment too long.

Snow flew in a flurry of sudden motion. With an impossibly fast blur, claws and teeth ripped into the rabbit's flesh, crushed its body into the snow before the thought *flee!* could fully congeal. There was a flash of pain too intense for consciousness to bear, and then numbness. It saw its own blood spatter onto the snow, its intestines fill the crimsoned mouth of its slayer. Then, there was nothing.

But the sound wound on. Now lilting, now stringent, the trilling of a flute coaxed by nimble fingers.

"Ar'tor!" The cry rang from a distance, and the music paused. Up above the bloodied twigs, a tuft of snow puffed out, and a boy thrust his head out of a slit in the rock beneath. If one hadn't known the cave was there, it would have been impossible to find, so well protected was it by snow and overhanging rock and dead brush.

The boy was as easy to overlook. His neck was thin and clumsily long. His hair was shadow-dark, shoulder-length, and looked perpetually windblown. His mouth and nose seemed too wide for his narrow face. His eyes were huge, dark, inquiring. Somehow, they made the balance work.

"Karls," he muttered, and popped his head back into his little hideaway. He had five more minutes before his brother would appear. Ar'tor twirled his flute like a baton, then set his lips to it again. *There* was the thread of melody that he sought. It vibrated in the cave, a clear, intoxicatingly mellow tone.

He should have been scouting for strays, as his brother and friends had for the last three days. But there was no pleasure in that, or in the hundred small and large duties that fell to him as youngest nephew of the chief of the Windrunners. Ar'tor's greatest satisfaction was to recreate the songs that the old men sang and played around the campfire. To feel them vibrate in his flute, to hear the music buzzing in the back of his head.

Leadership of the Windrunners would never be his. Regardless of his lineage, he would be a songsinger, a Bard, not a warchieftain of the Hilltribes. He would see his sixteenth spring in two more moons, but his brother Karls had seen twenty summers, and was already a blooded warrior. Better for Ar'tor that he accept the gifts that Spring had given him.

The thought of Ar'tor leading the Windrunners was absurd. His singing and playing were tolerated, but not totally understood. He was of a warrior line. His father had lived a warrior and died a warrior's death, a Lowlander sword in his guts. His uncle, the mighty Syman, was like Karls, a giant in physical strength and a leader of men. Syman was respected by all hundred factions of the Tribes. Ar'tor could never bind them with the power of his words, negotiate treaties, make war on the savage Lowlanders. The very thought terrified him.

Uncle had parlayed with Lowlanders, the mighty Horseclans themselves, winning an honorable peace. Then again, the role of peacemaker came easily to the leaders of the Windrunners, whether such peace was won by treaty or force of arms. Ar'tor remembered seeing his uncle contending with the chief of the Steelteeth for water rights. His cudgel had broken on the second pass, but his mighty fists lashed out, striking Old Keeshan senseless by the light of the council torches! The Windrunners celebrated loud and long, the hills ringing with their songs and drunken revels until dawn.

No, that was not a role that he could claim for his own.

Ar'tor tucked his whittled bone pipe into the leather pouch at his waist and felt out around himself in the dark. His fingers closed on his spear. Had he forgotten anything? This was *his* hidey-hole, but if he ever made the mistake of leaving something edible it would be quickly discovered by the scavengers that haunted the hills.

Ar'tor crawled out of the crevice and looked around.

"Ar'tor! Where are you, boy?" Karls's rough growl of a voice called him, echoed by the laughter of his two companions, Rollif and Marrin. Ar'tor knew that his backside would sting if Karls found out that he had been loafing again.

Ar'tor brushed the dirt and snow back into place, tidied up the trail, turned the rocks so that the damp sides were down, and prettied up the brush. There—anyone who came across it now wouldn't know what was there.

The wind changed, and for an instant he smelled it. Oh, yes, it was a cat, and it was strong. Ar'tor was not the hunter that his uncle and brother were, but his senses were sharp in ways that theirs were not. And when the wind shifted for that moment, he smelled Old Cat, strong and clear. Ar'tor froze, sudden terror bitter in his mouth.

True, Old Cat had never been known to hunt Man, only cattle, only the wiry goats and chickens of the Hilltribes, and those mostly in the wintertime. But hunters sometimes vanished into the howling wind, never to return. When this happened some said that the 'Ginni Truce had been broken.

But there were also whispers that Old Cat had lost his taste for goat, and now found manflesh more to his liking.

The Hillpeople had hunted him for more years than Ar'tor had been alive. They had never found Old Cat. The flowing feline shape floated through Ar'tor's dreams like a bleeding moon. Mothers hushed the cries of their children by telling them that Old Cat would hear and come.

Ar'tor slid his right heel back to brace himself and gripped his spear. Terror made his stomach feel heavy and hot, made his breath sour.

"There you are, boy!" Karls laughed. He grabbed Ar'tor and spun him around, spanking his broad hand against Ar'tor's narrow leather breechbottoms. "Where've you been?"

Ar'tor winced, but threw his shoulders back. "Patrolling. Keeping the edge secure."

Bearded Marrin howled with mirth. "Secure from songbirds, certain!y. They flee when they hear that noise you call music."

Ar'tor shaped a retort, then considered: Marrin was as large as two of him, and not renowned for his even temper.

His brother laughed. "Come along, little one, and we'll get back to the camp." Karls had two small goats roped before him, half frozen and three-quarters starved. They would be happy to be led back to the village, even if they were eventually destined for the stewpot.

Martin herded along three sheep, while Rollif One-Eye had two more goats at tether.

With his brother's warm arm around his shoulders, Ar'tor feared nothing. Karls was almost as strong as their gigantic uncle, and he feared nothing. One day Karls would be leader of the Windrunners. Ar'tor would be content to be storyteller, to chronicle the adventures of his brother, and his uncle, and his uncle's uncle, and one day passing on the job to his own nephews.

The two brothers climbed up through the ravine, by the fall of rocks that formed a staircase. Ice cracked and tinkled with every step.

They guided their strays through the shallow creek which fed into the river bordering their land from the Lowlanders'. The smaller waterway bordered their land from the Steelteeth, the wild men who traded with all and paid tribute to none.

"And what if I tell Uncle you've been slacking again? Dreaming?" Karls's broad strong hand felt around Ar'tor's belt, discovered the offending musical instrument. "Playing music rather than hunting goats."

"Don't," Ar'tor wheedled. "And I'll write you a love poem for Eloi."

Karls barked laughter. "I might take you up on that, small fish. Hah!" Karls had a big, square face that resolved their mother's fineness and father's broad strength into an elegant but utterly masculine profile. The men followed him willingly. The women groomed and prettied themselves when he passed. He might choose a bride from them, but he would probably take his cousin Eloi in marriage, thereby sealing his succession. Whoever he chose, Ar'tor knew that he would make strong, healthy children.

Ar'tor could smell the cookpots before he heard the voices or saw the rise of the village fence. As they crested the hill, Ar'tor saw the Hollow, the home that his granduncles had carved here in the hills.

The houses down in the Hollow were built into the trees, carved into the mountain, pitched against shelves of rock. Snow was swept clear of the ground in patches, revealing the sunbaked adobe paths which separated the little clusters of sloped roofs. Feathers of smoke rose from a hundred rooftops, savory wisps from a hundred cookpots. They tickled his nose, made him suddenly, maddeningly aware of his stomach's emptiness.

The gate dogs barked and squatted back on their haunches, welcoming Karls and Ar'tor with arfs and passionate licks.

Ar'tor scratched one of the great hounds behind her ear, then froze as a ghastly howl rose up from within the encampment.

Rollif cursed. "What in hell is that?"

Karls banged his spearpoint against the earth at the row of

wooden posts that made up the main gate. "Hear! Karls Windrunner, nephew of Syman, demands entry!"

Randii, the man on the other side of the gate, swung it open. He was normally a model of humor and warmth, but there was little save grave concern in Randii's expression today. He chucked Ar'tor under his chin and fought unsuccessfully to force a smile. "It's good you've returned," he said. "Your uncle is sick."

Karls's eyes narrowed. "The bellyache again? Damn green beer . . ."

"It's no bellyache," he said grimly, and spat through his beard. " 'Tis something worse. Far worse."

Karls's back grew spearthrust-straight as he walked through the Hollow, and Ar'tor threw back his own narrow shoulders to match. This was no time for display of weakness, no matter how small. Now the village needed their strength more than ever.

Their uncle's hut was at the far edge of the village, just past the pit of the great council fire. It was set into the bole of a great, broad-barreled fir tree. The house had been Syman's uncle's and his granduncle's before him, and over the years the tree had twisted itself around the house, sealed up like a wound. It accepted the house as the hills themselves accepted the Windrunners and their kin.

Ar'tor was tautly conscious that every eye in the village was on them, on the four of them as they strode up to the door. Again he drew his shoulders back. They left their spears at the door and opened it gingerly.

The lights within were dim, the tallow candles allowed to burn low in their dishes.

Syman's daughter Eloi met them. She was a tall young woman, healthily curved, and Ar'tor felt himself burn at her glance. Her hair was as yellow as the sun, and her smile brought an early thaw to the mountains. Ar'tor turned away in embarrassment, betrayed by his body. She was Syman's only child, and Karls's betrothed, although she sometimes listened to Ar'tor's songs with what seemed unsisterly intensity.

Karls gripped her shoulder, and she hugged him briefly. "How is Uncle?"

"Not well. It is good you return. Your mother is with him now."

Karls nodded and then recoiled in shock as a bellowing cry

rang from the back room, a brother to the cry heard at the gate. It was the sob of a soul broiling in the depths of hell. Through the pain and torment they could make out individual words: "Karls! Karls! Come to me, boy."

The outer rooms of the house were filled with hand-carved items: trophies, weapons, gifts, little things that Ar'tor's small clever hands had made over the years. Small baubles, images of tree and mountain and stalking cat, made for his uncle's pleasure. Now they brought darkness to his heart. There was a low table where meals were taken and small councils kept, and a shelf, carved from the very substance of the tree itself, covered with trophies and mementos. Uncle had always kept these things more for his people than himself, and Ar'tor had wondered why. Now, for the first time, he caught an inkling. What did they matter? What did anything matter when all men's lives hung by such a slender thread?

Beyond this was the master bedroom. They turned the corner, and Ar'tor caught his breath.

Whatever had struck their uncle down was no clean sickness. In three days the stench had become hideous, shrieking of corruption, and unclean things devouring him from within. His great, strong hands gripped at the ribs of his bed, square blunt fingernails gouging splinters from the wood. He screamed, thrashed. A yellowish netting hung suspended from the ceiling, diffusing the candlelight into a coppery glow.

Spit and blood-speckled foam flew from Syman's lips. His eyes glistened like hot glass marbles and bulged in their sockets. His entire body arched from the bed. "Ahhh. The bug. The cursed bug. Treacherous was its bite . . . ahhh!"

A vile, milky fluid leaked from a bandage on his side. Their mother, Syman's sister Gretcha, rushed in at the crescendo of his scream and pushed the boys back. She gingerly peeled away the bandage. Ar'tor turned his head, gagging. The wound was infested, a gigantic swollen black mass that actually *moved* under his skin.

"Ahhh!" Syman's eyes rolled to expose swollen-veined whites as Gretcha touched the wound. She turned to Karls, despair writ plainly in her face.

"There is so little that I can do," she said in a low, flat voice. "Hand me the dish."

She blackened the point of a knife over a candle flame,

then touched it to the dark pustule. The bad skin split like the flesh of a rotten melon. With nauseated fascination, Ar'tor watched a mass of tiny, legless grubs wriggle out of the wound. Gretcha cursed bitterly.

"Hold my brother," she commanded.

Rollif and Karls held Syman down, or did their best to, as she poured oil into the wound. She touched fire to it. Syman's scream was deafening. The stench of burnt human and insect flesh filled the room. Ar'tor ran, his senses swirling.

Ar'tor dried his eyes and looked up into his brother's square, somber face. "Uncle is dying, isn't he?"

Karls nodded soberly. "It is the insect that the Flatlanders call fireworm. It is no native of the hills. Someone introduced it into his bedding. Someone has killed him. We must find why."

"And who," Ar'tor said, mind racing.

"And who."

The two of them sat together on the steps outside the house, listening to their uncle raving into the tree, until the sun dropped below the western hills and the torches of night were lit.

They did not have long to wait for their answer.

The main gate rattled, and a low, booming voice carried across the Hollow, above the thin, keening wind. "Entrance! You give me entrance, by the Code of the Hills."

Curious, Ar'tor hefted his short spear and stood. Karls broke into a run, and Ar'tor followed as best he could.

"And who are you?" Randii challenged in return.

"Tluman Carpter, and his Huntmaster Carraign," the voice answered.

"And who are you to invoke the Hillcode?"

"Warchief of the Steelteeth."

"Lying dog. Old Keeshan is head of the Steelteeth."

With a loud and vulgar laugh, Tluman shouted, "Aye, that he is!" Something sailed over the gate, landed in the dirt, spinning to a stop near the fire.

Even from where he was, Ar'tor could see the glint of Keeshan's metal-capped teeth.

"Fair fight?" Randii muttered.

"Fair fight. The old man's rules. I challenged fair and

square. He lost. Now I be head of the Steelteeth, and no man opposes me. I have business! Open.''

Randii cursed vilely and swung the gate open.

The man who swaggered through was almost Syman's size, but wirier. He wore furs across his shoulders that made him even more monstrous. The shadow he cast by the blazing council firepit was barely human. He dwarfed any other man in the village save Karls.

Accompanying him, carrying one of the short sturdy bows of the plainsmen, was the lithe, almost womanly figure of Carraigh. Ar'tor disliked him at once.

Karls extended his arm to the burly Tluman.

"I am Karls, nephew of Syman."

Tluman ignored the proffered arm. He was a hard-eyed man, his face crisscrossed with scars. Ar'tor had the feeling that some of those scars might have been ritually inflicted, perhaps at the hands of the barbaric Horseclans. He had heard things about them.

"I didn't come here to palaver with infants." He grinned, sizing up Karls and discarding him in a single moment. The rest of the Hollow had gathered, some twelvescore men and women, not counting infants and those too old and sick to move from their beds. Tluman scanned them quickly, his gaze returning to Karls. "Where is the man himself?"

Karls's cheeks reddened at the insult. He left his arm extended for a few seconds, then lowered it.

"Indisposed."

"Nothing serious, I hope." Tluman's voice oozed concern.

"He will be fine soon. In the meantime, you can deal with me."

He grinned. "I've never gotten used to your system here. Where I come from, it is the sons who hold the reins when the father's hands weaken."

"No doubt why your northern kingdoms are so weak. They're full of bastards. Only the mother truly knows whose blood runs in her child's veins. Your sister's children are more certain kin." Karls pounded the butt of his spear upon the ground. "And I am not here to justify our blood customs. What is your business?"

Tluman swirled his skins about his shoulders, a flamboyantly large gesture. "I claim the rights of the 'Ginni Truce,'' he answered. "I claim the right of personal combat with the chief of the Windrunners."

"What grievance?"

"Old Cat," he said.

Karls was genuinely puzzled. "What of him?"

"He lairs on your ground, and hunts in ours. We say you have been remiss in your duties. Long before now, his worm-eaten black hide should have been stretched in the sun! It is time a proper Huntmaster tracked and trapped the devil."

"Never. Our Steelteeth cousins might have won the right to hunt on our ground. But never at such insult, and never outsiders." He regarded Carraign's piercing violet eyes and oversized lashes. "I am certain your bed bitch has many night skills. He'll never practice them here."

Karls stood toe to toe with Tluman. Although shallower through the chest, he stood inches taller, and Ar'tor was heartened. "Now, let's hear the truth. You did not cross the stream to discuss your flocks. Your challenge has nothing to do with Old Cat."

Tluman grinned. "You're not as dull as I thought." He raised his brawny arms. "The whelp speaks the truth. I have no grievance," he said. "And there need be no bloodshed. Listen to me!" He raised his voice now, and Ar'tor could hear the fox behind the bear. "People of the hills! Too long have your cattle been kept from fat grazing. Too long have your bellies been denied the spoils of good hunting. Down on the plains is food aplenty. I have been there! I know it!"

An old woman raised her voice from the shadows. "But what of the plains people? Fierce warriors they be. You know this for fact. You were once one, before they thrust you out."

His answering smile was warm and kindly, but for some reason Ar'tor had an image of the man ripping the head from a chicken and sucking the blood from its twitching body.

"Aye, and now I hunger to take back what is rightfully mine. People of the hills! I call you to come under my banner! Follow me, and my army! I *will* unite the hills. I will sweep these fierce, free people down and wash the plains in a river of blood. By Fire and Steel, this is my destiny, and nothing in heaven or earth can stop me."

Ar'tor felt himself sway, not so much from the words themselves as from the power of the feelings behind it. This man was a warrior, and a great one. A man who had seen many battles, had charged on horseback to the middle of the fray, his great sword rising and falling, rising and falling, until the sun hid itself from the fury of men.

The image of Tluman standing triumphant on a battlefield, sword or spear lifted to the sky, flashed to mind with blinding clarity. For a moment Ar'tor imagined himself there with this man, his own hands running with blood, his back bent with the weight of silver and jewels.

He saw his people sway around him, pulled by the same dream, and Ar'tor shook his head desperately. Something was wrong. These images of death and rapine were not the product of his own mind. It felt as if someone had prized open his head, jamming alien thoughts and emotions into place.

Fully in Tluman's grip, Ar'tor fought unsuccessfully to clear his head.

Ar'tor howled as he drove his short spear into the belly of a gigantic warhorse, then slitted the throat of its injured rider.

He laughed hysterically as the sky darkened with the smoke and flame of a hundred ravaged cities. He drank in the sweet, cloying smell of human flesh rotting in the sun. In a darkened cabana, he bent captive, helpless, butter-haired wenches over his silk-sheeted bed and . . .

"Hold!" Ar'tor's vile dreamworld was suddenly punctured, and he sagged. He heard sobbing exhalations all about the fire, and knew that he had not been alone in his insanity.

"Hold!" Syman screamed. The Warchief of the Windrunners staggered down the path from his house. Gretcha and Rollif supported him, helping drag him foot by painful foot down to the council fires. Syman, dying with fever, his bones eaten out from under him, still possessed the strength of spirit to leave his deathbed and look Tluman in the eye, measuring him. He coughed, hawked painfully deep and spit something dark and viscous into the snow.

"Never," he said. "Never will it be. You have your hatred for the Horseclans, who rightfully ousted you and your lover Carraign. I know! I have heard the story! You took a war captive, a young boy. To cut his throat would have been one thing, but the two of you used the body, and cut his tongue out that none might hear his cries in the night. They found his body a week later, in a ravine. Your own men turned against you."

"Lies," Tluman said peaceably. "You are too wise to squander your strength telling such lies."

"Old Keeshan was a fool to let you marry into his tribe. And where is his niece now that you gallop the hills with your catamite?"

"She tends my fire, one of the few things she does well." Tluman's dark eyes rolled up, as if reminiscing. "She is fat, thick-ankled and bucktoothed, but will do for a broodmare. It is no concern of yours."

Syman trembled with disgust. "My people will never fight for your twisted purpose. You have no concern for us, or the Truce we have shed so much blood to win. You wish conquest! And revenge! And the bodies of more children to vent your sickness upon—" Whatever frenzied strength had sustained Syman seemed to drain out of him all in a rush, and he sagged into the arms of Gretcha and Rollif.

Tluman stepped toward the fallen chieftain.

Karls snarled and leapt between them, lowering his spearpoint. "Back—"

Tluman reached cross-belly to touch his sword hilt.

Karls, disdaining all decorum or pretense of politeness, angled his weapon so that the point lined directly with Tluman's throat.

"Child, do not oppose me," Tluman warned. "I am sorry that there are no men here." He sheathed his sword. "I had heard that the Windrunners were great warriors! In two moons comes the Rite of Spring. Then my challenge will take flesh. Then, after I have slain your chief"—he made that short, ugly bark of laughter again—"or your chief's nephews, I will find out if any of you have the stomach for good honest bloodletting." He pulled at Carraign's arm. "Come!"

He turned and stalked out, Carraign following, his bear-skins swirling in the campfire light as he passed back through the gate.

The gate swung shut behind him.

Gretcha helped Syman to the stone seat at the head of the council table. He sat hunched over, staring into the fire. She wrapped furs tightly around his shoulders. The flames danced hungrily before him, but still he shook with chills. "My life seeps from my body," he whispered. The eternal winds quieted as if struggling to hear his words.

"Uncle!" Karls leapt to his feet, lithe body twisting like a

living flame. In Karls's skillful footwork Ar'tor heard the
sound of the pipes, the cry of a soaring hawk, the rush
bubbling of ice-slushed streams. He writhed, and mimed
rapid spearthrusts. "I will go, and I will climb the sacred
rock, and bring you the berries which cluster there! I will
brave all of the knives of the Steelteeth to bring you the
sacred medicine. You will heal, and grow strong. You will
fight again, Uncle, and gut this Flatlander lover of boyflesh!"

Syman nodded his approval of this ritual challenge, the
ceremonial promise. "And if the Winter sees fit to take me
before your return?" Syman's red-rimmed eyes were closed,
his lips darkly crusted with blood. He rocked back and forth,
trying to edge closer to the fire. Rollif held him back, kept
him from charring his own flesh in a fruitless attempt to
warm his worm-ridden bones.

"Then I myself will fight the Flatlander, and I will feed his
liver to the wolves!" Karls whooped and twisted into the air,
and the men and women of the Windrunners stamped their
feet in appreciation.

Syman nodded his head. "And you, little one?"

Ar'tor wanted to shrink away. Suddenly every eye was
upon him, and he knew what they expected him to say. *I will
bring the hide of a deadly snake*, or *I will spy out the land of
the enemy*, or some other moderately dangerous and bold
action. And then they would applaud politely. Syman would
die, nothing could prevent that. And if Ar'tor completed his
quest and Karls did not, then Ar'tor would be the Hollow's
champion. The Flatlander would kill him, and lead the
Windrunners down to their fate on the plains. He gulped, and
spoke in a rush, before he had time to call the words back.

"I will bring the skin of Old Cat."

Only hushed silence greeted him as the people of the
Hollow absorbed his words. For a moment he believed them
himself. Saw himself stalking the wise and ancient enemy of
the Windrunners, of cornering it in a ravine. Piercing its heart
with a mighty cast of his spear. Freeing its feline spirit to
walk the mountains, telling all of the mighty warrior who
slew it.

Then he heard the laughter. Karls was first, and then some
of the others, and spears dashed against the ground in appreciation of his bravado.

"Tell us," Karls said when he managed to catch his

breath, "tell us, Mouse—what will you really do to win the leadership of the Windrunners?"

Ar'tor withered, then looked across the firelight, and his eyes met Eloi's. Her tongue flickered out and moistened her lips. Her eyes grew huge as she absorbed what he had said. The sheer braggadocio had, for a moment, swept her up as it had him, and her heart reached to him. She might be the betrothed of his brother, but for that instant she was his.

Ar'tor straightened up and glared at them defiantly. "I have told you." The golden moment faded, and he knew his words to be a hollow lie, knew that they knew. Be that as it might, with Eloi's eyes upon him he could not back down.

"Hold," Syman wheezed painfully. "Do not laugh. Every boy becomes a man when he is ready, not when others mark him so." Syman stretched his hand up to the body. "Take my hand, nephew."

Ar'tor did.

There was still strength in Syman's grip, but what Ar'tor felt most strongly, what he would always remember feeling, was heat, as if the essence of his uncle's strength poured out of him like wine from an uncorked keg. Uncle seemed to be shriveling, draining, even as Ar'tor watched. "I see things in you," Syman said. "I see things that others may not. There is in you the essence of a warrior. A great warrior, if only you will let it free. Do you truly have this thing in your heart?"

"Yes," Ar'tor lied, and shame filled him for the cowardice.

Syman smiled through what must have been horrendous pain. "Then go forth, and prove yourself. Bring back the skin of the hellcat who has clipped our herd these many years. Today, I deem you a man, and not a boy. I, Syman Windrunner, declare it so!"

The voices around the fire echoed the sentiments respectfully. "This day a man. This day a man."

Karls slammed his spear against the ground, chanting with them. And across the fire, Eloi, too, stomped her feet. And Randii, and all of the others.

Never had Ar'tor felt such burning, all-consuming shame.

The morning sun hung low on the horizon, seemingly reluctant to rise farther and warm the air. Ar'tor was wrapped warm in shirt and buckskin cloak and leather boots. A waterskin hung on his back. His belt was laden with knife sheath and four pouches containing his pipe, flint, steel, dried goat meat, and other necessities. Ar'tor was ready to leave. Karls stood next to him, outfitted in the same manner for his own trek.

The gate closed behind him.

Karls searched Ar'tor's face. There were so many things to say, and Karls could find no proper words. To speak his true concern would discount Syman's proclamation. To speak now would be to admit what everyone already knew: that Ar'tor's words were a lie, a sham. Instead, he laid his hand on his brother's shoulder and said, "Good luck to you."

"And good hunting to you, Karls," Ar'tor said quietly. Without another word, Karls turned and set off by the western trail toward the border of the Steelteeth.

Ar'tor traveled east until out of sight of the village, then circled around and doubled back west, following his brother, staying far enough back to elude detection.

His brother was the one to win, there was no question about that. His brother would kill the terrible Tluman, and when he did, there would be no room for two chiefs. Ar'tor could be Bard, as he had always dreamed. To sit at his brother's side, teaching the children and spinning his stories.

His brother moved swiftly but warily, never suspecting that he was followed, never knowing that his every movement was imitated by a smaller shadow. And when Karls slipped across the stream toward Steeltooth territory, Ar'tor climbed up into the hills, up into his cave, and hid himself there, and cried all night.

Toward dawn, Ar'tor smelled it again. It was a hot, gamy odor, and Ar'tor was suddenly aware that the smell had been with him all the night long. There was something in the cave with him, something alive, and oh, by the gods of Spring—

Ar'tor felt his pants moisten with the sudden shock of his fear, and he opened his mouth to scream a death-scream, and die fighting.

Before a sound could leave his throat, he heard something, only it wasn't a sound that came through his ears. It came in through his head, directly through his skull, and he was stunned into silence.

Be quiet, manchild. Be quiet and we may yet both live.

!!!

They hunt us. They hunt us both. If they find us, both will die. Be silent.

Ar'tor was shaking, yet something unexpected forced its way through the terror: fascination. What *was* this? What was happening to him? Legends had spoken of men who could speak to animals, but no man, or animal, in the hills had ever had such ability. Was he dreaming?

If it was a dream, it was a dream hot with fur and sharp with fang, and a dream that seemed a living part of the darkness.

There was yelling outside, jeers and obscene, threatening jests from across the stream. Ar'tor wanted to see, but was terrified to make any noise at all.

Come. But be quiet. Come and see.

Ar'tor wiggled up. As he stuck his head through the lip of the cave mouth, he was careful not to disturb any of the rocks.

It was dark, but in the valley below there were men with torches, and they ran howling. One man was in the vanguard, riding a great black stallion. Ar'tor was startled. Such beasts were rare in the hills! Their legs were far too easily broken in chuckholes.

At first he couldn't make out faces, then he heard the voice, and it was one that made his hackles rise instantly.

Tluman Carpter.

"Hiiiiya!" he screamed, working his horse down the hill. He, and his men, were herding something. Something that stumbled on two legs toward the safety of the creek.

A word rose irresistibly up in Ar'tor's throat, almost escaping before the dreadful presence in the cave crushed the breath from him with a paw that felt like the underside of a mountain.

Yes, it is your brother. He is a dead man. Do not cry out, or we all perish. Would he wish you dead?

As Ar'tor watched, Karls staggered to the stream and waded across. Ar'tor held his breath. *He'll make it. He'll make it. Just a few more steps and he will be on our ground, and the Steelteeth—*

Tluman hied his horse down into the water, and his sword flashed overhead. Karls dove for the bank, stumbled, and then turned, defiant. The gigantic Tluman dismounted.

"So, boy." The words carried distantly. "You stand and fight. The better for you."

"You poisoned my uncle."

"Of course. That is the end of him, and of you. Perhaps your younger brother will have the sense to give me what I want. In that case I may allow him to live as a figurehead." He laughed speculatively. "He is not entirely without interest to me. You, however, must die. I give you first thrust."

"I see no honor to—"

In the middle of his words, Karls lunged forward, the tip of his spear flashing in at Tluman's neck.

"Hiiii-ya!!" he screamed. That blow should have severed Tluman's head from his shoulders.

Karls was larger, and, Ar'tor thought, stronger. But Tluman's sword parry batted the spear aside effortlessly. With Karls's second thrust, Tluman gripped his hilt with both hands and swung with preternatural timing. He clove the spearhead from the haft.

Another man might have frozen a fatal beat, but not Ar'tor's brother.

Karls whipped the butt of his spear into Tluman's ribs, and Tluman grunted at the *crack* of ironshod spear against bone. Karls spun the haft like a quarterstaff, and the end cracked against knee and forehead, missing the temple by an inch.

The haft banged against Tluman's swordhand, and the blade fell from nerveless fingers. Without hesitation, Tluman leapt forward, seizing the spear. The two men were frozen for a moment, exerting unimaginable strength against that length of banded wood.

Then Karls gasped. Tluman's teeth glinted in the moonlight. Inch by desperate inch, Karls was forced down. He twisted the staff to the side, wrenched it from Tluman's grasp. Both hands streaked for the shorter man's throat. Together, they fell into the stream.

Two bodies rolled in the flashing wet, torqued to and fro, striving wordlessly. Then a great, balled fist rose and fell.

A moment's pause, and that fist filled with a gleaming blade that plunged down once, with awesome finality.

Karls staggered up to his knees, opened his mouth . . .

As if in some bizarre dream, Ar'tor's brother toppled over onto his face, the life seeping from his body in a dark tide.

Then the other men gathered around, and their blades rose and fell, rose and fell . . .

Ar'tor started to scream, and then there was no breath. *If this is death, I welcome it.* . . . .

Ar'tor woke slowly. The first impression that pierced his consciousness was a smell. It was a heavy, meat-eater's aroma, and it swarmed into his mind with hooked tendrils.

But there was no sound to accompany it, and no warmth, and he knew that he was alone.

Ar'tor sat up with a jolt. Even in the cold, sweat was a sticky glacier under his arms, on his browline, in the palms of his hands. His lungs labored in the confined space, made the whisper of his breath a rasping thunder.

Perhaps he was wrong. Perhaps it had all been a dream.

He crawled to the opening, clawed his way out, pushed himself out into the snow. He blinked and wiped the frost from his eyes, and choked back a cry of grief.

Ar'tor half tumbled, half ran down the mountainside, toward the small, crumpled form of his brother.

Karls lay hideously mangled. Blood had seeped from his body until the snow beneath was tarry with it. Ar'tor's head whirled, and he fought to control vertigo. This could be no act of men. It had to have been a beast. A hideously depraved beast.

Old Cat.

Ar'tor sank to his knees. What could he do? If he told his tribe what he had seen, Tluman would merely call him a liar. Tluman would demand a test of steel. Syman had formally declared Ar'tor a man, and he would have to undergo the test—only a man can bear witness against a Warchief of the Hilltribes.

He stood no chance against the Lowlander. He would be killed.

Perhaps the Windrunners would try to stand against the Steelteeth and allied tribes alone. And they would be slaughtered. Or he could bring his brother's body back, and lie, saying he had found it as it was, allowing them to draw their own conclusions. And in two moons, as the last of Syman's nephews, he would have to face Tluman.

And die.

Karls's eyes were still open, staring at him with open

accusation. With horror Ar'tor saw that the insects had already begun to investigate.

With shaking fingers he closed those eyes. Then he wrapped his arms around his sides and cried until there were no more tears left. And then sobbed without tears.

For his brother, for his uncle, for his lost honor. For the insanity and death that had so suddenly and unexpectedly descended upon the Hollow.

With trembling hands, Ar'tor broke branches and laid them out in a mat. He crisscrossed and wove them, binding with vine and wood fiber until he had a sled that would bear his brother's weight.

Still crying, he rolled Karls onto it, then set his heels into the snow, beginning the arduous task of dragging his brother's body back to the village.

Each mile was murderous, a torment that started in his legs and burned his lungs with savage flame. As the cold, white sun rose above the eastern mountains, Ar'tor cursed his cowardice, his damnably small hands, for his inability to be a warrior and fulfill the obligations of his blood.

There was nothing for him now. He had hidden, choosing to play the coward rather than fulfilling his quest. That was the part he had chosen, and he deserved no better role now.

By the Rite of Spring, he had lain *next* to the dreaded Old Cat, and hadn't even tried to execute his duty. He had watched his brother die, and had not rushed down to deal death to as many of his killers as possible before they brought him down in turn. In each instance, he had clearly understood his duty. In each instance, he had failed it.

Before Ar'tor crested the hill that led down into the Hollow, the woods shook with a low, groaning wail. Ar'tor dropped the sled, overwhelmed.

The dirge horn. Syman was dead. The mourning call's message chilled him to the bone.

"Uncle . . ."

His mind numbed with the grief. He felt trapped in a blizzard, lost in an emotional whiteout, blinded and deafened with the shock of loss.

Panting, he pushed the sled up over the hump. He bent, kissing Karls's bloodstained forehead a final time, remembering all of their good times together. The hunting. The endless hours running in the mountains, their long, economical hillman's stride eating the endless miles. He thought, as all men do, of the thousand things left unsaid, the deeds left undone.

His mind buzzed with fragments of thought. If he reentered the Hollow, there would be nothing but shame for him. Shame, and confusion. Someone else, a warrior, a fighter, should take over the clan. While he lived that could not happen.

He was even afraid to die honorably. He cursed himself for ever having been born.

Ar'tor turned and vanished into the woods.

Ar'tor ran, ran faster as the shout of his kinsmen said that they had found his brother's torn corpse. The cold, barren branches whipped against his face. The pale light of the winter sun glared in his eyes as he ran, and he didn't care. Nothing seemed to matter anymore. There was nothing left, no family, no home. And most especially, no honor.

He ran until the legs beneath him trembled and failed. Ran until he was blind with sweat, and his feet turned beneath him. He fell, caught himself, stumbled on a few more paces. He just let himself go, let his body fall sweetly down the side of a hill, tumbling toward the stream, the blue sky and green earth and blinding white sun tumbling and tumbling together in a mosaic, until he struck the bottom, and lay there.

For a time his only sensation was that of water rushing over the side of his face, cascading, foaming up and then over. Nothing more. And again he cried. So much loss. So much . . .

Your brother. My cubs. My mate.

Ar'tor snapped his head around, sat up in the water, and looked directly into the liquid, golden eyes of the Old Cat.

Old Cat's fur was dark brown shading to black, and it was, most certainly, an ancient beast. Gray dusted its whiskers, and a patch of hair was torn from the left shoulder, leaving a ragged scar. Yet as Ar'tor watched it, as it moved ever so slightly, wagged its head from side to side and examined him, he had the impression of immense, controlled power. If the fury of a summer storm were touched with winter's chill and fleshed as a living beast, that beast would be Old Cat.

It looked at him, and Ar'tor read sadness in its eyes.

For long moments he said nothing. Ar'tor found his voice. "Did you . . . speak to me?"

Old Cat cocked its head sideways and took a step out into the water, gingerly, as if testing with its paw.

Ar'tor backed up, scrambled backward on all fours. This was the end. This was death. In a bare moment the creature would spring, would tear the life from Ar'tor's body, finishing the job that his own terror and cowardice had begun.

He backed until his head hit the roots of a tree and he could go no farther. Old Cat followed him one rhythmic step at a time. Ar'tor found the presence of mind to steady his breathing.

Good. GOOD.

"W—what is good?"

Ar'tor noticed that Old Cat hadn't come any closer. Perhaps, just perhaps it did not intend to make a meal of him just yet. He tried to catch a peek at its belly. Did it look full? Or like other cats, did Old Cat enjoy playing with its food? "Good for what?"

My cubs. My mate. Your littermate. It cocked its head sideways. *Your mother's littermate.*

Ar'tor blinked. "What are you saying?" Hearing words without hearing, seeing this creature speak without speaking, was giving him a headache. "What is happening to me?"

Mindspeak. Not all of your people have the talent for it. You do. I felt it in you. Feel what I feel now.

Ar'tor felt his head open, a sensation frighteningly similar to what he had felt in Tluman's presence. This was even stronger, seered him as if with white-hot irons. Never had he felt such blazing hatred. Hatred for all living things, for life itself. For a concept of fate more primal than anything that could have been birthed in the mind of a man. It was as if the creature before him hated him too much to kill him.

For the first time Ar'tor felt true fear, not the paralysis, or the self-pity that had shaped his actions, but a devouring awareness of death that went beyond concern for flesh, that threatened his very soul.

Why didn't Old Cat kill? Ar'tor fought to steady himself, to understand what was happening.

There.

There was another figure, one that stood out from the generalized burst of loathing for all things human.

Tluman Carpter. As Ar'tor watched, Tluman went through an amazing, impossible metamorphosis. He saw Tluman's skin clawed away a strip at a time, and then saw the raw, wet flesh beneath grow puffy with corruption.

He whipped his head away from the stench as the maggots began to swarm.

I hate you. All of you. But this one most.

"He . . . killed your cubs?"

We will not speak of it again. You can mindspeak. I can use you, if you have the courage. Otherwise, I kill you now. Your answer!

Ar'tor looked into those eyes, and his terror numbed. There was something that the Old Cat's incredible mind could not conceal from him. Grief.

Do not pity me. I will kill you!

Ar'tor drew back against the tree. "All right. I . . . have no choice."

Neither of us has a choice. We have no time. Old Cat looked Ar'tor up and down. *You are a poor cub, even for your kind. You will probably die.*

"I'll live long enough," he said, not even knowing what it was he was saying.

Old Cat's massive old head nodded in approval. *Perhaps you will. Come. Come with me. Do not try to run away, or I will kill you.*

Ar'tor set off, and looked over his shoulder just to be sure that he wasn't dreaming. No, he wasn't. The enormous black creature followed just behind him, stalking him, as he walked upstream, pushed through the thicker brush, heading into . . . what?

II

By the time that Ar'tor reached the plateau, he was utterly exhausted. He had crawled through ice-crusted bushes and climbed over treetrunks and finally climbed the side of the mountain his people called Misttop until every muscle in his body screamed for mercy.

But always just behind him, implacable and gilded, stalked Old Cat. And when he thought about falling back into those waiting jaws, Ar'tor redoubled his efforts and pushed onward and upward.

When at last Old Cat mindspoke, *Now. You may stop,*

Ar'tor dragged himself up and looked down on the valley, the Hollow, the distant silver thread of the stream dividing Windrunner territory from that of the Steelteeth. And beyond that, he could see the beginning of the Lowlands. The rest was lost in mist. With a strange, warm pride, he realized that he might well have been the very first human being ever to see this vista.

And Old Cat stood next to him, looking down over the valley, and when he mindspoke, there was something that Ar'tor took almost for wistfulness. *You are not the whelp I feared. I can use you, manchild. Be grateful. If it weren't for that . . . if you fail me . . .*

Old Cat switched his tail and snarled, mindspeaking a blast of directionless rage. *Now. Rest. You will need it.*

Ar'tor wandered across the plateau. It was no more than two hundred yards long, and fifty deep before Misttop began to rise once again. It was thinly wooded, with little grass, but clutches of bushes and a few straggly trees fought for survival. He found a place where the mountain rock split wide enough for him to crawl into. There, protected from the elements, he pulled his cloak from around his shoulders and balled it up, making a pillow of sorts.

Old Cat slept in front of the fissure, staring out at the lip of the plateau. Ar'tor tried to close his ears, but there was no way to close his mind. The grief poured out from Old Cat like a pall.

Something was being pushed against his face. Ar'tor coughed himself awake. He reflexively pushed the object away.

It was the haunch of a goat, still oozing blood. Ar'tor jerked up in shock, and looked at Old Cat, who wagged his dark head side to side.

Your reactions are pitiful. I could have chosen more wisely.
"Chosen for what?"
Eat.

Ar'tor grumbled, but crawled out of the rocks. He gathered moss, and scraps of wood. He searched them carefully for ice crystals, then heaped them together with tinder from his pouch. Flint and steel produced sparks, and in minutes he had a small fire. Chip by chip he fed it, until a decent cookflame had been built. He spitted the haunch and roasted it.

While the joint drooled goat fat into the flame, he watched

Old Cat, who sat watching him. The feline considered his every movement like a seer examining the contours and textures of deer spoor.

Ar'tor ate, still keeping silence. What did the animal want? It looked at him. Perhaps it meant to torture him, to exact some particularly cruel and lingering revenge.

He managed to keep bolting the food down even when the thought of those yellow eyes squeezed his stomach.

When at last he was finished, Old Cat said, *Take your knife.*

Ar'tor drew it, and suddenly the fear did rise up, without anything to hold it in check. He stood before Old Cat, three hundred pounds of venomously murderous animal, growling now, teeth bared, flanks heaving.

I am going to kill you now, Old Cat said. *Prepare, manling. I want my teeth in your vitals, my claws ripping at your testicles. If I cannot have Tluman, I will have you. Prepare to die.*

Old Cat stalked forward. Ar'tor stopped breathing, panic binding his chest. Then he realized that if this was the last moment of his life, then the least he could do was to die like a Windrunner. He crouched and held his small, pitiful blade before him, baring his own teeth.

Old Cat leapt, and Ar'tor slashed with the knife once, twice, all resolve suddenly disappearing before the onslaught of fang and claw. A mighty buffet struck his arm, and it went numb to the shoulder.

He found himself on the ground, dazed, wondering how to spoon his spilled brains back into his head. He rubbed his hair and checked his fingers: no blood. He groped for his blade, but couldn't find it. He mentally searched himself for wounds, and found none. Old Cat stood over him, one paw pinning Ar'tor's chest to the ground. Old Cat stared deeply into his eyes. Its breath was hot and wet and ripe, the smell of an animal that liked its meat still quivering.

Gods of Spring. It is going to eat me slowly. Old Cat will reach out now and bite away my face. It will chew my ears and lips and leave the eyes, let me watch as it pulls my guts out and plays with them on the ground. I don't want to die. I don't want to die. . . .

Old Cat stared at him.

Death. There were no options, there was no hope. This

was his moment, the moment that came for all creatures. In a moment he would know the answer to the question that had plagued wise men since the beginning of time.

And somehow, through the terror, a voice that was definitely Ar'tor's whispered: *Then let it be.*

And another voice joined it, this one the sibilant growl of Old Cat.

There is a place, it said. *A place in you where there is no fear. Your dying place. Every animal knows it. Those of your people who are called warriors know it. To let the place they stand be the place they die. The sights they see to be their last. With that nearness to death, you can kill. This you must find.*

"What do you want from me?'

I WANT NOTHING FROM YOU! I DEMAND! Old Cat's slitted eyes blazed with sudden hatred. *This is my price for your life. This, and none other. You do just as I say. You will . . . or you will die.*

Old Cat walked back over to the knife. It curled a paw, batting the sliver of steel back to Ar'tor.

Pick it up! Try again!

Ar'tor picked up the knife again. Flushed with embarrassment and confusion, he braced himself and waited.

Old Cat insolently walked up to him, staring into his face.

No. You are not ready to die. You are not ready to kill. Perhaps . . .

Suddenly the cat didn't seem the utterly invincible, terrifying killing machine. Suddenly it was an old, tired cat, and Ar'tor once again felt pity.

I WILL HAVE NONE OF YOUR PITY! Old Cat screamed, and lunged at Ar'tor with a paw. Ar'tor stumbled back, slashing frantically with the knife. He thumped onto his butt.

Old Cat glared at him, then licked at the shallow cut along his paw with an enormous pink tongue. His eyes were more thoughtful now.

"I'm sorry . . ." Ar'tor said, not realizing quite what he was saying.

He had to be mistaken, but it suddenly seemed that Old Cat smiled. *Don't be. Perhaps. Just perhaps. Do not question. Do not ask. Do you love your people?*

"Yes."

Do you hate the man who killed your brother and uncle?

"Of course."

I'm going to give you a chance. Just a chance, to kill him.

Ar'tor shook his head.

"The only way I could do that would be to ambush him . . . to kill him from behind. That would solve nothing."

You do not understand. I mean for you to kill him in fair combat. To shame him, to humiliate this great warrior, is my aim. For him to be slain by a stripling would be my greatest revenge.

"Revenge for what?"

Quiet! Do not ask! Do not ever ask.

"I can't do this . . . I cannot do this thing."

Old Cat dropped his head, yellow eyes rolled up to his head as he stared through Ar'tor piercingly. *You can. You will.*

"We have only two moons. You saw him. He can kill any man in the hills."

Any man, yes. You will not be a man. You will live with me. Eat with me. You will learn to be a cat. He will expect a man, but this you will not be. . . .

And so began the strangest apprenticeship that any human being had ever undertaken. For the remainder of that day, resting only long enough for the sweat to dry on his forehead, Ar'tor attacked the fearsome Old Cat again and again, every time rebuffed with another swiping paw.

Over and over, all day long, until Ar'tor forgot the meaning of fatigue. Every time he believed that he could go no further, Old Cat bared his terrible teeth, and panic swept away the exhaustion.

Until finally, as the sun dipped behind the mountains, Ar'tor could literally lift his knife no longer. There was no more strength, not even when Old Cat's teeth closed around his neck. Ar'tor gasped for breath, his legs become lead, his blood acid.

And as he slipped into unconsciousness, he heard Old Cat mindspeak gruffly, *Perhaps. Just perhaps, young cub. . . .*

Every muscle in his body ached, felt as if he had been stretched over an anvil and pounded out like sheet metal.

Ar'tor uncurled from his ball and crawled out into the morning light. There was no goat this time, merely a small bird. He crawled out toward it. Old Cat snarled, stopping him dead. *No! Stretch first. Stretch always.*

"Stretch?"

And Old Cat showed him. With a luxuriant rolling motion of his body, Old Cat extended his claws out, gripped the ground and arched his hips up into the air. His spine crackled with the extension. Old Cat turned his huge head and glared at Ar'tor. *Now you.*

Ar'tor pulled and torqued until he felt as if his poor stiff body were being torn into pieces.

And when he was done to Old Cat's satisfaction, he was given the bird. He cooked it hurriedly, finally ripping it off the spit before it was done. He wolfed it down, watching Old Cat's yellow eyes staring at him, always staring.

And now we run.

Ar'tor grinned. "That I can do. We are great runners! My brother and I used to run up in the mountains all day."

That is not running. Cats do not run foolishly, squandering their strength. They pick their time, and then they spring. You must learn to spring.

Old Cat backed Ar'tor against the rocks, facing him toward the lip, fifty paces away.

Now. Run there. As fast as you can.

Ar'tor loped across the dead, frozen grass, turned and grinned back at Old Cat, who was nowhere to be seen.

What . . . ?

He turned again, and looked behind him, and there the great feline sat, looking up him disgustedly. *I didn't tell you to crawl like a crippled lamb. I said RUN.*

Old Cat fetched Ar'tor a buffet that fair straightened his hair out. Ar'tor tumbled to the ground. He shook his head and looked up into the cat's flaming amber eyes. They held nothing but the promise of death.

Down. Crouch. Relax your legs. Dig your toes into the ground. Now RUN!

Old Cat was right behind Ar'tor now, jaws snapping, and Ar'tor ran, sprinted almost without breathing, ran as fast as he ever had in his life. He dug in his heels as he neared the rocks, stumbling to a halt.

No! Turn and RUN!

Ar'tor didn't bother to plead for mercy. He turned and ran, every muscle and ligament in his body burning.

Over and over and over again he ran, until he had to stop to chew mushy snow, to heave for breath. To stretch out his cramping leg muscles.

And then, after a meal of the rest of the bird, he picked up the knife.

Cover your belly! Old Cat's mindspeak was a scream. The cat emphasized the point with a paw swipe so much faster than Ar'tor's sweat-stung eyes could follow that his attempted defense was a travesty.

Old Cat's claws raked Ar'tor's midsection, leaving three roughly parallel lines that seeped blood. Ar'tor stared at them in astonishment. Surely in another instant his intestines would gush forth, and he would die howling in the snow.

You disgust me. It's a scratch. Next time, a little deeper. Now crouch! Cover your belly! Up on your toes! FIGHT!

On and on they went, Old Cat mindspeaking Ar'tor through the movements, until the boy wasn't sure who controlled which body. There were times that he felt Old Cat in his mind, command and response so close together it seemed he had no volition at all.

And other times, as Old Cat stalked toward him, the feline's mind was open and talking to him, so that he felt what Old Cat felt, understood the tensions and relaxations that gave a cat its power and speed.

And other times, most of the endlessly long and exhausting day, Ar'tor felt like the clumsiest and most stone-footed creature that the gods of Spring and Summer had ever let live.

That night, Ar'tor tried to escape.

Quietly, oh so quietly, Artor crept out from between the rocks and peered around. There was nothing in sight, no sign of Old Cat. Perhaps the old bastard was out hunting. If so this was a perfect opportunity to . . .

He scampered across the plateau, and began to climb down. Good. Nothing to stop him. He'd be gone before . . .

That was odd. What was under his foot didn't feel like a rock. Not like a branch, either.

Even in the freezing cold, Ar'tor began to sweat.

He looked down, directly into a pair of narrowed yellow eyes.

RUN!

Old Cat just behind him, Artor ran so fast that his feet barely left an imprint on the ground. He dove the last few feet into the rocks, rolled losing skin, and lay there panting.

Well. There was a little speed left in you after all.

And this time, for the first time, there was a trace of amusement in Old Cat's "voice."

For some reason that Ar'tor couldn't totally understand, he slept the rest of the night curled onto his side, smiling.

The days began to flow together in a pattern. Every morning, Ar'tor would rise and stretch his body. Then he would eat. And then run. In the afternoons, he would fight, and fight, and fight. And when he had no more strength, Old Cat made him stretch, and then run some more. Not the invigorating, healthy loping stride of the Hillpeople, but a sudden, start-stop movement that drained all of the strength in his body and made his limbs flame.

After the first week, he stopped thinking about the pain, because it was a constant, enveloping thing.

He accepted that this was his lot, and with that acceptance, the pain began to recede. Yes, his limbs hurt, but the agony was more a signal of growth than a warning, and he was able to push it from his mind.

Making room for other things. First, and now most important, Old Cat himself.

On the ninth morning he left his fissure and found no meal sitting out on the edge. Old Cat sat at the lip of the plateau, gazing out over the valley. His tail moved slowly from side to side. He turned to see Ar'tor coming.

Ar'tor could have sworn that he heard a purr of welcome. *Hello, little one.*

"No food today?"

I found nothing last night. I am sorry.

Ar'tor sat next to the creature, for the first time looking upon it as the beautiful animal it truly was. Beneath its black-brown coat, muscles rolled fluidly. Though the skin was loose now, it was easy to imagine Old Cat in his youth. What an unutterably magnificent creature it must have been.

"There is still goat from yesterday."

It is not fresh. It is not good.

"I'll survive."

Old Cat said nothing.

At length, Ar'tor asked, "What are you?"

I am far from home, Old Cat said.

For long minutes Ar'tor thought Old Cat was going to speak again, but he didn't. *Come. It is time for our lessons.*

Ar'tor warmed up, loosening his back, flicking the knife with controlled, whiplike motions. *Speed is loose. Speed is like a hiss,* Old Cat had told him once.

"You've known men before, haven't you?"

Many, the cat replied. *Once, long before you were born, I ran the plains with men. I loved them, and they loved me. I had a place in their society.* Old Cat shook himelf. *But come.*

For once, Ar'tor stood his ground. "No. You bring me here, and run me until I cannot stand, and then make me fight until my arms are on fire. I want to know. I have a right to know!"

Perhaps you do, stripling. You will know. You will know someday. Eventually, a being wants a mate. A creature to sleep next to at night. To give cubs to. Something to love. I was a creature of the plains, but I found my mate in the mountains. It seems insane now. I could have stayed with my friends, and fought, and lived . . .

"But you didn't."

I didn't. She would not come with me to the plains. And I loved her too much to leave her. So I came here, and I stayed. And we lived together. We had no cubs for many years. Men have a word for this. I don't know it. Only last winter did I finally feel my seed burn within her. Come summer, she would bear my cubs. And so it came to be.

Then came the one you call Tluman. A renegade, a mumbling mindspeaker, one who came after my separation from the men of the Horseclans. He had done something terrible, and failed the Test of the Cat. He hated my kind, and when he found that I lived in the hills, he hunted me. By the Great Cat, how he hunted me. And at last he caught my mate, and my cubs, and he skinned them slowly, trying to bring me out. And I did not come, because I knew that my only chance to kill him would be to use stealth. I would kill him in my own time, in my own way.

Old Cat looked at Ar'tor. *This is my time. You are my way.*

"What did men call you when you walked among them?"

They called me Yelloweye.

*   *   *

Ar'tor crouched in the brush, watching. On the other side of the clearing, Old Cat was moving. He didn't know where; the hunter had disappeared into the snow three minutes before, and Ar'tor had since seen no sign of it—of him—since. Yelloweye was a male, from his story.

Here the bushes were odd, twisted white lumps in an icy, flowing carpet. But between two of the lumps, nibbling through to a bit of twigs, a small doe was in sight. She stopped eating even as the thought *doe* crossed his mind. Her slender brown head quivered, the black rings of her nostrils quivering as she tested the air.

Ar'tor held his breath. A dozen trees separated him from the deer. Thirty yards behind her, trees broke from the snow, forming Yelloweye's closest possible cover.

The deer turned back to the twig, stripping away a scrap of bark. Then her head snapped up again, and Yelloweye exploded from the snow. Somehow, in a manner that Ar'tor couldn't quite understand, he had worked his way ten yards closer than the nearest tree. The doe panicked, bolting directly toward Ar'tor.

Ar'tor exhaled and leapt as he heard the hooves pounding against the snow. One part of his mind screamed, *Too soon! Wait until you can see her!* Another listened to the sound of the feet, working from some instinctive timing more precise than vision.

Ar'tor catapulted smack into the doe. Her hooves struck him in the face, but he managed to snake an arm around her neck and drag her to the ground. The terrified creature bit and kicked as Ar'tor found his grip on the knife, twisted so that he wouldn't stab himself in the buttock, and drove the blade in.

The deer's convulsions tore the blade from Ar'tor's hands. The two of them lay on the ground, panting, as Old Cat padded up. *A great victory. Will you live?*

"Long enough to wish your worms a hearty appetite." Ar'tor got to his knees and pulled out the knife, cutting the deer's throat. He set to stripping away the meat.

I liked that. You did well.

Despite his punctures and scrapes, Ar'tor smiled as he worked.

*   *   *

Ar'tor sat on the lips of the plateau and looked down over the valley. Distantly, he could make out the cookfires of the Hollow. The night was impossibly crisp and clear, and it seemed as if he could see to the edge of the world.

Karls would have liked the view. He would have made a joke about how far one could cast a spear from here, but it wouldn't have fooled Ar'tor. Karls would have found great beauty, would have asked Ar'tor to write a poem for it. A poem Karls would later give to Eloi.

Ar'tor felt suddenly, terribly alone. He took his bone pipe from its bag, slid his fingers gently across its polished surface, and plucked the first low, cool note.

He was immediately lost in the song, something slow and lonely. He barely noticed when Yelloweye walked up to sit behind him.

The big feline began to growl along with him, the sound climbing to a howl. At last Ar'tor reached out to feel the warm scruff of Old Cat's neck. Old Cat rolled against him, and together they sang to the moon. The sounds mingled with the wind itself, was carried across the valley. And those few who heard that wind wondered what form of demons haunted these hills.

The weeks passed. They spent their days fighting and running and hunting. Sometimes Ar'tor would abandon the knife and wrestle with the big cat.

Yelloweye's reflexes were impossibly quick. In twisting and flashing from beneath the paws, Ar'tor found himself moving faster and faster. Working with a blunt stick instead of a knife, Ar'tor found that he could dart in and out, and that he could touch Yelloweye now and again.

And the cat would scowl, and leap, brushing the knife aside, and the two of them would wrestle. On the few occasions Ar'tor won, Yelloweye gave a huge cat grin, letting him know the victory was a gift. And sometimes Old Cat would pin the young man and sit there with his paws atop Ar'tor's shoulders, pin him to the ground, and lick his face.

My cub, Yelloweye said once, impulsively. Then, as if embarrassed, turned and stalked away, tail twitching.

Ar'tor came up from behind him. There was no pity in his heart, none in his mind. As he sat down next to Yelloweye, he slipped his arm around the big cat's shoulders, and the two of them sat there for a while. And when he leaned his head over against Yelloweye's shoulder, the cat didn't move away.

The moon came and went, and as it did, Ar'tor felt the changes in him. He ran the short sprint, feeling his lungs stronger, his heart more powerful by the day. He climbed, and he fought for hours, under Yelloweye's watchful tutelage.

And they hunted. Skies above, how they hunted. They roamed the hills, and stalked as man and animal had hunted together in a more ancient place and time. Never had such hunts been seen in the hills, and the harvests were bountiful.

Then, one day, they were hunting a goat, using Yelloweye's pincer maneuver. Ar'tor saw Yelloweye moving into position, and a sliver of shadow flew out, hitting the old cat just below the ear.

Ar'tor would have screamed, but for the warnings imprinted in his mind by Yelloweye over the past weeks. He knew that there was an enemy near, but didn't know if he had been seen.

Without conscious thought, Ar'tor suddenly ceased thinking in words or sounds. His world became one of images, of feelings, of smells and shapes.

Had he been seen? And if so, by whom? He tried not to breathe, not even to think too loudly. Just became a part of the leaves and the trees for moment after long, achingly vulnerable moment.

Then finally there was movement, and sound.

From the opposite side of the glen, two men stood. Ar'tor recognized one of them as the man who had accompanied Tluman Carpter to their camp, Carraign.

Here? In the depths of Windrunner territory?

Ar'tor grinned mirthlessly. He could see what they could not—the arrow in Yelloweye's neck still moved slightly. His friend was alive.

Ar'tor had no bow and arrow, only the knife. Never had he learned to throw it, and to attempt such an insane thing now would accomplish nothing. It would merely disarm him at the same time it alerted his enemies. No. This called for something very different. Gingerly, he peeled his shirt back and smeared a generous handful of mud over his chest. He carefully tucked his knife out of sight at the back of his belt.

The two men stood over Yelloweye's motionless body, and one laughed, and made a motion with his sword.

Ar'tor rose from his cover and sang out, "Oh-hoo! Great and wise are they! Oh-hoo! Powerful and keen of eye, swift of foot, are the slayers of Old Cat!"

He spun as he stood, dancing as if drunken.

Carraign's bow whipped up instantly, fixing it on him, and what a sight he must have been! A half-naked mud-daubed boy dancing through the reeds, singing as if mad.

"What in the . . . ?" The arrow point remained steady. The other man with him finally put his hand on Carraign's arm. "Don't bother. It's clear that the boy is crazed."

Ar'tor danced closer. "Aye! And they are sweet, and strong, their forms pleasing to boy or beast. The beasts must fall, and the boys yearn to submit. . . ."

Carraign's brown tongue touched his lips, and Ar'tor grinned without mirth. He had indeed read the pervert correctly.

Ar'tor skinned back his shirt, exposing more of his smooth, sun-bronzed skin, corded with new muscle, and he moved, spinning, revolving heel to toe, singing more loudly. He was within three steps now, and from the corner of his eye he saw that Yelloweye was watching him, but he heard no mindspeak.

He spun to a halt in front of Carraign. "Oh great hunters, let me give you—death!"

Much too quickly for the swordsman to respond, Ar'tor's hidden knife flashed out to stab deeply into his stomach. The man screamed and reared back, screaming like a castrato. Ar'tor had already turned his attention to the bowman, who was struggling with shock, stumbling backward trying to get a pace of distance between himself and the whirling dervish who had suddenly unleashed death upon them.

But it was too late. Ar'tor's blade licked out once, twice, and Carraign was down, fingers fruitlessly attempting to stem the tide of blood from a gashed neck.

Ar'tor turned back to the other man and finished him with a thrust up under the ribcage.

Only then did the grief sting his eyes. Ar'tor crouched close to his friend. Yelloweye licked at Ar'tor's hand.

You have done well. It seems that we have no more time together.

"It was enough." He examined the wound. The arrow had

driven down, piercing the lung. Yelloweye's flanks spasmed, and he coughed blood.

Stripling, Yelloweye said, *there is one last thing you must do, in order for our work to have meaning.*

"What is it? I will do anything."

Ar'tor listened closely. Although he refused at first, Yelloweye finally convinced him. *Good,* the big cat said. *You . . . you were not such a bad cub after all. I think . . . my other cubs would have approved.*

"And my uncle would have approved of you."

Do not fail us, Ar'tor.

Yelloweye exhaled one final time.

Ar'tor sat hunched there for a long time before he moved again.

Before Ar'tor left that place, he built a mound of brittle twigs and branches over Yelloweye, with the corpses of Carraign and the swordsman at his ass. It blazed to the heavens, and Ar'tor watched it flare, mindless of the tears starting from his eyes. He wiped them with the back of his hand. Now was no time for sentiment. It was a time for deeds.

III

It was the night of the Rite of Spring. Snow had melted from the ground, and the first warm day of the year breathed life into the mountains.

This should have been a time for a celebration of life and love, but the songs of the Windrunners' village were muted with shame. There were champions who would resist Tluman, but none was of the Blood. The line, the fragile cord that bound the Hilltribes together, had been severed. Their chief had died, one nephew had died, killed by Old Cat, and the other had disappeared. Though they had combed the mountains for him, no sign had been found. The only possible answer was cowardice. He had run away from his birth duty, leaving the tribe to fend with only Steel, without Blood.

But by the flaring light of the council firepit, a hundred spear-carrying warriors stood ready. It was in vain. Without Blood, the lineage of the tribe would revert to its older line: that of the Steelteeth. Opposition of the rightful successor to the Steeltooth tribe would place them in disharmony with the other Hilltribes. They could refuse to war, and find themselves at war with the entire Nations.

It was a trap, a brilliantly executed trap, and they knew it.

And when Tluman Carpter entered the compound, he entered knowing himself already to be the winner.

Half a hundred of his warriors accompanied him, moved behind him as silently as ghosts. Among the Steelteeth he was a veritable giant; none of them stood higher than his shoulder.

"Who speaks for the Windrunners? Who speaks for Steel and Blood?"

There was silence for an awful moment, then Gretcha spoke. "There are none who speak of Blood. But every man of the tribe speaks of Steel! Just this once, let Steel speak freely. Let us have our choice of actions."

"You know the 'Ginni Truce." Carpter laughed, baring sharp white teeth. "I act within it. You also, or you are not of the Tribes. How say you?"

"Damn you," she whispered. "I see. I see. You may win, but sleep lightly, Tluman—"

There was a banging at the gates, and a hushed murmur from the crowd. "Hold within!" Ar'tor cried, and the gate swung open fully.

"What . . ."

Ar'tor entered. He was crusted with dirt and blood, and carried something lumpy and blood-crusted rolled on one shoulder. He limped, his left ankle bandaged.

Tluman narrowed his eyes. "The nephew? But the nations all know that you fled your duty. You have no part in this, boy."

"I fled no duty. I swore to bring the skin of Old Cat, and here it is!"

He unfurled the untreated skin of his friend, and stood, fists knotted on his hips, trying not to let the fear or the acid rage sound in his voice.

The tribal elders murmured in hushed tones, and one of them examined the dark skin. "It is Old Cat. It is!"

Gretcha strode to Ar'tor. "You are blood of Blood. Kinsman, do you speak for Blood and Steel?"

"I do."

Their eyes met, and such pride as Ar'tor had never known

a human voice could carry lived in the next words. "Kinsman
Ar'tor speaks for Blood and Steel!"

Among the warriors that accompanied Tluman, there was a
ripple of uneasiness. A battle between equals was one thing.
The slaughter of a child was another.

"Listen," Tluman said, shifting uncomfortably. "I would
as soon not kill this crippled boy—"

Ar'tor drew his knife. "I challenge you, great bag of feces.
Eater of offal and buggerer of babies. I challenge you!"

Tluman purpled with rage. "Are you so eager to die,
boy?"

Ar'tor bowed floridly. "Aye. With the taste of your blood
in my mouth."

Tluman gritted his teeth and unfastened his leather buckler.
"Then I shall give you half of your wish at least. All right,
boy, prepare to die."

Tluman's body was enormous. Ridges of muscle girded his
waist and framed his back like metal bands on a barrel. He
drew a dagger three inches longer than Ar'tor's and slashed
the air with it.

"Are you sure this is the way you want it, boy?" Tluman
was confident, almost pitying.

Ar'tor felt the fear squirt up into his mouth again. He
couldn't do it. No one could do such a thing.

Then he remembered Yelloweye. *Don't look at the sharp
claws. Look at the soft belly.*

Ar'tor moved in clumsily, dragging his left leg, the bandaged ankle still trailing.

Tluman shuffled in, bladed right hand in the front, left just
behind, fingers sensitively spread.

Ar'tor circled and circled, and then slashed out clumsily,
his ankle turning under him. Tluman flashed in, eager to end
this charade. Ar'tor's ankle suddenly straightened, and Ar'tor
lunged out, gashing Tluman's right wrist with a speed and
precision more feline than human.

Tluman's hamlike left slammed out instinctively even as he
realized he had been tricked.

Ar'tor tried to retreat from the blow, tried to roll with it,
but was too slow. The grazing backhand snapped something
in his chest.

He hit the ground and tumbled backward almost into the fire.

Tluman examined his wrist. Blood squirted out of it, puddling onto ground. He squatted to snatch up the knife, then struggled to find a tourniquet for the wrist. A scrap of torn shirt, a belt, anything.

Ar'tor didn't let him have time. The only hope was *now*, before Tluman fully absorbed the shock.

He bore back in, feinting and slashing now, putting everything he had into the attack. There would be no second chance, no other opportunity. For this instant, the mighty Tluman was confused. He stumbled back, guarding with his left, fighting to stop the blood that gushed from his right wrist.

With the blade in his left hand, his own blood smeared over his chest and drooling onto the ground, Tluman was still dangerous.

But Ar'tor moved insanely, darting in and out like a striking snake, his spine so fluid that Tluman couldn't make contact.

Ar'tor couldn't score another wound, but Tluman was totally off balance, with no chance to fix that gushing wrist.

Finally, bellowing with rage and frustration, Tluman charged in blindly. Artor twisted to the side and pounced, literally swarmed up Tluman's back, stabbing and slashing like a mad creature.

Tluman slashed Ar'tor's ankle, grabbed it and stabbed into his leg. Ar'tor screamed and levered the point of his blade under Tluman's ear.

Ar'tor frantically kicked Tluman in the jaw and twisted away, staggering to stay on his feet. His crimsoned leg wobbled beneath him, and he made it wobble more, trying to lure Tluman into imprudence.

Blood squirted from Tluman's slashed throat as he lumbered after Ar'tor. The council was no longer silent. A chant of "Ar-tor! Ar-tor!" had grown up and up, and even the men who had accompanied Tluman took it up, slamming their spears against the ground in tribute. Tluman's face was covered in blood. He stopped, staring at his men, who now chanted the name of his hated adversary.

He screamed in hatred and frustration and jammed his gushing wrist into his belt. He wanted only to get his hands on the limping demon sprite that still mocked him, still sneered at him, waving that puny blade in his face.

With a final despairing cry, Tluman lunged. Ar'tor tried to twist out of the way, but Tluman caught his ankle again, and both fell into the fire. Tluman had him now, and Ar'tor's world became black tinged with red as the brutal hands touched his throat.

There was no air. The coals burned horribly into his back, and the stench of his own charring flesh filled his nostrils.

So be it. This was his dying place, as it had been his uncle's. If he could but take this bastard with him . . .

As Tluman pressed him back, Ar'tor stabbed and stabbed and twisted the blade, and stabbed again.

Then the pressure at his throat was gone, and Ar'tor felt strong hands pulling him from the ashes. He windmilled frantically at the air, until he heard Rollif say: "That's it. That's all. It's over."

The mists finally cleared. There on the ground lay Tluman's gashed body, the great hands still twitching at the air, the mouth gasping to speak.

"Finish it," Rollif said, handing Ar'tor his spear.

Mind swimming crazily, he took two halting steps to stand above Tluman. For a dozen breaths he just stared into the dying man's face. Then he gasped, "Carraign waits for you in hell," and drove the spear into his throat.

He turned. All he could think of was collapsing, but this was not the time for it. Now every face was on him. Gretcha, Rollif.

And there, shining with pride, lovely Eloi.

"I speak now," he said. There was great pain in his chest, and he fought for each breath. He pulled the spear from Tluman's body and leaned on it.

His thin, wiry body quivered as he fought to remain erect.

"We have had peace in the Hilltribes, until this outsider came and tried to turn us against each other. He killed my uncle, and my brother. In vengeance, I killed his lover, and I killed him. That's the end of it. That is the end."

He turned and walked away from the council. If he was careful, he would make it all the way to Syman's house.

He grew dizzy. He couldn't make it. He couldn't . . .

"Let me help you," a warm voice said, just behind his ear.

"No, Eloi. I have to . . ." All eyes on him, he managed to stumble across the threshold before falling to one knee in his uncle's house.

Wrong—his house now. His, to live in, to heal in. To raise his and Eloi's children in.

To fill with his own trophies. He hoped he lived to have many of them, because one he would not have would be the skin of Old Cat.

That most precious of gifts would be buried in the hills, next to the graves of his brother, his father, and his uncle.

It did not matter that his people would never know why, or begin to understand.

Ar'tor knew why.

And Yelloweye knew.

And some secrets should remain between kin.

Ties of Faith

by Gillian FitzGerald

Gillian FitzGerald is five feet two, red-haired, blue-eyed, and Irish; more personal statistics are available on request. She has acquired several interesting but useless degrees, and has, in the best writerly tradition, held the normal number of weird jobs. When not avoiding writing, Gil is usually sewing costumes for SCA events and convention masquerades, listening to Irish music, or petting Corwin, her seventeen-pound black cat. Her short stories have been published in *Elsewhere, Amazons II, Dragon,* and *The Magazine of Fantasy and Science Fiction,* with another story in the forthcoming second volume of *Heroic Visions.*

Giliahna Sanderz, Undying High Lady of the Confederation, was beginning to regret her decision to return home to Sanderz Hall. Perhaps she should have taken her stepson Gy's advice and gone instead to Theesispolis. She could have talked to Mara about her feelings. Surely Mara would have understood how hard it was to adjust to being an Undying. Right now she would have traded her eternal youth and her regenerative abilities for the look of quiet contentment she had seen in the eyes of Gy's young wife, Decahna, as she suckled their first child. She would never hold a child of her own in her arms. So she was running home to Sanderz Hall, where she had grown up, where she had first known Tim as lover, where they had been reunited after long years of separation, where they had learned that they were Undying. If she could, she would have run to his arms, but he was off fighting on the western borders, so going home was the only choice.

What she had not counted on was the late-summer storms which had made many of the roads impassable and forced them closer to the mountains than she would have liked. She had left her baggage train at a Kindred holding and ridden on with an escort of ten men, hoping to make better time without the encumbrance of the slow carts. Even without the baggage train, however, they were still four days' ride under the best of conditions, and the conditions were far from optimum. The horses slogged through mud which splashed their clothes, and the near-constant warm drizzle left their light cloaks soggy.

She could put up with the physical discomforts, however. Like any Kindred woman she had been raised to hard riding, and her father had taught all his children that dry lodgings and a warm, soft bed were luxuries, not necessities. While she did not enjoy the unpleasant warmth of her riding leathers or the chafing of the breastband with which she had confined her bosom, she didn't bother to complain. Her men suffered just as much as she, so why play the spoiled lady? No, what nagged at her was the possibility that her thoughtless whim might be leading them into danger, danger which could have been avoided if she had stayed with the baggage train and the ridiculously large troop Gy had insisted on sending with her.

For the last two days she had heard disturbing reports of bandits and even more disturbing reports of raiders. The bandits were no surprise. In this outlying area they were only to be expected, and even the great Bili the Axe could not be everywhere. But these raiders were something different. They struck with the swiftness of the lightning bolt that was the symbol they left pinned to their victims' bodies, and what they left behind was death. Not clean death, either, but half-grown boys raped and strangled, grown men castrated and tortured, women mutilated. Young children were taken away, for some dark reason. She did not like the sound of it at all. It stank of the Old Church, and she had no love for that vile band. If the raiders who left the sign of the lightning bolt were somehow allied with the Old Church, Bili would want to know.

If they were able to make it to Morguhn Hall safely.

"Time to make camp, my lady," said Nik Smith, the heavy-set lieutenant who was the ranking officer of her escort. He was one of Gy's best men, and much in awe of the young and beautiful High Lady, who was also Dowager Princess of Cumbuhluhn.

"Thank you, Lieutenant," she said, smiling slightly. She

was used to his reaction by now, though she still found it a trifle disconcerting. Beauty was such a stupid reason for men to value a woman. It faded so quickly, while quick wits and a kind heart endured.

She allowed him to help her dismount, though she was perfectly capable of climbing down unaided. She had given up trying to help while they pitched the field tents. It was as if they believed her rank had somehow rendered her helpless. When the camp was set up, she had coaxed them into allowing her to cook the evening meal; once she had proved herself a better cook than any of the soldiers they were more than willing to let her handle the chore. Besides, it freed them to keep watch. After she had eaten, she retired to her small tent. She had learned that her presence left the men unable to speak for fear of offending her. That had made her giggle; she had been Djylz' wife and Tim's lady; she doubted they could think of anything she hadn't already heard from those two seasoned campaigners.

In the darkness of her tent, she listened to the quiet voices of her troopers around the fire and thought of Tim, who would be sitting with his own men somewhere to the west. She missed him with something close to desperation, and it did not help that Aldora, beautiful, arrogant, sensual Aldora, rode at his side. Oh, it made great sense for Aldora to accompany him. She was as good a commander as the best of Milo's generals, and she and Tim made an excellent team, his hard-earned caution balancing her natural recklessness. If Aldora had been a different sort of woman, one who did not want to come between pledged lovers, then Giliahna would not have worried—but she knew that not all women shared her sense of honor where a handsome man was concerned. She closed her eyes and tried not to think of Tim locked in Aldora's arms.

Oh, she was not so idealistic as to expect anyone to stay faithful on a long summer's campaign. But Aldora, who hated her, who had hated her from the moment they had met, was different. Mara, Milo's intelligent, sophisticated wife, had tried to explain Aldora's behavior to her. "It is not you she hates, but your happiness and your ability to love," Mara had told her. "Aldora has never been content with any man for long. If only Bili had been Undying . . ." Like Mara, Giliahna had taken to avoiding Aldora whenever possible.

She woke early, before the men, and dressed hastily. By the time she emerged from the tent in the pale-gray light of dawn, her troopers were up and beginning to strike the camp. They were on their way before the full force of the sun broke through the clouds.

The attack came without warning. Twenty bandits poured out of the trees lining the road, backed by archers. Giliahna wished she had her bow; she was a better archer then most men, and at least she would have been some use. Her men formed a protective circle around her, but three against one was not good odds. She drew her dagger and used it when the opportunity arose, but the next few minutes were a chaos of sword against sword, screams of wounded animals and shouted oaths, and she was in the middle of it all. The tide was not turning in their favor.

She turned to the curly-haired trooper near her, a young man named Barnes, and said, "Whatever happens, Bili must know about the attacks on the farms—the ones Grant told us about. Fight your way out and ride to him!"

"But, my lady—"

"Ride, man. You can do no good here."

She turned back to the fighting as one of the bandits fought his way through to her. She raised her dagger to parry his swordcut, tried to bring it down into his armpit, and took a cut herself in the process. There was no longer time to think at all, just to react and try to stay alive. And then there was a sudden jolting pain and she knew nothing more.

Stefanohs Penglees had been making his way through the forest on foot when he ran across the bandits' trail. The Reverend Father had ordered him to check out the truth of recent rumors that one of the High Lords of the Confederation was en route with only a small entourage. If it was true, and one of the hated heretic leaders could be taken hostage, it might provide the Faithful with a bargaining point, and even if the Confederation would not give in, the death of one of those who had caused such humiliation to true Ehleenee would be a major cause for rejoicing. Stefanohs was pleased that the Father had placed enough trust in him to allow him to handle such a delicate task. True, he was the best tracker and spy they had in Stronghold, but he was not a full member of the Swords of the Lord, and normally an assignment of such importance would have been given to one of the sacred warriors who had dedicated their lives to wiping out the scourge of the Confederation.

He followed at a safe distance behind the bandits, watching from hiding as they attacked the small party. It wasn't a long fight, over in a matter of minutes. The bandits stripped their conquests of anything worth looting, slit the throat of any survivors, then headed off again. It was all very matter-of-fact. There was none of the savage joy he had seen in the faces of the sacred warriors as they slew the ungodly—but then this was not the sacrament of death, only murder. Still, he could not help noticing that he did not feel the need to fight back nausea as he did when he rode with the Swords of the Lord. Clean death was something he could bear; mutilation and torture, even if done in the name of the Lord, went against some basic instinct. But he was weak in faith, unfit for the service of the Lord, as the Reverend Father had told him often enough.

When he knew the bandits were gone for good, he stepped out from the trees and crossed to the road where the bodies lay. He needed to verify that this was not the group he was looking for. One by one he stopped at each body and examined it. Typical Confederation troops, a mixture of Ehleenee and Kindred—mongrels, the Reverend Father would have called them, as Stefanohs himself was, a fact he cursed each day along with his unknown sire. The bandits had carried off weaponry and armor and purses, and in some cases jerkins and boots, if not too bloodstained to be sold.

Now who had these men been defending? They had formed a protective wall around someone important enough to die for. The object of their loyalty lay among them, a small lad in a richly embroidered leather jerkin which had only been spared the bandits' looting because it was covered with blood from the wound which had taken the young man's life.

Or had it?

As Stefanohs came toward the boy, he saw the slightest movement of the boy's chest, as he breathed shallowly. How could he have survived a blow like that? From the position of the rip in the jerkin, it had to have pierced his heart, and even if it hadn't killed him immediately, he would have bled to death in minutes once the knife was withdrawn. Stefanohs tore open the jerkin, to see how bad the damage was, and got the surprise of his life.

One full breast peeked through the gaping hole in the linen shirt. The survivor the others had given their lives to protect was a woman. And the Undying he had been seeking was rumored to be the High Lady Giliahna.

Perhaps his efforts hadn't been in vain after all.

He ripped strips off the shirt of one of the slain troopers and returned to the woman's side, just as her eyes fluttered open.

"Quiet, lady. You're in no condition to make any sudden moves. You've lost a lot of blood. Lie still and let me bandage your wounds." With his knifeblade he slit open her shirt and cut away the blood-soaked breast bindings, to reveal a wound that was already beginning to close. He had found what he sought.

"I would not move, Lady Giliahna. My dagger is inches from your throat, and I could behead you in a moment. That is one way to kill you Undying monsters, or so I have heard."

Giliahna woke to a dull pain under her breast, and knew that her body was beginning to heal itself. She also knew that the agony in her chest bespoke a major injury and massive blood loss, which meant she would be weak for several hours. Her body might repair itself rapidly, but it still took time to replace a large amount of blood. Slowly, carefully, she opened her eyes to see a man bending over her. A dagger in his hand, he spoke softly threatening words in a dialect of Ehleenee. Through the haze of pain it penetrated that he knew who she was.

"Stretch your hands above your head, lady. You can move them. The wound was in your chest, not your shoulder."

She did as she was told. The look in his eyes told her he would use the knife in the manner he had described so calmly, and she was not ready go to Wind just yet. Not while there was a chance to escape. Not while Tim still lived. Quickly and efficiently, he bound her hands, then ordered her to sit up. When she did so, he tied her hands to her belt.

"Now I think you can't get away, even with your sorcerous tricks. I know who you are and what you are."

"And who am I?" She was prepared to lie.

"High Lady of the Confederation, one of the thrice-cursed Undying Sorcerers. And," he added, "a useful tool for the Stronghold."

For the first time, she took a good look at him. Below average height, whipcord and muscle, dressed in woods-green breeches and jerkin. Dark hair, but not black as a pure-blood Ehleenee or Ahrmehnee's would be, and his skin was fair beneath the tan. Green eyes. Undoubtedly there was Kindred blood in his veins, though he professed hatred for the Confederation.

"What is the Stronghold, and why do you want me? How can I be a tool for you?"

"You will buy us our revenge—and perhaps our freedom." Methodically he cut a piece of stick, forced her mouth open and tied a strip of cloth to hold the gag in place. "I'd rather you didn't try to cry out. In a few hours it won't matter if you scream. There won't be anyone to hear."

The bandits had taken the horses, so he tossed her unceremoniously in front of him like a sack of meal. Giliahna resented the indignity of the position almost as much as she did the gag. She tried to keep track of where they were heading, but banging upside down like that made her dizzy after a few minutes. He kept to his word, however, and when he made camp late that night, he removed the gag. He did not untie her hands, though.

"How am I supposed to eat?" she asked reasonably.

"I didn't think you Undying had to eat, that you drank your blood of your victims," he told her, surprised.

"And where did you hear that stupid story?"

"The Reverend Father Zakareeohs told us about your ways, which are an insult to all true believers."

"We may be that, but we don't drink blood. We have to eat and drink just like you *kath'ahros*. We even make love the same way." She cocked her head to one side. "Or do you prefer boys?"

His pale skin flushed so deeply she could see it even under the light of the moon. "Those who are the Swords of the Lord embrace only each other, but I was not chosen for that honor. I—was not found worthy, by the Reverend Father."

Her mind touched his briefly, and before he could slam

down a shield, she felt a strong awareness of herself as a woman. He had mindspeak, though untrained, and he was not a boy-lover. Perhaps she could use both facts to her advantage.

"Why were you unworthy?"

She tried to make her voice sympathetic, questioning but friendly. If she was to make an escape, she needed to understand her captor and his people. Any information she could gain would be worth her weight in gold for Bili the Axe.

He bowed his head. "I am not *kath'ahrohs*. To serve in the Sacred Band, one must be of pure blood—but I am tainted. One of your accursed Horseclans soldiers raped my mother when she was only fifteen. When my grandfather found out, he brought my grandmother and my mother to the Stronghold, where they would never be bothered by your kind again. I was lucky enough to be born in the Stronghold, where I might learn the truth from Father Zakareeohs' own lips."

He was a fanatic, she thought, and she shivered. If he were an ordinary bandit, she might seduce him into getting close enough for her to somehow get his knife free, but with an Ehleenee fanatic that wouldn't work. Especially one who had been brought up to regard the embraces of a woman as something to be tolerated, far less desirable than coupling with another warrior—or a young boy. He might want her, but he would never admit it to himself, much less to her. If he took her, it would be to humiliate her only, and she had no desire to be raped if she could avoid it.

He looked across at her in the wan moonlight, and it threw the sharp lines of his cheekbones into relief, like a carving from pale marble. "We will win in the end because the Lord is with us. You will see. We will win."

Giliahna felt a quick stab of fear, and tried not to think of her dead half brother Myron and the knife he had wielded so ruthlessly. The physical scars of that night had faded to invisibility, but she would never forget the terror. If it came to a choice between a pawn in the hands of this Reverend Father or a clean death, she would die. But until the moment came when hope was gone, she would do her best to stay alive and get word of the danger to Milo and Bili.

Chuhk Barnes had barely made it away from the ambush with his life. He had been forced to literally hack his way down the road, and then he had spurred his horse to a gallop. At the first holding he came to he had flashed Prince Gy's insignia and explained that he bore an urgent message to Bili of Morguhn. Those two names were enough to convince the man to exchange his mount for a fresh one. It was no warhorse, and it lacked mindspeak, but all he cared about was that it was not exhausted. He rode halfway through the night until he reached another outpost, and repeated the process. At his third stop, he was forced to sleep for a few hours and gratefully ate the home-cooked meal his host's pretty daughter provided for him.

It was midday of the third day—the mud had slowed him down, he felt—when he ran into a patrol wearing Bili's device. They approached him suspiciously, until he identified himself.

"Are you riding ahead of the High Lady Giliahna?" asked the head of the patrol. "We expected her days ago."

"The rains held us up. But I do come with news of her and her party." The thought of his comrades lying slaughtered by the bandits, and of his lady in their hands, made his young face grim.

"Not good news, eh? Best to bring it to the *arkeethoheeks* soonest. Come with us, lad. We'll take you by the shortest route."

An hour later, he sat in Bili's private study, drinking strong ale and telling that legendary warrior what had befallen Bili's Undying half sister and her escort.

"Gy's men must be getting soft when ten Freefighters can't hold off thirty bandits," Bili said softly.

Chuhk leapt to his fellow fighters' defense. "They were better armed than most bandits—"

Bili waved him to silence. "No need to make excuses. I know the lot you ran into. They're renegade Freefighters themselves—no honorable burklord will hire them; they're too disreputable even to find favor in the Middle Kingdoms. My men have been harrying them for days. So they have Giliahna, do they?" For one moment he smiled, and it was not a pleasant smile. "They will pay us to take her back, if I know my little sister. She's a fighter, that one."

"She may be of your blood, and I know she is a courageous lady, but she is only a woman, after all."

"Don't let her fine gowns fool you, boy. She may wear Ehleenee clothes, but she's Kindred through and through. She'll be alive when we find her, and she'll slay any who abused her with her own hand, I promise you. Do you not know the story of how Tim Sanderz regained his hall?"

Chuhk shook his head. He had heard bits of the tale, gossip mostly, but the chance to hear the story from one who had been there would have prompted him to deny knowledge even had he heard the truth. He listened as Bili told him how Giliahna had come riding from Kuhmbuhluhn with a dozen horseguards to hold her brother's hall for him, how they had been reunited there after so many years—and how her step-mother had plotted to enstate her own mewling son as the chief. He spoke of the final siege of the hall, when Myron had caught Giliahna off guard. Myron had carved her beautiful face into a terrible travesty, and she had thrown herself on his dagger rather than allow him to use her as a hostage against Tim. Broken-hearted, Tim had fallen on his sword because he could not face the empty years without her—and both had learned they were Undying.

"It sounds like one of the old stories the bards tell," Chuhk said, when Bili had stopped.

Bili finished sipping his ale and nodded. "But it happened, and just as I told you. So don't fear for your lady; she's lived through far worse than a few days with some renegades."

Chuhk then told him about the reavers who left behind the sign of the lightning bolt amid complete destruction. Bili's grim face grew even grimmer, and his large fist hit the table with a resounding thud.

"More Ehleenee fanatics! Will they never give up?" He began to pace the length of the room. "I promise you I will find them and clean them out wherever they may be hiding—as soon as I find my sister." Bili ordered two patrols to ride in the general direction Chuhk had come from, and then dispatched teams of scouts to question the outlying farmers about the reavers. The cold fury that burned in the aging *arkeethoheeks'* did not bode well for those who bore the lightning-bolt insignia when they fell into his hands.

For three days they had ridden into the mountains, west-ward. Where was he taking her? Giliahna wondered. The mountain people did not like strangers in their country, and they were known to be fierce fighters. But Stefanohs seemed certain of his destination. The Stronghold, he called it, founded by renegade Ehleenee who had been willing to wait for two generations until they had sufficient warriors to take on the Confederation. So much she had managed to piece together from what he had said, and he was remarkably close-mouthed. She still had not found a chance to try an escape. He was extremely careful to watch her—and to keep her close-tied when he could not.

The third night, the rain had begun to fall again, heavier than before, and cold on the skin because of the higher altitude. Stefanohs had found them a cave to sleep in and had made a fire of some dry wood left there by other travelers. Or perhaps by Stefanohs himself; the cave seemed to be provisioned as a way station with firewood and dried meat. He placed some water on the fire to boil and threw the dried meat into it. Then they sat in silence around the smoky fire, watching the wind blow the wisps out the cave entrance.

"How far are we from your Stronghold?" she asked finally.

"We should reach it by tomorrow night."

"And you'll give me over to your Reverend Father?"

He shrugged. "He is the head of the Stronghold. It will be up to him to decide how best to use you."

"Stefanohs," she said softly, "what do you think they'll do with me? Use me as a hostage to negotiate some sort of truce with Milo and the Confederation?"

"Our freedom should be a small price for the Confederation to pay for the life of one of its High Ladies."

"Do you really think they'd send me back alive? They couldn't afford to. I know the way to the Stronghold. Once Milo had me safe, he'd use that information to lead troops against you. He'd have to. There can be no peace between the Confederation and the Old Church. Too much blood has been shed."

"The Reverend Father would keep a treaty made in the Lord's name," Stefanohs argued.

"Would he?" She fell silent again, gazing at him across the fire.

It was hard for Stefanohs to feel her eyes on him that way. He was far too aware of her as a woman, and women were only for the begetting of children. A true man would not feel his loins tighten when he smelled a woman's scent, nor long to touch her soft skin. No wonder Father Zakareeohs had found him unworthy. Even this Horseclans bitch could arouse his lust.

But she was beautiful.

He tried not to watch her in the flickering firelight, at the way it gilded her long red-blond hair, at the soft shadows it cast along her throat, leading down to the cleft between her full breasts. She was everything he had been taught to hate and despise, not only a woman of the enemy but a sorceress as well. Then what did that make him? He was cursed with mindspeak, inherited from the rapist who had given him his pale skin and green eyes.

"Have you ever seen a farmstead after your sacred warriors have finished with it?" she asked him.

"I told you, I am unworthy to cleanse the land for the Lord."

"Cleanse? Is that what you call it?" She told him then what his comrades did. Told him stoically, unemotionally, in words as stark and grim as the details she revealed. She spared him nothing, and when she had finished her recital of facts, he was shaking.

"Don't tell me these things happen in war, Stefanohs. I know about war, and I know what men do in wars. But this—this was the work of monsters. A child cut living from its mother's belly?" She shook her head. "That's not warfare. It's madness. And I know about madness."

She leaned close to the fire. "Look at my face, Stefanohs. Oh, the scars are very faint, you have to look close to see them, but they are still there. My brother put them there, because I was Kindred, not Ehleenee, and his bitch mother had raised him to hate all that was not Ehleenee. I know about madness very well."

His hand came up and slammed down hard against her mouth, drawing blood. "Shut up, woman. You will not make me doubt my faith. Shut up."

She turned away from him then, and they were both locked in their own private hells, she thinking of Tim, whom she might never see again, he hoping that she had lied to him but fearing that she had only told the truth. It was in the sudden quiet that they first heard the unvoiced cry for help.

It was faint at first, then grew in power and desperation.

Who is it? Giliahna asked.

A picture formed in her head, a triangular face, bright dark eyes, red fur, and a name, Silkfur. A vixen, and with mindspeak. Well, Milo had said it was spreading. Fear and concern, and then a wordless picture of two small fox kits. And then a question: *Who asks?*

Giliahna tried to make her thoughts soothing, but she knew this was a wild creature whose contacts with humans had probably not been friendly. *I am a friend, little sister, though I walk on two legs, not on four.*

Two-legs! Fear and anger, and memories of traps that had killed her mate.

Not all two-legs are hunters, Silkfur. Your kits, where are they?

"What's going on? I can feel that animal's thoughts, hear them as clearly as when I speak out loud," Stefahnohs protested.

"It's only mindspeech. She has it, just as you and I do. A lot of animals have it, especially horses and prairiecats, but you know about them."

"I was taught that your horses and cats were demons, familiars."

"As we are sorcerers? Shhh, and let me talk to Silkfur."

Your kits, little sister? Why are you afraid for them?

The two kits, trapped on a ledge where they had fallen. The vixen could not reach them, nor could she climb down and carry them up. Could the two-legs help?

Giliahna felt the vixen's terror and despair at her kits' fate. The ledge they were cowering on looked none too secure, and if this rain kept up, they might be swept down into the river below, a river that threatened to flood its banks.

Little sister, if I could aid you, I would. But I am not free to do so—

But I am. It was Stefanohs, clear and determined. *Show me the way, little sister. I will get your kits to safety.*

"Why?" asked Giliahna.

He shrugged. "I have to. I can't let them die, when I can save them. I just can't."

He gathered up a saddlebag to stuff the kits into, and riding gloves to protect his hands; even with their mother's mindspeak to calm them, he didn't want to risk the teeth and claws of two terrified fox kits. He glanced around the cave—his sword was on his belt, his knife in his boot. There was nothing Giliahna could use to cut her bonds.

"I'll be back," he told her.

She waited until he was gone a short distance, using the three-way link to follow him. Then, shielding her thoughts carefully, she inched her way over to the fire. He had tied her ankles together soon after they had made camp, to keep her from taking any foolish chances, he'd said, so she had to pull herself along the cave floor. It took an unbearably long time. Then, when she was close to the fire, she squirmed so that her back was toward it and plunged her rope-tied hands into it.

The first touch of the flames on her skin was agonizing, and she had to bite her lip to keep from crying out. She pulled her hands up, maneuvering so that just the rope was in the fire, but still she could feel the heat, and every so often the wind would blow the flames high enough to lick her wrists. Sweat broke out on her forehead, trickled down her cheeks. Her lips were bloody from her efforts to keep from making a sound, because she really had no idea how far away Stefanohs was and she didn't want him to be warned.

After what seemed an eternity, she felt the rope give, and she pulled her hands free and unwrapped the bonds. Her wrists were raw and starting to blister in places, but she knew they would heal quickly, though at this moment she was only aware of the pain. Ignoring it, she bent and untied her ankle bonds. She was free. Quickly she glanced around the cave to see if there was anything she could use as a weapon. Nothing. Stefanohs had not been careless.

But the horse was there, tethered under an overhang of rock which kept off the worst of the rain—the cave was too low to accommodate a horse; even she had to bend her head a little, and she was a small woman. She drew on her cloak, semidry from the fire, and started out.

She wanted to know where Stefanohs was, though. No need to run into him. She wanted as much time as possible before he discovered she was gone. Carefully, she reached out to his mind and looked through his eyes.

Stefanohs had followed Silkfur on a winding trail that led

partway down the side of the mountain. It was rough going. The mud made it hard to get a safe footing, and it wasn't easy to explain to the vixen that what would hold her small weight was not safe for him. Finally she had stopped before an outcropping.

Here, two-legs brother. My children are below. He felt her concern and fear for her kits.

All his life he had had a rapport with animals. He had always been able to gentle horses without having to break them to the whip. His hounds had always been faster and more loyal, and he had almost seemed to know what their baying meant. He had often wished he could know, because animals never made him feel an outcast as humans did. Half-breed, son of the enemy, unworthy . . . horses and dogs neither knew nor cared. If his grandfather had not been *kath'ahrohs* and from a noble line, he would most likely have been assigned to tend sheep and cattle, and he would have been happy enough—but he was his mother's son (his father's too, as they never allowed him to forget) and he was meant to be a warrior.

Now he could feel an animal's thoughts, and the vixen's need and desperation overrode everything. It didn't matter that this was a curse inherited from his father's people. This blending was a marvel.

I will fetch them for you. Be calm.

He inched out toward the outcropping of rock, lay down on his belly, and peered over. At first he couldn't spot them, because their bright fur was caked with mud, but at last he saw two bedraggled, very young, and very frightened kits peering up at him with terrified shoe-button eyes.

The larger kit growled and tried to bristle. *Leave us, two-legs. I will protect my sister from your kind.*

Hush, Bannertail, the two-legs is a friend. He has come to help. Let him touch you. He will not hurt you.

The growling and the bristling stopped, dissolving into relief at his mother's mindtouch. He was no longer a would-be hunter, but a frightened kit trying very hard to hide it.

Stefanohs tried not to laugh at the kit's ferocity. It reminded him of himself at that age, fighting with every bully who dared to call him a half-breed. He'd had his fair share of bloody noses and blackened eyes before they'd learned to respect his courage, if not his prowess.

The kits were on a ledge beneath the cropping, a ledge made mostly of mud and grass. He didn't want to have to climb down there if he didn't have to. He wasn't sure it was secure enough. First he'd try to reach the little devils.

Come to me. Your mother is waiting beside me.

The little male denied needing any help, he'd just been about to figure out how to climb up himself, but if the two-legs insisted, he would allow himself to be lifted to safety.

Stefanohs moved forward as far as he dared and then reached down. He could see the kits, but there were eight feet between his hand and their fur.

They were already at the edge of their ledge, and the dirt was beginning to crumble.

All right. That left him no choice. He'd have to go down to them. He took the rope he'd brought, tied one end around his waist, the other around a sturdy tree. It would give him some security if the ledge gave way. At least he wouldn't tumble headfirst into the river, which lay a dozen or so yards below. Slowly, carefully, he picked his way down the cliffside. Several times he almost lost his footing from the mud, but finally he was within reach of the kits.

Do as he asks, Bannertail, came Silkfur's firm mindtouch. Meekly, but with soft growls, the male kit allowed himself to be picked up and stuffed unceremoniously into the saddlebag. His annoyed comments made it plain that he did not care for his temporary home. The small female was easier to handle, and while there was a tinge of fear in her mind, she seemed to regard him as a hero. Stefanohs fastened the leather ties on the saddlebag, assuring them it was only for a few minutes, that they would soon be with their mother.

He held on to the rope and began to swing himself onto the trail he had come down, only to realize that it was not there. The mud had been crumbling under his boots, and when he had pushed off to jump onto the ledge it had collapsed. He couldn't quite make it to the next foothold. There wasn't enough slack in the rope.

For an awful moment he dangled there, then he used the rope to haul himself back onto the narrow, crumbling ledge.

*   *   *

Giliahna felt his fear and fought it back. He was an enemy. He had taken her prisoner, he had hit her, he would turn her over to that Reverend Father of his if he had the chance. She owed him nothing, nothing at all. But she could not quite banish the momentary glimpse she had had of the loneliness he had known all those years—nor could she forget that he had been remarkably gentle with her in a situation in which most men would, at the very least, have indulged in rape. It was almost customary, with a female captive. And he had wanted her, she knew that too. But he had not touched her. She couldn't let him die.

She had to. She had to think of the Confederation's needs before one man's. This Sword of the Lord matter was a threat to the Confederation. Another Ehleenee plot, so soon after the last one, could tear the duchies apart, especially when they were already fighting on the western borders with the hill clans. Determinedly she strode over to the horse. Unlike the warhorses of the Kindred, it lacked mindspeak, but she could use her thoughts to soothe it and calm it. She stroked its nose reassuringly and managed to get it saddled.

But she couldn't stop seeing Stefanohs, trapped on that ledge. What if it had been Tim?

She was never able to explain even to herself why she didn't mount the horse and ride away, leaving Stefanohs to his fate. She only knew that when it came to a final choice she couldn't leave him like that. She tied the horse's reins to the bush, ordered it to stay, and called to Stefanohs to guide her to him.

He was startled at first by her mindcall, startled enough nearly to let go of the rope. *How are you free?*

Ask questions later. Guide me now.

He showed her the way, and she moved along the path as carefully as he had, until she reached the cliff. She saw the rope tied to the tree and heard him call out to her. The situation was clear enough: She had to tug him to safety. She began to pull up the slack on the rope, until it was wound tight around the tree and taut on the ground. Then she dug her heels in, bracing herself against the tree trunk, and began to pull him up.

"Climb, damn you!" she told him, as little by little she yanked his weight upward. At last she saw his hands clear the top of the outcropping and knew he was nearly safe. One more tug, then the ache in her arms would end and she could rest.

He got a good grip on the rock and pulled himself upward. She stood for a long moment just looking at him, and then she read what was in his mind before he had a chance to slam his shields up; he could not let her escape, because if she was free, she would ride to Bili and bring him here. They were too close to the Stronghold.

She broke into a run, but her feet hit a patch of mud, and she went down face forward into the dirt. He was on top of her instantly, and while she turned and went for him with her nails, tried to free her legs to kick, he had pinned her to the ground. He didn't outweigh her by all that much, but he had her in a hold she couldn't break out of.

"I shouldn't have saved you," she said bitterly.

"No, you shouldn't. Why did you?"

She turned away. "The same reason you saved the fox kits, I suppose."

"Lady Giliahna," he said formally, "I give you my word you will be treated as an honorable hostage. No harm will come to you. I stake my life on it."

She wondered how much his life was worth.

"Your word I trust, but not your Reverend Father's. Tie me quickly. If I get another chance, I will kill you, if I have to."

He met her gaze squarely. "I know. And I also know that I owe you my life."

Bili's men had found the bandits' camp early on the second day. They had caught them by surprise, and when the reavers tried to run, Bili's men cut them to pieces. He had ordered that at least a few prisoners be taken, if Giliahna was not to be found among them, so that they could be questioned at length as to her whereabouts. But even the combination of mindspeak and torture could not get any information from them. They knew nothing about a woman. So far as they were concerned, only one of the travelers had gotten away, and that was Barnes. But they did have some interesting tales to tell about the raiders who left behind the sign of the lightning bolt. They had had run-ins with them once or twice—and lost. One of their scouts had followed a party back into the hills. Over three days southwest, he'd said.

And that was where Bili of Morguhn and his men were headed now. He had sent out riders to look for Giliahna, and search parties had already combed the forest around the ambush site, to no avail. There was nothing more to be done for his sister, and those Ehleenee madmen had to be cleaned out, like lancing a festering abscess.

It was almost nightfall when Stefanohs rode through the gates of the settlement, into the heart of the Stronghold itself. Giliahna was securely tied in front of him. They both looked muddy, disheveled and exhausted; their appearance mirrored their feelings. Stefanohs dismounted and heaved her into his arms. He was taking no chances this time. He carried her into his grandfather's house and deposited her on a chair. Then he called for a maid to fetch water, and one of his mother's gowns.

The commotion brought his mother, Sohfeeya, from her sewing room. She was a small woman, her black hair streaked with gray, her tired face still showing traces of her younger loveliness in high cheekbones and large eyes. "Stefanohs, what is this about? Who is the strange woman the maids came running to me about?"

"This"—he waved a hand toward Giliahna, who felt like an untidy package—"is the High Lady Giliahna, and our guest for the time being. She needs a bath, and clothes."

"You also need a bath and clean clothes," his mother told him.

"It can wait until I have seen the Reverend Father."

"You can't go to the Reverend Father's house looking like a—a cleaner of stables!"

"Just this once, I think he will forgive me, Mother."

"No, send for him. You can wash and dress properly, while you wait. He will want to see your captive with his own eyes."

She was right, and he knew it. He had to admit, too, that he liked being in the position of requesting the Reverend Father's presence rather than running to his summons. It was perhaps a half hour later, freshly bathed and dressed, that he received his august visitor in his grandfather's reception room.

His grandfather, Pehtrohs, was not far behind the priest, as were the other members of the council.

"Well, Stefanohs, where is the witch?"

"Dressing, I would think. It will take her some time to dry that hair of hers."

"You ordered a bath for a Confederation witch?" Zakareeohs thundered. He was a tall man, heavy-boned and beginning to run to fat now, though he did not have the flab of most of his fellow priests—he had dedicated himself to the Lord's service at twenty-five. His face was regular of feature, aquiline of nose and full of lip, the effect of nobility and high-mindedness spoiled by the beginnings of a double chin and jowls. Still he was an impressive figure in his stark dark garb, contrasting richly with his silver hair.

"She saved my life. She is my hostage, and I gave my word that she would be well treated." Stefanohs tried to make his voice level, but his awe of the Reverend Father showed in the tightness of his speech.

"Why would one of the Undying help an enemy?" his grandfather scoffed.

Stefanohs told them the story in as few words as possible. When he had finished, he saw sympathy and some approval on the faces of his grandfather and the council. But the Reverend Father's face was carefully blank.

"Have the woman brought to me," the priest said neutrally. "I will question her in the privacy of my home."

He swept out.

Stefanohs strode toward the women's quarters, where he found Giliahna garbed in one of his mother's simpler gowns. The pale rose set off her pallor as well as it did his mother's olive skin, and she was brushing out the tangles from her long hair. Her beauty was more than he could have imagined from their days of hard riding. She looked up at his footsteps and began to braid her still-damp hair.

"I've come to bring you to the Reverend Father. He wants to speak with you alone."

"I'm sure he does." Her voice was heavy with an irony even he could not ignore.

"There's no need to be afraid. I've given my word, and I've told him how you saved me."

She said nothing, but gathered up her white himation and arranged it to fall in graceful folds. "I'm ready."

They were escorted by six of the Swords of the Lord, all armed. Giliahna wondered if they were so afraid of her, and realized they were, when she saw one old woman back away making a sign against demons.

The Reverend Father's house was an impressive dwelling, grand enough to house the lord of a small duchy. She was brought inside to his study, where they found him sitting in a richly carved chair, his small, pudgy hands tight on its leather-padded arms.

"So this is the sorceress. No wonder she has bespelled you, Stefanohs. You were always weak when it came to women. She is beautiful." He spoke dispassionately, as if discussing a vase or some other *objet d'art*.

"Her beauty has nothing to do with it. I gave her my word that she would be treated with respect, as we would wish one of our own to be treated if she was a hostage."

"And how would your people treat one of my sacred warriors?" the priest asked her.

Giliahna said nothing. The man's shield was tight as a barrel sealed with pitch. She could pick up no thoughts at all. But she did not need to. The malevolence and hatred that burned in his dark eyes spoke loudly enough.

"They'd torture my fighters until they broke—but the Lord's chosen do not break! This time we will beat you, and drive you into the sea. We will cleanse this land of your unbelieving filth—"

He stopped himself. "Would your Milo Morai give up a portion of his land for your life?"

She said nothing. There was nothing she could say.

"Will you admit you are a demon-worshiping sorceress and repent your crimes against the Lord?"

Giliahna laughed.

She knew he wanted to hit her, but he was restraining himself, with an effort.

"Your kind tried to break me once. I preferred to die." She said it calmly, conversationally. "But know that my death will bring the Confederation down upon you. I sent a messenger to Bili of Morguhn, and sooner or later he will find you, and we'll see who does the cleansing then."

It was late, and Stefanohs could not sleep. If he was going to act, it would have to be very soon, while there were still

hours of darkness to cover their escape. He had sat through the
council meeting, listening to the self-congratulatory speeches
of his grandfather and the others, trying not to let what he felt
show on his face. For one moment, when the Reverend
Father had ordered Giliahna to be held under guard in the
temple, his mask had slipped, and Stefanohs had been able to
see into his mind, and it was like staring into a cesspool.
What he had planned for Giliahna was not to use her as a
hostage, but to give her as a sacrifice to the Lord—to save
her soul by killing by inches, knowing that as an Undying her
body would heal itself within minutes.

He could not let that happen. He had given her his word,
and he owed her his life. He had added a colorless liquid to the
watered wine that would be brought to the guards with their
evening meal. It would put them into a sound sleep. There
were advantages to being a scout and a spy after all; an
ordinary warrior wouldn't have known of the potion nor
thought to use it. By now the guards should be fast asleep.

The shadows hid him as he made his way through the
courtyard to the temple. The side door was less conspicuous,
so he went in that way, slipping by the guards. No one
noticed him. The whole Stronghold, except for those on duty,
were still celebrating—madly. He had drunk his share, but
had retired early, pleading exhaustion from the last few days
of hard traveling. After kneeling for the Reverend Father's
blessing, he had left them to their revels. Their shouts covered
any slight noise he might make.

Giliahna was bound with leather thongs to a chair in the
sanctuary. Her eyes widened when she saw him, but she
made no sound because of the gag. He pulled it free, made a
shushing noise, then sawed through her bonds. Then he gave
her breeches and a jacket in dark cloth.

"Put these on. You can't ride in a gown."

She didn't waste time with modesty or foolish questions
but pulled on the garments. He had a brief glimpse of full
breasts and white thighs before she had the breeches on, and
then the jacket.

"I'm ready. Where?"

"How good are you at climbing stockades?"

"You should ask Tim that. He taught me when I wanted to
be out riding with him instead of sewing. We both had our

behinds blistered, but I spent more afternoons riding than I did at my needle.''

"Good. Come on.''

They exited by the side door, and he led her around past the house of the junior priests, who were mostly passed out from the copious amounts of wine they had drunk earlier, judging from the snores. Then he boosted her over the wall and scrambled up beside her. They jumped to the ground, landing hard and rolling.

"Pray the guards don't hear us.''

"They won't. I drugged them.''

"Which way?''

He pointed, and together they darted past the outbuildings to the place in the woods where he had managed to tether two horses earlier, while the guards had been distracted. Again he blessed his years of getting revenge on larger enemies by stealth and craft. It had made him a good spy. Now it was helping him to escape.

He looked back over his shoulder for one last look at the Stronghold. He had grown up there, but he had never belonged there. Even to his mother he was an unwanted reminder of rape. The only thing holding him had been ties of faith, and Zakareeohs had shown him how misguided he had been.

But he did see the Stronghold one last time. Halfway through the following day, they ran into one of Bili's patrols, who recognized Giliahna from her visits to Morguhn Hall. They brought her as quickly as possible to Bili's camp, where Stefanohs was shocked to see that hard warrior wipe away what looked suspiciously like a tear as he embraced his sister.

He was even more surprised when Bili, who was known for his loathing of anything Ehleenee, did not have him placed under guard but treated him as an honorable prisoner—once Giliahna had told him her story. Bili's face darkened with rage at the way Zakareeohs had abused her—he had had her beaten while she was under his care, before he had had her taken to the temple.

"For that alone, he deserves to die.''

"It's nothing to what he would have done if Stefanohs had not come to my aid.''

"It was my doing that put you in his hands in the first place," Stefanohs said.

"Enough apologies from both of you," Bili thundered. "We must move against them at first light. Giliahna, can you give us directions to the place?"

"There's no need. I'll guide you there," Stefahohs said.

Bili looked at him silently for a long moment, probing for a lie, but Stefanohs allowed him free access to his mind. "I see you have reason to turn against your own."

"They were never my own. I just didn't know it until now."

"I can't ask you to take up arms against those of your blood."

"Why not? Zakareeohs did." His smile was grim.

Giliahna called him to the tent Bili had had vacated for her. It was small, but there was warm bedding to sleep on, and after her recent trials it looked like a palace.

"What do you want, High Lady?"

"Three friends were looking for you." Three triangular faces appeared out from beneath a camp stool. "They must have followed us here, somehow."

We came to thank the two-legs for aiding us. Though I would have done fine in just a few minutes. It was the arrogant little male.

Giliahn held out a hand to him, and he padded forward to sniff it, then curl up beside her contentedly. She scratched his chin, and he made a contented sound deep in his throat.

"Can foxes purr?" Giliahna wondered aloud, and then she glanced up from the kit to see Stefanohs watching her with hunger in his eyes. She pushed the kit to his feet and shooed him back to his mother. She patted the pile of blankets on which she was sitting. "Sit down beside me."

He did as she asked, carefully not making contact with her. She ignored that, and took his hand in both of hers. "You never told me why you saved me. It wasn't just what your Reverend Father had planned for me, was it?"

He shook his head. "I—I touched your mind. I knew what you were like. I— Everything they taught me was a lie, Giliahna. It was all lies. But you never lied to me, even about escaping."

His world had been shattered with the realization that

everything he had held sacred was so many lies. No truth anywhere. Except in her, the woman of the enemy who had chosen to save his life rather than escape. Gently, he reached out to touch her face, starting to draw back when she moved, only to find that she had leaned down to kiss his palm.

Ties of faith. He had broken all those ties. But she was bound by ties of faith too—promises she had made to Tim. But how did this night, and what she was about to do, touch what she felt for Tim? He had been her first love, her first lover. What did it matter who lay in her arms? She and Tim had centuries of life ahead of them. If Aldora wanted a few months of that time, let her have them. They could spare her so little.

As she reached out to embrace Stefanohs, Giliahna smiled.

The Courage of Friends

by Paul Edwards

Paul Edwards has been an actor, director, and playwright, but now divides his creative energies between professional engagements playing and singing blues and boogie-woogie, and writing fiction. He is also a bard and a Knight of the Society for Creative Anachronism. Mr. Edwards practices medicine in Tucson, Arizona, where he lives with his wife and two children.

The soldiery of Prince Gonzalo were too late to roust the citizens of Peony and Phlox from their beds to witness, at the dawn, the hanging of Suzor Daughter-of-Shrake. They were already at the crude gallows, standing and staring in silence, when the advance guard marched up, their heavy boots, extravagantly shod with iron, crushing the sparse grass into the red mud. The winds of autumn were filled with the creaks of leather armor and saddles, the scrape of mail against plate, heavy footsteps, and the whistle of the swirling air against the swaying noose.

The initiative to show Daughter-of-Shrake such honor demonstrated a totally unacceptable insolence to the Prince, who rode up with the second company, digging his spurs into his recalcitrant mount. Frowning, he peered into the faces of the somber men and women and youths and little children, standing behind the fence of armored men. *I can't impale them all,* he thought to himself. *I must think of the harvest, and the next spring.* The destrier snorted once, and then stood immobile beneath the conqueror.

The darkness to the east was compounded by the heavy black clouds plumping on the horizon, obscuring the very moment of sunrise, when life should commence its departure from the young woman. As the sergeants began deploying the men, the Prince enjoyed a brief reverie on the fateful night he had so anticipated, companying in love with the black-haired beauty from Phlox. She had smiled and breathed and moved just so! How eagerly she had come to his bed, braving the sneers and jeers of every single peasant and freeholder! He remembered her flawless skin, and large, taut bosom. Absently, his hand touched the ribs above his heart where the rip across his chest from her flashing knife had still not completely healed.

The rumble from the stockade was like a roll of distant thunder, so loud it seemed against the voiceless throng: the solid wheels of the cart turning angrily against wooden axles and wooden bearings, and standing straight within in it, unmoving, alone, her guard tramping near, Suzor Daughter-of-Shrake. Her thick, glossy hair now hung in greased, knotted strings; her smooth face and high cheekbones, which had given her such an air of grace, were softened by purple swellings; yet her shoulders were straight and she seemed not to feel the stout, coarse ropes which bound her wrists too tightly behind.

Kral Raus-son stared at her, awed by the beauty which shone through the ugliness, feeling the same guilt they all felt, shamed by her courage. He remembered the one kiss he had had from her, two years ago when she was fifteen. He had just won the most important horse race of the year despite the sneers of the other riders. How she had laughed, and giggled a promise to meet him that night. But of course it was too busy that night, and the next, and the next week, and then the moment was gone, the smile she had for him never fading, but the spark never kindling again. The cart passed by, and Kral could see that she was breathing slowly, her eyes downcast, almost shut, her mouth tightened into a frown more of anger than misery. The dangerous rage he must contain cramped his heart. He willed the tears in his eyes away. How could he be less strong than she?

The gallows rose above a little hillock which had been selected to best afford the crowd a good view. So there was no one who failed to see the soldiers roughly push the young woman beneath the rope to wrench the coarse hemp over her head and snug it against her neck. She never moved.

The Prince coaxed his horse toward her and nodded to his

man, who reached for the stained, frayed rag which was all her protection against the cold and ripped it away, exposing her precious body to the sight of all. The dried blood and bruises could leave no doubt as to the treatment she had received from the soldiers. She turned her head a little and clenched her eyes, the most she would allow such a trivial feeling as embarrassment.

Garva, twenty-two and huge, when his father was slain by the Prince's men, had been restrained from sudden vengeance by the sword at his mother's throat. He had sometime courted Daugther-of-Shrake. At the sight of her abuse, he stepped forward, but the sound alerted the woman no less than the soldiers. Spearpoints came down to rest against his chest, but it was Daughter-of-Shrake who stopped him. He looked up at ice-blue eyes piercing him, telling him clearly not to throw his life away. She was too strong. He backed off, and the soldiers lifted steel death away from him.

The Prince turned to the crowd.

"It was a stroke of cleverness to send an assassin against me. But useless, as you can see. I grant you that she is beautiful, charming even; but an assassin all the same. This is how Gonzalo deals with treachery!"

At his signal, one of the men thrust his hand between the girl's legs and lifted her up, as others pulled the rope. Then his hand was gone and the noose slowly tightened on the girl's neck. The briefest flash of hopelessness flickered across her face, and then it was only the struggle for air, and the choked gasping, and she fought against the indignity of her spasms and twitching, until the veins bulged from her temples and a faint violet hue colored her face and then the rest of her. Darker and darker she became, and finally sightless; the kicks and spasms became impersonal, and then, blue from head to foot, she moved only with the wind, all movement stilled. Her face relaxed into the countenance of anger, and with a final indignity, her bowels and bladder relaxed as well.

Even the Prince would later admit that it was a good death.

"She shall hang until nightfall, then whoever so wishes may take her corpse." Then Prince Gonzalo applied his heels to the horse's flanks. The beast did not move. He kicked it again, and then again even harder, and finally the huge animal began to turn as the Prince pulled the reins. He felt the eyes of the villagers on him, hating him, sneering at him, condescending. It was not to be borne. He halted and turned in the saddle to the throng.

"I demand again: Where are the horses?"

No one moved.

"Where have you hidden the horses?" The faces were unflinching, sullen, immobile and defiant.

"So your fabled mounts are that valuable, eh? Sebastian!"

"Yes, your highness?" Capitán Sebastian della Verruca came up to the Prince.

"Select one of these mutinous dogs and bring him to me."

"Sì, your highness."

The *capitán*, with a dozen soldiers, walked into the crowd. His eyes flicked here and there, measuring every man.

Garva stood impassive but for his clenched fists. His dark, low brows were an insolent challenge, and although Capitán Sebastian saw him, he figured that the man's resistance could cause a loss of face. He memorized the big peasant's features for the future and moved on.

Kral was sweating. He was afraid of pain, afraid of his own lack of nerve. If they took him for torture, there was nothing he could say to appease them, since there were no magic horses despite the Prince's insistence. He began to quake as the *capitán* drew nearer.

Sebastian saw the terrified boy and smiled to himself. He had flushed out a useful tool from these recalcitrant *peones*. This was too good to waste on the Prince's rage. He stared with a grim half-smile, and watched the blood drain from the boy's face, and then marched straight toward him, smiling at his trembling, seeing the cramp in the boy's bowels reflected in his staring eyes.

At the last minute, the *capitán* reached to his side and collared Lui Morgan's-son and yanked him into the circle of soldiers. They pinioned his arms and marched him to the Prince.

Gonzalo delicately placed the point of his sword over Lui's heart. Quietly he asked again: "Where are the horses?"

Lui shook his head. "There are no more. You've stolen them all."

Gonzalo frowned and jerked his arm straight. The blade slid between Lui's ribs, and as the blood gushed along the blade and down his chest, he sighed and collapsed.

The Prince shouted to the villagers, "That did not have to

be. But if you persist in thwarting me, more of you will die. You will give me the secret of your horses, or not one of you shall live to see the next full moon!'' He barked to his men, ''Bring the body!'' And with a savage kick to his mount's hide, he rode down from the hill toward the stockade. The men did as ordered, and followed, leaving a few guards, the fresh blood in the dirt, and the swaying body of Suzor Daughter-of-Shrake.

It was many minutes before the first of the women began to weep, and the sound of her sobbing broke the horrible spell which had overtaken them. Truly they were dead. So many had died, but somehow, this was the worst of all. Many turned to go, but more than a few stayed to guard the dead girl's flesh.

Kral remained immobile, staring at the body, not even noticing the graybeard that came up behind him. There was nothing startling in the quiet voice of Glaze. The old man had raised Comet, the sire of the three-year-old stallion Kral had ridden to victory at the Harvest Festival race. If the conquerors had known, they would have tortured the old man for the information he would give them, and then impaled him on the spot. He leaned up to Kral's ear.

''You're attracting attention,'' he said. There was no answer. ''Don't think that you're the only one who wants to do something about this. If you want to get in on it, turn around and come away with me now.'' Kral turned to him, and Glaze could see the tears on the boy's face. ''I know, son. Support me as if I were crippled. We'll take the time for tears today. More than that, Daughter-of-Shrake wouldn't approve.'' The old man and the boy left the dead girl and took the road back to Phlox.

By midmorning, Suzor Daughter-of-Shrake waited in her eternity above the gaze of eight villagers, and the gallows hill was guarded by only a single squad of the *conquistadores*. Slowly and sadly, the folk of Phlox and Peony had trudged back to the timeworn tasks of daily life. Prince Gonzalo stood at the battlements of the wood-and-adobe fortress, looking past a small forest of sharpened stakes firmly planted in the ground, and surveyed this paltry corner of his demesnes.

''They're holding out on me,'' he said quietly.

Don Arturo, his second-in-command, shook his head.

"They've no place to hide horses, much less anything to feed them with. We've got what they had."

"Then where are these mythical beasts to be found, these horses that can be trained overnight, and follow a rider's every whim?"

"I'm sure I don't know, sire."

I'm sure you don't, either, thought the Prince. *The wealth those horses could bring! I could become master of all four Mexicos!* "We may have to put more of them to the Question."

"I'd advise against that for the present. We're very outnumbered here. Push them too far and there will be open revolt."

"Bah! They're terrified sheep."

"The assassin was very well liked."

Gonzalo smirked. "Not surprising." He turned to the stables, which were bulging with his own and the confiscated animals. A score of peasants were at work expanding the facility, but only his men were allowed near this equine treasure. "How many do we have now?"

"Enough to provide a mount for every man. Enough for the largest cavalry this side of the Big River!"

If only all the men could ride as well as they fight! Gonzalo turned for the stairs. "Then let's not delay the training any longer. Get the maps! The men can start searching every hidden canyon while they master moving in columns. Those horses must be somewhere!"

They crowded into the false back end of Lon Farrier's huge barn, all who dared to ease through the afternoon under the noses of the patrols. Sheets of dusk's red light slashed through the heavy louvers of the shutters to illuminate the desperate courage of the peasants. The older folk led the meeting.

"Who do we have who's working at their stable?" Glaze asked.

A tanned and wrinkled man raised his hand. "We're making the bricks and stacking them up," he said. "They won't let us near the compound. They threaten us with whips, but they haven't beaten anybody yet. I think they're afraid of us."

Garva spoke for all their hopes: "They'd better be!"

Glaze looked around, not trying to stop the murmur. *As if*

we had weapons they might fear. In a moment they fell silent.
"We have to get to the animals," he said.

"The bastards don't trust us."

"Then who Speaks the strongest?"

All eyes turned to Kral Raus-son. "Not me!" he shouted.
"The captain marked me today! They're going to kill me! I
don't want to be impaled!"

Glaze put his hands on the boy's shoulders to calm him,
seeing the others out of the corners of his eyes: *Thank the
gods it's him and not me,* their faces said. "They're going to
kill us all if we don't stop them," Glaze said.

"But the captain marked me!" the boy wailed.

Glaze ignored it. "You Speak well with the horses?"

"Well enough to win the Harvest Race," Garva muttered.

Kral tried to put the truth of it into words. "I know
Comet's-son heard me," he said.

Glaze had let the boy take care of Comet's-son, and the
young stallion gleamed from the boy's brushing. The horse
would jitter a bit when anyone else managed his hooves, but
he always stood still for Kral.

The boy was afraid of the race, but Glaze had encouraged
him. The mass of riders leaped forward when the flag was
waved, and Comet's-son pushed through the pack to the
front. By the time they reached the great oak tree, a mile
distant, Comet's-son was in front. Kral was thrilled, a broad
grin on his face all the others could see. He leaned over the
left side of the saddle as Comet's-son rounded the huge trunk.

A hoof hit a root, and suddenly there was terror as Kral's
feet slipped from the stirrups. Comet's-son fought for his
footing, head down, with a twist of his hard-muscled back.
Kral bounced up and grabbed for the cantle as his mount
finished careening around the tree, ending half off the broad
seat, his legs gripping sweaty flanks, the powerful limbs of
his steed hammering him, smashing him looser and looser
until he barely had the strength to hold on, before falling
beneath the crushing onslaught of a hundred galloping hooves.

He stared behind, trembling in terror, unable to pull himself up. *I don't want to die!* shrieked out of his mind over and
over.

Then, something happened inside his head, a thought that
he did not think.

?

Please don't let me die!
You will not die. I will not let you die.
Get me away from them!
If I go faster, you will fall.
Please! PLEASE! Take me away! And Kral knew that he was speaking to Comet's-son, and that Comet's-son heard him and understood.

Hold tighter. I will run as never before.

Ever afterward, people remarked that there was never such a race. The boy felt a surge of energy as Comet's-son leapt forward, a dream-horse flying over the ground, sparks flying from his steel shoes against the flinty soil. Kral blinked and watched the rest of the horses and riders recede. Then they passed through the riband, the cheering townspeople, continuing on slower and slower, until Kral could dislodge himself.

I—I cannot go on; you must—must let me—

No! You have to keep walking, let the heat leave you slowly!

Comet's-son stopped, but Kral pulled on the bridle and kept the horse moving.

I won't let you get overheated and die!

The townspeople came running and soon surrounded Kral and Comet's-son. The horse was thoroughly lathered, panting, stumbling. Kral ignored them all, talking quietly to the animal which had saved his life. He let Comet's-son drink only small amounts at a time, and soon was alone in the stable, currying him, watching him until he knew he was safe.

Comet's-son never raced again. None but Kral could ever mount him, and he never again went faster than a trot. And though Kral could feel Comet's-son's confidence in his care, he never felt the great horse's explicit thoughts in his mind again.

"Comet's-son knew that I was afraid," Kral said. "I begged him to save me. He heard me, he—he spoke to me. You all saw what happened!" He looked up at the silent, staring faces, and blushed.

No one laughed or jeered. "We all believe you, Kral," the old man said. "Can you do it again?"

"I don't know. There's other people here who can Speak with the horses!"

Garva stalked over to the boy. "Yes, but you're the best.

My animals know me, they obey me, they—you know! But I have never Spoken with them.''

"But I—"

"You *cannot* be afraid now. Not any more than the rest of us!"

"How easy for you to say—"

"Do I have a saber? Do we have pikes? They'll butcher me too, if they get the chance. But my anger is greater than my fear, and I want to live as much as you, but if I'm to be killed, some of them'll be joining me."

He had seized the boy's shirt and hauled him to his feet. Kral stammered; no words came out.

"We can't afford your cowardice, you sniveling—"

"Garva! He's just a boy—"

"Quiet, Glaze!"

There was silence as an ominous smell perfused the air. Garva dropped the frightened boy; stood, sniffing the acrid stillness. Suddenly they all noticed the haziness even in the dark.

"Fire!" Garva shouted, and everyone jumped for the door. "They're trying to burn us out!"

As if he had given a prearranged signal, the thin boards of the door shattered into the room as the Prince's soldiers crashed into the little space, the deadly partisans in their hands punching red holes into the nearest of the terrified peasants. Screams of pain and shrieks of fear, and above it all, Garva's wordless bellowing. He wrenched one of the short spears away from a young bravo, swung the haft below the helmet into his jaw, and began to fight his way out.

The survivors shook off their startle, picked up the debris of furniture and waded into the uniformed men. Pressed up close, the troops couldn't wield their weapons; they began to fall back. The peasants cheered with one voice, the sound of a beast of prey. Before them, a young man with his first beard gurgled his death rattle, his throat ripped by a splintered board, but he couldn't fall; he stood, his white face lolling at the trapped villagers.

Capitán Sebastian della Verruca stood with the reserves outside the barn watching in disbelief as his men were pushed out. *It must be a tactical blunder*, he thought disgustedly, *as if Sergeant Lopez could conceive of tactics*. He decided on the garrote for the cowards who had complicated such a simple assault.

He was not prepared for the sight of his men turning and running from the barefoot peasants, more than one of whom had captured weapons in their hands. In the dancing yellow light from the burning thatch, the brown men and women seemed positively gleeful. Capitán Sebastian heard the moist crunch as a huge man lunged forward, the short broad blade of his partisan piercing a soldier's skull.

Praying that his own neck might escape the embrace of the garrote, the *capitán* shouted orders and commands, his razor-sharp saber aloft in his white fist. The uniformed men fell back to a ragged formation, and instantly it was trained troops against a rabble, and the briefest pause in which the momentum of the horde drained away. The huge man in front frantically looked around and saw death in uniformed ranks before him. The peasants wavered.

With a storm of sparks and a thump, the roof collapsed inside the adobe walls, and everything became darker. Terror welled up again; the peasants turned to race into the safety of obscurity. It enraged the *capitán* that such mice had routed the men he had trained. The mice weren't even dropping their hastily captured weapons. Those had to be collected. They must! The *capitán* ordered his men to charge after them.

Running, slipping and falling and scrabbling to foot again, down the lanes of the little village, through alleys the invaders couldn't know, breathing so hard the ribs grated one against the next, sharp pains in the chest, hollows in the gut, rivers of sweat, a glimpse of some others far away, the tramping of booted feet, the death screams of the caught, yells of triumph, and more running and running, searching in the dark for the little cranny where the deadly eyes of the soldiers couldn't reach, reaching in with humiliated, furious hands, and then red steel in the gut, or the stakes planted around the makeshift castle, dreading tortures, running harder and faster, running, running . . .

Juan Carlos had built the grandest dwelling in the village, with three steps up to a wood floor; naturally he had been the first killed so that the Prince might have a decent place to sleep. A small orchard provided shade during the summer months and gave a small amount of fresh fruit for the crude fortress which the soldiers had erected beside it. There, between the foundation posts of the old home, as far from Lon Farrier's barn as he could safely flee, went Kral Raus-son, darting from tree to tree until, out of sight of the sentries, he could creep to the crawl space unseen. He pushed himself in, pulling his long legs after. Then he could be still at last, and as his panting slowed, he began to shudder with weeping. A calloused hand slapped over his mouth.

"Quiet, or we're dead," whispered a familiar voice.

"Garva!"

"We wait, and get out of here when we can."

"Where's Glaze?"

"I don't know." The big man moved, trying to settle himself more comfortably into the muck. "There's nothing to do now except wait, and try to rest."

Kral listened as Garva's breath became slower and deeper. How could he rest? Or sleep? Kral made a pillow of his hands and tried to listen for the soldiers. Eventually he heard a single tread, running toward the building and up the steps. A fist pounded on the door, and several voices muttered and shouted together. Locks clicked and the man was admitted.

"Your highness! Your highness!"

"Sergeant, get this man some water—"

"There isn't time! Your highness, the peasant conspiracy, the revolt—"

"What? What are you talking about?"

The soldier gasped out the story, tripling the number of the peasants and halving the number of troops. It was still a tale of failure, and the Prince was apoplectic. With a storm of curses he struck the soldier to the floor, called for his war clothes and his weapons and began shouting to his staff.

"Sound formation! Open the armory! I want every man armed and mounted at once! We're going to cauterize this arrogance before the infection spreads! At once! And get me that villain Sebastian now!"

The white-faced troopers ran to awaken the garrison, and in minutes hundreds of voices began hollering, complaining and commanding. In the cramped space beneath the floor, the two fugitives listened, wondering how they could survive. The shouting and the footsteps rose and then died away as the men clattered down the steps and into the fortress.

"Now's our only chance!" whispered Garva. "Follow me!"

He slid on his belly to the edge of the stubby pilings and stared out. The gates of the fortress swung open, and a wedge of lanternlight illuminated the sharpened stakes planted before it. There was already a corpse speared through the anus on one of them: Lui Morgan's-son, whose crime had been to tell the Prince the truth.

"Don't look," Garva said. "We'll go the other side."

It was much darker there and the trees gave at least a little cover. Garva muttered a plan: to get out from Juan Carlos', pass through the orchard, and escape into the village, where there would be more and better hiding places than this.

They felt emboldened just to be standing up, stretching in the night. Kral knew that Garva would fight like a champion if he had to. He still had the bloody partisan. There wasn't a safer place to be than by Garva's side. Seeing no one, they ran to the trees.

They had barely gotten to the edge of their cover when the troops came marching out of the town, straight down the dusty road toward the fortress. The two men stood frozen, seeing the severed heads on the short pikes, as they came closer to the light, thin here, streaming from inside the fortress.

Kral clutched at Garva's arm when Glaze's vacant stare turned toward them. He moaned, and Garva slammed his hand over the boy's mouth, cursing him. They waited, and saw heads turn in their direction.

"You fool!" Garva hissed. Kral felt the strong hand almost twist the jaw from his face. "I ought to kill you now!"

Several soldiers began to move toward the woods.

The fugitives squirmed a moment, trying to figure their best chances. They had no choice. As one, they spun around and ran.

The soldiers shouted and the rest of the troops charged.

The plains around the fortress offered no concealment at all, so all Kral and Garva could do was head around the stockade, straight toward the adobe walls, and try to outrun the killers.

The shouting and running alerted the sentries, who peered into the night, and seeing little, sent more men out of the compound to quell the disorder, which could only further madden their already enraged sovereign. Mounted men galloped out to help the foot soldiers.

Garva and Kral sped into the labyrinth of scaffolding and

piles of freshly dried adobes which had been cast for building
the new stables. They were exhausted. There was nowhere
else to go.

"We have to fight here," Garva said. "I can take at least
three of the dogs. Here's where you can pretend to have the
courage you lack. There's nothing else."

Horses whinnied behind them, and the sounds of men
harnessing their mounts, too loud in the middle of the night,
too loud for the men inside to hear the butchery to come. Kral
found a rake handle on the ground. There were no other
weapons.

From a distance, the soldiers and the two peasants saw
each other. The soldiers slowed to walk, savoring the kill to
come, as Garva and Kral walked backward, until they felt the
rough adobe walls against their shoulders.

"Even if you kill us, there are thousands more just like me
behind every bush! If not this month, then next! Save your-
selves and go home!" He brandished his weapon.

Someone laughed, and a voice called, "You know how to
use that thing?"

"Come forward and find out!" Garva waited. "Come
forward, you craven, stinking cowards!"

Three spears arched through the night. Garva batted one of
them away, but the other two struck home, one in the thigh,
the other straight into his paunch. "Kral, the horses!" he
cried, and toppled into the dirt.

As the soldiers moved to grab him, Kral dropped his stick
and leapt with all his strength for the top of the adobes. His
fingertips caught the crumbly edge, and as spears clattered
against the dried mud, missing him, he pulled himself up and
over, into the forbidden stables of the Prince.

The horses had all been jammed together, with no space
for them to move at all. Kral dropped to his knees and ran
between the spindly legs of the beasts, close to the back wall.
He was too afraid to stand, terrified, alone, the soldiers all
about. His knees shook, and the sweat poured from him, and
at every human voice he shuddered and farted, waiting for the
sharp steel to cut him in half.

Why are you afraid, young one? came a thought into his
mind.

Kral jumped. "Who—who speaks?" he quavered.

I do, came the strange thought again. *You are Comet's-son's friend.*

Help me! Kral sobbed.

I don't know what you want. What do you want?

Don't let the soldiers kill me!

I am afraid of the soldiers, too. They put the steel in my mouth to cut me, and prick my flanks with the steel on their boots, until I bleed.

But you're so much bigger than they are!

If I throw them off, they tie me and beat me.

Please help me!

Gauntlet-shod hands grabbed the boy and jerked him up. With a wordless wail he struggled as the men twisted his wrists behind his back. The horses all around them began stamping and snorting, and the soldiers shoved through them to seize the doomed thrall.

With kicks and sharp stabs they forced Kral into the paddock, where the officers waited, already mounted. At the center of them sat the Prince.

The haft of a lance smashed into Kral's shoulder, and he fell to his knees.

"Conspirator!" the Prince called. Kral looked up. "Impale him!"

"No! Please, dear gods, no!"

The few unmounted men grabbed Kral and dragged him to the gate. Beyond, the sharpened posts stood in silent rows.

What are they going to do?

"Don't let them put me on the stake! I beg you! Help me!"

The soldiers laughed. "Who are you talking to, you little wimp? The horses?" They laughed some more.

We will try, Comet's-son's friend. We need you to help us, too.

The Prince's huge horse began neighing and twitching, stamping and prancing. Kral turned and for the briefest moment caught the eye of the beast and knew in his soul that this was the horse he had Spoken with. He wept, begging destiny for this chance.

The Prince had lost control of his mount. His long crop thrashed down again and again, but the horse paid no attention. Finally it kicked out at Don Arturo's mount, who likewise snorted and began to buck.

The mounts, whom the soldiers had thought so well trained, all began to rear and scream. A few riders were thrown, but most stayed on, raging at the horses and trying to master them. Then they began to run.

Kral was forgotten as the crazed beasts began to circle inside the fortress walls. Around and around they went, the riders hauling on useless reins.

What should we do with them, friend?

Take them away! The gate! Take them through the gate!

The Prince's horse pulled away from the swarming mass, leaping and screaming. Kral saw the man clutching the mane with both hands, his legs flopping against the saddle, as terrified as the peasant he had doomed minutes before.

In a flash, Kral saw that he was master of an army, too—an equine army. And he knew what Garva would have done. He was safe amid the horses.

"Follow me!" he yelled, running alongside the tide of horse flesh. He pushed through, beaten by the hooves and shoulders of the animals, feeling no pain, but exulting in freedom, and the strength of his allies.

The horses charged through the gate. Before them rose the stakes, their white points gleaming.

"Now!" screamed Kral. "Throw them off! Now!"

The Prince, aghast, heard that voice of command and stared for a heartbeat at the youth he had condemned. Then his horse went berserk. He held on as tight as he could, but his strength was too puny, and with a desperate, futile grab for the horn of his saddle, he felt himself lofted into the air. There was a moment of peace, and then searing, unimaginable pain as he came gut first down upon a cottonwood spear. His screams were lost in the noise of men and horses. Those who looked saw two feet of reddened wood penetrating the man's back, and his wretched thrashing and kicking.

The horses saw and understood. Rider after hapless rider found himself charging into the array of stakes and then facing a hellish tortured death. Those who hit the ground died faster, beneath iron-shod hooves.

Kral ran among the riderless horses, the knife of a dead man in his hand, cutting the bridles off as fast as he could. The sound of riot and war had summoned the villagers, and soon Kral saw other friends, two-leg friends, coming fearlessly into the stampede, to kill the few invaders who managed to remain on their feet.

Then it was over and the horses slowed their manic battle. Not one of the Prince's men would survive to see the dawn. The villagers were free. It was hard to believe.

Slowly they came together in two quiet groups, the horses and the people. The peasants watched as Kral went up to the huge horse the Prince had once had the arrogance to ride.

Thank you for saving me, he Spoke. *You saved everyone here. We all thank you.*

The one who rode me killed your friend, because your friend would not let him ride.

Comet's-son?

Yes.

Kral stood silently. There was nothing to say.

We learned that we need not obey the iron in our mouths. Tell the other two-legs that. We would be friends and allies, not servants.

Kral did so.

Is it true that there are tribes above the Sun where we and the two-legs all Speak as you and I do?

I have heard it, but I don't know.

We wish to look for them. I'll take you with me, on my back, if you wish.

Kral Raus-son considered it. Raus had long since died, and his mother too. His friend and mentor, Glaze, had been murdered. And Garva, who would have been his friend if he had lived through this night. Who or what was there to keep him here at Peony and Phlox?

I'll go, Kral Spoke unhesitatingly. *I'm not afraid.*

The Swordsman Smada

by John Steakley

John Steakley has led a busy life. He has been a stock-car racer, a semipro football player, a private detective, an actor, a car salesman, and, of course, a writer. He has been writing for the movies for the last nine years, has completed one novel, *Armor*, and is awaiting publication of another, entitled *Vampires*.

It made sense that we were there.

It just made sense. That's how come we could accept it so easily. It was where we were *supposed* to be. It just made *sense*.

At least, that's what we thought before the slaughter began.

Lanny and me—that's Lanny Weaver, my best friend— were big into the Horseclans like you can't believe. Like even I can't believe, looking back on it. We ate 'em and drank 'em and *talked* 'em! God, how we *talked* 'em! We'd stay up all *night* all the *time* talking Horseclans stuff. And of course we always ended up talking about how neat it would be to really be there, really *live* in that world. To know Bili the Axe personally and hang out with him. And Milo. We wanted to meet Milo Morai more than anybody, of course. But we didn't really care if we never even saw him if we could just *be there*! Hot damn! Really be there! Carrying swords and petting prairiecats and wenching and just traveling around kicking ass whenever we wanted to without any cops or anybody to bug us. The Horseclans world was infinitely better than our own, we believed, and we talked about that a lot, too.

We dressed like 'em, too. We had tunics and stuff. And chain mail made special by some retired army tank guy in Richmond, Virginia. And swords, too, made by the same dude. We had everything. Really. Daggers and stuff. Wineskins. Leggings.

And we wore them. At science fiction conventions and at meetings of our club and at SCA tournaments, which is really how all this happened. What, as Lanny said, "tipped us over the edge."

Anyway . . . you know what the SCA is? The Society for Creative Anachronism? If you know about Horseclans you probably know about them. But anyway, the SCA are a bunch of folks heavy into medieval life-styles. They dress up like those days, women too, and they have big feasts and tournaments where knights fight to establish the pecking order and determine who the king is. The king is the best fighter of everybody and he gets his choice of queen, which is sorta how the trouble got started, except Lanny and me weren't trying to be king—it wasn't that big a tournament. We were just trying to get laid.

You see, there were these two new girls just moved to town. They were sisters and they were . . . well, dynamite-looking. Gorgeous. And sexy, too. Really sexy. Blondes. I've always loved blondes. Lanny, too. So we set out to win their hands in trial by combat. And they'd made it real clear that it could be done. Win more than their hands, if you get what I'm driving at. Oh, those two were really something. They had us huffing and puffing. And they were eating it up the whole time. They had every dude in the club ready to kill himself—or anybody else—to get some of what they were offering. And the girls loved that, too. The funny thing was, we didn't care. I mean, we knew what it said about those two if they liked causing all that trouble and strife and the rest of it. But we didn't care. They would smile these smug little smiles—dimples and the rest—and then wag away real slow and we'd just stand there like idiots until they were out of sight.

And then we'd go practice like crazy. Huffing and puffing and pawing the ground.

Then the tournament came. It was in the spring and everything was real and pretty and we were all camped out in the country with trailers and tents and stuff. It was really nice.

Sunshine and green grass and long flowing dresses and the like.

And we—Lanny and me—we were ready. Ready and psyched up and, most important of all, in shape. We had been working out together all winter long. Before the two sisters even showed up, even. I mean—we were ready.

And then the Incredible Hulk showed up and entered the tournament.

We called him the Incredible Hulk because . . . well, if you'd seen him you would too. His real name was Something Jones but he went by Bubba.

No kidding. Bubba.

But the point is, he was as big as a house. Slow as hell. Much slower than Lanny and me—but then that was our big deal, speed, and always had been. We were faster than any of the rest of them. And strong, like I said, because we were in shape from working out all that time. Stronger than most and faster than anybody and . . .

And it didn't help. Bubba pounded us both. Badly. I mean, really. We must've struck him ten times for every time he hit us, but the thing is, every time he hit one of us we'd bounce. It was frustrating as hell. Not to mention painful. Of course, you really couldn't get hurt too badly with masking-taped cane swords. All the weapons had to be taped up heavily. That was part of the rules. Nobody wanted to get skewered. But, see, that was the point. While we were getting dribbled by this guy we kept thinking: If this was *real*, we'd have killed him ten minutes ago.

But none of that made any difference. Bubba won and won so decisively that he got *both* sisters and then to top it all off was loud and obnoxious about it and then rude and crude to the girls, and you know what? They didn't even seem to mind. They let him get away with it. He was a jerk and clumsy and loud, but . . .

But he had *won*.

Dammit!

The party afterward wasn't much fun. Lanny and I spent most of it gritting our teeth. Oh, we were nice and all—what choice did we have? But it wasn't much fun. Maybe it was that awful mead stuff we were drinking that somebody had made in his garage. Or maybe it was watching Bubba feeling up both girls in public.

Anyway, we left. Supposedly to go back to our trailer and get the tequila, but mostly just to get away from the rest and talk.

Only we didn't. We sat there across from each other, both covered with grass stains and humiliation, and didn't say a word for several minutes.

Then Lanny spoke: "Mr. Felix?"

"Yes, Mr. Weaver?"

"Let's get dressed."

I grinned, said: "Yeah!"

And we did. Put on our best tunics, not the junk we wore for tournaments. The realistic stuff. The chain mail and the rest.

And the real swords. And the real daggers.

And then we opened the bottle of tequila and took a swig apiece, toasting ourselves, and stepped outside.

It was the next part that I don't understand. I mean, there was a lot of it I didn't understand at the time and still don't. But what happened next has always been a mystery to me. I mean, how could we be so stupid and naive not to . . .

Anyway, we stepped outside into the darkness and headed toward the campfire and the rest of the party. They were singing over there and laughing and sparks were climbing up flickering above them and they all seemed to be having a great time, and suddenly we didn't want any part of it. We turned without a word and stepped into the woods to get drunk on our own.

We sure did that—get drunk, I mean. Just Lanny and me and the branches up against the stars and the tequila bottle. And our voices, of course. Because we were having our same old conversation in no time at all. About the Horseclans world and how we wanted to be there. Hell, by now we were so drunk it was how we *deserved* to be there and *ought* to be there and other things so terrifyingly stupid that even now when I think about it I cringe.

But at the time it all made perfect sense. I mean that: *perfect* sense. There was something especially strident and clear about that night with Lanny and me all alone in those woods with our dreams and tequila. More than those things should've added up to. And we felt it.

We didn't *say* we felt it. We never acknowledged it out

loud. We didn't have to. It was there. I could see it in his grin.

We ended up sacrificing the last third of the tequila to the Horseclans God, which is just as well, seeing as how we were already so drunk we couldn't hardly move. But we made it a real solemn deal, praising His vision of glory and honor and combat. We ended it by making a formal request to be allowed to go there.

Then we sat down.

Then we passed out.

And when we woke up, we were there.

And, for the life of me, I still don't understand why we weren't scared! God knows we should have been.

Soon, very soon, we were. But not soon enough.

The man astride the horse was a very serious piece of work. It wasn't so much what he was wearing as how he was wearing it. Everything from the broadsword to the piercing stare was real. Real!

"I said, 'Stand aside!' Must I assist you?" boomed out through his graying goatee, and only then did I realize he had spoken before. It had been his voice that had waked me up.

Us up, I mean. Lanny was there a few feet away, sprawled as I was on the dusty thing that passed for a road.

I looked at him. "I don't believe this is happening!"

Lanny's eyes were as fierce and blazing as his red hair in the sun. "*Sure* you do!" he replied. And grinned.

He was right, of course. I did believe it. And, God help all fools, loved it.

"Lads!" boomed out from the same place as the rider spurred his horse forward between us. We scrambled out of the way.

Lanny was a lot quicker than me, as usual.

"Beg pardon, m'lord. We did not mean to impede your journey. We were momentarily dazed by—"

"By drink, from the look of you," snarled the rider. But he pulled his horse up and turned it about to face us. I noticed then how foamy it was. He must have had quite a trip himself.

"Nay, good sir. Bewitched!"

The rider's gaze narrowed even further, if that were possible. Lanny chose to ignore it. He stepped forward and started

to babble a tale about how we were both good men and true
and fine swordsmen from good families, clans, he said, and
had been waylaid by a wicked sorceress who had taken
offense at our nobly attempting to rescue a fair damsel from
her clutches—which we had managed to do despite a fearsome
struggle and great personal loss to ourselves. But then the
witch was so offended by our interference that she loosed
upon us one demon after another, which we barely managed
to escape each time, so then the witch cast a spell which
flung us from our homelands (after first robbing us of all our
coins) to this very spot where he found us just now, alone,
penniless, lost, but without a single regret at having done the
right thing—nay, the only thing a true gentleman and swordsman could have done.

It was great shit.

Even better, it looked like it was going to be effective shit.
The rider sat silently throughout the entire tirade, seeming to
eat it up. And I figured it was going to work. "It" being
whatever the hell it was Lanny was trying to scam.

Then the man started laughing. He laughed and laughed
and laughed and laughed. He laughed so hard tears flowed
down his cheeks and his great belly rolled like a waterbed.
He laughed so hard it wasn't even embarrassing after a while.
Well, not completely.

When he finally got control of himself, he spoke.

"What are your names, lads?"

"Lanny Weaver, m'lord."

"Brad Felix, m'lord."

"Odd names you have."

Lanny just smiled. "Did I not just tell you of our having
been whisked away from our native lands? In our world, our
names are— "

The man held up a hand in a firm gesture. "Aye, lad. I did
hear your tale. And enjoy it much." He smiled. And then the
smile went away in a flash. "But I do not wish to hear it
anew."

It was not a request. Lanny and I looked at each other,
nodded, said: "Yes, m'lord," in unison.

The man leaned back in his saddle and rested a hand lightly
on the hilt of his broadsword. It was not necessarily a threatening gesture. It was just to get our attention.

"You lads are indeed far from home. Young men seeking

your fortune. Seeking adventure and amusement. Lost and poor, no doubt, due to some foolish trusting of a clever wench. I know not how you came to be fast asleep on the road, and care not.'' He paused, looked pained. Then he smiled rather paternally. ''Indeed, I know not why I should care about you at all, such as you are. But I was young once. And foolish.'' Then he peered right at us as he added: ''And a liar.''

We knew better than to take offense. Lanny even knew enough to smile.

The man nodded, satisfied, and went on. ''So I shall offer you employment. It so happens I am in temporary need of a few extra swords in my personal guard. Have you horses?''

''Nay, m'lord,'' Lanny replied.

The man sighed. ''I thought not.'' He paused for a moment. An idea seemed to occur to him. ''It matters not. Several of my riders shall be along on this road. They have been lagging behind due to laziness and sloth. Tell them you are of my personal guard and are to take two of their freshest mounts. Then I shall expect you to catch up to me on this same road by sundown.'' He leaned down toward us and his voice got hard. ''By sundown, lads. I'll be damned if I shall put two wastrels afoot just to horse two more. Is that clear?''

''Aye, m'lord.''

''Aye, m'lord.''

''For your sakes I hope it is.''

''M'lord?'' Lanny asked next. ''Could we not have you name as well?''

''Trebor Smada.''

''Trevor Smada,'' I mispronounced.

''That is Tre*bor*, lad! Not . . . whatever it was you said. You would do well not to get my name backward.''

I was thinking that missing only one letter hardly consisted of getting it backward when suddenly two coins were spinning into the air, one toward each of us. Lanny caught his in the air with one hand. It took me two hands and some juggling, but at least I didn't disgrace myself by dropping it. And then, of course, I did drop it. I bent down, red-faced, and picked it up.

Smada was already on his way down the road. ''That's to seal our contract. Perform well and faithfully and there will be more. Much more.'' He started cantering away. Lanny shouted after him.

"Lord Smada! How will we know these men with the horses?"

Without even slowing down, Smada boomed back over his shoulder: "Take the first two horses from anyone seeking Trebor Smada!" he shouted and then was gone around the bend.

Lanny and I were the ones really around the damned bend. We had bought the whole thing. We spent the next hour congratulating ourselves for having conned a job right off. Idiots! Stupid, trusting, numskulled idiots!

Oh, there had been a con, all right. But we hadn't even *seen* it. We just stood there on that road, like the dumb shits we were, waiting to die.

It was a couple of hours before anybody showed up on the road. Somehow Lanny and I managed to spend that time getting deeper into trouble. It started off innocently enough, though. We were just sitting there grinning at each other and noticing how pretty everything was.

Because it really was. I mean, gorgeous. The sky was so blue, the trees so green and pretty. Everything. The woods, the smell of the air. Even the dust of the road was somehow just right.

Us, too. I felt terrific. I felt healthy and . . . pure. I had even lost my desire for cigarettes. Well, my craving, anyway. After a while we noticed our clothes were different than they had been. The same, too. That is, they looked the same. But different. More realistic. Zippers, for example, had been replaced by buttons somehow.

It was neat.

In fact, I realized I felt as good as I ever had. I felt like I belonged. Oh, we had no excuses.

A thought occurred to me after the first half hour.

"Lanny?"

"Yeah."

"I don't think this is the Horseclans world."

Lanny laughed. "Of course it is. It's perfect."

"I know. That's the trouble."

Lanny laughed again. "What do you think it is?"

"I dunno. A movie."

"Huh?"

"That's what it feels like."

It did. It was too perfect. And I should have started to get scared right then with that thought. And maybe I did feel a little something, but then I got sidetracked when Lanny started talking again. This time it was about how we had to establish ourselves right away with these "peon types coming up the road." The idea, according to Lanny (and, to be fair, I liked it, too), was that we had to set these dudes straight. These and all the rest we met. Two kinds of people in this kinda place: the nobles and the gophers. And we were in no mood to gopher anything. Therefore we had to let everybody know right away that we expected to be treated like the upper-crust types we were.

"And," Lanny added, "what's the best way to get treated with respect?"

"Overtip the bartenders?"

"C'mon, Felix. Be serious."

"Sorry. How then?"

"Act like you expect it, dummy. Act like you're used to giving orders instead of taking them. You know, a little arrogant."

Which made perfect sense to me. I was already a little arrogant, feeling as good as I did.

So, anyway, that's how Lanny and I managed to get in trouble before anything even started.

Like I said before: no excuses.

An hour later they came around the trees riding at a slow walk. They looked tired and dusty and out of breath. About like Smada. Only these guys were a helluva lot less impressive. For one thing, Smada had been a big guy. Hard to tell when somebody's sitting a horse, but I'd guessed he was at least six three and two hundred fifty pounds or so. These guys were short. Five eight tops. We probably outweighed them by twenty pounds each.

They didn't even look particularly suspicious when we stepped into the road and held up our hands to stop them.

But why should they have been scared? They had no way of knowing how stupid we were.

They weren't too bright, either, thank God. They were off their horses and gratefully guzzling from the wineskins we offered before even asking who we were. I tasted the wine myself in turn. We had left with Robert Mondavi Table Red.

This was something awful and realistic. The riders seemed to like it well enough.

And then the shit started.

It didn't take much. One second we were all standing there smiling and drinking and the next second there were swords flashing in the sun. We didn't even get around to mentioning about taking their horses. We just introduced ourselves and told 'em who we worked for.

Gordon, the only one whose name I got, choked on his swig of wine. He stared at us.

"Trebor Smada?"

"The same," replied Lanny smugly. "We're his personal guards."

And then the one closest to me, not Gordon, had his sword out and was swinging with both hands right at my head, and I ducked instinctively and yelled, "*Hey*, watch it!" and stepped inside his guard and grabbed his wrists and said, "What the hell do you think you're doing, prick?"

And you know what? He just stared at me for a second. Totally unbelieving. But why shouldn't he be surprised I hadn't just immediately attacked back at him? He didn't know anything about stupid twentieth-century young-punk parking-lot slugfests. He didn't know anything about would-be posturing machismo. He lived in this world. If you fought then you fought. And if you won you lived and the other guy died.

In his world you didn't spend twenty minutes first standing around saying, "You better watch out, buddy, or else," while you took turns shoving each other in the chest until other friends came in to pull you two apart.

He was going to kill me. Just like that. And the fact that I didn't seem to know that startled him. Which is probably why when he ignored my idiotic grip on his wrists and flicked his blade at my face he didn't do it hard enough to cut my head off.

But his edge cut the shit out of my cheek. I stepped back and put my gloved hand up there, where the cheek stung. My glove came away bloody, and I lost it.

Which is what saved my life. I could just as easily have run away screaming. Instead I got mad and lived.

My sword was suddenly in my hand, bigger than his, and so was I, and swinging at him. There was a burst of sparks and a godawful clang I'd never heard before outside of a movie, but I didn't stop to think about it—I just swung again, swung so hard and missed him so completely that I lost my balance and fell forward just as his first thrust sliced through, not my skin, but my hair.

That scared me. It also pissed me off. I growled and screamed and leapt to my feet, swinging again as hard as I could. He blocked me easily enough, parried me well the second time, but I was just too strong for him. Too strong and too mad and too scared and too adrenaline-zapped to be stopped. I broke down his guard with the sheer force of my blows. Broke his guard and then a rib and then when he stood there staggering I laid into him with both hands toward his throat, but I was too excited and too a-jumple to get it right. My blade got turned in my hand, and the flat of it hit him in the nose with a mighty *whack* and he sat down right where he was and keeled over.

I stood there a second puffing and staring until I heard a groan and a clump and saw Lanny tripping backward over his own feet, his sword flying over his head, and Gordon above him bracing his back foot for a quick thrust, and somehow I was right there behind him and slamming the hilt of my sword against the back of his neck, only I missed this time, too, and there was a truly awful crunch as the pommel bashed a hole in the skull and he died before he could fall.

Then he did fall, and I stood there, knees wobbly, until I sat down with a sudden plop and looked at the sight of that mashed gray and bloody head.

"Lanny! Lanny, I think I killed him!" I wailed, and the tears were already coming to my eyes.

Lanny was a lot cooler. Always had been. He was already back on his feet and retrieving his sword before he said: "Don't worry. He would've died anyway." Lanny shoved the body over with his foot, and I saw the blood. Lanny had been doing pretty well after all. The man's thigh was cut almost to the bone. What do you call that artery? The femoral?

I got pretty sick. After that I stayed crouched there beside the road on my hands and knees while Lanny made purposeful movements around me. I wanted to help, knew I should, but just couldn't stand to look at them right then, particularly after seeing that my guy was a lot more than knocked out. Seems I'd driven the nose straight back into his head.

Shit.

I stayed out of it until I felt Lanny pressing a cloth against my bloody cheek and putting my hand up to hold it there. It stung from the wine he'd soaked it with. But that made sense. Alcohol to kill the germs, like in the movies. And fortunately, the resulting infection wasn't serious.

I didn't really have it together until a few minutes later when we were already astride the horses, and moving down the road. Lanny's voice was sort of a dull irritation at first until I started paying attention to the individual words and realized he was trying to bring me out of the shock by reminding me of the point of the whole deal.

Such as: We had wanted to be here. We had wanted to kick ass. We had.

Plus: They had started it.

After a while it started to work, bless him. He got me calmed down and then coherent, and then even I started to look back with satisfaction on what I'd done. Only then, when I realized I'd broken every fencing rule I'd ever known and *still* gotten away with it, did I get really scared the way I should have been all along.

I had to stop my horse and get sick again. Lanny sneered and looked disgusted, but an hour later he had to do the same thing.

But that seemed to work it out of us, damn our silly hides. That seemed to settle us down. A couple of hours later, I'll be damned if we weren't grinning and cocky again.

Incredible.

"Wait a minute!" Lanny said suddenly, and pulled his horse up short.

"What?"

"We were set up! Smada set us up."

My reply showed how it had been done. "Huh?" I muttered.

"And we fell for it! Dammit! We were so busy trying to impress him we didn't even see what he was doing. He wasn't hiring us. He was using us to slow down whoever those guys were that were chasing him. Don't you see? He was running away from them. And he suckered us into buying him some extra time." He stared at me, his face furious with anger. "You get it, Felix?"

I did. Too late. Way too late. But I got it. Finally.

"Hey!" I burst out. "We've got to get off this road. If there are any more and they find those bodies in the ditch . . ."

Lanny was way ahead of me again. "Not only that, there's Smada."

"Whaddya mean?"

"He said he'd meet us down this road. I guarantee you that means he's on another one. We gotta go cross-country until we find him."

"Okay. Which way?"

"Guess."

And I did, and once more dumb luck (or, thinking back on it, maybe something else) worked. We not only found the other road, we came across it at the inn with Smada's horse corralled outside.

Along the way an odd thing happened. I asked Lanny if he was sure we wanted to find Smada. He looked at me funny and said of course we did and I let it go. Because it was true. I really did want to find Smada. Supposedly to teach him a lesson for messing with us. But in my heart I knew better, and so did Lanny, though neither of us admitted it.

We wanted to find Smada. But not to fight him. We wanted to find him to brag about what we'd done.

See what I mean? We were slow learners.

The fight started when, somewhere knee-deep into the party, I turned to the innkeeper and asked to use his phone. Don't know what possessed me to do that. The thing is, there was this dude standing at the bar between Lanny and me when I said this, a real jerk this guy, and . . . well, as soon as the words were out of my mouth I realized how silly it was, being where we were and all, and Lanny did too, and we looked at each other and started laughing. And this obnoxious dude, who had been spoiling for a fight all night long, thought we were laughing at *him*, and the next thing I knew I was fighting again.

Which was okay with me. The guy had pissed me off long ago when he'd been messing with Smada, and even though I was just stumbling into it more or less unexpectedly, it was all right, it was okay, I was ready.

Thinking back, we stumbled into the whole mess. And then stumbled from one step to the next. Like the inn, itself.

Thinking back, we didn't enter that inn at all. We dove

into it headfirst. Dove into it like it was the ultimate hot tub, steamy smoky air and spilling wine and healthy fun-smelly wenches and roaring fires and roaring laughter and loud music and barking dogs and gritty cool stone floors ideally positioned to catch you when you fell over with a mug to your lips.

It was a wonderful place. Truly. Exactly as I'd always imagined such a place to be. I mean *exactly*. Which shoulda made me wonder, only I was too busy having fun to think to be scared.

We didn't have any trouble with Smada. We stomped in to confront him, and there he was, pillowed in a corner like a sultan with wenches framed all about him and servant types fetching and carrying. And the first thing anybody said was me saying: "What happened to you?" Because lying there like that instead of astride that huge mount of his he looked so, I dunno, *un*formidable.

Underrating Smada was, without doubt, one of the major mistakes we made. Bad as it was, though, we managed to compound it later on.

The argument we had stated our intentions of having never got very far. For one thing, our hearts weren't much in it, and for another . . . well, he looked so goddam. jolly there on those pillows filling his hands with whores and his belly with wine. We didn't want to fight him. We wanted to join him.

We did.

Smada, reading us like a book as always, laughingly pointed out that it was *we* who had begun by trying to con *him*, which was true. And it was *we* who had begun the day without a cent but had ended it safe, healthy, blooded, rich (from the coins Lanny had taken from the bodies) and mounted. So what had we to complain about?

Put that way, nothing. We laughed and looked a bit sheep-faced, I guess, and then we joined right in. It was wonderful. There were all *kinds* of folks there. It was one of the biggest inns in the territory and situated well along the major trade routes. There were merchants with their entourages and young swordsman types like Lanny and me and old swordsman types like Smada. One of them, the general, a big old tough dude with a full beard and scars, turned out to know some-body who knew somebody who was a cousin of somebody Smada knew well before she died, and on the basis of that intimacy the two decided to combine parties at once, and within an hour the old general and his bunch, along with Smada trailing us, had all but taken over the place.

All but. There was this obnoxious punk I mentioned before who was feeling left out, I guess, on account of our bunch having bought up all half-dozen whores for the evening or maybe just because he knew what a jerk he was and was embarrassed about it. Or both, I dunno.

Anyway, he went out of his way to make a big deal of it when Smada, quite by accident, bumped into him on the way to the outhouse and spilled his tankard of ale.

Smada apologized. Profusely. More profusely than I would have, and a lot more than I expected him to. But the punk still wasn't satisfied.

"If the old man is too befuddled by drink to make true his steps, then he had best learn greater care in a public inn or someone else will leap to instruct him."

And I thought: Whoops! Here it comes! And I was looking at Lanny, who was already looking for *his* sword.

But all Smada did was bow and say: "An excellent point, young sir."

And my mouth just sorta fell open. But there was more to come. The punk kept pressing it.

"Perhaps, old man, I shall trouble myself to give you this lesson here and now, lest you forget the point that must be made."

And I thought: Here we go for sure! Smada will *never* take that!

But while I was thinking that, he was doing that very thing. With another bow, he said: "A generous notion, young sir. But I fear the very drink which provoked my unfortunate mishap might further besmear my appreciation for your kind instruction."

I couldn't believe it. But there was more still. When the punk was still standing there uncertain about what to do, Smada groveled some more.

"Pray, young sir, perhaps another time when I am not so clumsy with wine?"

And the punk stared. Then he nodded, abruptly and rude as hell, and just turned away back to the bar. Smada waited a beat and then trod on off to the can.

Lanny and I looked at each other. He was the first to speak.

"That chickenshit old fart!" he hissed. "Can you believe that?"

"No, dammit!" I replied in the same harsh whisper. "And we thought he was such a big deal!"

"Well," Lanny mused, "he was the first swordsman we found. I guess that's why we thought he was something. And on that big horse and all. Dammit!" he muttered a few seconds later. "I just hate being embarrassed for people."

And I nodded to that.

Later on when Smada reappeared from the outhouse we had trouble looking in his direction. But, interestingly enough, no one else did. We assumed it was because no one else had seen it. Lanny and I *had* been the closest ones to the exchange. And the party hadn't stopped at all while it was going on. So we just figured nobody else had noticed.

Wrong again.

With everybody else apparently immune to the tension, Lanny and I felt it was pretty hard for us to maintain it. And Smada really was the life of the party. In no time at all we were right back into the swing of things.

We thought. Hell, we *never* picked up on the rhythm of that place!

It was storytime that did it. Smada insisted on a story, and the old general echoed his sentiments loudly, and then the girls cheered and encouraged the idea. The first guy was this little short thin jester type, the old general's official storyteller. He cranked out this tale about—who else?—Bili of Morguhn, and then another one about the legend of the Undying One, who Lanny and I knew damn well was none other than good ol' Milo but nobody else considered anything but a fairy tale.

Then it was our side's turn. And Lanny did *The Mummy*.

No fooling. He did the whole damn movie. Got a bunch of white cloth and wrapped it around his head and legs. He had one wrist tied to his chest and the other arm stretched out in front of him reaching for victims' throats and dragging the one dead leg behind him and the whole bit. It was great. And the people at the inn absolutely ate it up. The whores squealed and held each other and us when the mummy snatched the beautiful archaeologist's daughter and everybody cheered like hell when the evil Egyptian got zapped by his own monster.

Lanny was a tremendous hit. He should've been a writer.

After that was singing and dancing by the whores. It was, trust me, worth seeing. By the time the food came I was so horny my mug shook. But the food took care of that. I use the term "food" loosely.

Ate something they said was owl and tasted like one—that or anything else that had stayed up several nights in a row. Probably drinking that ale stuff the whole time. Let me tell you about that ale: It was no Budweiser. Though it probably would sell well in Milwaukee or anyplace else where they have trouble starting their cars on icy mornings. A little shot of that shit in the carburetor and "Zoom, *zoom*!"

The wine was—how shall I put this?—worse. In fact, the whole meal gave me a Big Mac Attack. I remember thinking about all the preservative fuss always going on back home and thinking that Ralph Nader, who had never manufactured anything and never would, didn't know what a glory he had.

Anyway, the men got to dance after that. Lanny and I needed to do something to work this stuff through our tummies. And we got into it full steam. We sang and danced and fell over benches and laughed so hard we couldn't organize arms and legs enough to get back up, and *that* only made us laugh all the more and on and on and on.

It was a blast.

About then is when I asked to use the phone and Lanny and I started laughing and the punk who had backed Smada down (*we* thought) got upset and demanded to know what was so bloody amusing and stupid me said he probably wouldn't understand it.

A lot of it was the booze I had downed, and a lot of it was the women watching. Some of it had to do with Smada being (in our minds, at least) such a weasel to this punk before. Maybe I just wanted to show how much neater I was. Or something.

At any rate, I said what I said knowing damn well the punk wasn't going to like it. And, sure as hell, he got mad and pushed off from me at the bar and reached for his sword. At first I thought it was just a bluff. I mean, he was moving so damn slowly! But then I got a look at his face and it was plenty grim enough to make this serious. Then I realized my sword wasn't on but over there across the room with the pillows and the whores, and by this time his, the punk's, was almost out.

So I slugged him.

Clouted him good with an overhead gauntlet-fisted right cross right on the button, and he careened back against the bar and sat down with a plop. There were the usual gasps and cheers associated with a barroom brawl. Because that's all this was all of a sudden, on account of having hit him with my fist. The punk was hep to that, too. He loosed his swordbelt to the floor where he was and came up swinging.

At least you could call it that. I'm pretty fast, like I said before, but he was so goddam *slow!* His first roundhouse missed me by days and left him staggering in a circle three feet past me.

That got a big laugh.

So I decided to get cute. The next time he swung and missed I ducked underneath his arm and tapped him on the shoulder from behind and said: "Here I am!"

That got boos. No kidding. The crowd was ugly. I'd never been in front of an audience before, but it was clear to me that making fun of your victim was a definite no-no. Lanny's look told me he'd read the same attitude. So I set about finishing it.

Which was damned hard. He was slow as hell and no bigger than me, but he just kept coming. I'd jab him and punch him and knock him staggering or, more rarely, knock him down. But he just kept coming. I was really starting to admire the guy, all bloody and puffy and nose broken but not giving in an inch.

The only time he hit me was when, like an idiot, I stopped right in front of him, held out my paw to shake and said: "C'mon, man, let's call it a draw." He ignored my hand and hit me so hard you can't believe it. I felt the stones smack the back of my head and looked up kinda dazed to Lanny peering over me and hissing, his voice furious with anger and concern: "Finish this, goddammit! You're not at *home!*"

And that kinda woke me up. I laid into him hard and kept at it. But it was getting a lot tougher. My right hand was swollen and sore, and I've never had a decent left, and the punk was still coming on.

I remembered Lanny saying, "This isn't home," and realiz-

ing the naked fatal facts of that. I *wasn't* home. I wasn't
anywhere else but where I was, and this was not only happening, it was gonna keep on happening until it ended. That
thought, and the punk still coming on, got me a little scared.

Which is what I damn well should have been all along.

The first time I kicked him I got a few more boos, but by
that time I didn't give a shit. *I* was the one doing the fighting,
and nothing else had seemed to work. So I kicked him some
more, once in the chest and once toward his balls. I missed his
balls—you almost always do—but his groaning wince as my
booted toe slammed into his thigh muscles opened up his
bloody face again. I tried one more right cross, laying all my
weight and momentum in behind it, and missed his chin and
hit his throat and felt something awful go crunch and col-
lapse, and then he was down and turning blue and wheezing
and everybody tried to help but they couldn't get the wind-
pipe clear in time and all of a sudden I had killed someone
else.

It was quiet while they drug the body out and Lanny sat me
down on a bench in front of Smada and the old general and
the girls. Smada was clearly disgusted by something, and for
a while I thought it was because it had taken me so long. And
then I thought maybe it was on account of my using my feet.
And then I didn't know *what* the hell was bugging him and
was starting to get a little pissed off myself and said so:

"You got something to say to me, old man?" I snarled,
calling him what the punk had called him on purpose. "Then
say it!" I added.

Smada sat up and eyed me coolly. "Very well, lad," he
began, and leaned forward and put his hands on his knees. "I
don't know where *you* are from. But in this land there are far
too few opportunities to be gentle instead of murderous." He
paused, looked disgusted, added: "And you have just wasted
one."

Then he stood up and went to the outhouse.

Conversations lamely shuffled ahead after he had gone.
Lanny sat down beside me and handed me a mug, which I
downed thirstily in a couple of swigs. Under the sound from
the others talking I leaned over to him.

"Do you know what he's . . . ?" I began before Lanny
shook his head to say, no, he didn't understand what was
bugging Smada either.

But now I think he *did* know. He was just too embarrassed to tell me. Lanny was always quicker than me, and I think he did see Smada's point. The punk had been slow and ponderous and, while a jerk, still a harmless one. And we would have noticed how slow he was, as everyone else had, because everyone else had been paying attention to who was armed and drinking in a public inn from the first moment they had entered. You know, the way *we* should have been?

Smada reappeared suddenly with an apparent willingness to forget the whole exchange. "Now, pray tell, what *is* all this about a phone?" he asked gruffly. But he smiled as he did it. "Just what would a phone be, lads?"

We were tired and feeling a bit odd and, I dunno, glad that the snarling was over, so we did. We told him everything. We told the exact truth about what had happened. And we described America. We told all about it. About telephones and telegrams and television. About cassette decks and pornography. About panty hose and heart transplants and internal combustion and Watergate.

We described freeways and democracy and Walt Disney World and women's lib. We sang them some rock and roll.

They loved it. I mean *loved* it. Not that they believed us much, I don't think. But they ate it up anyway. Maybe Smada believed. He asked some incredibly penetrating questions anyhow.

What happened next was absolutely . . . I don't know. Stunning, I guess. What was stunning about it was the logic of their next question. Everybody listening agreed that this America was one helluva neat spot, all right. So the obvious question was: Why weren't we still there?

Lanny and I just stared at them. Then at each other. So they tried again.

Was there a horrible war or plague?

No.

Were we driven out for siding with the wrong king? Nixon, was it?

No.

Were we being pursued because of having been involved in some indiscretion (read: crime)?

No.

Then why were we here?

We wanted to be.

Why?

We think this is better.

Long pause. Exchanged looks.

No kidding, we assured them. We like it here more.

And then they really didn't believe us. Except Smada, I think, who looked at us like we were absolutely and completely stark raving stupid. And we were. We were.

And it was going to cost us.

But in the meantime we were just sitting around still getting drunk at the inn. The topic moved on to more important (or more believable) things, like the best whorehouse in the district and the worst way to break in a new slave. I tried to interest the prettiest whore in a little you-know-what. She was attentive enough. And friendly. But she never left Smada's side. None of them did, spread around him on those pillows like a doughnut. It was discouraging as hell.

Lanny and Smada talked a long time. I don't know about what, but at least some of it was a continuation of the America description and Smada's resulting amazement at our choice.

It was starting to get really late. Most of the other folks had retired to their rooms or headed back out on the road. Only the old general & Co., Smada and the whores, and us were still about.

And drinking. I had to give Smada credit for that much, anyway. He was the most incredible drinker I had ever seen. Drank like it was water, like there was no tomorrow, like he was to be hung the next morning, like . . . well, you get the idea: The sonuvabitch could by God drink.

I got up to piss toward the end and offered to do the same for Lanny but he said, no, he needed the exercise, so we went together. The outhouse smelled just like what it was: an awful place where people put their awful things forever.

When we came back in, everyone else was gone.

Everyone else. We had to wake up the innkeeper to find out what was what. And when we did, we were pissed. There was nothing wrong with our rooms. It's just that we didn't need separate ones, seeing as how Smada had taken *every single whore* to bed with him.

Our first knocks on the broad oak door that was the entrance to his rooms (the best in the place, of course) were tentative and shy. But then we got mad, thinking that we had also paid for the damn women and therefore had a right to at least *two* of them! There was a lot of giggling from inside before a cute little redhead poked her head out and assured us that two of them would be out to join us in just a little while. Then she handed us another flagon and two more mugs and directed us to a little bench there in the hall to wait. We sat down, suckers that we were, and waited. She closed the door.

The giggling this time was a lot longer and louder. But we still just sat there with our little swords and our little mugs. And waited.

But even that wasn't as dumb as the conversation we got into. How is that Lanny and I, just by talking, could screw things up still to come? Incredible.

We talked about Smada, of course, and what we really thought of him. Which *wasn't* what we really thought of him at all. It was what we really *wanted* to think of him.

He *had* been a chickenshit with that young punk, no matter what he said.

"Right?"

"Right!"

And there really wasn't anything stupid about us wanting to come here to this world, it was just our being so adventurous and all.

"Right?"

"Right!"

And his amazement at our wanting to be here just showed even more what a weasel he was.

"Right?"

"Right!"

If he'd really been a *real* swordsman he'd *never* want to live in wimpy twentieth-century America.

"Right?"

"Right!"

But even if he was a sniveler, we weren't. We were damned glad to be here where men were men.

"Right?"

"Right!"

And if anybody else doubted it or just wanted to make something of it, we'd kick their ass.

"Right?"

"Right!"

In fact, we were just hoping somebody'd mess with us.

"Right?"

"Goddam right!"

You see how bad we could get?

The last thought I had before passing out on that bench waiting for the whores was of Smada's face earlier that night when we'd been explaining why we were glad to be there. He had held up a hand for quiet. And once he had it he fiddled pensively with his goatee a second. Then he spoke, all the time looking back and forth between Lanny and me.

"Lads, I wish to have this clear in my old head. You have traveled here from a land of plenty where most men live threescore and twenty winters, may transport themselves one hundred leagues in a day, may expect to live a long and honorable life without once having need of violent resort and where the most compelling issue of the kingdom is the debt incurred from overpaying the poor?"

"That's it," I replied brightly.

"M'Lord Smada," Lanny rushed to say—which surprised me—"we wish you could understand just exactly *why* we undertook this journey of—"

"I do, lad. I do."

"Do you really, sir?" asked Lanny, seeming terribly relieved for some reason. "I do. You are, both of you, idiotic fools."

We woke up a little before dawn with the son of the innkeeper and a servant helping us stagger down the narrow hallway to our rooms. Room, rather, since the sight of the other bed in Lanny's room was too sweet a sight for me to move another step. I shouldered in past the innkeeper's son and slammed down upon it.

Lanny had been mumbling something the whole time we'd been stumbling along, mumbling it over and over again under his breath. Just before I went under again I recognized it.

"Alka-Seltzer . . . Alka-Seltzer . . . Alka-Seltzer . . ."

I knew just how he felt.

This time, we were just too smart for Smada.

He came into the room in a rush, looking . . . well, gorgeous. His hair was neatly trimmed, his goatee meticulous and . . . you get the idea; those damn whores had spent all night long preening him instead of servicing us, dammit! But this didn't do too much more than add to the anger we already felt for him. And when he tried to con us *again* . . .

It seems there was a feller named Lord Grey-something. Greydon, I think. Anyway, he was coming in from the west. He was the lord who had been pursuing Smada. He was also the one now shy a couple of outriders, thanks to Lanny and me. He would arrive at the inn by early afternoon or thereabouts.

He was not in a good mood.

The east road, according to Smada, was the way out of "our little difficulty."

Lanny and I looked at each other. *"Our* little difficulty?" Lanny retorted sarcastically. "Whaddya mean, 'our'? You're the one he's after."

"Yeah," I offered indignantly. "Besides, his men died in self-defense."

Smada raised an eyebrow quizzically. "And?"

Lanny and I looked at each other again. "They attacked us first!" I pointed out.

Smada just did it again. "And?"

"Would you stop saying that?" I snarled.

Smada half smiled. "What would you have me say, lad?"

"C'mon, Smada. You know damn well he isn't after us. He'll understand once we tell him what really happened."

"Will he?"

"Sure he will!"

Smada stared a few seconds. "I see. Lads, if ever I had uncertain thoughts as to your tale of transport in the past, I do hereby now lay them low. I doubt not at all that you spoke truly of your native land."

"You believe us?" Lanny asked.

"I do."

"How come?" I wanted to know.

He smiled. But it was a grim one. "Because in no way could you have lived so long in this land."

And then he walked out.

Lanny and I sat up on the edges of our beds and talked about this awhile. The gist of it was this: That fat old smoothie was *surely* trying to con us again. Into doing his fighting for him again, most likely. And the smart thing for us to do was just stay away from him. If he wanted to run away—and that seemed to us to be the only thing he *ever* did anyway—then let him go. We weren't scared of this Greydon dude. Oh, maybe a little. But we were sure we could work things out with the guy.

At least that's what we said.

We *liked* Smada. We really did. But he was a con artist and a chickenshit and . . . facts were facts. Best to go back to sleep. God knew we needed it.

Facts *were* facts. Facts *are* facts.

And fools are fools. We slept.

It wasn't until some hours later, when the innkeeper burst in to demand payment, that we realized our money was gone.

"Ah hah!" smirked the innkeeper. "Just as Lord Smada suspected."

"Smada!" Lanny and I shouted in unison. "He's the one who took it!" Lanny added.

It was obvious, Lanny explained to him, that Smada had done the whole bit. Lanny was smooth and persuasive and reasonable. He was as good as I've ever heard him.

And the innkeeper bought it. It seems he had suspected Smada all along. And when it had been Smada who suggested that the two young sirs asleep upstairs had no coins . . .

But we could still catch him. He had only just left down the east road. If we hurried . . .

"We're way ahead of you," said Lanny as we gathered ourselves together to ride.

We were gone a full mile's gallop when it hit us.

"Wait a minute!" yelled Lanny, pulling up his mount sharply. "Wait just one goddam minute!"

I pulled up alongside. "What'sa matter?"

"He did it to us again!"

"Who?" I asked, looking around like an idiot. "Smada?"

"Hell yes, Smada. And that bloody innkeeper. Look, here we are going down the damned east road just like he wanted. Right?"

"Uh, right."

"And that innkeeper—who doesn't know us from Adams, by the way—is suddenly trusting us to leave owing him money, catch up to the thief that stole from us, retrieve it, *and* return and pay him back? Doesn't that sound just a little fishy to you?"

"Uh . . . yeah."

"Well, let's go."

"Where?"

"Back to the inn, stupid. For whatever reason, Smada wants to get us away from that place."

"He says it's because of that Greydon guy."

" 'He says! He says!' Dammit, Felix. I'm gonna go back to that innkeeper and kick his butt through the roof of his mouth until he tells me the truth. Are you coming?"

"Yeah!"

"Right?"

"Right!"

You have to understand, this made perfect sense in the stage we were in. That is: hungover and stupid.

So we went back. Despite everyone's attempts to save us, Smada's, the innkeeper's. Despite everything, we went galloping straight back into the nightmare to come.

We were sitting there drinking on credit when the Bad Guys strode into the inn. We were able to get credit by taking it. We were pissed off. The innkeeper had been surprised when we showed up back at the inn. Surprised and then guilty-looking when we accused him of having set us up on Smada's orders. When we saw his expression we were sure we were right. So sure, in fact, that we didn't also notice the sad look on the man's face that came right after.

We should have.

Anyway, we sat there and ate first and then drank some and then drank some more waiting for Smada to show up again. We were sure he would. We had no idea what scam it was he was planning but we were pretty certain there'd be some loot in it for somebody. And since he wanted us *away* from the inn, that's where it had to be.

"Right?"

"Right!"

We did that a lot. We also drank a lot. And waited. Ducks in a barrel.

And then, like I said, the Bad Guys came in. I call 'em the Bad Guys because that's damn well what they were. To begin with, they were huge. Every one of 'em was as big as I was or bigger, and they all wore black and carried polished swords with shiny handles and had big broad shoulders and big black helmets with little slits showing eyes that by God *should* have been blood-red and they slammed that front door open and stalked in two abreast in *formation*, for Chrissakes, all six of 'em, and set up a semicircle just inside the doorway where they could survey the room and then just stood there, poised, looking like they just *hoped* they'd get a chance to slaughter everybody in sight.

Then came Lord Greydon, and he was worse. I mean, the man was a walking ghoul. White hair. Not gray—white. White pasty skin stretched like dead hide across cheekbones that shoulda been knuckles and a forehead that loomed over his eyes like the Frankenstein monster's. His eyes really *were* red. Bloodshot, anyway, like the look of somebody who spent his nights at a graveyard catching bats and cracking their bones with his teeth. And his voice . . . I'll never forget that voice. Husky and dry and dead and . . . piercing, somehow, like he had some sort of dead man's amplifier.

It was the voice that did it for me. From the first sound of it all my illusions were swept away. And you know what kind of illusions I mean. All the old clichés: "There's no such thing as a bad boy" and "Criminals are made by society" and "The Soviets are just people like us" and "Any man can be reached" and, best of all, "There's no such thing as Evil, only mental imbalance"—all of these thoughts were slapped pitifully down by that voice. It was as if I could hear the devil chuckling softly offstage, saying: "Welcome to the *real* world, boy."

I want to tell you, I was scared of that guy. Scared of his men and terrified of him. Terrified and . . . caught. That's it. Caught. It was as if I had been given every opportunity in my life to face reality but had been too lazy and too much of a punk and now it was too damn late. I had been caught pretending the whole thing was a game I could call off, but that wasn't up to me anymore. It was up to this ghoul. And he didn't *want* to call it off. He was *here* for death.

I glanced at Lanny and saw it in his face. He knew it too: Somebody was going to die.

Somebody did. Right then. For the first rasping words from Greydon's dead lips were: "Kill him."

The guy he was pointing to was some merchant standing closest to the door with a mug in his hand. We hadn't talked to him much and didn't know anything about him except that he was just what he appeared to be: an aging overweight penny-ante fur dealer who liked dirty jokes and barmaids when on the road away from his wife and kids and who carried a sword for absolutely no reason other than for show.

But none of that mattered, because a second later he was dead when the closest black guard to him drove a blade as wide as your leg right *through* his spine and six inches out of his back with a horrible grating *chunk*.

It was so fast and so incredibly brutal that nobody else moved. The three guys at the bar and Lanny and me at our table just sat there while the blood spurted and the body sagged and a great black boot shoved against the deflating chest to give the murderer leverage to drag his sword noisily from the body. And then there was a blade at my throat and at Lanny's and at everyone else's and before we knew it we were disarmed and helpless and surrounded and Greydon was standing there smiling a grin full of wickedness and almost sexual delight.

"Where is Smada?" he asked the room.

And nobody knew. You could feel it. Not even the innkeeper. I could tell by looking at him. And I could tell something else, too. It hit me in a flash. Smada had been trying to save us. He had been trying to get us away from the inn, all right. Away from what was about to happen to us. But we had been too smart for him.

"Lord Smada is gone," said a frightened voice just over my shoulder. I turned around and saw the old general sitting there with two of his entourage, the storyteller and a personal servant.

A lot of the next was a blur to my blood-pounding eyeballs. There were cries of fear from the bar girls and fearful protestations from the old general and those with him and one of the black swordsmen lit a great flaming torch but nothing could stop what was about to happen. It was all a preamble to . . .

Look. I'll make it short. For calling him *Lord* Smada, they cut off the old general's hand with an axe.

Then they used the torch to cauterize the wound.

Then they slapped him awake.

Then they slapped him to stop his moaning.

Then they rapped his cheek with a sword hilt until he talked. And he babbled like a child. So would I. And so I did when my turn came after they had found out from the old

general and everyone else who knew that it was us who were
riding Lord Greydon's outriders' horses.

We told him everything. We would have told him anything. I'd have given anything to know where Smada was. I'd
have given my mother, my dog.

I would have given Lanny.

Yes, I was that scared. Scared and broken and beaten and
willing to do anything to please the ghoul. I couldn't even
look the black guard guarding me in the eye after the first
second. His gaze seemed to drill right through the soft me I
knew right then I was and had always been and always would
be. But these guys . . . they lived here and killed here. Had
grown up killing here and loved it and always would and this
was just a lark to us, a game and . . .

And nothing. We were going to die. And right there. Right
then. Horribly. Slowly. Painfully.

Lanny's voice while he desperately tried to explain broke
my heart. He was too scared to even try to sound persuasive.
He was merely plaintive. Almost begging. So was I, trying to
help him. Help me, rather. Help make the ghoul just let us
go. Let me go!

The ghoul loved it. It was the kind of thing he loved,
watching us squeal and squirm like piglets. We were so
scared we didn't even hate him. We were so scared we would
have *loved* him if he'd let us leave in peace. We were so
scared we didn't deserve a chance to live.

But we got one anyway when Trebor Smada, all six foot
three and two hundred and forty pounds and mile-long broadsword and, incredibly, smartass grin, kicked open the side
door and strode across the room to our table.

And the whole world . . . changed. More light seemed to
stream into the room. More breath seemed to come to my
lungs. Maybe it was the way the black guards moved back at
his appearance. Maybe it was the look of hope on the innkeeper's face or the one of . . . not fear, but wariness, on
Lord Greydon's.

Maybe it was none of these things. In fact, it wasn't. It
was . . . I dunno, the truth. I'd been shivering in my seat so
petrified at the price to be paid for my arrogant manhood.
And then Smada showed up and reminded me that . . .

"So, Smada, you've come back to die," scratched Greydon
into the heavy air.

"We'll all be dead someday, Greydon," replied Smada evenly. Still, his voice boomed of life.

"You'll be dead today, Swordsman!" snarled Greydon, but did nothing else. In fact, no one did anything at all for a second.

Smada moved at last. He did a curious thing. He was clearly responding to Greydon's remark when he spoke. But as he did he turned and looked down at Lanny and me, saying:

"We shall all be dead for ten thousand thousand years

floating in the darkness and remembering that,

for a time,

some of us,

but not all of us,

were Swordsmen."

I can explain what that meant to me, but it would take forever. Leave it at this. I was still scared. I still expected to die. But, well . . . no more piglet. No point to it. Never was.

"Bah!" rasped Greydon. "You and your foolish Swordsman rituals. What good will they do you now?"

Smada's voice was dead-cold: "Watch."

He turned his back on them and looked at us. "Now, lads . . ."

"Now what?" we answered in sloppy unison.

"Now I'm going to retrieve your weapons," he said softly with a gesture to the bar, where they lay now unguarded. "And the fight will commence." He looked back at the rest of the room and spoke so all could hear: "I shall kill the three on the right. You get the rest."

I couldn't believe he just said that out loud. Neither could anybody else. We didn't have a prayer and everybody knew it. So did Smada.

But he was saying: "Screw it!"

Lanny gulped and asked: "When?"

Smada smiled and looked at us and said, "Right now."

And then Smada was spinning impossibly fast around to the bar and the swords were flying toward us and we caught 'em somehow and managed to grip them and I spun around and a black guard slammed into me full-face and we went over the table together smashing it flat with splinters flying up into the air and seeming to hang above us while we grappled and he tried shoving the edge of his blade into my

temple despite my grip on his wrist and his on mine. I got
him over and got on top of him—I don't know how—and
smashed at him with my hilt and kneed him in the thighs and
then the stomach. His grip slid on my sword arm and I
twisted my hand and popped free and drug my edge across
his face, shedding sparks from the edge of his helm and blood
from the underside of his chin. He gurgled and spat and I
shrugged halfway up and shouted with triumph or bloodlust
or something and two-handed my point into his chest and
then screamed as a dagger ripped through my tunic and waist
between chain mail and belt.

I spun about, still screaming, and saw the bloody face of
the guard upon me, his helmet long gone and he long dead
from a gaping thigh wound (Lanny's trademark) but not
knowing it yet and maybe not caring. He threw himself at me
again, his dagger blade flinging drops of my blood into my
eyes. I dropped underneath his wide swing and drove upward
with my point, but I skittered off to the side and suddenly the
two of us were down, arms around each other and hissing
hate and fear into each other's face.

He butted me with his forehead. It broke my nose and hurt
like hell, but something else, too—it so, I dunno, *offended*
me that I started doing it back to him and kept doing it until
long after he was still.

"Brad!" Lanny shouted out and woke me up. I lurched up
from the still form below me and there was Lanny, blood-
soaked and swaying but alive. Smada was there, too, dragging a blade from another guard.

There were bodies everywhere and blood everywhere else
and the women and the others were cowering in a corner
whimpering and we'd done it! We had by God *done* it!

I had just noticed that Greydon was nowhere in sight when
he burst back through the open front door.

He was leading the other guards. Six more.

We did pretty well, considering.

Smada was nothing short of spectacular. Lord, he was
strong! Once, during a pause in my own struggles, I saw him
backhand his blade at a guard's throat, miss the man when he
ducked, but still manage to literally behead the guard behind
the first with his off-balance follow-through. He was fast as
hell, too. And he knew how to use all that weight. Even

without all of that wrist speed of his, he could have bludgeoned through almost anything.

My own lot was a blurring mist of terror and rage and exhaustion, of swords sparkling slippery through the air and grunts of pain and many, many wounds from dagger edges and sword edges but never again from points. I just hacked and drove ahead and kicked and punched and screamed in pain and fury and fear. I never fought so well. I never did anything so well. I needed to. I had three ribs smashed right through the chain mail when a guard slammed his hilt at my groin and missed. I broke my own left wrist hacking downward with my dagger against the side of a helmet but still managed to punch it in there through the space caused by knocking it askew. Once I plunged my blade in so deep I was too tired to draw it back out until somebody slammed into me and popped it loose.

All was confusion. And horror. And heartsick misery at what just goddam *would not ever* seem to be finished.

I saw a lot of what Lanny did. He was something to see. He skewered them and stabbed them and carved at them. He threw punches and furniture and karate kicks, of all things. I saw a lot of his fight. It was wonderful. He was wonderful. Once I saw him make a move I didn't know the human body could make at all, much less with power. I saw a lot of his fight, like I said. I even saw him kill Greydon.

I didn't know Greydon had already killed him.

Nothing in my life had ever been so horrible. Nothing hurt so badly. It was over, goddammit, and we had *won*! But Lanny's wound wouldn't stop pulsing. The life just kept throbbing out, and I remember thinking that any decent paramedic unit could have saved him. Saved him at the scene and, using the siren, have him at the hospital within seconds.

But there were no hospitals there and Lanny died. He died. In my arms, his body shivering, his face white and dying, too weak to speak.

I could not stop crying. I could not stop wailing. I couldn't stop. I couldn't do anything except catch my breath and wail some more. But it did no good. They wouldn't take me instead. Lanny never moved again.

Smada, tears of pity running pink down his own face, held me in his lap and rocked me and rocked me for what seemed like days. Then, exhausted from fatigue and loss of blood and heart, I fell asleep in his arms.

And I had the most incredible dream. I *knew* it was a dream. And I also knew it was real. It was incredibly fast but also incredibly detailed. It was . . . hell, I don't know what it was.

Smada and I rode together, in that dream, for twenty years. It was awful. It was also wonderful. I mean, there were some wonderful moments. Some truly amazing parties, for example, with some truly amazing women. Lots of women, Smada being as he was. And lots of friendships and lots of swordly triumphs plus times of great but temporary wealth. But the money got spent and the friends all seemed to die, one after another. Some of them badly and dearly. It was like Lanny all over again with three of them, one of them for Smada.

It was such a grinding tragedy of a life. Flashing glory only meant more aching scars and bloody wounds and long lines of dirt-poor trudging peasants to pass on the roadway. And the whole time the thought of the wondrous age I had left behind.

When I awoke I was still on Smada's lap and Lanny was still dead in front of me and I began to whimper some more. Smada was infinitely caring. He rocked me until I stopped whining. He spoke to me in a dull but reassuring monotone. He wiped my bloody forehead with his glove and once, tenderly, with his damp soft beard. I just stared, mostly, not thinking of anything for a long, long time.

When I came partly out of it and looked up into his eyes he smiled lovingly at me and said: "Time to go home, son."

I began to cry. "I don't know how," I whispered plaintively. "I don't know how!"

But he just rocked me and said, "Sure you do."

And, of course, I did. I looked upon him one last time, teacher, father, brother-in-arms, and then I closed my eyes and slept again.

When I woke up it was night and I was back in the forest and the SCA party was still going on by the campfire and the tequila bottle was empty and Lanny was alive beside me.

He looked pale—bet I did too. We stood up and embraced and walked back to the trailer and took off our sword stuff and put on blue jeans and got drunk all over again and slept.

It was a three-day SCA event, but we left bright and early—
and hungover—the next morning.

Lanny and I are still best friends, more than ever now. I
never told him about my dream and he never told me about
being dead, and I don't blame us. We still go to SCA stuff
but we never fight. Mostly we just point and laugh.

We still read the Horseclans, too. Now more than ever.
Because now we understand just what they were about all
along. And the heroes in those stories are no less real to us
than before. Hell, just the opposite. Now we understand that
for a man or woman to rise to heroism in such a brutal place
is what heroism is all about. We had wanted to go there
because we thought being great was automatic. Now we
know it's miraculous. It is awe-inspiring.

Read it.

No, I do not wish to go back. I think about it a lot, what
happened, but I never think I want another crack at it. Not
me. Not ever.

But I do miss Smada. Whoever or whatever he was—or
is—I miss him. Every day I miss him.

Every single day.

Sister of Midnight

by Shariann Lewitt

Born in New York City, Shariann Lewitt began writing seriously in her teens. Her first play was produced Off-Broadway when she was nineteen years old. Educated as a playwright, she holds an M.F.A. from the Yale School of Drama, where she was named Lord Memorial Scholar, John Golden Fellow and a Graduate Fellow of Calhoun College. Her undergraduate degree is in anthropology, with a specialization in physical anthropology/ evolutionary biology. In addition, she has done graduate work in Middle Eastern anthropology and studied at the Université La Source d'Orléans in France, and she speaks French and Arabic.

In the tradition of writers, she has held numerous jobs, including teaching at Catholic University, directing plays in New York and Connecticut and working as a drama therapist in a rehabilitation program for heroin addicts. She has also worked on archaeological digs and had a short stint as a commercial model.

When not writing, Lewitt sustains an active interest in aviation, ballet and international travel. She makes her home in Washington, D.C., with her husband and three blue hippos.

The men of Harzburk had made short work of the Ehleenee rearguard. Here along the road were scattered the remains of the previous day's work, and already most was gone. The larger scavengers had come first, and now the crows and worms were feasting on what was left. The feast was a generous one, men and warhorses alike strewn in a mass of torn limbs and innards set in congealed blood. Even from a good distance the carnage rested heavy on the air, the stench overwhelming any other scent.

Emhelee gagged slightly, then took a deep breath and held it as long as she could. A small knife rested in her left hand;

she held her nose with her right. She settled deeper into the brush and *listened*, her mind alert for any stray thought-sending of any creature in the area. She did not want to be noticed.

Assured that she was alone, she edged closer to the scene of the slaughter, still careful not to draw attention if there were any lurkers beyond. Her knife was ready. If it was small it was also very sharp, and Emhelee knew how to use it. It was not the kind of blade anyone but a noble would carry, made of the finest steel. Not a proper thing for a young girl, her mother had said. What kind of scullery maid could wield a weapon so well?

At eleven, she was no real scullery maid yet, but her mother had hopes. And the girl was unwilling. Which was why she was out on the road at twilight so very far from home. Gingerly she crept forward toward the scene of the fight.

"My father would be proud of me," she told herself over and again. "He would not let the smell make him sick. He will be pleased to hear how I came, and took what I needed . . ."

Emhelee leaned against the bole of a tree and was sick in spite of her good intentions. She heaved, then spat out the bad taste and forced herself on. She could not possibly get sick again. There was nothing else in her, and she had no more food in her bag. The last of it was lying uselessly spit-up on the grass.

"Stupid, stupid," she berated herself, not permitting herself to cry. She was sure that her father would not approve of girls who cried. When she met him she would present the knife, which he would surely have to recognize, and she dared not cry.

Now for the men. She pulled her courage around her fiercely and forced herself toward the scene of the battle. Little enough there would be, and she could not miss any of it. Not if her plan was to work. Over and over she told herself that this was the most fortunate good luck that could have come her way. There was nothing to fear from the dead, and what goods they had she could surely use. Food would be gone, taken by those who now picked at the remains of men and horses alike, but there should be some money, plate, maybe a fine sword.

Not that she could use a sword, but Emhelee did believe that she could recognize a particularly good one. All she had to do was to match the blade to her knife, to the strange wavy patterns of subtle color that danced down the length of it. Plate could be traded on the road for food. A truly wonderful sword might be the beginning of a dowry when she arrived in Morguhnpolis.

The odor overcame her once again, and she dropped onto the hardpacked road. And began to sob. It was growing late, the shadows long and the light deep yellow. Soon the chill of evening would creep in, and Emhelee had no idea how far she still had to travel. The terror of it spread cold fear through her, and she began to mindcall, without control, for anyone to hear. It was so lonely, lonely, she sent out the message without precise words, and she was frightened.

"Who bespoke me? Who calls on Midnight to kill their enemies?" A mind had touched hers.

Emhelee whipped around and sought the speaker. Midnight was not a man's name, nor a woman's either.

"I! I! Supid two-legs, I should show you the Steel of my warhooves. I should trample and kill you, mash you to redness! I am over here!"

"*Here* is not very helpful," Emhelee beamed back, offended. She understood it was a warhorse who bespoke her, yet she had done nothing to incite the stallion to such anger. The only horse she had ever bespoken in Harzburk, the ancient mare Meehah, had warned her about the stallions.

Then Emhelee heard a rustling sound and a leggy black colt stepped elegantly from the woods. The young stallion had certainly chosen a name that described him well. His shining jet coat was unbroken by any white markings as he trotted closer to Emhelee.

"You're beautiful," Emhelee beamed, remembering that Meehah had told her to always praise young stallions. "Midnight is a perfect name—how clever of you to have chosen it. And surely I could use your aid against enemies on this road as I travel to Morguhnpolis. How do you come to be here and alone, Midnight?"

"I should ask you just as well, two-legs. As yet I do not even know your name as you know mine. Midnight is as brave as the Moon and as bold as Steel itself. But you look to

be no warrior. You are too little and wear no armor." The
black colt nosed the girl suspiciously.

Emhelee thought fast. "Yes, that is true. My name is
Emhelee and I am going from this place to find my father,
who is one of the greatest warriors in all the Confederation. I
do not know exactly where the Confederation is, but I shall
find it. And when I do, if you care to come with me, there
will be more fine fighters and warhorses than we have ever
seen in my father's army. I am sure that such a noble brother
as yourself could choose between as many bold young Kindred as he pleased, and perhaps become King Midnight ere
the year grows cold."

Midnight pranced around a few steps, inspecting the girl.
"You're a filly! And a baby one, too, only a two-legged
foal."

"True enough," Emhelee agreed. "So there is neither use
nor honor in fighting me. Victory is too easily assured and
proves neither your valor nor skill. But escort me to my
father's home and you shall have stories and deeds that all
will tremble to hear. And it is truth that we are both young to
be away from home."

Midnight snorted, and then nuzzled Emhelee. "Do you
have any apples?" he asked. "I am very fond of apples."

Four days on the road passed peacefully. It was late enough
in the spring that Emhelee found early berries and tender
greens. With a sling she could bring down birds, at least
those who did not flee at the thrashing she and Midnight
made as they journeyed. For his part, Midnight found enough
tender young grass to keep well filled, and if he complained
about the lack of apples and other delicacies it was all for
form.

On the morning of the fifth day they left the main road for
a smaller track. "The army is well ahead," Emhelee beamed
to Midnight, "but it's safer this way, I think. They need the
road, so any fighting, of course, will be there. I would avoid
battle as best we can, and that means we should stay well
away from the army."

"Avoid battle?" Midnight bespoke her, contempt shading
the meaning of his thought. "I do not avoid battles. And you
promised me stories of valor to tell."

"You don't have any proper armor and I don't have a good

sword,'' Emhelee improvised. ''It is not noble to ride into
battle without armor. It is just stupid.''

The argument had become old on the road, and now was a
source of solace to them both. The girl knew that the colt was
only posturing, even if he believed his own words. No proper
herd would permit a mere yearling to begin war training, let
alone do the deeds that Midnight longed to boast of. She
walked without looking, thinking about the colt and why he
was here alone.

A mindspeaking war stallion, though only a yearling, was
surely worth more than she could imagine. When she had
been the lowest assistant scullery maid in the kitchens, she
had heard whispers of this horse or that, how one was ill or
another had saved the lord's son. She remembered Kahl, the
heir of Harzburk, often came into the kitchens at odd times
hunting for a fine apple or carrot or other treats for his
brother. Why a colt like Midnight was wandering far from his
ilk she could not even begin to understand. Nor could she ask
Midnight. Since they had first met, he had refused to answer
any of her questions. She wondered if he was like herself, in
search of a truer home.

For herself Emhelee was not afraid. She had always planned
this, ever since her mother had first told her about the valiant
young fosterling of the house who had become her father.
She had been only eight when her mother had brought out the
knife and showed it to her, setting it in the place of honor in
front of the hearth of their tiny hut.

''Emhelee,'' her mother had said carefully, ''you are
soon to be a young woman and no more a girl, so it is fitting
for you to know of your father. He was a nobleman, the heir
to the House of Morguhn of the Confederation.'' Her mother
had recited the names by rote, as things learned carefully and
not to be forgotten, but not to be truly understood. ''He was a
great warrior already so young, and now will be greater still.
His name is known by all, and honored as high as the God
Milo, for your father is called Bili the Axe.''

Emhelee had gasped and held fast to the leg of her stool.
Even she had heard that name. But her own father?

''When he was here as a fosterling,'' her mother continued, ''I was lucky enough to catch his eye for more than one
night. He left to return to Morguhnpolis before you were
born, but a good and thoughtful man he was. Two nights

before he left he visited me and gave me this knife. He told me that if my child was his son, to give the boy the knife and send him south when he reached an age to be trained to war. And that if my child was a girl, then the knife should be sold for no less than three silver pieces, that she should be properly dowered and wed.''

That had seemed enough and more to Emhelee. It was a good and generous lord who left some inheritance to a by-blow with a serving wench. No, Emhelee had first wanted to go south to see this fine person who was her father. The next year there was much gossip in the kitchen about another girl, the daughter of nearby Kindred by a servant much like Emhelee. This girl had been properly given in marriage to one of her father's sergeants because the girl had strong mindspeak. All the girls in the kitchens, and the woman too, had talked of nothing else for days. The Undying had urged those with mindspeak to marry others with that particular gift, but still it was amazing that it should lead to a laundry helper actually marrying a sergeant. With gifts from the family too, it was said, a fine bed with a down coverlet and copper and one silver plate and a mare from the lord's own stable.

If some other wench could marry so well, Emhelee thought, she could too. She had been able to use mindspeech since before she could remember, since before she could talk aloud. Of course, it was rare for her to bespeak a person. Most everyone of her rank was mind-deaf, and she dared not bespeak one higher. So she had sought out those animals who would have conversation with her, the mare Meehah being her best friend.

Surely, she thought, if her father knew that she had inherited his talent she would be welcomed in Morguhnpolis. Most likely he had never mentioned this possibility to her mother because he was sure that his child would be mind-deaf, as was the usual case with such unions.

Her thoughts so occupied, she did not notice the rustling of the leaves behind her, the man-noises on the trail. Midnight had gone up ahead to find some tender grass, as he had done every day of their travels. Two-legs were too slow, he had insisted, especially silly, mooning fillies. So it was not until she was stopped by a spear pointed level at her breast that she noticed there were others in the woods.

Emhelee began to scream. There was nothing else to do.

She knew these men, the kind they were. She had seen them often enough, villagers with airs who thought themselves Freefighters when all they were was rabble. She had heard Meehah say so many times.

As she screamed they laughed. The largest one came over and pinched her arm. "Not much meat there, is there?" he boomed. The men leered.

"No, she's not for you," the large man said. "For the thrice-damned Ehleenee priests, blast their black robes. But they pay well enough. Well enough for an untouched one, that is. So keep your hands off and we'll have more than enough to feast on soon."

Emhelee became very quiet. She understood at least a little of their meaning. They were not going to violate her, at least not now. They were going to bring her to the Ehleenee priests, of whom she had heard no good, but no real evil either. What they would want with her she couldn't imagine, but whatever it was precluded permitting these men their natural vices. She stayed still as they bound her and set her on a pony.

"My father will pay well for my release," Emhelee broadbeamed to the little band. She waited for an answer, for the feeling of touching another mind, and then tried again. There was no answer. Mind-deaf, they were, and that suited her perfectly. She had hoped but had not expected it.

"Midnight!" she beamed out in the direction he had gone. "Midnight, help! Two-legs have me! Stinking ones!"

There was no reply. She didn't know where Midnight was, or if he was close enough to hear her. In panic she tried again, this time sending out broadly, trying to catch a touch of her companion.

The silence that answered her echoed in her mind. She could not find Midnight, and without the stallion, colt though he might be, she was truly alone. She began to sob quietly.

"Stop sniveling, girl," the large man commanded her. "Or you'll never get to the priests. Damn if we need you— there are others here. And they aren't all that careful who they take, if you get my meaning."

Emhelee gulped softly and pressed her eyes shut. Perhaps the priests would be kind. She knew that the Ehleenee were soft, decadent, not in the least admired among those of Harzburk. But it was possible that among them she would be unbound and could slip away. One thing she had heard was that mindspeak was rare among the Ehleenee, a thing she found hard to credit. Among those of Harzburk it was nearly as likely as not, no matter a person's rank.

They stopped for food. The men did not untie Emhelee, but she was given a few swallows of water and a bit of cheese, which she could hardly keep down in her fear. Even the taste did not help, although it had been many days since she had had such a luxury. Her arms ached and her skin was chafed from the coarse rope that held her tight.

Then, as the band remounted and Emhelee was settled roughly on the pony, she caught a flicker of shadow between the trees. "Midnight?" she beamed cautiously.

"Sister Emhelee." The reply was firm, though wavery and distant. It was hard to communicate over the distance, for Midnight kept himself well back in the foliage.

"Midnight, enemies, help!" Emhelee sent. "Careful, careful." She sent again and again, hoping only that the colt could pick up her thoughts as he followed. She was aware of the black shadow behind them, far enough away to avoid immediate detection, but real communication was difficult. Still she reinforced her warning. She was not so frightened now that she had at least one friend who knew of her plight and who could be counted on to help. Not that Midnight was a properly trained war stallion. He was still a very young, leggy colt without the killing weight and thick bones of an adult.

Emhelee closed her eyes and her mind to such thoughts. Midnight was her best hope now. He could surely help her escape from the priests, no matter the purpose for which they wanted her.

They arrived at a large gate just past twilight. Emhelee was not familiar with this place, even where it was. She knew that they had come farther south, which pleased her, but exactly where and how far she couldn't say. She was sure from the sun that they were slightly more to the east than when she had been captured, but there was no city here, no town or village with a name she knew. Instead there was only this large holdlike building.

A thin man with watery eyes in a black robe came out. "Oh, yes, very good," he said, examining Emhelee. "Bring her in. The father abbot will see you shortly."

The men grumbled, but the gate groaned and opened. A thought brushed Emhelee's mind lightly. The priests would not notice one more horse nosing behind the rest, a black one in the quickly darkening night. "Be careful," Emhelee repeated once more as the priests took her away.

They did not unbind her. Instead she was carried like a sack of potatoes over the shoulder of one into the stone edifice and down a flight of stairs. They had not taken her knife, strapped against her thigh in proper feminine manner. She twisted slightly so that the priest carrying her would not feel the unyielding hardness of it. Down they went again, and this time Emhelee was taken to a small chamber, where she was unceremoniously dumped.

The priests left, taking the lamp with them. She was alone in the dark, her hands still bound. "Midnight," she beamed, knowing full well that the colt must be too far to hear. Still, against all hope she called out, the only thing she could think to do in this place. They had left her tied and had given her neither food nor water, nor even a pail to use in the corner. As her eyes became accustomed to the dark she noticed that there was no window, no spot of stars anywhere in the room. That she had expected. She was underground.

"Midnight!" This time panic boosted her sending. If she had been glad before that the men who had captured her had waited to do ill, now she was not so sure. With her knife at least she could have tried to fight or sought an honorable death so that her father would have been proud. Now there was only the dark and the terror of what would come. If they didn't give her food or water they didn't care much if she lived long, and somehow she suspected that was exactly the case. "Midnight!" It was almost a warcry, stronger than she had ever believed she could send.

A moment of recognition, of contact, and then there was nothing. Still, it reassured her. Midnight was here and had not been found. If only he lived up to his boasts, or only a quarter of them, she would find some way out.

Later Emhelee could not say if she had slept or dozed or had been awake the whole of the night. Time ran strangely locked up in the darkness without contact with any creature. When she heard the footsteps coming closer to her cell she was relieved to have the monotony broken, if only by danger.

In the flickering light, the priests' faces were sepulchral and threatening. Emhelee shrank away from their thin-lipped grins and grasping hands. "Come, girl, it's an honor you're lucky to receive," one of the priests said, which reassured Emhelee not at all. The other shrugged, grabbed her and threw her over his shoulder. Emhelee was too exhausted to fight, even had she not been tied.

They went down a long corridor and up a flight of stairs. After another hallway they emerged into the light of day. Emhelee blinked against the brilliance of the morning sun. She could hear chanting in the distance, strange cadences in a language she could not understand. Then, from the corner of her eye, she caught a dark movement near the corner of the building.

"Midnight!" she called, hoping that the colt was close enough. Familiar thought brushed against the edge of her mind as Midnight tried to contact her.

"Where do they take you?" he demanded brusquely.

"To the building with the chanting. Midnight, I fear they mean me no good," she mindspoke urgently.

She thought she heard a snort and the stomping of a hoof. Desperately she tried to impress Midnight with the fear in her, the certainty that these Ehleenee did not plan to let her live.

"Midnight loves battle." The words rang clearly in her head. She whimpered. The unlessoned colt could say anything, but he was still too young and unable to do anything against the many Ehleenee gathered here for the ritual. A fully trained warhorse of years, with his full weight on him and heavy shoes to crush the fragile bones of enemies, might have been able to save her. A yearling like Midnight was no help at all.

Amid the chanting the priests tied her to a stone altar, dark with rust-colored stains. Around stood not only the black-clad monks, but others dressed as lesser nobility and soldiers. Soldiers. Emhelee whimpered again. This was not meant to be. She had not been born and raised, the daughter of the great *thoheeks* of the Confederation—albeit illegitimate and unacknowledged—to be used as a sacrifice in some decadent religion. Sun and Wind were honest and fair, and she wondered briefly if the Wind would take her up, sacrificed to an unnatural god.

The chanting went on and on. One of the black-clad monks produced a silver chalice of delicate work. Emhelee shrank against the cold stone. She did not plan to do it. Anger merged with fear, anger above all, and flowed through her. Even though she had been bound all the night and had not slept, energy coursed through her. She could feel it like sparkling sunlight on frost, blazing in her body. Then the fear was gone and only the power was left. Emhelee was no longer aware of herself, of the priests and their chalice. Strength merged with strength, power with destiny and heredity.

It was horses she knew to seek, Midnight she had found before. Midnight and Meehah converged into a single image in her mind as she sent her thoughts clearly to those who had minds to hear. There were no words wrapped in her power and terror, nothing to direct the current she poured forth. There was only the one ringing note/image/concept of revenge.

A thundering came at the door, the sound of Steel and hooves against the heavy oak. The priests turned white. They dropped their implements, and swords came out from behind long robes. The soldiers, who had stood quietly to this point, now turned, weapons in hand, to face the splintering portal.

Emhelee was not aware of what was going on. She could not stop the sending, the fury that drove the pictures in her head outward, outward over the quivering crowd. Midnight and Meehah and all the others she had seen she imagined at the door. The great chestnut and two grays who roamed the pastures of Harzburk, the roan mare and the bay with white stockings, all of them crowded into her memory and out in that sending. She bespoke all of them with all the power of her life, her being.

The door splintered open as the participants in the aborted ritual began to scream. They ran, not for the door but for the few windows. Some even managed to climb to the high ledges and jump in their panic.

Others, men armed with swords and axes and bows, began fighting phantasms. Emhelee turned her head and watched with amazement as the crazed men-at-arms charged an army of the unmounted warhorses of Harzburk. She knew them all, the horses she had called, and elation tinged the fury and fear in her as she watched the great chestnut trample the priest who had carried her here under his great hooves.

In her joy she tried to communicate with these noble

four-legs, but try as she could there was no mind she could touch. And as she stared a little longer, she found she could not focus on a single one of the great beasts. The chestnut's coat shimmered in the darkness, and Emhelee thought she could glimpse a bit of the wall through his bloodied bulk.

Suddenly she gasped, would have screamed out except for the surprise. The horses of Harzburk dissolved before her. The Ehleenee continued to fight, to run and fall before warrior beasts Emhelee could no longer see.

Only a single horse remained in her vision, a leggy black yearling who went from one downed man to another, stomping and rearing on the fallen, crushing flesh into bone in great killing blows until the place was empty of living Ehleenee.

Elegantly Midnight approached Emhelee on the altar. "I told you that Midnight is brave and great and crushes the enemies of his sister," the young horse mindspoke proudly. He leaned down to nuzzle Emhelee's cheek, and the mindtouch became stronger. "But why are you waiting? Why didn't you run away?"

"They tied me here with rope," Emhelee explained. "If you could pull it free or chew through it or something, then we can go away from this place. But I have a question, Midnight. Where were all the other horses? Where did they all go?"

"What other horses?" Midnight demanded angrily. "There were none but myself, although the two-legs acted most strangely, striking where there were no enemies. They fled from the sight of me, though, did you see?"

Emhelee beamed her affirmation and reminded the black colt about the rope, which was not too thick and rather old. He began to chew it contemptuously. "Sister Emhelee, it tastes very bad," he complained. "When you get up, will you give me some apples? I like apples very much and you never give me any."

For several more days of travel, Emhelee could not keep her mind on the country they passed or the journey itself. Enough that they kept moving south, she thought. The horses who had come to her aid with Midnight in the Ehleenee monastery haunted her. Still, they made progress, especially since Midnight insisted that Emhelee ride him and that they keep to the main road.

As they were scouting for a good place to camp, Midnight's ears pricked up. "Sister Emhelee," he bespoke her happily, "I hear the sounds of horses and an army. If we get near I can see if they're friends, and then we will be safe. For I am tired of this going always to nowhere. I don't know where any Confederation is, and my sire will be pleased to see me. It was him I went to follow, though all said I was too young. But I am not too young. I proved it, didn't I?"

Emhelee was too distracted to protest as Midnight carried her close to the assemblage of armed men. In the center of the great camp stood a silken tent, larger and more beautiful than any Emhelee had ever seen. Midnight filled her head with joyful wonder.

"My elder brothers and sire have described this many times," he informed her. "The High Lady Aldora's tent, her army. We are truly safe, sister. And my sire is here, I know. Now I shall be a real warhorse with a warrior on my back and shoes of Steel and armor."

Emhelee protested feebly as she slid off his back, but Midnight was determined. The young girl blinked back her tears as Midnight disappeared into the press, leaving her huddled in the brush much as he had found her.

Night came, and she slept without hope. The wonders and pleasures of her great destiny once she reached Morguhnpolis did not give her any comfort. Instead, as she drifted off, she considered going home and becoming a proper maid as her mother wished. Midnight was gone to his own kind now, and she lay abandoned.

"That's the girl. I would have known just to look at her." The soft words startled Emhelee awake. She looked up in fear only to find herself gazing at the most beautiful woman she had ever seen, flanked by an obsidian-colored colt.

"The High Lady herself," Midnight mindspoke proudly, doing the introductions. "I told my friends of our battle, and the High Lady was told by a King Horse, the sire of my father. And she wished to have speech with us." Midnight was practically dancing.

Dazed Emhelee rose and did proper respect.

"Now, come along. You need a proper night's rest and a good meal, and we'll talk tomorrow."

"And apples," Emhelee mindspoke sleepily. "Midnight needs apples."

It was not until late the next evening that the Lady Aldora had time to speak to Emhelee. The young girl had spent the day with the cooks, doing a better job of kitchen work than she had ever done before. Indeed, they seemed pleased to have her, and Emhelee made herself quite useful.

Ushered into the High Lady's presence, Emhelee became tongue-tied. Expertly Aldora helped her to overcome her shyness and told her about her father. Emhelee, drawn into the conversation, finally was able to explain about running away from home, about Midnight and about the horses in the Ehleenee chapel.

"Truly your father's daughter," the Undying High Lady muttered. Then she turned and addressed Emhelee directly. "Emhelee, what you have told me must remain a secret between you, your father and myself. More than any knife, this proves your paternity, and I myself shall ensure that you marry well. A gift like this is important, nor have I heard of it in any save one place. What you have done is throw an illusion. The horses were not there, Emhelee, only your gift made your enemies see them. This I have seen in one person only, your father, Bili the Axe. It is something we must encourage, but you must never speak of it again. Do you promise?"

Emhelee nodded seriously.

"Then, girl, get ready to ride. Midnight awaits you, for we leave for Morguhnpolis tomorrow."

Nightfriend

by Roland J. Green and John F. Carr

Roland Green was born in Pennsylvania, raised in Michigan, and educated at Oberlin College and the University of Chicago. He has been a resident of Chicago for twenty years. He has also been an officer of the Society for Creative Anachronism (Middle Kingdom Seneschal, 1969–72) and of the Science Fiction Writers of America (Vice-President, 1984–86), and is an inveterate collector of naval and military history. His published books include the Wandor series (and yes, there will be that fifth book), *Peace Company*, and collaborations with Frieda Murray (*The Book of Kantela*), John F. Carr (*Great Kings' War*, a sequel to *Lord Kalvan of Otherwhen*), Gordon R. Dickson (*Jamie the Red*), and Jerry Pournelle (two novels in the Janissaries series, *Clan and Crown* and *Storms of Victory*). He has also reviewed science fiction, fantasy, and military history for *Booklist* magazine (American Library Association), the *Chicago Sun-Times*, and *Far Frontiers* (Baen Books). At this writing he lives on Chicago's lakefront four miles north of the Loop, with his wife and collaborator Frieda Murray, daughter Violette, a black cat named Thursday, a Kaypro computer, and six thousand books, not all of them naval or military history.

John F. Carr lives in Southern California with his wife and two children. He has written three novels, the most recent, *Great Kings' War*, with Roland Green. He has edited four collections of H. Beam Piper's work and has coedited, with Jerry Pournelle, several different anthology series, consisting of some twenty individual books. He is a war-game enthusiast, active among collectors of miniatures and fans of medieval and Renaissance history. Recently he came in third in the Los Angeles Regional Monopoly Tournament. John is currently dividing his time between work on *Gunpowder God*, with Roland Green,

War World, with Jerry Pournelle, and the Vice-Presidency of
Science Fiction Writers of America. In his copious spare time, he
plays the guitar and, occasionally, sings.

Iron Claw stretched his eight-foot frame along the top of the
sun-warmed rock and caught himself almost purring in contentment. Purring was for females and cubs, not the chief of a
sixteen-member pride; he resisted the impulse.

The winter had been bad. Two of the kittens had frozen at
night. Iron Claw himself had felt the aches and pains of
battles fought before Silver Tip, his favorite mate, was born.
But none of this was any reason to turn kittenish just because
Sun had once again turned its warm face toward the earth.

Lately his mind had taken to wandering through the hills
and valleys of his past. Sometimes the memories were so real
that he could almost feel the body heat of White Nose, his
first mate. At times his wanderings reminded him of the
stray thoughts of some female two-legs. Was old age at last
creeping up on him?

He'd lived a long life for a prairiecat, like his sire and most
of his siblings. A few silver hairs nestled among the black
here and there, but he was still strong enough to rip the
hindquarters of a standing buffalo. Maybe all the winters
were just piling on top of one another.

The loud call of another male prairiecat tore the still morning air.

Iron Claw leaped up and gave an answering screech. The
hair around his neck bristled as the call was returned. His first
challenge of the year!

He hadn't had to fight much the past few years, not since
he'd learned that killing his opponent not only ensured that he
would not return next year but awed the other males in the
area. Last year's only fight had been with a scraggly old
range cat who'd decided to make one last foolish try at siring
a litter. The pride feasted off his carcass for two days.

"Come on, old cat," mindspoke his opponent. "It's time to
join your ancestors. Come down off that rock before I drag
you off."

Iron Claw was amused. The mindspeak sounded familiar,
but he couldn't place it. His mates were silencing the growling kittens as they hastily left the area. He heard another cry

and spotted the waving grass that gave away his opponent's position.

"Afraid, old kitten-eater? You should be. I'm going to take your bones and spread them with the pride's droppings!"

"You sound brave enough," said Iron Claw. "I will remember your words when I hang your tail from my enemy tree." Another way he'd found to spread fear was hanging the severed tails of his dead enemies on trees at the borders of his territory.

The challenger left the grass and strode boldly into the clearing before the rock. Iron Claw was astonished at the size of the young black-and-white male. He was a full third larger than Iron Claw.

Then the challenger turned toward Iron Claw, and the empty socket of his left eye revealed his identity. One Eye was one of Iron Claw's sons from half a dozen winters ago. As a two-year-old, he'd lost that eye when he'd tried to feed on his father's fresh kill. Iron Claw hadn't meant to harm his son, but the bloodlust had still been roaring in his ears. Also the rule of the pride was strict: Iron Claw first, then the nursing females, then the kittens and other females.

"So you have returned, my son, to try once again to steal what cannot be yours."

"No, old cat. Just to take what you can no longer hold."

He spoke with such confidence that Iron Claw felt unfamiliar stirrings of fear. He roared his defiance and leaped down from the rock.

He'd hoped to land full on his opponent and bury his teeth in One Eye's neck, but the larger cat moved with surprising speed. All Iron Claw felt was the scrape of his claws on the other's rump.

One Eye glared, then jumped. Iron Claw lunged, and they met in a tangle of teeth and claws. Both were now on their hind legs, whirling and lunging. Iron Claw felt pain blossom where his right ear had been and roared satisfaction when teeth took out a mouthful of fur and skin from One Eye's neck. He was maneuvering for his favorite trick of putting his right paw into the lower belly to gut his opponent when he felt pain tearing through his left hind leg.

Iron Claw fell clumsily, his leg burning. One Eye leaped on him, chewing fur and flesh from his shoulder and neck.

With a last desperate lunge, Iron Claw threw off the younger cat and ran.

His leg had been badly hamstrung, but he'd had enough hurt paws and legs over the years that he could run almost as fast on three legs as on four. His sudden retreat took a battered One Eye by surprise, and he was almost a score of body lengths ahead before One Eye took up the chase.

One Eye was faster, he knew, but if he could reach the stream he could climb one of the trees. For once, *he* was the lighter cat. He felt some sympathy for those few who'd used that trick to escape him in the past.

Then the unexpected—Silver Tip bursting out of the grass, to attack One Eye from behind. Iron Claw felt a surge of affection for his former mate, then mindspoke her a fond farewell, promising to return. He might not be able to keep that promise, but he had little fear for her. One Eye might give her a thrashing, but not kill the dominant female of a pride he hoped to rule.

Meanwhile, Iron Claw continued to cover ground as fast as his three good legs would carry him. It would be tempting fate to remain in this land before his leg was well and he could once again fight on equal terms. Well, healthy terms, at least.

Iron Claw ran toward the winter lands. There he could be sure that none of his enemies were lurking, either two-legged or four-legged.

Djoh woke up thrashing, to a pitcher of cold water thrown in his face. He could tell that it had been snowing again by the cramps in his lame leg. It was going to be another long day; not even a faint blush of sun showed through the scraped-ox-gut window.

"Up, lazy one. There's work to be done. Get dressed and meet me in the kitchen," ordered his father.

Djoh quickly dried his face with the bedclothes before the water froze, then hopped out of bed and began dressing. His room was in the eaves, with little between him and the shingles. It was almost as cold as outside. He only fell twice before he had his trousers on, then pulled on his homespun shirt and made his way down the ladder. If he didn't reach the kitchen before his father had finished, there would be no breakfast this morning.

He managed to arrive in time. Nee, his older sister, was serving hot porridge. His younger sister, Lilla, hung on to his mother's dress. She was only four years old, but even she had her chores; there were no idle hands in Peetuh the carpenter's house.

His father cleared his throat. "Today I want the joists for the supports on Oskah's barn done. I've already trimmed the logs and stacked the lumber."

Djoh shook his head in wonder. No matter what else could be said about his father, he never asked more than he gave. This morning he must have used some of their precious oil for light to get so much done before dawn. Oskah was a wealthy farmer and an important man in the area; his good-will was worth having. Clearly Peetuh meant to earn it.

Not that Djoh had any complaints about that. It would give him another few minutes with Oskah's daughter Marthuh. She was the beauty of Blue Springs, and Djoh's mindspeak let him know that she thought well of him. His brief visits with her were moments of light in a life that was otherwise mostly dark routine and hard work.

After breakfast his father showed him what was to be done and left on horseback for Oskah's farm. Djoh worked furiously all morning with a speed and deftness that might even have made his father smile. By not stopping for lunch, he managed to finish the first load by early afternoon. With some help from Nee he loaded it into the wagon and headed out.

Djoh reached Oskah's farm by late afternoon. He was surprised to see how much it had grown. Unlike most local barns, Oskah's new barn was built of stone, by the combined effort of all the stonemasons in the Blue Springs country. With the walls finished, Djoh saw that it was also three times as large as any other barn he'd seen. It could probably hold a good part of the town's population under its roof. Surely it had to be the largest building to go up in these parts since the Wasting.

"I see you're early," said his father. He immediately set his two apprentices to helping Djoh unload the wagon.

When that job was done, Djoh expected more work. It was too bad that Marthuh hadn't come into view while he was working, but you couldn't expect good luck in everything.

"You've done a good job, lad," said Peetuh. "Take the rest of the afternoon off."

Djoh tried to thank his father without stammering or staring. His father had never done such a thing before. Had he just possibly guessed his son's hopes of a match with Marthuh? With his father's support, Djoh's hopes wouldn't be totally vain. Peetuh was Blue Springs' only carpenter and a man widely respected for sobriety and hard work. His son and heir would be a fit match for any farmer's daughter, even a farmer like Oskah.

Djoh walked to the big sycamore in the northwest field, the place where he and Marthuh had first talked last fall. Snow blanketed the field, and the tree was only a skeleton's arm and hand stretching toward the gray sky. The sun's hint of warmth was already fading, and his breath swirled white. By the time he reached the tree, he was beginning to wonder if he should have used the time working. It would have kept him warm, at least.

He nearly jumped out of his skin when a hand brushed his shoulder. "Just me," said a familiar voice, teasingly.

"Hello, Marthuh. I was hoping you'd come." And if he hadn't been daydreaming, his mindspeak would probably have told him she was waiting. To hear another's thoughts, Djoh had always needed to concentrate.

Marthuh's blond hair and fair skin were almost as white as the fresh snow. She might have looked colorless, except for her sparkling green eyes, bright as gemstones. They made her the most alive and beautiful thing Djoh had ever seen—or ever would see, he suspected.

"The baking's done, so I can stay awhile."

"Me too," he replied. Unconsciously he moved around to the rear of the sycamore, where no one might see them accidentally from the house. Marthuh followed. Djoh's breath was becoming labored, and he no longer noticed the chill air.

"I don't like it out here," said Marthuh. "I want to move back into Blue Springs where it's not so lonely."

Oskah was so rich that he usually spent only spring and fall at his farm. This year he'd stayed on into the winter, to see the new barn completed. Djoh was the last man to complain about that, since it allowed him many more visits with Marthuh. His father had a countryman's disdain for Blue Springs and seldom stayed overnight even when work took him there.

Djoh had never spent a night in the town in all his eighteen years.

"If it was up to me, I'd build you a big townhouse . . ." Djoh trailed off in midsentence as he realized how hopeless that wish sounded, even to himself. It would take a miracle to even put them into a small cottage together.

"Do you mean that? Oh, Djoh, I wish we could spend more time together, but . . . every time I mention your name to my father, he just glowers."

Marthuh moved closer, until Djoh could feel her heart beating. Without thinking or trying to read her thoughts, he took her in his arms and kissed her. Her lips opened in response, until he felt as if he'd fallen into a whirlpool. He tightened his grip and ran his fingers through hair that felt like new cornsilk.

Before he knew what had happened, his coat was on the ground and then the two of them were on top of the coat, limbs twining. His fingers groped for the hooks at the back of her dress. She moaned softly. He was drowning in her warmth, her scent, her softness—

"What in Peeoryah's goin' on here?" roared a male voice.

Djoh lurched to his feet, suddenly aware of the half-dressed girl on his coat and the stinging cold. "I—I—I don't know! Nothing, really! We were just—"

"I can see, damn you!" Oskah punched Djoh in the chest, knocking him hard against the tree. He could feel the bark through his shirt. Then Oskah was trying to hit him again; he tried to push away the fist. Something jarred his head, and his nose began to bleed. His watering eyes made out half a dozen figures headed toward the tree, one of them in billowing skirts.

"You no-count half-caste!" shouted Oskah. "We know what you are! And everybody knows about your mama and that storyteller who came to town and stayed at her daddy's farm. We had to run that sumbitch off when we found him talkin' to one of the horses. Should of burned him like in the Old Days, but people hereabouts have gotten soft. Maybe you're a Witchboy yourself!"

"Watch who you call Witchboy!" said Peetuh. His tone boded ill for rich farmers who left the hard work to hired hands. "What's going on here?"

"That pretty-boy son of yours was 'bout to bundle with my

little Marthuh. I aim to put a stop to that kinda crap, if I have to geld the little bastard!''

"Girl don't look like she was pushin' him away none," said Peetuh, his voice clear and cold. "I say we let bygones be bygones and I'll keep him clear of here.''

Even through tears and blood, Djoh could see that Marthuh's red-faced father wasn't buying that idea.

"That little storyteller's get you call your son needs a good lesson, or he'll be back like an egg-suckin' snake that's got its first taste of yolk—''

A fist the size of a blacksmith's hammer sacked into Oskah's jaw. He fell as if he'd been laid out with a fencepost. He lay twitching for a few moments, then shook his head and tried to rise. His wife began to howl.

"You fat hunk of blubber," growled Peetuh. "You ever say another word about *my* son's blood or bein' 'cursed' and I'll come back here and pull your head right off'n your shoulders. Hear me?''

Oskah nodded cautiously. He was feeling his head as if surprised to find it still attached to his body.

Peetuh's arm rose again, this time to brace Djoh as they walked back to the wagon. Djoh's last sight was of a slack-faced Marthuh still lying on his jacket, a blubbering and cursing Oskah being helped to his feet by his hired men, and a wailing Marthuh's mother.

Djoh found he was still dazed. Was it the beating, or was it seeing his father throw away probably the best job of his life to stand up for a despised son? And what was all this about a storyteller?

About the time they reached the wagon, they heard a bellow from Oskah.

"Don't neither of you ever put foot on this land again! Hear me? You do and I'll have my man Jacot put an arrow twixt your eyes. My man in town'll settle our accounts, Peetuh. You hear me?''

Peetuh shook his head in disgust and helped Djoh up onto his seat. To Djoh the trip back home was like a dream. He was still half dazed, and something new ached every time the wagon jolted.

There were so many things he didn't understand—his mother, the storyteller Oskah talked about, his "curse." Since he'd been able to understand her, his mother had always cautioned him about his mindspeak. She'd told him it scared most people and that bad things might happen if they learned of it, but she'd never said that he was "cursed."

And why was his father so calm? He'd just been thrown off the best job of his life and he wasn't even swearing! It would also mean the loss of all future work from Oskah.

Of course, the Blue Springs people would have to go a long way to find a better carpenter than Peetuh. Enough of them also disliked Oskah to give Peetuh extra work just to spite the florid farmer. Still, it wasn't like Peetuh to take adversity this quietly, let alone defend a son he usually didn't have much time for.

One question was answered the moment they reached home. "Unharness the horses and put the wagon away," said Peetuh. "Then wait for me in the barn."

Djoh unhitched the team as if he were sleepwalking. His father's tight-lipped order to wait in the barn told him only too well what was coming. He also knew better than to spin out the work to delay his punishment.

He was waiting quietly in the barn when his father entered, carrying the whip and trailed by his mother and older sister. Djoh felt his knees beginning to tremble.

His father spun around to face his wife and daughter. "Leave us! We've men's work to do."

Nee fled. Uncharacteristically, his mother stood her ground. "What are you going to do to him? Just because he took a boy's liberty! What kind of man are you?"

"A cuckold, as you damned well know, woman!"

"You son of a bitch! You knew all about that when we got married. Otherwise why would I have married the likes of you?"

Peetuh's hand snaked out, and Behtee went sprawling. "Woman, I'll deal with you later!"

He turned back to Djoh and yelled, "Take off that shirt! Now!"

Djoh yanked his shirt off so fast a seam ripped.

"Turn around!"

Djoh turned around. The first lash landed seconds later, so hard that it knocked the breath out of his lungs. The second one knocked him to his knees. His father swung again, but he heard a loud scream as the third lash bit into his shoulder.

"You bastard! Hit him again and I'll leave you! Even if it means selling myself on the streets of Blue Springs!"

Djoh turned. His father was hunched over as if he were taking a beating himself. "Arrrhhhhhh!" he shouted, throwing the whip down. Then he ran out of the barn, not meeting his wife's or his son's eyes.

Behtee half crawled, half walked over to Djoh and cradled his head in her arms. "My beautiful boy, don't worry. He won't whip you again. I promise, I promise. I should have done this a long time ago."

Djoh's head spun with questions, but his throat hurt too much to let any words out. Then uncontrollable tears began to stream down his face as he buried his head against his mother's bosom.

Iron Claw watched intently as the doe's hooves bit through the thin ice crust around the pool. He continued to mindcall soothing reassurances as the doe slowly moved into striking distance, two body lengths away. He'd been here for two days and nights, trying unsuccessfully to ignore his growing hunger and painful body, patiently waiting for his next meal. He couldn't survive another two-day fast.

His luck had been bad ever since One Eye drove him out of the pride. In spite of his lead, the younger cat had trailed him for five days and four nights. It seemed that the son had learned the father's lessons about making sure opponents never came back.

Now Iron Claw was lost, farther north than he'd ever traveled before. His wounds and hunger made feeding himself desperately important, and this had brought him to the pool.

During the first few days, game had been plentiful and he'd eaten well. Few of the animals here had ever seen a prairiecat his size. But his wounds made him clumsy, too many would-be meals escaped, and far too quickly his presence was known and feared. If he'd been thinking clearly, he'd have moved on at least four days ago. He hadn't wanted to leave his half-completed den, though, and now it was too late.

The doe moved another two cautious steps. Iron Claw felt his heart beginning to race, preparing for the great leap. Then the doe paused, sniffing the air. Iron Claw willed his heart to slow down and tried to send a message of serenity, peace, and safety. The doe made a tentative half-step. Iron Claw felt his left hind leg begin its familiar throbbing.

With surprising speed, the doe leaped to the edge of the pond and put her head down to drink. Like most animals, she preferred water to snow when she had a choice.

Iron Claw was digging in for his final leap when his bad leg gave way, throwing him off balance. He landed on his side, with enough noise to alert the doe. She sprang into the air and in a moment was nothing but a patch of brown and white bobbing in the distance.

Iron Claw let out a roar of anger and frustration that silenced the forest. Then he slowly limped back to his den. Maybe there was still some meat left on that scrap of rabbit skin he could so clearly remember from an earlier meal?

Everything had changed and nothing would ever be the same. That single thought went around and around in Djoh's head as he approached the forest. His father had sent him to mark some trees for cutting and dressing, but it seemed to Djoh that this was more to get him out of his father's sight. They already had more than a year's supply of lumber stacked outside the barn.

His father had been even more silent than usual since the incident at Oskah's farm. For the most part he acted as if Djoh weren't even there. At first Djoh enjoyed the anonymity, until sheer boredom drove him to confronting his father and asking for some work. This makeshift tree-marking was all he'd been given.

Hazel, the old mare he was allowed to ride, suddenly reared up and tried to turn. Djoh pulled on the reins and mindspoke soothing emotions to calm her down. What *was* spooking her, anyway?

He dismounted and walked slowly through the trees, all his senses alert. Then his mind heard something discordant—a searing edge of pain, new and old pain mixed together, along with hunger and rage. He began to move more cautiously.

He would have missed the den if it hadn't been for the paw he spotted out of the corner of his eye. It was the largest paw he'd ever seen, ten times the size of a bobcat's paw. He'd heard tales all his life from occasional travelers about the great prairiecats, but he'd never believed them until now.

As Djoh moved closer, he could make out the great head. It was still, except for an occasional movement as its breath rattled. What was a prairiecat doing in these parts? What was wrong with it?

And shouldn't he be running like hell rather than standing here spying on a creature that could gut him with one swipe of that paw?

He was about to do exactly that when the cat's huge yellow eyes opened and it mindspoke.

"Who are you, two-legs? And what are you doing near my den?"

Djoh remember one traveler's telling about how to address the cats. It couldn't do any harm, at least.

"Forgive me, cat-brother. I mean you no harm. I heard that someone was hungry and in pain, so I came to find out who."

"Two-legs! More nose for trouble than head for safety!" A spasm shook the cat's body.

"Is it you that needs help?" Djoh mindspoke. He was almost sure it was. The cat's mindcall was surprisingly weak, and layered with pain, hunger, and exhaustion.

The cat shook its great head. "I have not eaten a real meal for more than fifteen days. It seems that I will soon go to Wind."

"Maybe I can help," said Djoh.

The cat's laugh rumbled in his mind. "I see no weapons, and I suspect that your true calling is far from that of a hunter."

For once Djoh wished he had one of the big fortress crossbows, like the one at Oskah's farm. But the carpenter's family did well to have the longbows and pikes that mostly hung over the fireplace, except when the local trained band held its annual muster after the harvest. The only time Djoh could remember it mustering any other time was four years ago, and then the rumored band of river pirates never appeared.

"I have a hunting bow, back with my horse. They say I'm a good shot."

"I hope you speak the truth, two-legs. Otherwise there is little that you can do for me." The cat's mindspeak faded away as it slipped into an uneasy sleep.

It took Djoh an hour's ride and four hours of hunting before he bagged a large badger. He gutted it and threw it on the horse. Hazel wasn't happy about the extra load but did carry him back to the big cat's den. He unloaded the badger and dragged it to within reach.

The cat's mindspeak was even weaker, but Djoh heard the sarcasm clearly. "A nice morsel, two-legs, but I'll need more than this to fill my belly."

"Be thankful for what you have, old grouch. This is the biggest badger I've ever seen in these parts. Even for you it should be a meal."

"Perhaps you speak the truth," said the cat, between bites that quickly grew lustier. He'd finished less than a third of the badger when he stopped. "I fear my belly has shrunk even more than my eyesight. I still owe you thanks, two-legs."

"Your thanks are well received, cat-brother, but my name is Djoh, son of Peetuh, not two-legs. What is your name?"

Iron Claw paused. He seemed to expect something more, and Djoh ransacked his memory for hints of what it might be. The memory that finally helped him was not of travelers or prairiecats, but of their old tom watching over his mate and her last litter. He also remembered his mother, with tears in her eyes, cleanly breaking the old tom's neck when he was dying slowly in constant pain.

"I will care for your kittens and your mate while she is nursing them. If you are dying, I will send you quickly to—to Wind."

The cat's approval flowed over Djoh like a warm bath, and with it came a name!

"Iron Claw. I am called Iron Claw, and legion have been my mates and kittens. By sharing names and giving the oath, we are now truly brothers."

Djoh realized that he'd been granted a very special honor by this magnificent creature. He cleared the snow from a patch of ground, sat down on his cloak, and listened to Iron Claw's tale of its—no, *his*—flight from the prairie.

During the next week Djoh spent almost as much time hunting as marking trees for his father. He suspected this suited his father well enough. Everyone was on edge around the house. His parents spoke to each other even less than usual, Nee seemed afraid of her father and solicitous of Djoh's welfare, and Lilla cried at the least provocation. Peetuh ignored his son, and Behtee seemed to avoid being left alone with him.

It wasn't until one night when his father returned from a trip to town that they had any real conversation.

"How's the marking and culling coming?"

"Well enough, Father. It'll probably take another week, though."

His father looked away. They both knew that it was a three-day job at best. *Does he even wonder what I've been doing out in the forest all that time?* Djoh asked himself. *Or doesn't he care anymore?*

Not that Djoh was complaining. Iron Claw was still too weak to hunt. Another couple of weeks, though, would give him back enough strength to seek prey on his own.

"I'm glad you're doing such a thorough job, Djoh. Just stay away from the river. Heard in town the pirates are out early this year. Big Everly and his crew lost their barge and all their gear to the pirates. Everly was cut up bad, and three of his crew didn't make it back at all. He says there was more of 'em than he'd seen in one crowd in twenty years of bargin'."

"There's two other boats missin' besides. Council's put out orders that no one's to leave the wharf without permission. They're thinkin' of gettin' all the boats together and makin' a convoy."

Djoh whistled. This was more excitement than Blue Springs normally got in ten years. "What about the militia?"

"Council's callin' out one man in four, right now. I'm one of 'em, so I'll be stayin' in town for a while. Djoh, you're goin' to have to come home early and keep an eye out for the womenfolk."

"I sure will. You don't think they'll come out this way, do you?"

"Nope. If'n I did, I wouldn't be goin' into town. We're ten good miles from the river. No pirate's goin' to go that far when there's better pickin's right on the river."

The whole house almost visibly relaxed with the news of Peetuh's departure. It might give them all time to come to terms with everything that had been said in the barn. Behtee smiled for the first time in a week.

*   *   *

The next morning, his father was gone even before Djoh was out of bed. The kitchen seemed almost lively, compared with its usual solemnity. Djoh guiltily wondered how it might be if his father didn't come back from a brush with the pirates. Lame leg aside, he wasn't as strong or as fast as his father, but he'd learned all the carpentry Peetuh could teach him. Times would be lean for a while, but they would survive.

After breakfast his mother asked him to stay, then chased out his sisters.

"Djoh, I guess you have a right to know the truth about some of what was said in the barn."

Djoh felt his skin crawling. He was curious, but he wasn't really sure he wanted that curiosity satisfied.

"Jo"—that was her pet name for him—"I wasn't always as ugly as I am today."

"You're not ugly now, not to me," said Djoh, almost reflexively. In fact, there was a good deal of truth in his mother's words. Eighteen years of hard labor had taken their toll. Her hair was limp and streaked with gray, her face blanched and prematurely lined. Yet her neat features and fine bones spoke of a past beauty that had known only a short, fleeting springtime.

"Thank you, Jo. My mirror tells me a grimmer story. But it wasn't always so. When I was Marthuh's age, I had just as many suitors, if not more, including both your father and Oskah.

"Does that surprise you? That's one of the reasons your father did so little work for Oskah until lately. Oskah was as unpleasant as a young man as he is now. In spite of his father's wealth, I've always believed I made the right choice, even if I didn't make it quite freely.

"The tales are true, Djoh. There was someone else. An older man, a bard and storyteller who most likely still wanders these plains. His name was Willee. He rode into Blue Springs on the most beautiful horse anyone in these parts had ever seen. He was a handsome man and he set all the hearts aflutter, whether they'd been spoken for or not!

"It was I who captured his heart. Yes, I say I captured it, because he was a great gentleman. He would not take anything that wasn't freely given."

Djoh felt himself blushing. This was the first time he'd talked with his mother as one adult to another.

"After the first time we lay together—no, don't stop me. It's about time you knew the truth. Anyway, after that first time he decided to spend the summer in Blue Springs. He was a smith as well as a bard, so Old Garth gladly put him to work.

"That summer was the best time of my life, for all that it's cost me since. Willee was loving, kind, wise—he told marvelous stories, even though you knew half of them couldn't be true. I remember particularly the ones he told about an immortal warrior named Milo. Sometimes he even tried to make me believe the horse was a gift from Milo.

"But Willee was restless, and he had your gift—the mindspeak. He showed me that it was a good gift, not the curse we are taught to think it is. That was his undoing.

"You see, my other suitors—particularly your father and Oskah—weren't happy at my spending all my time with an outlander. Now, I believe they suspected what we were doing on all those long trips into the country. But I was young and in love, and none of this was clear to me at the time.

"Willee, on the other hand—he was worried. He knew what I was risking and tried to tell me. Yet he found something in me that made him want to linger on, far past the time when he should have left.

"Then I discovered I was with child—you. Of course, it was Willee's son, but I didn't want to use you to tie him down here with me. So I never told him. One summer night when it was particularly chilly, I asked him if he would take me with him when he left.

"He explained that he couldn't, that his life was not one I could face. He sounded sorry, and I think he was. After that, he stopped seeing me so often and I knew that it would be wrong to use you to force him to stay.

"Willee's horse was very intelligent. Some people began to think he was *too* intelligent. Oskah spread these rumors, and claimed he'd seen Willee speaking in tongues to the horse. He accused Willee of witchmagic.

"When I heard of this from my father, I ran and told Willee that it was time for him to leave. That night we slept together for the last time. In the morning he was gone. Part of his heart and his son have stayed with me all these years. Sometimes I think that's all that's made them bearable."

"You mean, Bard Willee is my real father?"

"Yes."

"But why didn't you tell me?"

"Do you think it would have made living with Peetuh any easier, knowing that?"

"No—no. I guess you're right. I'd have hated him, maybe even enough to throw it in his face."

"Yes, and he doesn't deserve either. Deep inside, he is a good man. Hard, but always just. He deserves your love and respect. Hasn't he always treated you like his own son?"

"Yes, but why did you marry him?"

"You know how the town fathers feel about women with— who give birth out of wedlock. They and their families are disgraced. My father was all alone and sick. I couldn't do that to him.

"Oskah—I knew he'd never accept a child he had any doubts about. So I told your father. He was hurt, and for a while he was angry.

"But he got over it, then asked me to marry him so that the child would have a name. He has never used it against me or treated you other than as his own."

"I know, Mother. You would have been proud of the way he took care of Oskah at the farm. I—I think I've wronged him."

"Then tell him. He can be hurt too, for all that he tried to hide it. People like your father can be hurt the worst of all, maybe. And I wronged him too, even though I was trying to protect you, my one son, the son of my one true love."

His mother's voice became brisk again. "Oskah has never forgiven me. After your birth there was more talk, which he has never forgotten. He is a man who nurses on pain as if he were a suckling child. I don't think he's finished with us yet. Watch your steps, Djoh, and be careful."

On the way to see Iron Claw that afternoon, Djoh began to have the feeling that he was being followed. But he was unable to spot anyone, and there was no mindtrace. Maybe he'd been hearing too many stories about pirates. Certainly there was no treasure in the forest that would attract any pirate's interest.

Iron Claw actually came to meet him at the edge of the forest. The big prairiecat was beginning to fill, and Djoh began to realize just how huge his friend was when not half starved.

"Good hunting, Little Brother. Today I will follow you."

"Good, Iron Claw."

Djoh actually welcomed the company. They found the markings of a herd of wild pigs and followed them for two miles. Iron Claw easily kept up, then finished off a big sow Djoh had only wounded.

"This is good, Little Brother! To hunt again, instead of being fed like a just-weaned kitten!" Then Iron Claw was too busy eating to talk.

On the way back to the den, with the pig's hindquarters resting on Djoh's mare, he brought up the subject of pirates. "With my father gone, I won't be able to hunt for you except during the afternoons."

"That does no harm, Little Brother. My leg is healing quickly now. This fine sow should satisfy my hunger for three or four days. Soon I shall have to leave, although I shall miss my two-legs brother."

"And I shall miss you, oh hungry one. But let us not think of unpleasant things until we must. I will return in three days and we will hunt together again."

"Farewell, Little Brother."

As he approached the house, Djoh sensed many mindtraces, filled with anger and fear. Had the pirates actually come this far inland? Or had something happened to his father? He kicked the old mare into a trot toward the barn. There he was met by half a dozen grim-faced farmers and townsmen.

"What's wrong? Is it the pirates? Where is Peetuh?"

"In jail, for now," said the marshal. "He couldn't accept that his own son or whatever the hell you are was a slime-suckin' weasel."

Djoh would have fallen off his horse in surprise if the men had given him a chance. Four pairs of hands roughly yanked him to the ground and had him bound and hog-tied in a minute, while the marshal covered him with a crossbow.

"What—what am I supposed to have done?" he stammered.

"As if he don't know!" sneered one of the farmers.

"Somebody 'round here's been tellin' the pirates about

when boats are leavin' and when they're supposed to return,''
said the marshal. ''An' it's all come back to you, Witchboy.''

Djoh felt his stomach sink into his boots. Oskah! Who else
besides his family and a few trusted friends knew about his
mindspeak, or even thought they did? What chance did his
word have against one of the Town Fathers?

''How could I know that information, Marshal Nehil? I
haven't been to town all month. I haven't been near the wharf
since last summer!''

''That's true enough, Marshal,'' said one of the townsmen
who owned a waterfront warehouse.

''Don't need to be there, Witchboy, from what I hear.
Besides, it ain't up to us to decide. You'll have your trial fit
and proper, at the Shrine. It's up to us to get you to jail.''

Oh sure, thought Djoh. Nobody could complain about that;
the Sacred Caterpillars were fair-minded men. They were also
either business partners or friends of Oskah. The trial would
be a farce, for the entertainment of Blue Springs and with
only one possible end.

Djoh had the feeling that his luck had run out. He and Iron
Claw would both be leaving Blue Springs soon, but for very
different destinations.

Peetuh was released on oath to ''not interfere with the
judgment of the Sacred Caterpillars,'' so Djoh was alone in
the town jail from his first night there. That night he tried to
mindspeak Iron Claw. The cat was going to be on his own
sooner than he'd expected, so the sooner he knew about it the
better.

Djoh was the only mindspeak adept in Blue Springs. It was
as easy as ever to pass through the town's tangle of thoughts,
like a hand brushing away a cat's cradle of spiderwebs. Some
of the farm animals, horses in particular, had a rudimentary
mindspeak, but none compared with the prairiecat.

It took him about half an hour to reach Iron Claw.

''What is it, Little Brother? Something that makes you
uneasy, I sense.''

Djoh gave an edited version of the day's events, trying to
make it appear that he was in little danger so that Iron Claw
wouldn't try anything foolish. He promptly learned just how
hard it was to lie while mindspeaking.

''I will come and get you,'' said Iron Claw.

"No, you must not! They have bows and swords here, and you aren't well yet!"

"Well enough, Little Brother, to make short work of any clan of two-legs!"

"That is true, Iron Claw. But there will be a better time, when few of the two-legs are around." He wasn't sure about that, but he hoped he sounded convincing. There was no sense in this farce costing two lives instead of one.

"Very well. Be sure to call the moment you need me, little brother. It has been a long time since I fought bad two-legs, so I am looking forward to it. Without their weapons, they fight worse than kittens!"

"I promise that I will call you when the time is right, Iron Claw. Do you think you are well enough to hunt now?"

"Yes, Little Brother. I will start hunting early tomorrow morning. I should bring something down long before I run out of pig."

The next ten days passed so slowly that Djoh began to look forward to the trial as at least an end to the boredom. His only visitor was the marshal. He came in twice a day, bringing breakfast and dinner but rarely speaking except a few grunted monosyllables. Djoh found this worse than no visitors at all, since it only reminded him that he *was* in jail.

On the eleventh day he finally had a real visitor—Marthuh.

The marshal left her outside Djoh's cell door, with a warning.

"I don't know why your dad asked you to bring the prisoner a message, but if anything happens, it's goin' to be on his head, not mine. Don't you get too close, neither. No tellin' what this one might do."

The moment the door closed, Marthuh pressed up against the bars. Their lips touched; Djoh could tell that she shared his thought that this might be for the last time.

"Don't cry," he said.

"I just can't stand seeing you like this. And all because of me!"

"No, Marthuh. It's not your fault. It's not mine, either. I've never met a pirate in my life."

"I know that, Djoh. But my dad did this because I told him I loved you and that nothing would keep us apart. He swore to me that he'd keep you away, even if he had to kill you himself. Now he's found a better way.''

At that moment, with Marthuh's declaration of love in his ears, Djoh wouldn't have minded if they'd taken him out on the spot and stoned him. Marthuh loved him! What more could he hope for?

In another moment, common sense returned. It would be nice if they could have some time together. Also, the impulse to tell her the truth about what had kept him going to the forest all these weeks faded. It wouldn't make any more sense to her than Oskah's lies, and would only confuse her.

Besides, the fewer people who knew about Iron Claw, the better.

"I can't think of any other reason for my being here. But doesn't that make it dangerous for you to be visiting me?''

"No—well, not very. When my father finds out, he'll be angry. But without you, it doesn't matter. Djoh, I want to help you escape.''

"That *will* be dangerous, Marthuh. Besides, how could you get past the marshal?''

"I don't know. I just have to do *something*. Maybe I could steal one of my father's swords—''

"Marthuh, no! You'd get hurt and wouldn't accomplish a thing.'' He wanted to say "I forbid it,'' but the look in her eye told him that they'd have their first quarrel if he said that.

"Djoh, we have to do something soon. Father said last night, when he came in from the farm, that your trial is going to be at the end of the week. When I asked what would happen to you, he said that I'd never see you again. The look in his eyes when he said it was scary. Something awful is going to happen. We've got to get you out of here!''

Three more days. Suddenly the cell didn't seem so bad. They wouldn't really have him stoned for this, would they? Giving information to the pirates was a serious charge, but dammit, he was *innocent*!

Yes, and they didn't know that. All they had was his word against Oskah's—and he knew who they would believe.

"It will be all right, Marthuh. Really. I haven't done anything. The Sacred Caterpillars won't harm an innocent man.'' He hoped he could make her believe that without believing it himself.

In a moment he knew that he'd failed. Marthuh still stood

willow-straight, but tears were trickling from her eyes. Then
the trickles turned into streams, and sobs racked her body.

Djoh wormed his arms through the bars and tried to comfort her. They were in this clumsy embrace when the marshal
returned.

"What's goin' on here? Get your hands offa her!"

Marthuh jerked away.

"Wait till your dad hears of this! You didn't have no
message to deliver, did you?"

Marthuh shook her head.

"You git out of this jail right now. Your dad'll know what
to do with you!"

She gave a half-cry, half-gasp and ran out of the jail. The
marshal stood shaking his head. "I ain't too sure I know what
all this means. But one thing you can count on, boy, it won't
make your bed any easier to lie on, no sir."

Djoh knew that this was the truth, but he also knew
something else that really helped. With her father alerted,
Marthuh wouldn't be able to do anything foolish. Both she
and Iron Claw were safe, and *that* was a load off his mind.

Iron Claw woke up irritable, which usually meant that he
was hungry. This time not even three rabbits and a runaway
calf took the edge off his anger.

Something was wrong. Little Brother hadn't mindspoken
with him for two days. Was he in some danger he hadn't
foreseen?

Iron Claw tried to mindcall his friend, but the scent of his
thoughts was lost amid all the other two-legs in their great
den. Little Brother had the most powerful mindspeak he'd
ever encountered, but Iron Claw had neither his range nor his
power. Maybe if he came closer to the two-legs' den . . .

The idea of being so close to so many bad two-legs did
nothing to improve Iron Claw's temper. He loped off toward
Blue Springs in a thoroughly foul mood.

Today was the day of the trial. As much as he hated to
admit it, Djoh was scared. He'd picked at his breakfast for
over an hour, until it was a congealed lump of oatmeal.

He knew that the best that could happen to him would be
exile, which was just a delayed death sentence anyway.
Strangers were always suspect, and a wanderer with neither

home nor kin was fair game to both human and animal predators. Maybe Iron Claw would protect him for a while, but the prairiecat surely had his own plans, which wouldn't include wetnursing stray two-legs.

His musings ended abruptly as the door opened. Four men came in, wearing the hooded yellow robes of Sacred Caterpillars. The marshal followed them, and they waited while he unlocked the cell door. Then silently they bound Djoh's hands and escorted him out of the jail, up the streets of Blue Springs to the Shrine on its bluff.

The Shrine looked no different than any other day, except maybe a little cleaner. From the pole over the big iron-shod doors, however, hung the great banner showing one of the ancient Caterpillars at work moving a mountain.

As the party drew closer, Djoh smelled the fumes of the sacred oil. They must have more lamps than usual lit today, to make such a stink. He wondered if the sacred oil really was what the Caterpillars once drank to give them their magical strength, in the days before the Wasting. Or was the formula as much a product of somebody's imagination as Oskah's tale?

It didn't matter. People would believe what they wanted to believe. They'd wanted to believe that they still had some of the ancient magic, and now they wanted to believe that Djoh was guilty. The set expressions and hard eyes of the Caterpillars told him that plainly. The only question was how severe the sentence would be.

At the front of the crowd around the Shrine, Djoh saw his parents. Peetuh's hands were balled into fists and held tightly at his side. Djoh felt a wave of affection for this stern man, who'd been a father to him even while knowing better. He hoped his father wouldn't try to interfere with the trail; he couldn't fight the whole town.

Oskah stepped forward, as accuser, and one of the Caterpillars began to recite the charges:

"You, Djoh son of Peetuh the carpenter, have been brought before this body for the crimes of treason and murder. You have committed the second crime as a result of the first, by giving to the pirates information leading to the loss of four boats and the deaths of twenty-three men.

"How do you plead?"

"Innocent. I know nothing of the pirates. I have neither met them nor helped them in any way."

"Do you deny having the ability to cast your words, or hear those spoken in the minds of others?"

Djoh paused, knowing that this was the crucial question. If he told the truth, that would be as good as admitting guilt. If he denied his mindspeak, he'd be lying—and there were people in the crowd besides Oskah who would probably call him one.

Which would leave him right back where he'd started.

"Yes. I have the ability to mindspeak, but—"

The word "Witchboy" ran through the crowd. Djoh felt his heart sink into his boots again.

"So you admit to witching?"

"It's not witching. It's an ability, like hearing or seeing. Many animals have it too, the big cats and some horses. Are they witches too?"

The crowd was silent.

"Which animals?" snarled Oskah. "They gotta be put to death too."

The crowd pressed forward. For a moment Djoh caught sight of Marthuh's face, the color of new-fallen snow.

"Little Brother!" cried a voice in his head. "I am outside the two-legs' den. Many bad two-legs are approaching it along the big stream. They carry weapons, and their heads buzz with evil thoughts like carrion birds'."

"Stop!" Djoh shouted. For a moment he had everybody's attention. "The pirates are coming, marching along the river-bank! Run and get your weapons, before it's too late!"

"Liar!" screamed Oskah. "It's a trick to let him escape!" A few townsmen started running for their weapons. Most milled about in confusion.

"You've got to get ready now, before they reach the town! Hurry!"

"Stone him now!" screamed Oskah. "Before he makes more trouble! We cain't let him escape—"

The clanging of the town bell interrupted Oskah's cries. A distant scream followed, then the sound of a pirate war-horn. Oskah's face turned the same color as his daughter's. The crowd began to dissolve, as more men ran for their weapons while others herded the women and children into the Shrine for safety.

The four Caterpillars guarding Djoh stripped off their robes, ignoring him. One of them ran into the Shrine and came out with helmets and wicked-looking maces for all of them.

Oskah grabbed one of the Caterpillars. "Where you goin'? Cain't you see it's just a trick? They're comin' to save their spy!"

The oldest and tallest Caterpillar stared at Oskah. "Are you mad? The boy would never have warned us of their coming had he been their spy. Leave him be. We can sort out the real truth later. Now there is men's work to do."

"We cain't leave him here! He'll run off!"

"Only if he is guilty. Then so much the better, for we will be rid of him and his blood will not be on our hands. If he is innocent, he will stay to see that the truth prevails."

"Fools!"

Oskah snatched a knife from his sash and leaped at Djoh. The old Caterpillar caught him easily, then pulled his arm back and almost casually twisted it up behind him. Oskah dropped the knife and screamed.

"There is more here than we have been told," the old man said. "It may be, Oskah son of Looey, that you have sought a private vengeance by lying to the gods at their very Shrine. Think carefully what you do, if you do not wish to take Djoh's place here when we have beaten the pirates back to their dens!"

Oskah gave everyone a furious look but said nothing. The four Caterpillars hefted their maces and ran down the hill, and a moment later Oskah followed. Djoh stood in a daze for a few more moments, until he noticed that Marthuh hadn't gone into the Shrine with the other women and children. From down toward the river, he could hear warcries, screams, pirate horns, and the drums of the town rallying its defenders.

"Why aren't you in the Shrine? It's dangerous out here."

Marthuh picked up her father's fallen knife and began cutting his bonds. "My place is with you. The gods have brought the pirates upon us, to avenge my father's desecration of their Shrine. Let's not waste their gift."

The moment circulation returned to his hands, Djoh cupped her chin and kissed her. He knew little about the gods and right now he cared even less, but he knew an opportunity when he saw one.

"Marthuh, it's not going to be safe, and I don't know what

kind of love I'll have to offer. I still can't think of anyone I'd rather share it with, my love."

She squeezed his hand. "Me neither. Let's try for the river. Maybe we can find an abandoned boat there."

They skirted the town on their way downhill and made their way through the heavy second-growth woods to the river. The uproar of battle grew louder as they approached the water. It sounded to Djoh as if the pirates had been reinforced.

When they reached a point where they had a clear view of the town, Djoh saw that he'd guessed right. The pirates had sent one column overland, to seize the waterfront by surprise and hold it while the rest came up in boats as usual. The overland column couldn't have been very strong, or it would have been spotted. It still might easily have cleared the waterfront, if the Blue Springs townsmen hadn't had Djoh's— and Iron Claw's—warning.

Now it looked as if the townsmen were holding the two main streets leading up from the river. The pirates were extending their flank, trying to work around the townsmen. If they succeeded, they might take the townsmen in the rear. At best, the rest of the battle would be fought house to house in Blue Springs itself, which would ruin the town no matter who won.

A number of small boats were drifting slowly past the two fugitives. Djoh started to pull off his clothes, for swimming out and catching one of them, then hesitated. It wasn't fear of the cold water, being spotted by the pirates, or even being thought guilty as the Caterpillar had said.

Blue Springs had treated him unjustly, but dammit, the place was his home! He didn't want to see it destroyed. And what would happen to his parents if he ran off? He didn't care if everybody else thought he was a traitor, but Peetuh and Behtee—

"Djoh, don't you think we should hurry?" Marthuh asked.

"Not yet. Wait until the pirates start their big attack. Then they'll be too busy to watch their rear."

He was thinking that something could be made of that fact when a familiar presence touched his mind. Iron Claw was mindspeaking, seeking him.

"Are you well, Big Brother?" Djoh asked.

"Yes, but my blood is boiling. Oh, for a good fight against these stupid two-legs!"

Djoh almost heard a thump as his thoughts fell into place. "Iron Claw, the bad two-legs are preparing to rush the den. Can you help stop them?"

"Am I a kitten? They are many, but their hearts are small. Only give the word."

"I will, Iron Claw."

Djoh told Iron Claw where to go and wait, then watched as the last boatloads of pirates joined the flanking movement. The townsmen didn't seem to be noticing it. The sheds and warehouses on the waterfront probably hid the pirates.

On the other hand, the pirates had thinned out their men on the two streets. Also, the ones on the flank were getting very close to the forest. Once they had all their attention on the enemy to their front . . .

The pirate horns blared. The pirates surged forward, meeting the desperate resistance of the townsmen. Voices and weapons made an appalling din. Djoh forced himself to wait until he was sure the pirates had no eyes for anything to their rear, then mindspoke:

"Now, Iron Claw!"

Marthuh stared as the big cat came storming out of the trees. "What is *that*?"

"A friend. The one I was seeing so many nights."

The big prairiecat reached a flank guard, who seemed too paralyzed by surprise or fear to move. The man flew into the air as if he were a straw doll, then Iron Claw tore his way into the pirates' flank. They fell before him like wheat before a scythe. The ones who had room and a moment's grace started to scatter, tripping, colliding, screaming in terror as they fought to get away from this nightmare creature who seemed to have sprung from the earth.

The townsmen on the flank saw what was happening and charged. Some of the pirates rallied, while others kept on running, now heading for their boats. Word must also have reached the townsmen holding the streets. Djoh saw the two pirate bands there wavering, then thrust violently backward on to the waterfront. Townsmen poured out of the streets after them, just as the pirates on the flank broke for once and for all.

The townsmen swept in on the right and left of the pirates, catching them like grain between two millstones. Djoh saw

Iron Claw still in the middle of the pirates, a ring of bodies around him.

Then a churning mass of pirates and townsmen swept over and around him and he vanished from Djoh's sight.

Djoh wanted to dash into town and rescue his friend, but now the pirates who weren't taking to their boats were running along the bank, hoping to be picked up. If he left Marthuh alone, some of the fugitives might still spot her and carry her off.

Reluctantly he led Marthuh back into the shelter of the forest. His last sight of the fight was a handful of pirates rallying for a final stand on the town wharf. Archers were already climbing onto the roofs of waterfront buildings, to shoot them down or send a few parting arrows after the pirate boats.

As the boats started passing Djoh, he saw that few of them had all their oars at work. Most carried dead men, and some of the oarsmen were bleeding as they thrashed their way along.

It would be a long time before pirates raided Blue Springs again. It would be even longer before this band of pirates raided anybody at all.

Halfway back to the Shrine, Djoh had to stop to rest his leg. It was aching as if he'd been hard at work since before dawn. He took Marthuh in his arms, then tried to mindspeak Iron Claw. He'd almost given up when the answer came, very faintly:

"Little Brother, are you and your mate-to-be well?"

"Yes, cat-brother. I watched you send the bad two-legs running. I was proud."

A long mental sigh of relief, pain, and weariness. "Little Brother, it is my time to go to Wind. May Sun shine on you, may your kittens be many and strong . . ."

A long pause. Djoh was glad he was mindspeaking, because he couldn't have forced any words past the stone caught in his throat. Then:

"Do not grieve, Little Brother. I had a long time, and the end was—a most glorious fight. I thank you for it. . . ."

This time the silence in Djoh's mind went on, until he knew that it would last forever.

He tried to squeeze his eyes shut so that the tears wouldn't overflow, then gave up and clung to Marthuh as they streamed down his face.

"Djoh, what is it? You're hurting me."

"I'm sorry, Marthuh. I'm just glad you're all right."

"You won't be, if we stay here. Maybe now we can take one of these boats."

"The river won't be safe until that band's run all the way back to wherever they came from. Besides, I don't think we'll need to leave Blue Springs now."

"But my father!"

"He's not going to be able to chase me out of town with his lies anymore. The chief Caterpillar just about told him so. Besides, I've learned a lot about fighting today. I'm not afraid of your father anymore."

He took Marthuh's arm and started downhill again, toward the town. He wanted to be there when they found Iron Claw's body. No matter how many questions the people asked, he wasn't going to let Iron Claw be treated as just another dead animal!

He knew there would be no answer, but he still sent a final thought:

"Goodbye, Nightfriend. You taught me well."

About the Editors

ROBERT ADAMS lives in Seminole County, Florida. Like the characters in his books, he is partial to fencing and fancy swordplay, hunting and riding, good food and drink. At one time Robert could be found slaving over a hot forge making a new sword or busily reconstructing a historically accurate military costume, but, unfortunately, he no longer has time for this as he's far too busy writing.

PAMELA CRIPPEN ADAMS is living proof of the dangers of being around science fiction writers. Originally a fan, she now spends her time as an editor and anthologist. When not working at these tasks, she is kept busy by their two dogs and ten cats.

For more information about Milo Morai, Horseclans, and forthcoming Robert Adams books contact the NATIONAL HORSECLANS SOCIETY, P.O. Box 1770, Apopka, FL 32704-1770.

⊘ SIGNET SCIENCE FICTION

THE FIERCE CHIEFS & FEUDING CLANS
of the *Horseclans* Series by Robert Adams

(0451)

☐ **HORSECLANS ODYSSEY (Horseclans #7).** Milo of Morai promises the clans a return to their legendary homeland, but first they must teach their enemies the price of harming any people of the clans . . .
(124162—$2.95)

☐ **THE DEATH OF A LEGEND (Horseclans #8).** When they are driven into unfamiliar territory, Bili and his troops are spotted by half-human creatures. Will these eerie beings use their powers of illusion to send the troops to their doom? (129350—$2.95)*

☐ **THE WITCH GODDESS (Horseclans #9).** Stranded in a land peopled by cannibals and half-humans, Bili and his warriors must battle these savages, as well as the Witchmen, evil scientists led by Dr. Erica Arenstein. Fighting both these dangerous groups, even Bili's proven warriors may not long survive . . . (140273—$2.95)*

☐ **BILI THE AXE (Horseclans #10).** With the help of powerful inhuman allies, Prince Byruhn has persuaded Bili and his warriors to delay their return to Confederation lands and join in his campaign against the deadly invading army . . . but are Bili and Prince Byruhn galloping straight into a steel-bladed trap from which death is the only release? (129288—$2.95)*

☐ **CHAMPION OF THE LAST BATTLE (Horseclans #11).** The time has come at last for Bili and Prince Byruhn to rally their troops for the final defense of New Kuhmbuhluhn. But within the very castle grounds stalks a creature of nightmare, striking down the defenders one by one in a reign of bloody terror that may prove far more deadly than the enemy at their gates . . . (133048—$2.95)*

*Prices slightly higher in Canada

Buy them at your local bookstore or use this convenient coupon for ordering.

NEW AMERICAN LIBRARY,
P.O. Box 999, Bergenfield, New Jersey 07621

Please send me the books I have checked above. I am enclosing $_____
(please add $1.00 to this order to cover postage and handling). Send check or money order—no cash or C.O.D.'s. Prices and numbers subject to change without notice.

Name_____

Address_____

City_____ Zip Code_____

Allow 4-6 weeks for delivery.
This offer is subject to withdrawal without notice.

⊘ **SIGNET SCIENCE FICTION** (0451)

FROM A TIME OUT OF LEGEND . . .

comes Robert Adams' *Horseclans* Series.

☐ **A WOMAN OF THE HORSECLANS (Horseclans #12).** The frightened girl who Tim Krooguh had rescued from certain death was destined to become a living legend among the Kindred, a fighter whose courage would rouse the clans against a foul and dangerous foe . . .
(133676—$2.95)

☐ **HORSES OF THE NORTH (Horseclans #13).** "Kindred must not fight Kindred!" So said the ancient and unbroken law. But now, clans Linsee and Skaht were on the brink of a bloodfeud that could spread like prairie fire throughout the Horseclans. Could even Milo smother the sparks of hatred before they blazed up to destroy all of the Horseclans . . . ?
(136268—$3.50)

☐ **A MAN CALLED MILO MORAI (Horseclans #14).** In an effort to heal the rift between the feuding clans of Linsee and Skaht, Milo must take the assembled sons and daughters on a journey of the mind to a strange and distant place . . . back to the twentieth century! (141288—$2.95)

☐ **THE MEMORIES OF MILO MORAI (Horseclans #15).** Ancient treasure and sudden danger await Milo and the Horseclans in the heart of a long-dead city, where the heirs to a legacy of violence lie waiting to claim the men and women of the Horseclans as the final victims in a war that should have ended hundreds of years ago. . . . (145488—$2.95)

☐ **TRUMPETS OF WAR (Horseclans #16).** Now that chaos reigns there, can the undying allies of the High Lord's Confederation reconquer their war-torn lands? Or will traitors betray Milo's warriors to a terrible doom?
(147154—$3.50)

☐ **FRIENDS OF THE HORSECLANS edited by Robert Adams and Pamela Crippen Adams.** For over ten years, Robert Adams has been weaving his magnificent tales of the *Horseclans*. Now he has opened his world to such top authors as Joel Rosenberg, Andre Norton, John Steakley and others hwo join him in chronicling twelve unforgettable new tales of Milo Morai and his band of followers. (145989—$3.50)

Prices slightly higher in Canada

Buy them at your local bookstore or use this convenient coupon for ordering.
NAL PENGUIN INC.
P.O. Box 999, Bergenfield, New Jersey 07621

Please send me the books I have checked above. I am enclosing $_____ (please add $1.00 to this order to cover postage and handling). Send check or money order—no cash or C.O.D.'s. Prices and numbers are subject to change without notice.

Name_____

Address_____

City_____State_____Zip Code_____

Allow 4-6 weeks for delivery.
This offer is subject to withdrawal without notice.

⊘ SIGNET SCIENCE FICTION

COME OUT OF THIS WORLD

(0451)

☐ **CHILDREN OF ARABLE by David Belden.** In a distant future where males and females seem interchangeable, and babies are grown in labs to meet the needs of society, one *real* woman in search of love could launch a revolution that will alter the universe forever ...
(146603—$2.95)

☐ **THE GLASS HAMMER by K.W. Jeter.** Ross Scyuyler is a hero—a racer driving black market computer chips through hostile and dangerous territory. But when this microcomputer starts warning of conspiracy and doom, he must choose between familiar dangers and the perils of an all-seeing, yet faceless enemy....
(147669—$2.95)

☐ **BRIDGE OF ASHES by Hugo and Nebula Award-winner Roger Zelazny.** He was the "ultimate" man, the greatest telepath the world had ever known, and he was Earth's last hope against an enemy that had created the human race—and could also destroy it ...
(135504—$2.50)

☐ **TIES OF BLOOD AND SILVER by Joel Rosenberg.** To David, stolen from Elweré as a baby and raised as a thief of the Lower City, it is a dream of paradise, a treasure trove to which he must find the key, no matter what the cost. That is, if Eschteef—twice the size of a human, with glowing eyes and rows of needle-sharp teeth—doesn't get to him first ...
(146212—$2.95)

☐ **WORLDSTONE by Victoria Strauss.** When parallel worlds collide, who is friend and who is foe? Alexina Taylor, a loner, has always felt different—as if she's waiting for something. Then she discovers Taryn, a young boy who has come through a passage in a nearby cave that leads to a parallel universe—one powered by telepathy. Together they journey through the other world seeking out a renegade who has stolen the Worldstone—the heart of the Mindpower world!!
(147561—$3.50)

Prices slightly higher in Canada

Buy them at your local bookstore or use this convenient coupon for ordering.

NEW AMERICAN LIBRARY,
P.O. Box 999, Bergenfield, New Jersey 07621

Please send me the books I have checked above. I am enclosing $_____
(please add $1.00 to this order to cover postage and handling). Send check or money order—no cash or C.O.D.'s. Prices and numbers are subject to change without notice.

Name _____

Address_____

City_____Zip Code_____

Allow 4-6 weeks for delivery.
This offer is subject to withdrawal without notice.